oxygen

CAROL WILEY CASSELLA

Simon & Schuster

NEW YORK

LONDON

TORONTO

SYDNEY

SIMON & SCHUSTER
1230 Avenue of the Americas
New York, NY 10020

First Simon & Schuster hardcover edition July 2008

SIMON & SCHUSTER and colophon are registered
trademarks of Simon & Schuster, Inc.

For information about special discounts for bulk purchases,
please contact Simon & Schuster Special Sales at
1-800-456-6798 or business@simonandschuster.com

Designed by C. Linda Dingler

Manufactured in the United States of America

3   5   7   9   10   8   6   4   2

Library of Congress Cataloging-in-Publication Data

Casella, Carol Wiley.
Oxygen / Carol Wiley Casella
p. cm.
1. Single women—Fiction. 2. Anesthesiologists—Fiction.
3. Seattle (Wash.)—Fiction.
PS3603.A8684 O99 2008
813'.622   2007037542
ISBN-13: 978-1-4165-5610-7
ISBN-10:   1-4165-5610-9

This novel is dedicated to the center of my universe:
Will, Sara, Julia, and Elise;
and to my own twin star, Steve.

oxygen

· 1 ·

People feel so strong, so durable. I anesthetize airline pilots, corporate executives, high school principals, mothers of well-brought-up children, judges and janitors, psychiatrists and salespeople, mountain climbers and musicians. People who have strutted and struggled and breathed on this planet for twenty, thirty, seventy years defying the inexorable, entropic decay of all living things. All of them clinging to existence by one molecule: oxygen.

The entire complex human machine pivots on the pinnacle of oxygen. The bucket brigade of energy metabolism that keeps us all alive ends with oxygen as the final electron acceptor. Take it away, and the cascade clogs up in minutes, backing up the whole precisely tuned engine until it collapses, choked, cold and blue.

Two portals connect us to oxygen—the mouth and the nose—appreciated more for all their other uses: tasting, smelling, smiling, whistling, blowing smoke and blowing kisses, supporting sunglasses and lipstick designers, perfumeries and plastic surgeons. Seal them for the duration of the morning weather report and everything you had planned for the rest of your life evaporates in a puff of imagination.

There is a moment during the induction of general anesthesia when I am intimately bonded to my patient. A moment of transferred power. I squeeze the drug out of the syringe, into the IV line, and watch the face slacken, watch the last organized thoughts slip from consciousness, see breathing shallow, slow, stop.

If I deserted my patient—deep in that swale of sleep, as suffocation colored blood blue—the lips would turn violet, pink skin would dull to gray, and the steady beep, beep, beep of the heart monitor would fade, then falter. Like an archaeological ruin, the brain would die in levels; personality, judgment, memory, movement collapsing like falling bricks to crush the brainstem's steady pulse of breath and blood.

There are points in an otherwise routine day when I am struck by how precariously this unconscious patient dangles, like a hapless fly on a spider's thread. It is like drowning, but blessed unconsciousness precedes desperate air hunger. At the last instant I swoop in and deliver a rescuing breath, adjust my machine to take over what the brainstem can no longer command—make the lungs move oxygen in and out to keep the heart beating, transferring each oxygen molecule to the cells. It becomes so easy, after years of the rescue. It becomes so routine, to watch the ebb of consciousness followed by the ebb of breath, and then to spring up as the obligate hero. It no longer feels like power. It feels like a job.

I am an anesthesiologist—a practitioner of the art and science of anesthesia. The word means, literally, "no sensation." In our modern lexicon it denotes a temporary loss of sensation, an absence of pain during an otherwise painful procedure. That is how I see my job: to make painful events painless; to coax and manipulate the human mind to give up its fierce clutch on control, its evolutionary reflex to flee from dismemberment and violation.

Granted, most patients come to surgery out of choice: the shoulder that stiffens on the squash court; the gallbladder that pangs upon digesting a rosemaried leg of lamb; the nuisances of body fat or age lines. Then, of course, there are the unfortunate twists of nature that destine some of us to die before a graceful blur into old age: the cancers creeping into baseball-sized tumors while we pay our bills, prune our roses, plan our children's birthday parties. Or the silent shearing of aortic aneurysms and coronary vessels and carotid arteries that snap our smoothly humming lives in half while we argue with our teenagers or make love to our husbands and wives. These events bring us to the doors of doctors and emergency rooms, place us supine on the white-sheeted gurneys rolling down the long, green-tiled, fluorescent-lit hall-ways into the cold and windowless operating rooms of this nation.

Today is a day like any other workday for me. I shut off my alarm before five and stand shivering beside my bathroom heater while the shower runs to warm. Somewhere in the city my patients are also beginning to rouse, anxious about their operations, worried about the ache or illness that can only be cured with a knife, trying to imagine the inevitable scar, trying to anticipate the pain. Maybe even trying to envision me, a stranger, the only doctor directly involved in their care whom they've never met. People may select their family practitioners based on comfort and trust, and their surgeons through reputation or referral, but anesthesiologists are usually assigned to an operating room rather than a particular patient. Hospitals couldn't absorb car accidents and emergency C-sections and gunshot wounds into an already crowded surgery schedule without a flexible, interchangeable anesthesia team.

That anonymity almost kept me from choosing this specialty when I was in medical school. I wanted to be involved with my patients' lives, not just be a transient manager of their pain. I balked at the hubris of asking anyone to yield so much control to me after only a few intro-ductory words. But within the first week of my anesthesia rotation I discovered that I loved this work—its precision and focus, its balance of technical skill and clinical judgment; finessing the interplay of heart and lungs while the brain sleeps; titrating narcotics and nerve blocks to that sweet spot in which a cancer patient's pain is relieved and they can still enjoy the time they have left with the people they love.

And inside the scant space of my preoperative interview I've found an entire cosmos of healing: the quick read of trepidation or naive acquiescence; the flash of entrapment or submission; perceiving the exact phrase or touch that can transform me from stranger to caretaker, from assigned clinician to guardian. I can't prove that rolling into the operating room believing you will be kept safe improves the outcome of surgery, but it's where I find the artistry in my work.

I slip on worn blue jeans and a loose sweater, thankful that I only have to dress for the commute. The aroma of coffee lures me into the kitchen, still dark as midnight. Tasks start to crowd out dreams—my presentation on labor epidurals for the nurses is due next week, the pharmacy committee wants a rundown on muscle relaxants, I have a dozen phone calls to make, and I should have changed the oil in my car about 12,000 miles ago.

The phone rings just as I screw the top on my travel mug, one foot already out the door. I grab it on the last ring in a lunge across the kitchen counter that spills coffee down my arm and knocks over a neglected potted violet, more brown than green; bone-dry dirt skitters across the floor.

"Aunt Marie? It's Elsa." Her voice is muffled and I hear a squall of tears tangled in her throat.

I look at my watch. "Hi, sweetie. What's up? You sound kind of upset."

"Not much. I just wanted to talk."

"It's five thirty in the morning, honey."

"Seven thirty. It's seven thirty here."

"Right." I lock the phone under my chin and sweep dirt and desiccated petals into a ridgeline under the counter with the toe of my shoe. If I'm not out the door in two and a half minutes I'll be late. "So are you just getting up or just going to bed?"

"Ha-ha. School starts in forty-five minutes." Her breath blows loud across the mouthpiece and I know exactly where she is—curled on top of her tennis shoes and sling-back sandals, draped in folds of Gap T-shirts and Abercrombie jeans, the telephone cord snaking under her closet door. "Mom and I had a fight last night. Did she call you?"

I drop my keys into my purse and lean on my elbows across the kitchen counter. "No. I was working late, anyway. What about?" I shove the coffeemaker at an angle so the red numbers on the clock don't glare at me.

"She just doesn't get it!" Her anger erupts into sobs. She is fifteen, the eldest child of my sister, Lori, my only sibling. When Elsa turned fourteen I was suddenly promoted to autodial status; I am the non-mother with all the answers to the questions she can't bring herself to ask her mother. As honored as I am, I have to suspect she turns to me because she knows I'm holding both their hands.

"Get what, sweetie?"

"Anything! She blew up because my Civics essay is overdue. But it's only late because I had to practice for Debate."

"When did you join the debate team?"

"Not like *school* debate. It's a new club. We want to legalize marijuana."

I stand up straight and count to five before I answer her. "Elsa?"

"Yeah?"

"Would you tell me if you're smoking pot?"

"Oh God, Aunt Marie. I hate getting high! But this is, like, basic civil rights!"

This time I count to ten and decide to ignore her slip. "Well, maybe you've got a leg up on your Civics essay here."

Elsa calls out to my sister that she'll be down when she's dressed, stop bugging her. "What are you wearing?" she asks in a bright new voice, her distress forgotten.

"What am I wearing?" I look down. A faded cable-knit sweater in army green, blue jeans and water-stained clogs. "A drop-waist hot pink rayon skirt and creamy cashmere sweater. And I just got my nails done— one of those French manicure things. With polka dots. Also pink."

Elsa bursts out laughing. "Oh right, Aunt Marie. You are *so* lying."

"Caught me again! Remind me and I'll send you some scrubs. Tie-dye them for me, huh? My boss would love that. So, what are you wearing?" Her laugh could almost make me forget about time. Eight minutes later Elsa is out of the closet and on her way to school. If the traffic lights are with me, I'll be OK.

First Lutheran Hospital was built in the thirties, a castle of art deco facades, a fortress against disease. I've worked here for seven years— long enough to have a good parking spot in the basement garage, avoiding the cold drizzle of Seattle in these early days of spring. I push the gearshift into neutral and turn the heat vent toward my face to enjoy a last second of solitude.

At this early hour I'm one of the few physicians in the hospital. But the lingering night staff and arriving day shift are already filling the hallways. They chatter in Tagalog and Korean and Urdu and Spanish and English—beneficiaries of an international recruiting effort that annually scavenges the brightest graduates of foreign classrooms to staff American hospitals. It takes a small city of personnel to move each patient from the parking garage where they arrive intact to the exiting wheelchair ramp that spins them back into their lives, stocked with clean bandages, pain pills and a ten-day-follow-up appointment. All of us dress for work in the same blue cotton pants and shirts, wearing the same blue hair caps and shoe coverings designed to keep our personal bacteria out of our patients' open bellies, chests and limbs.

While much of the city still sleeps, we heave in to set up medicine's greatest show, the Barnum & Bailey of daring adventures inside the human body. Ropes of electrical cords are uncoiled between cautery devices, television towers, bypass machines, lasers, microscopes and mobile X-ray units. Scaffolds of surgical steel are autoclaved to cleanliness, instruments displayed like exotic cutlery along lengths of wheeled tables. A swimming pool of sterile saline is warmed to human temperature, ready to plug into blood vessels and pour into body cavities.

Bethany, our operating room manager, slides the jumble of planned and emergent surgeries, instrument trays, cameras, fiber-optic scopes, technicians, pumps and personalities together into a functioning organism. She's mastered a balance of fawning and authoritarianism that keeps our surgeons grudgingly cooperative. She sits at her high desk behind a sliding glass window, clacking away at her computer keyboard with long purple fingernails, a ruling priestess over the operating rooms.

I scratch my own bare nails across the glass to annoy her, and she looks at me over her rhinestoned bifocals, looped by a turquoise beaded chain around her neck. "Hi, Bethany. Where am I today?"

"Scratch that window one more time and I will tell Dr. Scoble you volunteered to take every holiday call."

"I'm already on three this year. You'll have to come up with something scarier." I steal a cinnamon candy from a paper cup on the window ledge and pop it into my mouth. "Speaking of call, I have friends coming to visit week after next. Any idea how busy things are looking? It's spring break, so some of the surgeons ought to be out of town."

She fishtails her computer mouse across the desk, clicking through screens. "Looks like . . . three generals and two vasculars are out. Should be OK." She slides a pad of paper toward me. "Write the dates down. I'll try to put you in light rooms. *If* you bring me more pralines." I gave the OR staff boxes of my favorite Texas pralines last Christmas and Bethany's now addicted.

"A whole crateful. How does today look?"

"Bad. Hope you slept well. Fifty-eight cases scheduled—three hearts—and I've already got six add-ons. Be glad you're not first call."

"I'm fourth. Any emergencies yet?"

"One. Subdural hematoma going in twelve."

Sometimes I think the hospital administrators would like us to staff every operating room twenty-four hours a day; it's one of the few sectors of hospital care that predictably generates money. But we at least make an attempt to accommodate normal circadian sleep rhythms by rotating the length of our days throughout our anesthesia group. Once or twice a week I take the first call duty and stay in the hospital all night doing whatever emergency operations come in. One of my partners takes second call, staying until late in the evening and being available to come back to the hospital if two of us are needed. Then the call peels down sequentially from there, a higher number designating a shorter workday. But all days are eventually ruled by surgical imperative—tumors encroaching on vital organs, the brittle, broken bones of old age, gangrenous limbs that threaten sepsis, twisted fallopian tubes and obstructed bowels.

Bethany says, "You start in five with Stevenson, then I've got you covering eight in the afternoon, unless I have to slide one of the add-ons into five. Hillary's in eight until you can relieve him—he was on call last night. McLaughlin got pulled away for a long case in radiology, so I don't have anybody free to give breaks until after twelve thirty. Sorry. If Janovich keeps to his schedule Kuciano should be free to get you out for lunch. Maybe." She lays out the day she has meticulously choreographed to move as many patients as possible through the system before overtime has to be paid.

I look at the immense whiteboard across from Bethany's desk that displays the entire list of surgeries and operating rooms, scheduled cases in black felt-tip pen and emergencies in red. Beside the number 5 runs a list of three short cases—a mastectomy, a ventral hernia repair and a central line placement—followed by one longer pediatric surgery. The first three anesthetics should be relatively simple and straightforward, if the patients are healthy. I'll have to talk to Don Stevenson, my surgeon, about the child. We don't take care of children as often as adults at First Lutheran, so those cases always seem more stressful. If Don can finish his surgeries reasonably close to the predicted time, I'll be able to move into room 8 by three o'clock and let Joe Hillary go home to sleep. But I've worked with Don for a long time and know his tendency to overbook his day.

I tell Beth, "Better get a backup for Joe. Stevenson will run late, which will push that last case past three, I bet. Who's on General Surgery call today?"

"Marky."

"Oh God. Marconi. We'll all be here late." Sean Marconi is famous for working all night. Even on fourth call I am at risk for a long day.

Bethany winks at me over her glasses. "God *Marconi* or God *God*?"

"Does Marconi know the difference?" She laughs and I add, "You never heard me say that, Bethany. We have enough gods here as it is."

• 2 •

Room 5 is at the end of a branching hallway off a central core of equipment storage rooms. The clink of metal and plastic echoes off the tile walls with every footstep; I sound like a fully equipped security guard with my stethoscope and keys dangling around my neck, my pager and cell phone clipped to my waist, pockets stuffed with pens and vials of medicine and syringes. The sky would just now be lightening, if I could see it. I sometimes spend entire days without sunrise or sunset, moving from windowless operating rooms through interior hallways to a windowless cafeteria.

An operation is already under way in room 8; Joe Hillary is hunched over the small desk attached to his anesthesia machine, papers lit by a narrow beam of light in an otherwise darkened room. I grab a surgical mask from the shelf above the scrub sink and tie it over my mouth and nose, then push open the heavy steel doors, wide enough to wheel an operating table through. The surgeon looks up and nods, but Joe doesn't see me until I'm nearly beside him. His patient is sleeping, her eyes carefully taped shut to prevent any corneal scratches, a plastic endotracheal tube jutting from her mouth. The tube rhythmically fogs and clears with each cycle of the ventilator. Beyond the blue drape that separates us from the surgical field, television cameras display the inside of her abdomen, inflated to the size of a pumpkin with carbon dioxide so the organs can be seen and dissected. The pale oranges, deep purples and soft yellows of her tis-

9

sues, crisscrossed by a netting of red vessels, shift on the screen each time the camera moves. The surgeon teases her swollen gallbladder away from her liver and her blood pressure climbs. Joe, sitting near her head, turns his anesthesia gas up in response. Anesthesia is not a static thing, any more than human beings are static. The soup of drugs and gases needed by each patient is unique, modified throughout the course of surgery.

I lean close to his ear so our conversation won't distract the surgeon. "Hey. Why are you doing a chole at this hour?"

"You see the board? The schedule was too full to add her on later today."

"Fielding's got two sitting craniotomies. I love those cases. I should ask Bethany to put me in neuro more often." The ventilator thrums in a slow drumbeat, whole notes below the high-pitched quarter notes of the patient's pulse. "It's freezing in here. Want me to turn up the thermostat?" I pick up a blanket lying next to Joe's chair and wrap it around my shoulders.

He shakes his head. "Keeps me awake." He is slumped on his high stool so that, despite his height, our faces are level. I can only see his eyes, bracketed between his surgical mask and hat, blushed with fatigue. "Did you get any sleep?"

He shakes his head. "Goddamn pager went off every time I put my key in the call room door."

I massage his neck for a minute. Joe likes to work hard—work hard and play hard. We both chose First Lutheran because of its reputation as the best of the multiple hospitals that crowd this area of Seattle. The cords of his shoulders and spine are taut.

"Why don't you go get a cup of coffee?" I offer.

"Don't worry about it. You've got your own cases to start."

"Go on." I nudge his side and, when he still doesn't move, rub my knuckles under his rib until he laughs and pulls away. "Take a break. My first case is an easy setup."

He finally gets up from the stool, stretching and peeling off his latex gloves as he gives me a quick summary of the woman's health history and her current status under anesthesia. I fill in the few vital signs that the machines have automatically measured over the last few minutes and sign the chart.

Joe comes back in under ten minutes, looking slightly less beaten down by the night, an aroma of coffee and mint on his breath. Clear droplets of water are beaded through his sideburns, eyebrows and across his forehead, and the front of his scrub top is splotched with dampness.

"Thanks," he says. "If I get out of here before sundown I'll pay you back."

"Save it. Pay me back next week. Gary and his daughter are flying into town for a visit and I might need to trade a day with you."

He raises his eyebrows. "So, I finally get to meet your ex?" Gary and I shared a house—completely platonically—with two other women when I was in medical school and he was a business major at the University of Houston. He's still a dear friend. Joe refers to it as my time in the commune.

I jab at his ribs again; this time I laugh, and the surgical technician looks up at us. I give her a tiny wave, turn away from the field and lower my voice. "Let's all go to Wild Ginger one night. But don't use that joke in front of his daughter—her mother might not find it very funny if it got repeated. I can't believe he's the father of a thirteen-year-old already."

"Does she look like you?" he asks in a wheedling tease.

"No jokes, Joe. Promise, or you don't get to meet him." I pick my pen up from the desk and drop the blanket across Joe's neck. "Gotta go. I'll be back as soon as Stevenson finishes up."

Joe is my best friend at First Lutheran. More specifically, he is my best friend. And for a few months, years ago, he was also my lover.

I knew better. Since medical school I'd drawn an ironclad curtain between my work and my love life, unwilling to offer up my private world as locker room entertainment for my peers. Operating rooms breed close friendships, but they can also be dens of gossip and slippery personal boundaries. Something about the collusion of working for hours together in these semisealed vaults of technological marvel and conceit, clustering around our patients like flesh-colored components of a great and mysterious machine, mass-producing kidney transplants and knee replacements and breast biopsies and rotator cuff repairs. It's like belonging to a secret society in which we all check our fallibility at the door in order to muster the utter gall to play gods over disease.

I consciously reminded myself of this when I recognized the tinge of nervousness I felt if he sat next to me in the conference room, the awkward awareness of my posture and the sound of my voice. Now I think the months of forestalling that came before the giving in may be the reason we have such a strong friendship, as if the sexual love between us had been an island in the middle of four years of mutual confidences and inside jokes and shared stamina over long workdays. It's almost as if that island of physical intimacy had bonded us, like the blood pacts I'd made with girlhood friends.

Anesthesia is like aviation—we have backups for our backups, safety nets stashed along the route. Only the human link in the chain comes without an installed flashing red light. By 6:15 AM, I am in room 5 setting up my work space and anesthesia machine—a ritualized check of vacuums, pumps, pressurized tubing, gas flows, monitors, warning lights, emergency drugs and alarms. The blaring tones and beeps sound like an out-of-tune orchestra warming up.

A red cart with multiple locked drawers holds my breathing tubes, IV lines, syringes, suction catheters, laryngoscopes for seeing the tiny passageway to the lungs through the caverns of the mouth and throat—all the myriad equipment I need to drift my patients safely into the timeless void of anesthesia. The top drawer holds drugs: drugs that obliterate consciousness and memory, drugs that paralyze muscles and then restore them to strength. I have drugs that raise or lower the heart rate, manipulate blood pressure, thin the blood, numb the skin, empty the stomach, slow salivation. On top of my cart is a small locked box holding my narcotics—morphine, Demerol, fentanyl, Dilaudid— the miracle drugs that make surgical pain bearable. Invisible chemicals, clear as water, the cousins and stepchildren of opium. Injected into the bloodstream, they seep into the brain to bind and block the molecular keyhole in the cobwebbed attic door to pain. I draw up each transparent syringe of drug and label it, then lay them across my cart like columns of soldiers ready for my commands, and relock the box with a key I wear around my neck.

Mindy, the OR nurse, and Alicia, the scrub tech, arrive and begin setting up their own territories, sorting through stacks of paperwork, unfolding sterile blue drapes across massive tables, adjusting lights, spreading out fields of stainless steel. The three of us have spent countless mornings in chilly operating rooms trading insignificant details of our lives. They have both been at the hospital longer than I have—long enough to know everyone's first and second spouses as well as a number of surreptitious lovers.

Alicia immigrated from the Philippines and relishes her new American identity. Her eyes are rimmed with black liner that slants to a point. Most women who work in surgery spend the majority of the day with their mouth and nose covered by a mask, their hair encased in paper. Some compensate by drawing all attention to their eyes, like veiled harem dancers. Her hair is an electric orange, and the first time I ran into her without a surgical head covering I didn't recognize her at all. She's so tiny she has to stand on a step stool in order to see the surgical field and hand out instruments.

"So are we going to have a good day today, Alicia?"

"Of course, Marrrrrrria!" she trills. "Is there another kind? I'm planning to put the tiniest drizzle of Valium in Stevenson's morning coffee."

"Careful—his wife might get used to it and you'll have to cultivate a steady supply."

"It's a good schedule. Too busy to get any add-ons in here. We missed you at the softball game Saturday. The ER staff shut us out." She places dozens of silver metal clips in perfect parallel rows, their tips marching in a precise line along the edge of the table.

I glance up at her from the head of the bed where I'm arranging EKG leads, splayed like a five-legged spider beneath the pillow. I like to have everything ready, the mechanics of my craft disguised below softer surfaces before my patient lies down and sleep steals in. "You didn't miss me. When I was in med school I was catcher in a pickup game.

They finally made me *roll* the ball back to the mound, my throwing was that bad. Sign me up for soccer."

"Hey, I got to take my daughter to get braces on her teeth today. You got any drugs for that? For *me*?"

"Hah! Nothing legal. My sister always gives her kids Tylenol before they get their braces adjusted." I tuck my bangs back up under my cap and scan my setup one final time. "Did Stevenson ask for anything special on the pediatric case?" Until I meet my patients and read their medical charts, I know almost nothing about them except their names and ages. But Stevenson wouldn't schedule a child at First Lutheran if she had any major health problems—complicated cases have to be done at Children's Hospital. Sometimes, though, the room staff can tell me if the surgeon has requested any unusual position or equipment that might affect my anesthetic plan.

"The cyst? Yeah. He wants to do her prone. He was talking about this kid yesterday. I think he said she is a little bit retarded or something."

I stop working and put my hands on my hips, playing out different approaches to her anesthetic induction, mildly irritated at Stevenson for not telling me about this earlier. With the right preparation I look forward to cases like this—calming a challenging patient in my preoperative interview. I'm playing psychiatrist as well as medicinal artist, a chemical hypnotist beckoning the frightened and the uninitiated into a secure and painless realm of trust. It's a private world I build with my patient, a world the surgeon never sees, a secret pact that never makes it into the hospital record or onto an insurance billing form. I like to think it is where I can make the most difference—spinning the first layer of the anesthetic cocoon with language instead of drugs.

"OK. I might need a little extra time then, to get some sedation going before we bring her into the room," I tell Alicia.

"You're the boss. I go home at three no matter how much time you take."

My first patient today is a forty-six-year-old woman who will lose her right breast to cancer. I greet her in the surgical holding area, smiling, cheerful, deflecting her anxiety with rapid-fire questions and explanations, reassuring her that she wins the lowest risk classification for undergoing anesthesia—ASA 1 on a scale of 5. She is sitting up in her bed, slender and tanned, wearing light pink lipstick and tasteful eye makeup (for whom, I wonder). It gives the morning a patina of normality, as if she were headed to the tennis club instead of cleaving this invasive parasite from her body.

I feel like I've met this woman before, dozens of times. She is the Junior League volunteer, the poised hostess, the sorority alumna usually referenced by her husband's full name prefixed with a *Mrs.*, polished enough to be mistaken for pampered. She is the woman who does not wince when I start her IV, who asks me about my work and my family and defies me to pity her. She will beat this and move on.

Wrapped warmly on the narrow operating table, I lean next to her ear as she slips beyond knowing, and whisper, "I am right here with you. I will take care of you. You will wake up safe and comfortable. You will recover and be fine." The faintest rise in her heart rate is the only fear she ever shows.

The case goes well. The steady high pitch of the pulse monitor tells me her red blood cells are richly saturated with oxygen. The slight valleys and peaks of her blood pressure and heart rate guide my mix of anesthetic gas flows, narcotics and fluids. We are in an unspoken physiologic communion, my patient and I. I stand like a sentry at the gate of surgical trespass.

Stevenson is in a good mood this morning, thank God. His kid has just been chosen first-string quarterback in tenth grade, so maybe he is hoping college tuition will be covered. He teases Alicia about setting them up together, the "things" she could teach him. When the patient's lymph nodes come back from pathology free of cancer the mood lifts for all of us and Stevenson asks for closing music—he likes to suture the skin to Led Zeppelin.

I can almost quantify how well a case is going by the volume of the background music and conversation. People on the outside seem shocked at the irreverence of listening to a hard-rock band while latexed hands split or sew the tissues of living flesh. But I reassure them—that is a good sign. That is the sign your surgeon is walking straight down the center of known territory, so at ease with this procedure his hands are driven by comforting familiarity. That is the sign your anesthesiologist hears the steady high tone of the oxygen and heart monitor and knows, intuits, exactly where in the operation the extra touch of narcotic or the lightened breath of gas will foment the precise balance of chemicals to keep you sleeping, unaware and senseless, until the last bandage is taped, the fresh sheet is pulled over your chest, and you hear the reassuring whisper in your ear, "Wake up, wake up, your surgery is over, and all went well." We have honed and streamlined surgery until the historical amphitheater with the suited students, the ungloved hands, the chloroformed handkerchief has faded to the initial lurch of an assembly line.

By the time I wheel my patient into the recovery room she is smiling, her cancer drunkenly forgotten in the absolution of drugs. "It looks good," I say, stroking her hair back from her forehead and handing the chart off to Julia, her recovery nurse. "Dr. Stevenson will be in to talk to you in a few minutes."

She reaches up to her face; it's such a common gesture after anesthesia. I've come to believe we must need some tactile reconnection with our own lips and eyes and nose to awaken. "It's over? The surgery's over?"

"Surgery's all done, sweetie," Julia tells her. "Are you having any pain?" My patient shakes her head and relaxes back against her pillows. Julia turns to me. "My niece is coming in next month for a rotator cuff repair with Nuezmann. Would you mind taking care of her?"

"I'd be happy to. Talk to her about an interscalene nerve block. Lots of those patients don't need pain meds till the next day."

The recovery room is already filling up, a dozen strangers parked at monitoring stations lined up along the wall like wounded soldiers, a community of catheters and bandages and emesis basins. Even the pretense of privacy is secondary to keeping patients and monitors visible in case an alarm should sound or an airway obstruct. I pull a sheaf of papers from the back of my patient's chart and start filling out triplicate billing pages and order forms and an anesthetic summary.

The top sheet will stay with her permanent record to document my work, while the copies will be parceled out among insurance companies, hospital supply centers, the pharmacy and the anesthesia office, where my professional care will be translated into accounting codes and invoices. One of the nurses has stabbed some freshly cut blue hyacinths into an empty plastic urinal, and I lean over the desk to bury my face in their scent. This may be the closest I get to the outdoors today.

Will Hanover, the senior partner in my group, bumps into me as he rushes from dropping one patient in recovery to meeting the next in the surgical holding area. "Hey!" He steadies me with an arm around my shoulder and slips his surgical mask off his face to dangle below his rotund chin. "Bethany may be adding another case in your room this afternoon. Are you on schedule so far?"

I glance at my watch. "Thirty minutes behind. Can anybody else get Joe out? He was up all night." First Lutheran hired four new surgeons in the past year, but hasn't been able to recruit any new anesthesiologists. Will is in charge of our call schedule and spends hours figuring out how to staff all the cases.

"Nobody's free. This'll be the third day in a row we haven't had anyone out of the OR before seven. We should yank Phil out of his meetings and put him back in the operating rooms full-time. Then he'd hire somebody." Will hikes his scrub pants up higher on his well-padded stomach and tightens the knotted waistband. It seems a gesture he'd like to use on Phil Scoble's throat right now. Phil is the chief of our anesthesia department and a board member of the hospital. The rest of us have speculated whether this makes him more our advocate or our nemesis, but I think the answer varies in proportion to our fatigue. He has to walk a difficult line, being both one of us and one of "them."

"Didn't he make an offer to that woman from New York?"

"He did. So did three other hospitals with better benefits and better pay. I'm gonna give him a Foley catheter for a Christmas present this year—see if he likes the idea of working thirteen hours without a goddamn bathroom break."

Will splutters in my face as he rants, and I find myself wanting to console him more out of concern for his blood pressure than for collegial bargaining power against the hospital's rigid budget.

My second case takes longer than expected, and we are an hour-and-a-half behind schedule by the time I greet my third patient. He is a sixty-three-year-old Starbucks executive with newly diagnosed lymphoma, and Stevenson is placing a catheter into the vena cava so he can be treated without the scorching infusion of chemotherapeutic drugs through the smaller veins on his hands and arms. When I meet him in the pre-op area he seems cool and stone-faced, giving me almost curt answers to my questions. I inject a milligram of sedation into his IV and the mask melts into a plea for consolation and hope, a stalling narrative about his newest granddaughter. The extra minutes have got Stevenson pacing in the operating room as he waits for me to bring the patient in. Now Stevenson's getting testy and he barks at the radiology technician who is helping out, then mutters an apology under his breath, more for himself than the intimidated young woman. His impatience pervades the room, and even Mindy and Alicia stop trying to humor him.

As soon as my patient is asleep I start getting fresh medications and equipment ready for the pediatric case to follow. A child needs more precise drug dosing than an adult; the margin for error is less forgiving, so I dilute the drugs into larger volumes and lower concentrations. Pediatric tubes and scopes and IVs and oxygen masks are all scaled smaller, reminding me of the dollhouses I played with in childhood with their tiny tables and kitchen stoves, their minuscule pans and dishes. The door swings open behind me and Joe walks into the room. He leans across my anesthesia cart on folded arms, his knotted blue veins branching over ruddy freckled hands. I sense Alicia pause in her concentration when she sees him—he has that effect on women.

"Hey. My pancreatectomy got canceled so I'm done. You need a quick break before I go? Coffee in the lounge is only three hours old." Joe has a way of making everything he says sound mildly humorous. If you don't know him very well it's easy to miss his sober side. He has a slight amblyopia, and when he is tired I catch his right eye drifting off center, like he is seeing the world from two points of view. Somehow it only compounds his charm—a detail of vulnerability women love.

"I'm fine. Brad's supposed to be able to get me a lunch break. You should sleep—seems like you're always at the hospital these days."

"My contractor just gave me the bid for my kitchen—I asked Will for extra call. Not like there's much to race home to."

"Where's Claire? Is she complaining about your domestic indifference again?"

"Like all my women." He winks. "Don't give me that wily smile."

"I'm not! I swear." I clap a hand up over my mask.

"You're thinking about it, though."

"You need a dog, Joe. Something loyal and warm to sleep next to you every night."

This gets him laughing, and under the harsh white operating room lights the wrinkles around his eyes crease all the way to his hairline. Some men really do look better as they age, though I detect Joe's feeling edgy about growing older. People rib him about being too cavalier, even in the OR, but he's a dedicated doctor. It's one of the reasons I like him so much. He put himself through medical school twenty years ago by working in a research lab at night, and he still drives himself relentlessly. He bought an Italian racing bike on a whim, and I teased him about how much it was going to cost him per mile ridden. The next weekend he rode from downtown Seattle up to Paradise Lodge on Mount Rainier and back again.

Stevenson snaps at me to wedge a rolled towel under the patient's back—he's having trouble getting the catheter into the vessel—and I have to dive under the surgical drapes to lift the shoulders and head.

Joe hands me a folded towel and whispers, "What's got him so agitated?"

"We're running behind. Big surprise. Don't worry, I'll get him cheered up. Would you draw up the rest of my drugs for me?" I slip my narcotics key from around my neck and toss it to him. "It's a child, so I want the fentanyl at five mics per cc."

"What else?" I hear him peeling open packages of syringes and needles, popping the plastic caps off glass bottles.

"Succinylcholine at two per cc, atropine at one hundred."

"How much does the child weigh?"

"I don't know yet. Not an infant—eight, I think?"

I stand up from under the drapes, my hair spilling out from under my cap and my stethoscope dangling by one earpiece from the front of my scrub shirt. Joe is labeling the last syringe, his forehead shines with sweat, and he's pushed the sleeves of his scrub jacket higher on his forearms. Under his mask is a day's growth of rough auburn stubble.

"Thanks. Go home," I say.

He slips my key chain over my neck and tucks my hair back under my cap. "Give me a call this weekend if you want to have dinner. If the weather's clear we could fly up to Friday Harbor."

"Hmm. Can't we do something at sea level?" Joe is a pilot, probably a very competent one—he bought his own plane a year ago. But I have an almost embarrassing fear of heights, and he's only talked me into flying with him once. My stomach was churning by the time the tires broke loose from the gritty friction of the runway with an alarming, gliding silence. Joe looked at me and reached for an air sickness bag, then burst out laughing when he realized it was only my nerves—his velour seats were safe. Banking over the islands of Puget Sound on a cloudless day, the view would have been glorious, if I could have relaxed enough to keep my eyes open. He kept trying to convince me to take the copilot wheel in my hands, until he finally accepted that my terror wouldn't budge. "It defies logic. You work in a field that depends on science and mechanics and you have no faith in the principles of lift and thrust," he chided.

"Oh, I trust the physics," I shouted over the engine. "What I don't trust are the humans who build and fly the planes."

· 3 ·

Jolene Jansen is sitting with her mother in the waiting room, twisting the arm of a frayed pink nylon teddy bear. The portable TV in the corner plays a video of old Looney Tunes cartoons, and Wile E. Coyote springs up after being pushed off a high cliff. When I come in Jolene jumps into her mother's lap and tucks her face into the open collar of her mother's shirt. She is small for an eight-year-old. The nurses have not been able to coax Jolene into changing out of her blue jeans, and I can see on her mother's face this is one battle too many for her this morning. I stuff my mask into my pocket, and pull off my surgical cap so my hair spills out around my shoulders, hoping to look less clinical.

Jolene's mother looks up at me from the toddler-sized chair she is squatting on. There are no other chairs in the small room; I sit cross-legged beside them on the carpet and try a peek-a-boo game, but Jolene won't look at me directly. Children often won't trust me until I've won the trust of their parent, so I offer my hand to her mother. "I'm Dr. Heaton. Marie Heaton. I'm Jolene's anesthesiologist. How are you this morning?"

She shrugs and blows a straggle of brown hair out of her eyes. A flash of nervousness twists her mouth before she answers. "I'm Jolene's mom. Bobbie Jansen." She hunches the weight of her daughter higher on her shoulder and drops her voice. "She's kind of shy, especially around doctors, you know, since she's been to so many."

21

The room is overly warm, and half-moons of sweat bleed under the arms of Bobbie Jansen's red T-shirt. She smells of woodsmoke and fresh soil and almond-scented lotion. A creased daffodil dangles from a safety pin on her shirt pocket and a matching blossom weaves through the lace eyelets of Jolene's blouse. I let my hand linger in hers for a moment before I open Jolene's chart. "Let me look through her records for a minute and we can talk about how I'll take care of her during her surgery." I keep my voice light and happy, glancing at Jolene's buried face now and then to try to catch her eye. Bobbie has a cautious, withholding look, and I wonder if it's from too little experience with the medical world or too much.

Jolene's anesthesia sheet is blank, indicating she is healthy enough to have bypassed our pre-op clinic. I turn past the reams of Medicaid forms to Don Stevenson's surgery clinic note and learn she has only recently moved here from Yakima. Her retardation is fairly mild and not known to be associated with any syndrome that might involve other medical problems. In the past few months she has had recurrent infections in a congenital cyst at the base of her spine, and a walk-in clinic doctor referred her to Stevenson to have it removed. It should be a straightforward, short surgery, the only complicating factor being she will have to be turned facedown on the operating room table after she is asleep. I don't have any medical documents from her past; no physician seems to have been consistently involved with Jolene, at least inside our hospital system. Her mother will have to tell me what she can.

Bobbie's eyes move from the open chart to my face and back again as I read, gauging my level of concern for Jolene, my mix of compassion versus science. We are at the balancing moment of trust, and I know my words and gestures will classify me with the caring or the callous doctors she must have dealt with.

I reach up and lightly stroke Jolene's back, smoothing the ruffle along the hem of her checked blouse. "Has Jolene ever had surgery before, Mrs. Jansen?"

"It's Ms. Jansen. I'm raising her by myself. No. No, they wanted to put her to sleep once, to do some kind of a test on her, because she was growing so slow, but I wouldn't let them. I never saw a reason to put her through some doctor's test that won't change her future. Only now this infection has made it so she can't even sit without hurting. That's why we've come." She scans the room, my nametag, my stethoscope, hesitant, it seems, to look into my face, like she's looking for something solid to hold on to.

I try to relax my posture, disguise the preanesthetic checklist inside my head. "Did any of her doctors ever say she had a heart murmur? Or any problems with her lungs?"

"She's healthy so far as I know, except for her mind. But she understands things. She'll talk to me—just not to strangers. She coughs a lot, sometimes, and she doesn't like to run around like other kids. But she's a good, sweet girl, aren't you, baby?" Bobbie softly rocks side to side, and I see Jolene relax onto her shoulder. Bobbie wipes the corner of Jolene's mouth with the hem of her T-shirt. Her earlobes and fingers are spare of jewelry; her nails are cut short, clean to the quick.

"When you say she doesn't run around much, do you mean she can't?" Bobbie looks quizzical, not understanding the relevance of this question. "I mean, does she seem to get short of breath when she runs, compared to other children?"

"Maybe a little. She's just always liked to stay quiet. She doesn't play with a lot of other children . . ." She trails off.

"But none of her doctors ever told you she had asthma, or any heart problems?"

Bobbie just shakes her head, and the space between us widens. I wait until our eyes connect again. "It's a difficult job, to raise a child alone."

"Do you have any kids?"

I clasp my hands around my knees and try to forget that Stevenson is waiting. "No. But I have two nieces and a nephew. My sister's children. Neil is the same age as Jolene. Do you still have family in Yakima?"

"Not really. Nobody close. Does your sister live here in Seattle?"

"Texas. We grew up there."

She loosens; a half smile. "I thought I heard some accent."

I try to weave medical questions, explanations and general conversation into a safety net, asking about allergies and medications and hospitalizations. I put my stethoscope against the pink teddy bear's back and ask him to take a deep breath, but when I place it over Jolene's lungs she whimpers and pushes me away. If I force it she'll wail and I'll hear nothing anyway. Bobbie tries to persuade Jolene to hold the metal bell herself, but Jolene cries and clings tighter around her neck. Bobbie's eyes glimmer with tears, and I wonder if I have pushed them both too far. She closes her eyes for a minute, then asks me, "So would you do this? Would you let your nephew have this operation?"

I take her hand again and nod. "I'm going to keep her very safe for you." She grips my hand like a last chance. Then I coax Bobbie into holding her only child while I inject four milligrams of Midazolam into Jolene's thigh, pick her up in my arms and carry her down the hallway into the operating room.

By the time we reach room 5 Jolene is drowsily grinning at all the strange masked faces circled above her like witches over a cauldron. The Midazolam has blurred her fear and blunted her memory, so she yields herself up to us. I'm struck by how pretty she is when she is relaxed and smiling. Her skin is perfect, as if it had never seen the sun, cream colored and flushed over the cheek hollows. Her eyes, a lovely, lucid blue, are losing focus and she laughs quietly at some fringe of a dream overtaking her. I wonder if this is the face her mother had before life wore her out.

I bring the clear plastic oxygen mask over her nose and mouth, and her eyes flicker with panic, recognizing strangers, missing her mother. I put my mouth at her left ear and sing softly, a song my mother rocked me to sleep with:

"Hush-a-bye, don't you cry,
Go to sleep my little baby.
When you wake you shall have
All the pretty little horses."

Her hair brushes my cheek. My right hand turns the dial on the gas canister and whiffs of sweet, languid vapors leak from beneath the mask into my own lungs. Jolene's breaths become quick and shallow, then slower and slower, deeper and deeper, until the regular, even breathing of gas and oxygen in and out tells me she is asleep.

Mindy and I move into action, start her IV, put on her blood pressure and heart monitors, get ready to turn her over. At the deepest moment of sleep I gently extend her neck and insert a metal blade into her mouth. The blade is lighted by a tiny bulb along its shining silver curve so I can see her vocal cords and the dark tunnel of her trachea. I slip a hollow plastic tube between her open cords and attach the other end to corrugated tubing connected to my machine. Now I will breathe for her. I will control the delivery of oxygen to her lungs, her heart, her brain. The nurse telephones the waiting room to let Bobbie know that her daughter is safely asleep.

Stevenson is back in good spirits. He must have had time for lunch between cases, so at least one of us is not starving. That or Alicia threatened to quit if he didn't stop pouting. He's telling some far-fetched story about driving his Porsche off the highway into a field of bulls, and his black, bushy eyebrows wiggle above his glasses like a pair of caterpillars. Jolene is floating in a smooth and steady state of anesthesia by now. The chemicals I've swirled through her blood and lungs and brain are perfectly balanced against the surgeon's knife.

Brad Kuciano walks into the room and immediately begins goading Stevenson about some baseball bet he owes him. Stevenson starts the story of the Porsche all over again and Alicia rolls her eyes.

"Hey, Brad. Please tell me you're here for lunch. I'm starving."

"Hell no. I just came in to ask Alicia if she's busy Saturday night."

Stevenson jumps in: "Too late, Kuciano. I'm setting her up with my son."

"*I'm* taking Alicia out on Saturday," I say. "You're both out of luck."

Alicia does a quick shimmy on her step stool. "Dancing. She's taking me to learn the tango, right, Dr. Heaton? We're *both* wearing high heels and low-cut dresses—getting out of these ugly scrubs." Her accent rings exotic in the words and I'm almost looking forward to our imagined date.

Brad taps me on the shoulder. "OK. I've got three lunch breaks to give in an hour." He picks up Jolene's anesthesia page and looks over the dots and dashes that mark blood pressure, heart rate, ventilator settings—sort of a two-dimensional snapshot of her physiology. "A drug rep left pizza in the lounge. Give me a quick rundown and go before the food's all gone." He raises his eyebrows. "This patient's only eight?"

"She's small for her age, so be careful with your doses. Her face is padded, but I'd check for any pressure points again if the table's moved." I fill him in on Jolene's history and my plan for her anesthetic, point out the drugs I'm giving: fentanyl—a narcotic to blunt her pain, a little Propofol to deepen her sleep, anesthetic gases. It's almost impossible to talk to Brad without focusing on an enormous Adam's apple that rides up and down the column of his trachea below his surgical mask. He's just out of his residency, still swaggering between academic confidence and inexperience, and I catch myself talking to him more like a teacher or mother than a colleague. "Are you comfortable with pediatrics?"

"Sure." He looks over my setup, checks the row of labeled syringes, gathers in the data he'll need to take care of Jolene while I eat. "Leave your key in case I need more narcs. And eat a lot—cases are piling up out there, so who knows if you'll get dinner."

When I get back from lunch twenty minutes later, I sense more tension in the room. The cyst tracks deeper than Stevenson had expected, and he's getting short-tempered again. Brad looks relieved to see me.

"She's been stable," he says, then leans closer to my ear and whispers, "Wish I could say the same for your surgeon."

"Sorry. Thanks for lunch. Did you change anything?"

"Gave a little Propofol, a cc of fentanyl, turned your gas up some." He puts the fentanyl syringe into my hand as he slips out of the room.

Alicia looks up at me and wiggles her eyebrows in imitation of Stevenson. She's learned to ride the waves of his moods. I look over the surgical drapes and see a much bigger incision than when I left. Jolene's heart rate increases and her next blood pressure is up, a sign that beneath the sleeping layers of consciousness her body is reacting to pain. I screw the syringe of fentanyl into her IV line and inject more into her.

Within minutes her pulse returns to normal and her blood pressure drops.

Someone has changed the background music to classical, Erik Satie's *Trois Gymnopédies*, an effort to soothe the sleeping giant of Stevenson's temper, no doubt. He reaches for the scalpel again to open up Jolene's sacrum. I inject another dose of fentanyl, this time in advance of the electrical jolt of pain that will sear up her spinal cord when he cuts intact skin.

That's when an alarm sounds. The flashing numbers on the machine behind me show Jolene's airway pressure rising. It's probably a kink in the breathing circuit. Or maybe a plug of mucous in her endotracheal tube. The monitors are sensitive and often register some inconsequential change. I reset the alarm but it immediately blares again; the machine strains to push oxygen into her lungs.

I throw a lever and begin to ventilate Jolene by hand using a breathing bag—but there is too much resistance. She might be reacting to the surgery, coughing against the ventilator. Another monitor alarms—her blood pressure has dropped by twenty points and her heart rate is going down.

Mindy looks up and sees the flashing red lights on the screen. "Everything OK, Marie?" She is used to the minor problems that happen during many surgeries and waits to hear the alarm go silent, to know all is under control.

"It will be. Could you mix up some epinephrine for me?"

The reassuringly high pitch of her oxygen monitor is starting to drop, and there is more resistance against the breathing bag. I squeeze it with both hands. I trace the tubing—it's clear; the blockage must be inside Jolene's airway passages. I put my stethoscope over her back on the right, on the left, and can hear only faint breath sounds, a high-pitched wheeze when she exhales.

"Mindy, get a suction catheter out of the bottom drawer and hook it up to the vacuum."

My voice is steady and calm, but I know she hears a new urgency. I slip the catheter down Jolene's breathing tube to check for plugs. The tube is open.

The numbers on the oxygen monitor begin to spiral down. Any reserve is going fast. Jolene is in bronchospasm. Her smaller airways are swelling and tightening, strangling her from the inside. It must be anaphylaxis—a profound allergic reaction, or undiagnosed asthma. But her heart rate should have increased, at least initially.

My mind separates itself from my body. I enter some hyperfunctioning realm where I race forward in emergency protocols, calling for backup help, telling Stevenson we have to stop the surgery, turn her over.

He stares at me as if I've lost my mind. "She has an open wound on her back. We can't turn her over." I hear someone command him to put sterile towels over her back and turn her over now. *Now!* It is my voice.

Her heart rate keeps falling, the pitch on the oxygen saturation monitor is in a steep decline. Nurses and technicians pour into the room, but no other anesthesiologists are available. I rip sterile drapes from the operating field, shove my hands under her shoulders and head, tell Stevenson to grab her feet, Mindy to push the epinephrine, give her albuterol, atropine, antihistamine. We logroll her onto the gurney as her monitors plunge in pitch, plunge in heart rate.

Her skin is white, her lips are dusky. I call out emergency drug doses, order another IV, a defibrillator and arterial line. I place my hands over her sternum for chest compressions—her heart is failing and can't circulate the drugs that might save her life. I tell Stevenson to squeeze the breathing bag. The pressure monitor bounces off the scale with each breath like a bicycle pump on a tire with a blocked valve. Jolene's chest compresses easily beneath the heels of my hands, her pulse shows I'm circulating blood. But blood without oxygen is worthless. Her face is gray now, her lips dark blue.

She is dying. My God, this child is dying. I can feel blood rush into my face, the team watches me, waits for me to pull off a miracle, all of us teeter on the brink of realizing that Jolene has already been starved of oxygen for so long nothing of her former self will survive. A sound buzzes inside my head, and the garish operating lights make my hands glow as they pump up and down on Jolene's sternum. I don't know how much time has passed. Ten minutes? An hour? The noise level has dropped from a cacophony of commands to a heavy, weighted silence.

I feel Stevenson's hand on my shoulder, a gentle, focused pressure. "Call it, Marie. Call the code off. It's over."

· 4 ·

There is a roaring in the background, maybe inside my head, as if some cavernous space has cracked open. Everyone in the room— Mindy, Alicia, Bethany, Don—stares in never-intersecting lines of sight. If we look at one another, or speak, or break open the tight circle we stand in, this disaster will become real. It will become irreversible.

Someone squeezes my hand. Don has grasped it, urging me back into the role I must play, the professional face I need to apply. I look up and clear my throat, try to make my eyes focus. "Thank you. Everyone. I appreciate your help. I know you all did the best you could." No one wants to meet my eyes. Several people touch my shoulder or brush my arm as they leave, some attempt at support that might leave me intact.

I have to look over at her, this child, still plugged with IVs and monitors, the breathing tube still taped so securely to her lips, arms stretched out with her palms up so we could access her veins, lying there in the shape of a supplicant. I have witnessed the deaths of any number of people since I began medical school, almost all appropriately at the end of full lives of mating and parenting, loving and arguing, worshipping God and wondering whether God recognizes them. I have stood at bedsides while life support was discontinued, and held warm and supple hands as they entered death, wondering if I discerned that imprecise moment when a soul and body separate. But I have never seen a dead child. It feels wrenchingly incongruous to see her pallid, inanimate death mask without wrinkles or gray hair.

Don must have led me to a stool, because I'm sitting down and he's kneeling in front of me holding my clasped hands inside his own.

"We'll need to tell her soon, Marie. She'll be asking why it's been so long."

"Right." I barely hear my own words over my breath. I have to think of what to say. I have to think of how to tell her. I don't know how to do this. I can't tell her she's lost her little girl. I rock back and forth on the small stool, grip Don's hands as if they could anchor me to this spot in time.

He stands and guides me up to him, holds me wrapped in his arms and whispers, "Don't think. Don't be Marie yet. Be her doctor. Be the highly competent and skilled physician you are, helping a woman understand the most probable medical causes of this death. Just one more hour, then you can let go."

He leads me to the door and opens it. Jolene is behind me. It is such an adamant, ingrained principle of anesthesia never to leave a patient alone in the operating room, even for a moment, that I hesitate before walking out, still unable to comprehend there isn't something more I can do to help her. I must leave Jolene to care for her mother in a crisis of my own creation.

The surgery waiting room is lodged in an afterthought of space created over the parking garage, down two linoleum-tiled hallways. They retain the sterile, tunnel-like quality of institutional America, the floors and walls marred with pocked tiles and black streaks left by gurneys and wheelchairs. Our paired footsteps are magnified in the awkward silence. I will be the one who tells her—the death is clearly not a surgical complication, even if I cannot yet answer the blaring question of why Jolene died.

Bobbie Jansen is sitting in the back corner of the room, flipping through the pages of a magazine. When she looks up at the clock she sees us, and I watch the knowledge overtake her. I watch her search my face for the composed and reassuring anesthesiologist who interviewed her three hours ago. I see her realize that I am no longer the same woman, and that because of what I will say to her, she also will never be the same.

I kneel beside her chair so my face is level with her eyes. It feels like the whole world has dissolved into those two black holes. My words come out in a raspy whisper. "Ms. Jansen, Dr. Stevenson and I would like to talk with you in a more private place. Could you follow us, please?" She allows us each to take an elbow, one on either side, and walk through the waiting room filled with expectant, cautious faces. All watch as we turn down a short walkway into a small, dimly lit room with a couch and two straight-backed chairs. All recognize that this one woman will hear the words they have imagined but suppressed. Just below their tension I sense the guilty relief believing that surely two tragedies would never happen together, and this woman must have absorbed the horror that otherwise could have struck them.

Don and I lower Bobbie to the sofa and we take the chairs facing her. A box of Kleenex sits on the side table. She sits stiffly, her arms straight, supporting herself on the edge of the seat as if poised to run. The door clicks open and shut behind me, and I turn to see Bethany standing in the corner with her hands clasped in front of her and her head bowed, trying to remain an invisible witness. Of course. She will have to notify the medical examiner's office and enforce whatever regulations First Lutheran has in place for an intraoperative death. Does she have a page inside her book of protocols that dictates how I should tell Bobbie that something I did killed her child? A spasm grips my throat and for a second I'm terrified I will start to cry. Then I divide myself, split the doctor from the woman, and start to talk.

"Ms. Jansen, there has been a complication during your daughter's surgery, a complication from her anesthetic." I study her face, try to gauge how much to tell her at once, how much she already knows. Her fingers are white, clutching the edge of the flower-patterned sofa, and I feel an overwhelming urge to take her hand in mine, some need to connect with her physically as I talk, but I can't. "Jolene suffered what I believe was a respiratory arrest. A breathing problem during surgery. Her airways, the passages that take air into her lungs, closed up, and we weren't able to give her the oxygen she needed. We couldn't open them up."

She stares at the floor, nodding to herself, as if she's acknowledging an internal voice. I see her torso sway and I reach for her, but then her body goes rigid, like a warning to keep away. "I . . . We tried everything. All the drugs that might have helped. We all did everything we could to . . ."

She clears her throat and breaks in, speaking in a flat monotone. "Tell me what you need to tell me. Tell me whether she's still here. Whether she's still alive. Tell me now."

My ears are ringing so, it's hard to hear my own voice. I keep scrambling for the right words, magic words that could make a brutal truth bearable. "Jolene died, Ms. Jansen. We tried everything we could to reverse it, to save her, and we couldn't. I couldn't. She may have had an allergy we didn't know about, a drug reaction, or asthma. It may be difficult to ever know for sure."

In slowed time Bobbie curls in on herself, clenches her arms across her stomach. She lets out a keening moan, an animal howl, both desperate and hopeless, as if she's trying to block out the sight and sound of us.

Don glances at me. He looks ashen, almost disoriented. He coughs and says, just loud enough to be heard above Bobbie's cry, "Mrs. Jansen, when things like this happen, when a death is this unexpected, we suggest—the coroner will suggest—that we examine the body . . . the person, in more detail afterward. Particularly for other family members who might need surgery in the future, finding the cause of death can give everyone more peace in the end. Sometimes . . ."

Bethany steps up behind Don and puts a hand on his shoulder. I look at him in stunned abashment, wondering if he has leapt to the only bit of science he could resurrect from this emotional maelstrom.

Bobbie lifts her head and stares, her mouth ajar, and his speech stutters to a halt. "You want to cut her open, is that what you're asking me? You come in here and tell me she's gone, and in the next breath you ask me to let you cut her apart?" Her mouth gapes, and every line on her face is creviced deep, and abruptly old, wrung out, as if all the pain she's tolerated in her life is crashing her open.

"I think Dr. Stevenson meant . . ." I start, unable to stop myself from reaching for her hands.

"Actually, the medical examiner will need to decide that," Bethany says, sounding so sane and calm the contrast is harsh.

Bobbie shoves my hands away from her and shouts, "Get your hands off me! What are you saying? There aren't any other family members to put at *peace*! There's nobody but the two of us. Jolene and me. Now. You take me to her. You take me to my baby!" She gasps in irregular, audible gulps of air, as if she were forcing herself to breathe. Then the breaths coagulate into a sob and she drops onto the floor clutching her head in her hands.

Don stands up and nods toward the door, signaling me to follow him out. I feel like I'm rooted in the chair, waiting for some conclusion. "Ms. Jansen," I say in a hoarse whisper, "I . . . I can't tell you . . ." Someone puts a hand on my back. The hospital chaplain has come in, recognizing that I have reached the end of what I can bear to say, the end of what Bobbie can bear to hear. He will sit with her until she seems ready, and then escort her into the curtained cubicle where they have taken Jolene, IVs and wires and endotracheal tube carefully left in place for the medical examiner, a white sheet pulled up over the discolored area on her chest where I did CPR.

I walk back to the operating rooms and begin the documentation that follows any medical complication: the detailed chronological description of each event that took place from the moment I met Jolene. Every sentence I write unravels a train of automatic responses I apply to an emergency, a train that has to move forward without hesitation during a crisis.

But now the damage is known. Now I stand back as the critical observer of my fallibility, rewinding the action from an omniscient standpoint, knowing the outcome and therefore knowing that every decision I made, every confident, assertive action I took, every command I gave, ultimately has proven wrong. The only salvation I can find in the act of writing my own perfunctory defense is that it keeps me from having to drive home from the hospital and be alone.

· 5 ·

I barely remember going out to my car or coming up in the elevator. Bethany shifted the rest of my cases to other rooms. I'm sure it made other people's schedules awful, but I couldn't have introduced myself to another patient. I don't think I could have given a safe anesthetic.

I should eat something. It's after eight o'clock and I haven't had any food since Brad got me out for lunch. I open my refrigerator and a wave of nausea sweeps through me. My living room is chilly. I stand by the windows pressing my forehead against the cold glass—pressing hard until my skin feels bruised. Like pulsing physical pain, I pass through seconds of forgetting into exploding images: Jolene's dark purple lips, Bobbie's mouth gaping in a ragged hole, the sound of her moan that felt like something sucked out of my own lungs.

My answering machine is packed. Three of my partners have left messages offering to give up their vacation days if I need some time off. Don Stevenson has called to tell me he knows I did everything possible and I have his full support. Joe has called, too, at first pretending to be insouciant and upbeat; then, dropping his voice, he reminds me it's part of the risk we all take being doctors, no one could have done a better job. The hospital chaplain has left his home telephone number, encouraging me to call at any hour if I need to talk. He had caught up with me just as I was leaving the hospital, still too stunned to cry. "You'll need to grieve almost as much as her family," he told me. "Grieve. And then forgive yourself." The minute he said it I knew the question that would become my cross: Did I miss a diagnosis in her? Could I have prevented Jolene's death?

I wonder who's calling Bobbie Jansen, offering to sit up through the night with her, make food or help with funeral arrangements. Who's letting her rage about the guilt and anger she must feel having entrusted her daughter to doctors, to strangers—to *me*?

The day after Jolene's death, I park in the same spot, take the same elevators to the same locker, hang the same stethoscope around my neck and dive back into my work. But there are oil splotches on the parking garage wall I've never seen before, deep chips gouged out of the cement pillars I'm sure weren't there yesterday. The carpeting in the elevator must have been replaced overnight. It's the color of blood—an odd choice for a hospital—stained with car grease and frayed to bare jute strands near the doorway. The locker room is bigger today, and there is a brown water stain across the acoustic ceiling tiles in the shape of a human heart. I eat breakfast because it is time to eat. I nod at the laundry woman because I can't fabricate a smile. And I gradually begin to understand that nothing in my life will feel or look or behave the same again. Even when this is years behind me, and I've successfully anesthetized and reawakened a thousand patients, there will always be the before and the after Jolene Jansen.

Phil Scoble has left a note in my mailbox asking me to drop by his office. On my way up I run into Will. His smile is too bright. "Hey. Marie. How're you doing?" Then he drops the facade and hooks his thumbs under the string of his waistband. "I heard about your case yesterday. I'm sorry."

"Thanks." Despite myself my mouth starts to tremble. Will pinkens with embarrassment. He shrugs his arms forward, as if he'd like to give me a hug but has discovered his hands permanently affixed to his waist. They flap awkwardly once and sag, a bird arrested at take-off, and he looks down at his feet.

"I'm on my way up to see Phil," I say, rescuing him. Then I put my hand on his arm and attempt a smile. "It'll be fine, Will. Thank you for being brave enough to bring it up."

I step into the closing elevator and Will wedges his foot against the door. "Marie, it happened to me once. Years ago. Lawsuit . . . the whole thing. It can get pretty lonely." The elevator door starts to buzz and he releases it. "Call me, if you want." I hear his disembodied voice as the doors seal shut.

Pamela, Phil's secretary, stands up as soon as I walk into his waiting area. "Hi, Dr. Heaton. He's expecting you. Need any coffee?" I would love to believe she hasn't already heard, but she's never stood up for me before. She hands me a Styrofoam cup and blushes the instant our eyes meet. She turns and begins stacking papers on her already tidy desk. "Go on in. Let me know if you want a refill."

Phil immediately walks over and hugs me. I've known him for eight years, had dinner at his home multiple times, even joked with him about crossing over to the "dark side" when he joined the hospital governing board, but he's never touched me in any way other than the most cordial handshake. He clears his throat and pulls a chair up to his desk for me. "Did you get any sleep last night?"

I shake my head and sit down.

"Sure you're up to working today? We'd all understand."

"Got to get back up on the horse, don't I?" I answer in a quavery voice.

"Well . . ." He purses his lips together and blinks. "You've probably already talked to the malpractice company. Do you have a meeting set up with them yet?"

I let my breath out. I've been concentrating so hard on not crying, I'm almost relieved to switch to the procedural mechanics of this death. "It was so late when I got home, I was going to call later this morning."

Phil nods, pressing his lips together in a taut line. His hands are clasped in a thick, square lattice, his nails thoroughly scrubbed. His blue surgical cap is pushed up high above his brow, leaving a red indentation across his forehead. "Sure. We've already talked to them, of course, so they have the basic information. I imagine they'll try to reach a quick settlement."

"A settlement? Is she . . . is the mother suing us?"

He grimaces briefly before adopting a perfunctory smile. "Not yet. I doubt any lawyers have gotten to her yet. But in a situation like this—a healthy girl and a low-risk operation—the hospital will want to move straight to a settlement offer. Resolve it before the media puts it on the front page."

I slump forward on my chair and press the heels of my hands against my eyes. "I hadn't even thought about that yet—any kind of legal thing. I'd been thinking about sending her mother flowers or food, or starting a donation fund or something." An involuntary laugh escapes me. "I guess that sounds stupid, doesn't it?" I trail off. He is staring at me with a mixture of sympathy and alarmed perplexity, as if I have no inkling of what he sees charging at my back.

"Actually, it sounds kind. I hope it stands in your favor." His tone is almost paternal. "Marie, I've worked with you for seven years. I know how thorough you are, how compassionate. No one here blames you for this death."

Tears start to well up and I have to hold my breath for a minute to get control. "It's a little hard to believe that right now. But thanks."

He returns to a more professional sobriety. "Let me know as soon as you talk to the insurance representative—I want to set up a meeting with all of us by the end of the week."

My hands are crossed in my lap, dry and chapped from washing between surgeries, and I have a sudden flash of them pumping on Jolene's chest when I gave her CPR. I blurt out another question. "So, if we settle, is that like an admission of a mistake?"

"No. Well, technically yes, in that it'll go into the national database, but outside of some miracle of ignorance, there's no chance this mother won't seek damages. If she doesn't think of it, someone else will. So you either settle or let it go to a full-tilt trial."

The database Phil is referring to is a public record of doctors who have paid an insurance claim to a patient. It doesn't matter if the claim was defensible, or justified, or even moral. It doesn't even matter if it never blew up into an actual lawsuit. It cost the malpractice insurer money, and is therefore published like a slash mark across the physician's reputation.

"Could a trial clear my name?" I ask.

"It could clear it, or it could cost you multiple times what a settlement would. You and the hospital. Not to mention the publicity." He drops his voice back to a more calming note. "Look, even if the mother—what's her name? Jason?—does get carried away and pushes this all the way to a trial, I can't imagine the autopsy will expose any problems with your care."

"Ms. Jansen refused an autopsy. There won't be one."

"She can't."

"What do you mean?"

"She can't refuse. This will be a medical examiner's case. The girl was ASA One, right? No health problems? Unanticipated deaths in ASA One and Two patients almost always get an autopsy."

A knot twists in my stomach remembering the horror on Bobbie's face when Don asked about an autopsy. Phil leans closer. "You should be glad about this, Marie. An autopsy will just confirm you did everything right. Maybe even . . . I guess we shouldn't talk about any particularities without the lawyers here. Look, are you sure you don't want to take the day off?"

I haven't thought about an autopsy before now. I've written all Jolene's death forms and reports assuming she died of bronchospasm, from anaphylaxis or asthma, even if I'm not sure what triggered the reaction.

"Where is she now? Jolene—the little girl?"

"King County morgue, I guess. The medical examiner took her shortly after the mother left."

I've had a picture in my head of Jolene lying in a trundle bed, with children's toys around her instead of flowers, her mother sitting beside her in an armchair, smoothing her hair. It's ridiculous—a fabricated scene I wasn't even conscious of until it metamorphosed into an eviscerated child on a pathologist's slab.

"Do you have any idea when the funeral will be?" I ask.

Phil blinks as if his eyes burn. "Marie, I know you feel for this family, but it would be foolish to show up at the funeral. Even if you're not to blame, you should keep your distance here. Anything personal has to come second to legal issues. Maybe you could make some gesture after there's a settlement."

Three hours later, in the middle of a laminectomy, Frank Hopper pages me, asking me to come to his office before I leave for the day. Frank is First Lutheran's CEO. Stepping into his office is like opening a door from Wal-Mart to Saks Fifth Avenue. The nubby print carpet changes to lush wool, the vinyl chair coverings transform to Italian leather. The only other time I was in this sanctum was when I signed my contract.

Frank invites all of us to address him by his first name, and begins every conversation with intense, direct eye contact that dissolves into a scan over my face, my hair, my clothes, my posture—a measuring assessment that usually leaves me feeling inadequate. He reassures me that he has complete faith in my medical judgment and how I handled the "crisis," skillfully avoiding the word *death*. He and the whole staff understand that these next months will be trying for me and they want to keep all avenues of support and communication open. His elbows perch on the arms of his swiveling chair, and now and then a cufflink peeps out of his sleeve—onyx, I guess, with what looks like a diamond embedded in its belly. It makes me wish I had at least worn earrings today—something in blue to complement my crumpled and overlaundered scrubs.

"We're working with a great malpractice company. Top-notch lawyers. John Donnelly—he's helped us before. The child . . . a girl?"

I nod.

"She was . . . from what Don Stevenson said, she was handicapped?"

"Jolene was mentally retarded. Yes."

"That's to our benefit, you know. No lost wages to compensate. When are you meeting with the insurance representative?"

"I haven't had a chance to call yet. Today . . ."

"Make it soon. You need to do it while you still remember details. You've charted everything, right?"

"Completely. Right after it happened. We called a code, of course, so Matt Corchoran was there—he'll have all the medication records." I realize my hands are twisted together in fists and I unclench them. "I've rechecked all my drug doses, gone over every step of it, Frank. I don't think there's anything I could have done differently."

He holds a hand up in the air. "This is your first experience with this sort of thing, am I right? So take my advice: don't talk about it. Only with the lawyers and insurance people. Anything else becomes fair game to be used against you."

My brother-in-law answers the phone on the first ring. I can tell he's disappointed it's me.

"Hey, Gordon. Is Lori free? She can call me back if she's putting the kids to bed."

"*Lori!*" I hear through a muffled mouthpiece. "She'll be here." His voice lightens some, as if he's given up hope that I will transform into whatever business contact he was waiting to hear from. "So how's the Sandman?"

"I'm OK."

I picture him running his stubby hand through his thinning hair, waving the phone at her and mouthing that he's waiting for an important call. I've worked to appreciate all that my sister sees in Gordon. He has a capricious sense of humor, laced with a keener edge, lately. But he has made Lori happy, for the most part, over seventeen years, three children, six houses and multiple cycles of real estate booms and busts. Boom for the last four or five years, which seems to have inspired enough self-confidence in him to probe into my own income.

"You make money putting people to sleep, and I make money waking them up. I wake people up to possibility. That's what real estate development is all about, when you boil it down. Possibility. Abandoned, weed-covered plots turned into bedrooms, restaurants and cash machines," he tells me at any chance, never deterred by my explanation that student loan repayments absorbed most of my disposable income for five years, and now the rest goes into the retirement account I'm a decade behind in funding. Tonight I am spared when Lori grabs the phone from him.

"Perfect timing. I was just about to call you."

"Claire Voyance here," I say, our joke for the startling frequency with which we both reach for the phone at the same time. But tonight my voice twists in the middle of the words. I tuck into my reading chair, and pull my nightgown over my knees like some small wood creature curled in protection. Everything I need to tell her is flooding up from my chest, pushing up against the base of my skull, churning into cries and images, begging for relief.

And I can't let go.

There is a wail in the background, and Lori shushes a child. "I need doctorly advice. Lia fell on her arm about an hour ago—jumping on a pogo stick wearing roller skates. Go figure! How can I tell if it's broken?"

And here is my alibi. Everything that hurts is instantly swallowed inside the emotional vacuum of logic and professional advice. "Is it swollen? Does it look crooked at all? Can she wiggle her fingers? Bend her elbow?"

I have Lori splint Lia's arm in a rolled-up magazine, give her Tylenol and call her pediatrician in the morning. Lori wants to know if it matters whether she chooses *Rolling Stone* or *Harper's*. From there she glides into descriptions of a disagreement with one of the teachers, how unusually rainy it's been in Texas, "as if we lived in Seattle," the fact that my father's birthday is approaching and we should plan something together for him. The telephone is wedged between my face and shoulder and tears flow down my cheek along the hard plastic receiver until it becomes slick. I wonder if it is possible to cause a short circuit should they flood the tiny holes that carry my voice over fifteen hundred miles between here and Fort Worth.

· 6 ·

It's easy to get the information about the funeral. I call up the medical examiner's office on Saturday, when only a low-level assistant is likely to be on duty (even so, I'm tempted to alter my voice, ready to conjure a pseudonym). She perfunctorily tells me which funeral home received Jolene's body; the funeral director consolingly tells me the date, time and place. Half my closet is on the floor by the time I've chosen a simple navy skirt and sweater, having given up on composing an outfit at once somber, tasteful and capable of making me thoroughly invisible.

The first truly springlike day of April, cherry trees quaking with proud blossoms, the air a purified blue, is the day Jolene is buried. I park across the street from a small chapel attached to Massins' Funeral Parlor and grip the steering wheel while I reiterate all the reasons I'm justified in being here: funerals are a chance for resolution, a chance to seek peace; funerals are events where wealth, power and status acquiesce to equalizing fate—events where cautionary legal prudence should hold no ground. I've come here to show respect for Jolene's life, for Bobbie's loss—to acknowledge that even if we end up in adversarial roles in lawyers' suites, I can grieve with her. I can do something to make her feel less abandoned. I have come here because I could not stay away.

A few minutes after the service is scheduled to start a man in a black suit walks onto the porch, checks his watch and closes the doors. I slip into the chapel and let my eyes adjust to the dim light. It is the simplest of rooms, no crosses or stars, everything cut to square without peaks rising up to point at God. I have no idea whether Bobbie is a religious woman. Is she having her daughter memorialized in this allegorical sanctuary because she is godless? Or just because she is poor? Did she raise Jolene to pray each night before sleep, begging the Lord her soul to keep? And when she did not wake, would never wake, was Bobbie prepared for God to take her child's soul? Sunshine spills through the dusty panes of a high row of windows in shining bundled blades. Only seven or eight other people are scattered through the pews.

In the absolute stillness all I can hear is my heart pounding. It's to be expected, I tell myself—so much guilt to work through. Of course I feel anxious about seeing Bobbie. I'm more ashamed to admit that I'm scanning the room for anyone here from First Lutheran who could recognize me. I slide onto the farthest edge of the last oak pew, as distant from the other guests as I can get.

Bobbie is sitting in the first row. Her hair is gathered into a loose bun at the nape of her neck, exposing the vulnerable bones of her cervical vertebrae, a rippling ladder from the collar of her black sweater to the curving base of her skull. She looks so much smaller than I had remembered. Jolene's child-sized white coffin is directly in front of her on a raised platform, a bouquet of star lilies and white roses draped over the half-closed lid. There aren't any other flowers—two large urns at the sides of the central stage stand empty. The teddy bear Jolene was clutching when I met her in the preoperative holding area must be lying on her breast—I can see the pink nylon of its stuffed belly curved above the wooden rim.

A middle-aged man and woman sit in the same pew with Bobbie, though not close to her. She seems isolated here, among the people I would assume she knows best. I glance at the faces I can see and try to guess at any family resemblance. The door swings open again and sunlight slices across the stone floor. Backlit by white light, two men, both dressed in dark suits, are silhouetted against the entrance. They're coming toward me, looking right at me. I know them—Phil Scoble and Frank Hopper. They must be here to represent the hospital. I should have anticipated this. It would be the politically smart thing to do—to show up in a gesture of sympathy. Smart for First Lutheran and foolish for me. I'm about to stand and face them both when they cross out of the light and I see they are complete strangers. My head falls into my hands as if I were praying; I'm enraged at my relief.

The man who closed the chapel doors stands up at a lectern, clears his throat and opens a notebook. He drops his chin to survey his meager audience over his glasses, then welcomes us to this service honoring the life of Jolene Marielle Jansen. He reads a touching, generic eulogy. I wonder if they have prewritten speeches at a place like this, abbreviated psalms for children. Bobbie doesn't look up. She doesn't even move.

The speaker takes his seat and the chapel is quiet except for a few stifled coughs. The silence builds to an awkward shifting of weight and creaking of benches until people gradually begin to drift outside. The woman nearest Bobbie stands up and walks over to her, touches her shoulder and says something too low to hear. I gather my purse and a small spray of iris and daisies tied with a pink ribbon. I recognize now that I chose pink because of the bear—guessing that was Jolene's favorite color. She was at an age when girls like to have a favorite color, I think. And the blue iris because her eyes were so blue, almost a cornflower blue, but I couldn't find any cornflowers.

I have it all planned out, how I will walk up to Bobbie at the end of the service and hand her the flowers, tell her how sorry I am for all she's going through, maybe touch her sleeve and then go before she feels like she has to talk to me. Nothing, certainly, that would upset my malpractice insurers or any lawyers. She might not even recognize me, dressed in normal clothes with my hair down. I can't introduce myself to her again here—the thought of it paralyzes me.

The two men I mistook for Phil and Frank stand up and approach her. One kneels down, blond and boyish-looking, out of kilter somehow with anyone who might be a relative. He talks to her for several minutes, eventually helps her up and guides her down the aisle. They pass me and I can't even stand up to intersect her. My heart turns over when I see her face-on. I've seen the same deserted eyes on trauma victims in the emergency room, a mask of stunned incomprehension as they struggle to recognize their exploded world. I am obviously invisible to her—we all are.

Walking out to my car, I see the three of them standing together under the boughs of a massive cherry tree, pruned into stubby wings bisected by a power line. A gusting breeze frosts them with a snowfall of petals. The blond man pulls a white business card out of his suit pocket and folds it into her hands, holding them in his own for a moment much as a minister might bless a parishioner after services. He escorts her down the street to an older beige Ford sedan with one mismatched blue panel on the passenger side. Then the two men walk to a black Lexus and chat together. In the daylight the balding man looks more juvenile, almost obsequious in the way he chuckles and agrees with the blond. There's an abrasive self-confidence about their posture that makes it clear they're used to choosing who stays excluded. Whatever they're discussing, it couldn't be the death of a little girl. It is suddenly as obvious to me as if I had read this man's business card. He's not a minister. He's a lawyer.

In the evening, after I've showered and changed into a nightgown, I pick up the strewn contents of my wardrobe. I hardly ever wear anything but scrubs or jeans or running shorts anymore. I bought most of these dresses in the first few years after First Lutheran hired me, when I could finally afford to treat myself occasionally. So many of them look dated now, if I paid much attention to fashion. There was another spurt of consumerism at the end of my last student loan payment, this condominium and some furniture. It was the first time I owned an entire refrigerator, not just one borrowed shelf. The first time I could sit up late reading a novel in my own living room and not worry which roommate would come stumbling in from a party. And a new car—at last. No mismatched door panels in my life these days.

The purchases almost seemed part of the rite of passage of becoming a full-fledged physician, like framing my medical degree, licenses and board certifications—documents I was expected to display, status symbols I was expected to crave. I think I mainly desired the proof that I could provide for myself. I put so much on hold.

I ended up never hanging the certificates on any wall. Instead I filled the blank spaces with family photographs—my nieces and nephew at christenings and birthdays; my sister and me at the beach, at a rodeo, doubled up bareback on the sagging spine of her pinto mare; my mother in her rose garden, still as slender and fresh as one of the unopened buds gathered in her gloved hand, an age before my clear memories of her. And one formal portrait of my father taken for his retirement announcement, propped up in the center of a bookcase from which he can judge the wealth and security I've accumulated without his help.

I arrange the wilting iris and daisies in an orange juice glass and set them on my bedside table, scribble a note to Gary apologizing that I have to attend a conference the week he's planned to visit, begging him to reschedule. Then I call Lori.

"It wasn't broken—only a sprain. Her doctor loved the magazine idea. We went with *Rolling Stone* in the end. How was your day?"

"Not so great," I answer. Then I take a deep breath and add, "I went to a funeral."

"Marie, I'm sorry. Who was it?"

I sit down on the bed and knot the phone cord in my hands. The iris hangs limply over the rim of the glass—I turn out the light so I can't look at it anymore. "It was a patient. Someone I took care of."

Lori is soothing and sympathetic. She's heard me talk about the lingering, often painful deaths of cancer patients who may undergo multiple surgeries before letting go. "Ah. That was kind of you to be there. Had you gotten close to the family?"

"No." I stop. A soft cry escapes me; I can almost feel Lori's tension at the other end. "It was a little girl. Eight years old. She died on my operating room table."

Lori lets out a low groan. "Oh God. What was wrong with her? What kind of operation?"

"Nothing. She was a healthy patient having a completely routine surgery." My breath reverberates against the mouthpiece; otherwise there is complete silence. I curl down onto my pillow with the phone snuggled under my cheek. "We were in the middle of her operation and suddenly I couldn't ventilate her. Her airways closed."

"There wasn't any reason? I mean, nothing you could predict?" She sounds almost panicked, and I know she's talking to me as a mother right now, not a sister. How can she help that? I hear another, smaller voice murmur in the background; Lori whispers, "Shhh, shhh, everything's OK, baby," and there is a rustling of fabric. Then she speaks into the phone again. "Lia's in my bed. She had a nightmare."

"I'm sorry. I should let you go."

"No, it's OK. She's back to sleep. I can't believe you're up there going through this all alone. Do you want to talk about it?"

The tug of loneliness stretches the continent between us. "They've told me I'm not supposed to talk about it. That's almost the worst part right now."

"But you know it wasn't your fault, right? I mean, do things just go wrong sometimes?"

"In sick people. Old people. Not in eight-year-olds. At least not very often. I think she had an anaphylactic reaction to one of the drugs. Maybe latex. And I treated her for that, but . . . it all happened so fast."

"Is that like an allergy?"

"The worst kind. The kind that kills people."

"But you couldn't have predicted that, right? I mean, that isn't your fault."

I don't answer her. How can I explain that blame is only one part of guilt when something goes wrong in a doctor's work?

"Do you want me to fly up? I could ask Olivia to help Gordon with the kids. I could be there tomorrow."

"Uh-uh. Don't even think of it." I try to force my voice to relax. It sounds hollow in the cove between my face and my pillow. "I'll be OK. I guess at some point I was bound to have a bad outcome, just based on statistics."

"Oh, Marie. I know you took wonderful—perfect—care of her."

I roll onto my back, brushing damp hair from my temples onto the pillow. "If I'd taken perfect care of her, she wouldn't have died. She was an only child, Lori. Her mother's only child."

. . .

Lori and I lost our mother twelve years ago this month, when I was twenty-five. I was in my third year of medical school. After twenty-four months bent over microscopes and cadavers and textbooks that broke the spine of my bookcase, my classmates and I all felt ready to apply our memorized Latin terms and lists of symptoms to flesh-and-blood patients. Finally we graduated to the hospital, and began to wear the emblematic white coat of a physician—pockets crammed with rubber stethoscopes, reflex hammers, tourniquets and antibiotic tables. We were the lowest tier of patient caretakers at that stage—even nurses' aides smirked at our flailing efforts to mesh aced exams with the practical realities of illness. No textbook can teach you how to insert an IV catheter into a vein or a nasogastric tube into the stomach, or to suture a kicking child. Egos collapsed under the weight of bedpans and Band-Aids taped over our botched efforts. Still, for most of us, that white coat implied some mastery not only of medical knowledge, but of medical morals— the ethics of life and death. At some point, though, we all had to face humanizing reality. I had to face it inside my own family's private crisis.

My mother had rheumatic fever as a young child, which damaged her heart valves. Over the five and a half decades of her life, her heart strained to push blood through a shrinking portal, building up its thick, muscular wall like the oil-slicked biceps of a weight lifter. Her heart strained and thickened while she ran with girlhood friends in her rural Texas school yard, fell in love with the older graduate student who lived in her mother's boardinghouse, worked as a waitress to buy her husband's books, tried for years to conceive a child and then bore my sister and me within fourteen months of one another. Her heart struggled and strained during all of this, quietly compensating for the misshapen valves so that all along she believed herself healthy, believed she would live to see her daughters marry, hold her grandchildren, help her husband into the infirmity of old age.

Her heart granted her this grace period of apparent health until it turned some physiological corner of irreversible damage and she became aware of a breathlessness when she mopped her floors, a pain in her chest while weeding her rose garden. By the time Lori and I were in high school she'd marshaled a standard list of excuses for missing picnics or walks or trips to the lake. Even then her quiet pride, her maternal endurance, kept her symptoms a private matter, each year without medical intervention diminishing any chance to reverse her decline. She kept her symptoms hidden until I began to notice how she paused in the middle of our staircase every time she carried up the socks, books, sweaters or shoes that we, her family, ungraciously dropped in the middle of our kitchen.

But it wasn't until I was in medical school that I understood it well enough to insist—in a newly respected voice, propped up by my fresh white coat—that she see a cardiologist and take advantage of what modern medicine could offer her. By then her only choice was open-heart surgery.

Her cardiologist explained that she would likely do well after the surgery. Yes, her risks were higher than they would have been in the early stages, but without the surgery her risks were higher still. My family turned to me to translate this foreign dialect of choice and consequence. And I could—even in that infancy of my medical life—explain ventricular hypertrophy, valvular areas and gradients, cardiac output, cardiopulmonary bypass. Those words I could look up in my *Stedman's Medical Dictionary,* dissect down to their Latinate origins and offer their meanings up to my parents like gifts, proof that my education had worth. What I could *not* give them, and what they needed most, was the perspective of experience, the critical filter of judgment that might have made their choice clear: without heart surgery she would almost certainly die within two years.

Somehow the choice seemed to paralyze them, having grown up in a world where illness rarely offered options. We talked in circles. I tried to persuade her, using simplified words and penned sketches of her circulatory system. She turned to my father, as always, for his opinion. He asked me to explain it all again, as if a more thorough description might guarantee her life would be saved. My mother sank into a depression that stalled her ability to see a future either way.

Then one morning she rose from her favorite chair and collapsed to the floor with a crushing weight in her chest. The pain so ripped the breath from her that she couldn't cry out. My father heard the shattering teacup and ran to the living room. She was still talking when we reached the hospital. But much of her heart was dying. The stiffening muscular wall that had granted her one last decade of life had grown so thick it squeezed shut its own blood vessels—retribution for its malfunctioning valves.

She was rushed into intensive care, the very unit where I was assigned to learn the intricate balancing of medication drips and electrical wires and breathing machines that can save a life or merely painfully prolong it. There was a chance still, said her cardiac surgeon. If the stress on her heart could be lightened enough to allow some healing, some trickle of oxygen-rich blood to its inner core, she might survive the surgery.

They slipped a small pump through the flesh of her groin into her femoral artery and up into her aorta to lodge just beyond her flailing valve. The pump was timed to the electrical rhythms of my mother's heart, inflating and deflating to siphon the blood forward, out to her body and her brain.

I sat in the half-light and listened to the rhythmic thudding of the mechanical pump, muffled through the layers of her living flesh. I envisioned the submarine-shaped pump expanding and contracting in the bright blood of her aorta, its cord snaking down the pulsing vessel to erupt from her groin and connect her to the machinery. The sound lulled me into a realm where memories of my life with her and hope for my future could weave together, connect as a continuous line, without the scar of grief I knew her death would leave inside me.

My father circled the floor like a confined animal, repeating the same questions over and over. I kept trying new words, new metaphors that might make the mystery of her failing body comprehensible to him. But as days went by and her kidneys stopped cleansing her bloodstream, her liver quit manufacturing enzymes and proteins, her bone marrow stopped creating new blood cells, waiting for surgery became moot. Now we were waiting for death.

A meeting was gathered of her medical team, my sister, my father and myself. This time her cardiologist's words were chosen haltingly, chosen to be soothing but without hope. He gently guided my father to the understanding that he must end this artificial extension of his wife's life.

I'm sure my mother never suspected she was raising a doctor. Female doctors were rare in her world. She taught me the things she believed I would need in my life: how to sew a bias-cut tie as a gift for my father one Christmas—a wide garishly flowered thing he wore once out of courtesy; how to separate the white from the yolk when making meringues, slithering the contents of the raw egg from half shell to half shell until the golden center swam naked in its clear membrane; how to pluck my eyebrows, put on a bra and pull sheer stockings up my legs without snagging the interlaced filaments.

She taught me all the things my sister has put to excellent use in her life, all the complexities of stabilizing a home and joining two people and the generation they create together into a new and whole family—critical facts that make families work, passed from woman to woman, never tested or graded or ranked, but invaluable nonetheless. I stored them up to share with my own daughter someday, after the temporarily consuming labor of medical training was finished. Once I regained some control over my life, after my residency, I always knew, I would rejoin the intended stream of marriage and motherhood. I never meant to dam myself off from those. I just knew they would require careful scheduling.

· 7 ·

After the first week people stop telling me how sorry they are or asking me if I'm holding up all right. Instead of being a disaster shared with everyone who works in the operating rooms at First Lutheran, it gradually becomes the silently screaming secret that sends an awkward hush over groups of surgical techs and nurses chatting at the coffee bar the minute I show up. I ask a question about the schedule, offer an opinion on the new epidural kits, give the most intentionally bland comment on the weather, and the responses return stained with pity.

The other anesthesiologists at the hospital are bolder: "It happens to a lot of good doctors; I might have made all the same decisions"; "I know how you must feel. But for the grace of God I could have been assigned to that room"; "You have to get up and go on, Marie." Only the vaguest shadow of judgment in their eyes, only the slightest drop in their voices dangles the question of doubt.

Within a few days after Jolene's funeral it becomes obvious that my closer friends are working harder so I can get out of the hospital earlier. Joe, Will, even Sandy McLaughlin, who is usually so private and self-contained, all seem to be coincidentally discovering my late case has been transferred into one of their rooms. They wind up unexpectedly free right around noon with nothing better to do than send me out to pick up Thai food for everyone. It's hard not to care that I'm never assigned any pediatric cases.

One morning the garage elevator opens and Brad gets in. As soon as he sees me I can tell he wishes he'd taken the stairs. It's the first moment I admit to myself that I've been avoiding him in the cafeteria and conference room. He nods at me and pushes the button for the next floor up, even though we both have to get to the fourth floor operating rooms. When the doors open, though, I get out with him in the deserted vestibule of basement offices.

"Brad." I hesitate, stretching for safe words. "Look. I never got a chance to tell you how sad I am that you're caught up in this. It was just . . . bad timing. Bad luck." I intend to stop with that, I know I should stop, but there isn't a soul around to hear us. "I don't think anything could have made a difference, on either of our parts, but if you noticed something, even some change that didn't seem important at the time . . ."

He is beet red, shaking his head. "I can't. I'm sorry, Marie. My lawyer says I can't say anything to anyone except a shrink or a priest." He reaches past my head to push the elevator button, and I feel my own face grow hot.

"Your lawyer? Why did you talk to a lawyer?"

He shrugs and pushes the button again. "I just needed to know where I stand. When . . . if a suit's filed." He steps inside the elevator and looks directly at me for the first time. His eyes seem sad, or disappointed, or maybe just afraid. "Marie, I'm the new guy here. I don't have any record to stand on. Who are they gonna try to hang?" The doors close between us and the cables hum as he is hoisted away.

A week to the day after Jolene's death I need to leave early to meet with my malpractice case representative and Joe comes in to take over my thyroidectomy.

"Got your speech ready?"

"I guess. Do I look nervous?"

He puts an arm around my shoulder, his mouth at my ear. "Just remember. You're paying *her*."

"Yeah. It's easy to forget that right now. Sort of feels like she's the whole jury."

I tell him my patient's medical history and allergies and my anesthetic plan for her. I'm about to leave when I remember her primary request of me. "She really wants her dentures back in as soon as she's awake," and I point out the clear container holding a perfect plastic grin.

Caroline Meyers-Yeager, my malpractice claims manager, is a petite woman, somewhat older than myself, wearing a crisply fitted ivory silk suit that matches her equally crisp blond hair. Her clipped New York accent cuts to the bone of historical payouts for pediatric deaths and the statistical odds against prevailing in front of a jury if this comes to trial. I'm sitting opposite her desk, unable to swallow the tea her assistant brought, uncomfortably aware that I haven't combed my hair in hours.

She listens to my well-rehearsed synopsis of Jolene's anesthetic and code—the version my own bathroom mirror confirmed I'd performed flawlessly. "I've gone over my notes repeatedly," I tell her in my most objective and collected voice. "The most likely explanation is anaphylaxis."

She jots a note or two on a long yellow legal pad. "But she had no history of allergies."

"Not in her record. Her mother didn't know of any."

She frowns and skims her notes. "You've done a good job with your charting. Very detailed—Donnelly will like that. But if you had to question your own diagnoses"—now she flashes a more conspiratorial smile—"if you were your own cross-examining prosecutor, is there anything that doesn't fit?"

I start to answer her, consciously composed, but she catches the flicker of doubt. "It's OK," she says. "Nothing we say here is discoverable."

"Her heart rate." I pause and bite my lip. "It should have gone up at first. Before her oxygen level dropped. That's the one thing that doesn't make sense."

"How significant do you think that is?"

I remind myself that for all her experience in the legalities of medicine, she isn't a doctor. "I'm not sure. I gave her a narcotic, fentanyl, and that might have kept it from going up."

She raises her eyebrows and waits. I add, "In the whole picture? It probably doesn't mean anything at all." Despite this blind alley, it is a relief to finally admit this fraction of doubt in a protected space. "Regardless, the autopsy should confirm anaphylaxis, if I'm right about that."

She nods and takes a sip out of her own teacup; her lipstick stays perfect. "Let's hope so. Keep in mind that whether you did everything right or not, First Lutheran has a vested interest in keeping this quiet, which means settling even if that implies some error. The degree of your error or competence primarily impacts the dollar amount of that settlement."

"When do you expect the autopsy results to be back?"

"Weeks, usually. We'll go forward on the presumption that they don't indicate any act of negligence."

Negligence. It's the first time anyone's spoken that word to me out loud. I've said it to myself. I even looked it up: "failure to exercise the care that a reasonably prudent person would exercise in like circumstances."

"Ms. Jansen hasn't actually sued me, though, has she?"

"No," she states with a finality that makes me almost relax. Then she continues. "But I expect she will. And if she does, she won't sue just you, she'll sue the hospital and everyone in that operating room. And if she sues this will get into the newspapers and cost us that much more."

"I understand," I say, not really sure I understand at all.

"This needs to be quick." She is back to all business, her fingers locked across her thin waist. A diamond on her left ring finger sprays flecks of light across my file. "I'm sure you know what a claim like this will do to your database, but we can't risk a trial. First Lutheran can't risk it and neither can you. If we settle we at least have some control over the costs. Remember, your policy has a cap. There's really no winning this, it's purely a matter of how much we pay her."

"What would happen if a settlement went above my cap?"

Her eyebrows dart upward for a second, and I realize how naive my question must sound.

"Well, anything above your cap would have to come out of your own assets."

Will Hanover is on call tonight. Well after eight o'clock I go back to the hospital and knock on the call room door, hoping he isn't still in the operating rooms. I hear the bed springs squeak under the pitiful excuse for a mattress we all rotate using.

"Hi, Will. I'm sorry, were you trying to rest?"

He runs a hand over his hair and scratches his scalp. "Not at all. I was reading the paper. We're starting an ex lap in an hour or so—waiting for the patient's son to get here."

"Who's the surgeon?" I ask.

"Marconi. Poor lady is eighty-six with an ischemic bowel."

"Do you need any help setting up?"

He laughs. "So you dressed up in your nice clothes and came back to the hospital to help me set up my operating room?" He shakes his head. "How did your meeting go today?"

I shrug and shove my hands into my coat pockets. "OK. I guess. How did you hear?"

"Joe. Want a cup of coffee?"

At a corner table in the cafeteria, I finally ask, and Will tells me the details of a lawsuit he went through in his first year of practice at a hospital in Portland. "It was a bilateral carotid in an obese woman. Not the best surgeon; I was fresh out of residency. I wanted to leave her intubated at the end and the surgeon insisted I pull out the tube. I was right, and he was wrong, but I didn't stand my ground."

He pulled out her breathing tube in the recovery room after she was fully awake, but she thrashed and her blood pressure skyrocketed. The carotid sutures ruptured and she bled into the tissues of her neck, closing off her airway. He couldn't get the breathing tube back in.

"She died?" I ask.

"Worse. She was vegetative for eight years before she died. I wanted to settle but it got too contentious. The family's lawyer pitted the hospital and me and the surgeon against each other so it went to trial. The award went way past my malpractice coverage. I didn't have much money at the time, but I lost what I had."

"Oh God, Will. I'm so sorry."

He stirs his coffee and takes a minute to answer. "The money's not the hard part. The hard part is convincing yourself that you should ever be allowed to take care of people again. The hospital, the insurance company—they all fixate on the dollars. But you're the one who tries to go to sleep every night with that patient's face floating over your head." The cafeteria is almost deserted; it smells of bleach and detergent and overheated coffee. The janitor begins vacuuming our section and we're quiet until he leaves.

"This lady, she had nine kids, eleven grandkids—every time I went by the ICU in the days after it happened, her room was filled with people. Wouldn't even consider turning off the ventilator. All praying and waving a Bible over her, waiting for her to wake up."

He looks up at me and folds his hands in his lap. "I shouldn't say that, should I? I don't mean to offend anyone by it."

I shake my head. "I was raised Catholic but we dropped it all when I was a teenager. So how did you get through it?"

"Youth. Jenny, my wife, was great—we had to sell our house. Phil Scoble gave me this job, which I was very grateful for at the time. And I've never gone against my own medical instincts again. If there's any good outcome, it's that." He sits back in his chair. "So on to you. Was this your attorney today?"

"No. My malpractice claims manager. She wants to settle it as quickly as she can—the mother hasn't sued me, but everyone's expecting that."

He nods. "Well. Yours ought to be more straightforward. I know you can't talk about it—I sure remember that part—but it doesn't sound like you made any mistakes. It's remarkable how many months these things can drag on, though. Lawyers bill by the hour."

I wish I could smile at this. "Phil's been supportive. Even Frank."

He nods again, more pensively. "Phil's a decent guy. Just . . ." He stops.

"Just what?"

He flinches for an instant. "Nothing. Personal philosophy. Always remember they'll sacrifice the soldier before they'll lose the war." His pager goes off and he has to leave for the operating room. The coffee feels like it's burning right through my stomach.

The following morning I'm called before the hospital's Internal Quality Control panel to present Jolene's case. Someone pours juice for me; I pick up my glass and a quake of tremors spirals across the surface. In voices tempered with sympathy, a panel of strangers in white coats convert my chart notes and dictated description of the catastrophe into a series of checked boxes on a standardized intraoperative death report. The chairman, a doctor who retired from First Lutheran before I went to college, shakes my hand as we leave the room. "This is all formality, Dr. Heaton. The doctors against the lawyers." He drops his voice to a whisper. "My daughter is a pediatrician. Got sued for giving a kid his measles vaccination. She walked away from her practice afterward. It's like everybody's forgotten how to make an honest living."

That evening, after my last patient is in the recovery room, I meet with the Physician Committee for Mortality and Morbidity. This time I sit at the end of a table filled with my own colleagues and friends— Sandy, Will, Peter Janovich, Sean Marconi—surgeons, anesthesiologists and internists assigned to objectively analyze my role in Jolene's death. Phil presides over the hearing. Finally I'm allowed to discuss the details of the case with other doctors—people who can understand all the possible consequences and rationale for the drugs and CPR I gave Jolene. With the record of her surgery and anesthetic in front of me, and the notes I composed after her death, I explain every incremental change in her status and the intervention I chose to correct it. I keep looking across at Phil, trying to interpret each nod or sigh or pause. Slowing the events down like this, removing the panic, it's clear to me—to everyone here—that I missed nothing, that I responded appropriately and promptly to every alarming number as it flashed on my monitor. No one points any damning fingers or flags my personnel file with condemnations. Phil concludes by commending my quick recognition of the crisis, my cool allegiance to emergency protocols, my stoic return to work, how appropriately I am putting remorse into its proper professional perspective. There can be nothing to fault, except that Jolene still died.

Will stops me on the way out. "That went pretty well, don't you think?"

I lean against the wall and hug the copies of Jolene's notes against my chest. "Better than I'd expected."

"So maybe there won't be any lawsuit. Phil told me nobody's filed anything."

He looks so hopeful, it's hard not to be inspired. "Well, if this committee didn't flay me alive, maybe the lawyers won't smell enough money to come running, huh?"

He holds his palm up for a high five and I meet it with a light slap, but then clasp it tight. "Thanks for being in there, Will. It sure helped to look up and see your face."

He shoves his hands into his pockets—now I've embarrassed him. "Jenny's picking me up for dinner at Chez Chez. Why don't you come?"

"I can't. I've got a hair appointment."

He weighs an invisible scale of pleasures. "Dinner out? Haircut? It'd be our treat!"

I laugh. "Believe it or not, this is a great sign—that I'm relaxing enough to even think about my hair. Maybe next week, though. You and Jenny can come over to my place."

James combs my hair back from my face, presses his palms against my temples and turns my head from side to side. "How about some more layering, around the front?"

He tips my head back into the sink and begins a deep scalp massage that puts me into a near trance. Over the sound of spraying water I listen to the continuing story of his tattoos: an evolving work of animal art that crawls, swims and flies over his arms and torso. "I interviewed an artist from Taos for the dragon scales."

"What happened to the guy from Laguna Beach? I thought he was finishing the dragon." Even my words are slowed down; I wonder if James can read my future through the bumps on my head.

"We ran into some artistic differences. This guy's got a better sense of color, anyway. New Mexico sunsets."

"Just make sure he uses clean needles."

"Of course, *doctor*!" He exaggerates the title humorously and starts rinsing out the soap. "So what happened to that kid at your hospital?"

The muscles in my abdomen go rigid. "What kid?"

"One of the surgical techs is a client and he told me some kid died on the operating table a couple of weeks ago. Makes me glad I don't have to cut anything that bleeds. I guess you have to get used to that kind of thing in your business."

The water is so warm over my face I can't be sure if I'm crying when I answer him. "Nobody with a heart could get used to that."

Driving home, I go over and over the questions I answered for the committees, replaying their supportive comments and reassurances, waiting for them to sink in and make me believe in myself again. In all the medical minutiae I recited, nobody asked me about the hour I've never had to document—the hour I spent trying to help Bobbie understand what had happened to her daughter in the operating room. I can close my eyes and see Bobbie's face going white, watch her slide onto her knees as if something solid inside her were dissolving.

I never had a chance to tell her I was sorry. The chaplain interrupted us. *Sorry* feels like such an insignificant word in the irrevocable context of death; such an obvious sentiment—Bobbie may have heard me say it even though I didn't. But now, absurdly, it feels like some vital conclusion we both needed. As if, if I could only go back in time and tell her how sorry I am, the outcome could change.

· 8 ·

A certified letter from Feinnes, Reames and Peynor, Personal Injury Legal Specialists, arrives at the end of the second week. We are all named: Don, Brad, Mindy, Alicia, the pharmacist, Matt Corchoran, even Joe—everyone who was anywhere near that room during Jolene's surgery, whether because they'd been randomly assigned to her case or because they'd been compassionate and dedicated enough to come running when I called the code. Caroline Meyers-Yeager assures me this shotgun approach is common. After the first scattered blast Bobbie's attorneys will quickly focus on the most exposed and lucrative targets— the hospital, the surgeon and me.

Lawyers seem to rain out of Seattle's skyscrapers, clustering around First Lutheran's mahogany conference table so every named soul can be pulled out of the operating rooms in shifts. Boxes of Krispy Kreme doughnuts and vats of coffee are passed around while they interview all of us. Mindy sits next to me, and she keeps squeezing my hand under the table in a maternal way. She answers every question with an emphatically optimistic note, like a mother defending her child before the school board. They hammer Brad for more than two hours about his twenty minutes in that room. He sifts through pages of typewritten notes he made right after the death, blushing and stammering every time he answers a question about my choice of anesthetic technique, drugs or equipment, or the way I managed her resuscitation.

If self-confidence could win a legal case, it's hard to believe John

Donnelly's ever lost one. He is not an overtly handsome man, but his height, his tan, his graying hair, even the hook of his nose, evoke all the principals and college deans and medical board examiners who have ever unnerved me, and I'm thankful he's on my side. He conducts my interview in a resonant, assured voice. He guides me through hundreds of questions in practice for my deposition—reiterations of my degrees, my medical experience, my certifications—guides me with the skill of a slalom racer, avoiding the red flags of litigation. I relive those hours of my life a dozen times in a single day, while charts and records are checked and rechecked, notes are scribbled and passed between hospital administrators and insurance executives, and attorneys rhythmically tap their pens through the silence that follows each of my answers.

I keep wanting to blurt out my own questions: Do any of *you* see the mistake I'm blind to? Would you trust me to take care of your own child? And, reverberating always, below words, is the germinating concept that the more we lose, the more Bobbie Jansen, who has already lost everything, could gain.

Phil walks me to my car at the end of the day, filling up silence with complaints about our litigious age. Just before I open my door he becomes more serious. "You look like you haven't slept all week."

I sort through my keys so I don't have to see his expression, unsure what to say. "It's hard. I'll get through it."

"Look. Some tragedies are just unavoidable in this job. It's normal, almost expected, that you'll begin to doubt yourself, even though you did everything you could to save this kid's life—absolutely by the book. You can't let this interrupt your career. You're one of the best doctors in this department, and I don't want to lose you." His jacket is slung over his shoulder and faint rings of perspiration darken the blue fabric under his arm.

I try to answer him but my throat closes up. The garage is empty, lit by spotlights that pock the vast space in cold white cones. I clutch my sweater tighter, shivering. "Thanks." It comes out barely audible until I swallow and repeat the word.

"We can give you some time off if you want. Anything you need."

I shake my head vigorously, terrified of idle hours at home. "Oh

God. That's the worst thing you could do right now. Work is the only place I feel sane."

"You're able to concentrate?" he asks, the crease between his brows a black gash.

"Of course," I say, holding my breath while I look straight into his eyes. "I wouldn't be in the OR if I couldn't." But I see on his face that he hears my own doubt.

Four days later I'm coming home after a night on call, fragile with exhaustion after twenty-four hours of labor epidurals and emergency cesarean sections. A gaunt woman with stringy blond hair and chapped skin rushes at me from the curb beside my building, her cigarette still burning on the pavement. "Are you Dr. Marie Heaton?"

"Yes, I'm Dr. Heaton, what can I . . ."

"I've got a subpoena here for you." She pushes a long white envelope into my hand, jabbing a finger at the black letters of my name, a relieved look on her face, knowing she has earned her pay. She runs back to her car before I can open it, her cigarette still disintegrating on the sidewalk in a graceful twist of smoke. I've been expecting this for weeks, but I still feel the affront—like running into a piece of familiar furniture in a dark bedroom.

In the weeks leading up to my first actual deposition I start coming to work earlier, often arriving before the night cleaning crew has finished—an institutional odor of disinfectant rising like morning fog off stainless steel, the hallways so dim and still they have the aura of a morgue. It becomes the only peaceful part of my day, opening the heavy swinging doors into the dark operating room, the ventilator and pumps and monitors looming in the shadows like mechanical mannequins. I almost hear their robotic voices interrupted by my living presence.

At home, in the sleepless single digits of the night, I scour textbooks in search of answers. I read about anaphylaxis, an unchecked death spiral of the immune system. I study biochemistry, evolution's masterwork of elements shot from the first exploding star, cohered into

a living being. I rememorize pharmacology, the molecules we manu-
facture to stall nature's culling of the ill and aged. I read as much as I
can of the ocean of knowledge we have accumulated about our physical
bodies since the days of leeches and humors, the ocean of knowledge
that encompasses only a fragment of all there is to know about what
holds physique and soul in union for the flicker of a lifetime. Knowledge will be my magic wand; knowledge will reclaim my control over
the anesthetized patient spread like a crucifix on the operating table.

My answering machine gradually fills up with messages I barely
listen to, invitations I won't accept. Anyone who knows about the suit
wants to ask if I feel prepared, if I'm completely confident in my lawyer,
if I'm sleeping all right. Anyone who doesn't know can't tolerate my
silences, the puzzled stare I give to their jokes, the full plate of food I
push away at the end of dinner. Lori coaxes me through sheer persis-
tence. She threatens to get on a plane within the hour if I don't pick
up, then fills our short conversations with stories about her children
instead of questions.

And Elsa. I always answer Elsa. I recognize her calls by their late
or early hour, only when her parents are sleeping. Her adolescent self-
centeredness is a gift, a secret room where time rolls back and I am
me again. Sometimes I huddle on my own closet floor when we talk,
a long-distance comaraderie of solitariness. "Why don't you think she
believes you?" I ask her, my knees folded against my chest, curtained
between my wool coat and flannel bathrobe.

"I can just tell. With both of them. They tell me how great I am and
then they watch every little thing I do, like they think I'm a juvie. It's
driving me crazy."

"They watch you because they love you, Elsa. You know that. In
your heart. Don't you? Learn to trust that voice inside yourself."

I wonder if she knows that the lifeline I've been holding out to her
has become my own.

My first official deposition falls one month to the day after Jolene died.
I arrive so early the janitor has to unlock the conference room door
for me. The room has one tall, thick-paned window looking out over

Puget Sound where an early spring fog floats the Olympic mountain peaks like a grand ship. My palms are so damp I wish women still wore the short white gloves my mother used to put on my sister and me for Easter.

Men arrive lugging scuffed briefcases weighted with papers. The room takes on a jovial atmosphere, a breakfast outing away from the office routine. Everyone seems to know one another, regardless of which side of this suit they represent. Donnelly shakes my hand and pulls out a chair in the middle of the polished table. As people take their seats along either side, the divisions of loyalty split: defense team over here, plaintiff's over there.

After I am sworn in, Bobbie Jansen's lawyer, Darryl Feinnes, smiles at me cheerfully and waves at a video recorder set up in the corner, pushing the bridge of his glasses higher on his nose with a stubby index finger. "You don't mind the video, do you, Dr. Heaton? It just helps us all be sure we get the information right." An assistant punches the silver button on the recorder down with a sharp snap that abruptly shifts the convivial mood.

I answer and reanswer the questions Donnelly has prepared me for, but now my answers feel false and overrehearsed.

"How long have you been an anesthesiologist, Dr. Heaton?"

"Have you ever completed a fellowship in the specialty of pediatric anesthesia, Dr. Heaton?"

"How many children have you anesthetized? Fifty? Two hundred?"

"When did you last study pediatric resuscitation?"

"What were your board scores, Dr. Heaton?"

He keeps rocking back in his armchair and sucking his lips in between his teeth, as if he is tasting my vulnerability. The video camera's steady red light reminds me that every hesitation in my voice, every stutter over my career statistics, is being seared onto a permanent record.

After a few hours Feinnes suggests we all break for coffee, and there is a general scraping of chairs and loosening of ties. He is a short, puffy man with back-combed hair and blushed cheeks better suited to an English schoolboy. Feinnes leans forward over his Styrofoam cup and makes a chuckling remark to Donnelly, who throws his head back and laughs. I use the moment to go to the bathroom, where I sit silently in the stall, holding my forehead against tight fists.

After the break another lawyer, some junior partner, repeats all the same questions. Every time I answer I look at his face to see if I have missed a date, a number, given some inconsistent answer that will damn me. The court reporter, a shrunken, osteoporotic woman, hunches over the muffled keys of her steno machine like a muted pianist.

During the final three hours of the deposition the lawyers dissect every moment of the day Jolene died.

"Which drug did you give first?"

"Why did you choose that drug?"

"How much did you give?"

"Are you sure you gave that amount?"

"Was that the correct dose?"

"How many patients have you anesthetized in the prone position?"

"How much sleep did you have the night before?"

"Did you have anything to drink the night before?"

"Do you tend to drink very much? How much is not much?"

Donnelly objects to this and I shrink as if I'd been scolded. He tells me that I'm still required to answer the question, but at least his objection will be on record. I shift my clasped palms into my lap and see a damp outline of their shape on the tabletop.

Near the end of the deposition Donnelly does his best to piece me back together. He reassures me that I'm doing fine, turns me by the shoulders to face his groomed graying hair, his creased, authoritative face. "Try to keep to the facts, tell the truth, stay calm. Just tell them exactly what steps you took in the operating room that day, to the best of your knowledge."

To the best of my knowledge I let a healthy eight-year-old girl entrusted to my care, my medical expertise, die. But until we have a pathologist's report and a final settlement, who could tell me this was not my fault? Forgiveness can only come from myself.

Donnelly reassures me that once we have the autopsy results

Feinnes's case for negligence will be even weaker. Still, he warns, the discovery phase of the mediation will probably take months. He walks down the hall with me after my deposition listing the records he'll need to pull from my medical school and residency and years of work at First Lutheran, discussing the expert witnesses he plans to hire, explaining the tedious seesaw of haggling and bartering between legal teams that will finally affix a price tag to Jolene's life.

We wait for the elevators opposite another plush room, nearly identical to the one in which I've just been deposed. The door swings farther back and a young woman carries out a tray of dirty coffee cups and crushed sandwich boxes, leaving me a clear view of the gleaming conference table, the walls hung with paintings of flowers and fruit and English hunting parties. Bobbie is sitting at the table. If she looked up now we would be facing each other for the first time since Jolene's surgery.

Darryl Feinnes pushes a stack of papers in front of her marked with red stickers. I can hear snatches of their conversation—accounts and fees, funeral costs, pain and suffering, lost companionship—as he calculates the final tally of her tragedy. He twirls a pen in his fingers with a pinched mouth that suggests he finds her exasperatingly slow to comprehend. She watches him curiously, as if she's hearing a foreign language dribble out of his mouth, the concrete details and dollars irrelevant. The bones of her face seem more angular than I remember, disproportionately prominent, her eyes and cheeks hollowed in purple shadows as if she'd forgotten to eat. The top buttons and holes of her blouse are misaligned. The fluorescent panel lights wash the flesh tones from her face and highlight gray strands seeded through her brown hair as her hand mechanically fills in the signature lines. I feel like I'm spying on her own private wound. We are coupled, she and I, through this lost child who has skewed the orbits of our lives.

The elevator door buzzes and I turn to see Donnelly holding it open, patiently waiting for me to follow.

It is almost dark by the time I get home. I should have left a lamp on—something, if not someone, to wait up for me. I call Lori but she doesn't answer and I don't have the heart to talk to a machine. I pick up the phone again intending to call my father, then put the receiver down before I dial.

I pull a leftover wild rice salad out of the refrigerator, pour a glass of wine and sit in my study watching the last light give up the day. Downtown city windows scatter just enough glow to cast everything in the room gray or black, familiar in shape instead of detail. My father stares at me from his picture frame, ghostly in the low light, nailed square in the center of a wall of books—a suitable setting for him. Maybe this is how the world looks to him right now as he loses his sight.

After twenty-two years of sharing only the most neutral and essential information with him, of studiously living without his advice, I suddenly wish I could repeat to him the perfect summary of Jolene's anesthetic, memorized after days and days of telling it to lawyers. Maybe we are far enough away from each other by now that he could listen and reassure me, convince me that I missed nothing, overlooked nothing, did nothing that might have precipitated her death. There was a time in my early life when he would have done that for me. But the woman I am today is too remote from the favored child I once was, and if forgiveness is what I need, he taught me well not to look to him.

For the tenth time in a month I pull my pediatric anesthesia textbook off the shelf and read about anaphylaxis and cardiac resuscitation, convincing myself once more that nothing could have made a difference, hoping I find enough peace to sleep.

· 9 ·

I'm sitting on a beach, and a breeze combs the fronds of
three coconut palms rising into the cloudless canopy of sky; they ruffle like
frayed emerald sheets. I hear the rattling crescendo before my hair lifts in
the cool wash of air. The ocean stretches taut against the world's curve,
bright and blue, striped light and dark above hidden hills and valleys. The
clean sweep of the horizon is notched by a dark scratch, a bobbing boat
filled with three or four children. They are singing. Words ripple to me on
gusts of air:

> *The Owl and the Pussycat went to sea*
> *In a beautiful pea-green boat.*

I walk into the blue, and cold creeps up to my ankles, my knees, my
thighs. My abdomen contracts and then relaxes as my skin shunts blood
back to my core, warming my heart, my lungs, my gut, my womb. A wave
lifts me, buoys me up to swim across the sea to the boat. The children's
voices beckon, their flushed faces shaded by sun hats; light and shadow
cleave their bodies as the boat rocks and they stretch over the gunwales to
splash the sea. I reach up to the polished wooden railing, the shadow of my
hand splayed across it like a glimpse into the future, ready to grasp hold.
I push my torso up and over the edge, poised, when a sucking tug in
my pelvis, a vortex of gravity, pulls me, drags me below the water, beneath
the boat. Salt washes into my nose and stings my open eyes. I hear the

swallowed sound of the children's singing over the humming pressure of the ocean, see the barnacled bottom of the boat above me, swaying on the water in the sunlight, marking the sharp break between air and ocean.

The sea is so beautiful I don't struggle at all, even as the water gets colder, heavier around my skull. Only at the last minute do I think of breathing, only just before the burning in my chest reminds me. Miles of ocean stretch over me and I am still swirling down, down until the evolutionary root of my brain, planted long before the higher fluff of my frontal lobes—site of all the judgments that make me unique among humans—forces my diaphragm down, gasps in whatever substance surrounds me, reflexively inhaling any possible source of oxygen.

The breath wakes me up. In the disoriented space of near dreams I'm only aware of my heart pounding, rocking inside my skull, racing with the panic of impending catastrophe. My heart—the central organ of immediate survival that links all organs together through the oxygen-rich bath of circulating blood. It is as sensitive as a precision-tuned Ferrari—contracting and accelerating, throttling blood and oxygen and life ahead at the first physiological inkling of disaster.

Jolene Jansen's heart should have been racing when her body plunged out of the controlled and level plane of anesthesia into the strangling spiral of anaphylaxis. Her heart rate should have sped up before terminal oxygen deprivation checked it. Something was wrong with her heart. Something was wrong with Jolene's heart even before I put her to sleep.

I rest the tips of my fingers against my carotid artery and count my pulse as it slows down from one hundred to ninety to seventy to sixty. Outside I hear the last of the revelers leaving Pioneer Square as the street transforms from night to day, from bars to businesses. Circling red lights on my ceiling reflect the city's sweep to bustle drunks off to emergency rooms or jails before the Starbucks and French patisseries open. In another two hours, pale-skinned baristas clothed all in black, silver rings ladder-stepping up the curves of their ears, will begin picking their way through the broken glass and oil-sheened puddles to turn on their espresso machines. It has been thirty-two days since Jolene's autopsy, and the report is still not back. I creep down the hallway in my nightgown, padding on tiptoe as if there were anyone else here to awaken. My alarm is set for five. I have an hour to begin reading about congenital heart defects.

Karen Leece, one of the gynecologists, pages me during my first case to say she has an extra ticket to the symphony at Benaroya Hall tonight. Her husband, Rick, travels a lot as a manager for Alaska Airlines, and she often adopts me as her spare date.

"There'll be eight of us—Glenn and his wife from my old practice, and some of Rick's colleagues. We're coming back to my house after for a drink. Please come, Marie—it's Ravel. We'd all love to see you getting out again." There is a brief moment of awkwardness as she realizes where she has trod.

The thought of making small talk with strangers feels ludicrous. But she's right, I've cloistered myself since Jolene's death. So I accept.

Benaroya Hall's arcing glass wall fractures into glistening panels that rise three stories above the symphony patrons. Karen meets me at the front entrance with my ticket just before the auditorium lights go down so I won't have to socialize until after the concert.

"Do I look OK?" I ask her. I threw on a gauzy summer dress just before the taxi came, and couldn't find the right shoes.

Karen kisses my cheek and guides me past the usher with an arm around my waist. "Gorgeous. Are you eating anymore? Your belt is slipping off. How come I only gain when I'm stressed?"

There is a swell of applause, and the pianist bows and sweeps the tails of his coat over the piano bench. Notes gather and swirl into imagined shapes; Ravel's minor chords and runs stir a communion of unresolved pathos that cuts to my core. We are two thousand strangers revering music composed almost a century ago, discovering emotion evoked through vibrations of air. I close my eyes and let the piano crescendos wash over me, penetrate me, sweep me into a universe where these last weeks of my life could dissolve into inconsequential bits of fallen stars.

After the concert we share cars to Karen and Rick's house in

Madison Park, a boxy glass and stucco structure plunked between two pastel Victorian-style mansions, its front porch overhung with evergreen clematis, the fading white blossoms fluttering like small ghosts against the dark leaves. Karen pops some fancy hors d'oeuvres out of the Sub-Zero refrigerator and pours champagne into gold-rimmed flutes. Glenn builds a fire of pressed-wax logs, unnaturally colored flames incinerate the paper on the fake wood, and we pull armchairs and kitchen stools around a pink marble coffee table. I'm hungrier than I've felt in days, and the champagne feels like it's untangling something inside me.

Louis, one of Rick's trainees, and his wife, Jeanne, are over from France for a year. Their fourteen-year-old daughter is enrolled in the public high school.

"She wants me to drive her everywhere," Jeanne says. "At home she walked to school. If she wanted to see friends, she took the bus or the subway. Now she says she would be too embarrassed—her friends would laugh at her. Be glad you have boys, Karen. It is too difficult raising a teenaged girl."

"Well, don't trade her away too quickly." Karen shakes her head. "You should have been here to clean out the washing machine last summer when they forgot to take all the tadpoles they'd caught out of their pockets."

The conversation circles around the myriad trials of parenting until Glenn includes me with a remark about the financial freedom I'll have without a college savings account to worry about. And then, as always in a gathering of physicians, we debate the U.S. health-care system. Glenn's wife, Sharon, a public health physician, talks about funds redirected from a community clinic so her hospital can create a bioterrorism office. "They want me to prepare for smallpox while my older patients are dying of the flu."

"I'm always reading that America has the best health care in the world, yet you give new hips and knees to eighty-five-year-olds, and nothing to millions of children," says Jeanne, crossing tanned legs so one high-heeled sandal dangles from a scarlet-nailed toe.

Glenn deflects the medical criticism back onto the legal system, pointing out the outrageous malpractice premiums driving obstetricians out of the state.

"I've heard about this. And Marie," Jeanne says turning to me, "it sounds like hell what you are going through with the lawyers. Do they really videotape your testimony?"

I rise and pick up plates and crystal from the table. "Hell would be a close approximation. Next year you must find me a job in France, Jeanne." A hot flush floods my face and I tip my head so my hair falls forward in a veil.

In the kitchen I run steaming water into the sink and pour in an iridescent blue soap. Laughter and competing voices rise and fall through the half-closed doors. I jump when a hand rubs my back. Karen has put on an apron covered with dancing black and white cows. She stands a head taller than me, with wide gray eyes pregnant women must find soothing. Her front teeth overlap. I suspect her parents couldn't invest in nonessential dentistry, that Karen must have worked hard for scholarships and living wages so her children could grow up in a well-padded lifestyle, a lifestyle that would safely assure them long and happy lives. She grabs a dish towel and plucks wet stemware from the stainless rack beside the sink.

"I'm sorry about that. We shouldn't have talked to them about the suit. I can't excuse myself for it." She twists the end of the dish towel deep into the funnel of the fragile crystal to polish the inside back to clarity.

"Well, I might as well get used to explaining this—it'll be on my permanent record." I keep my voice light, but she stays self-consciously silent for a minute. We both know that from now on, every year when I renew my medical license or my hospital privileges, I will have to write a detailed description of the malpractice claim.

"Marie," she says, pointlessly buffing the gleaming steel faucets. "What *do* you think really happened? What caused it?"

She can't help asking. She is searching for the consoling nugget that will guarantee her own child is not vulnerable, that her own child can proceed to the tonsillectomy, the appendectomy, the ear tube placement, and come back home alive.

I'm on the verge of telling her what I suspect. I'm on the verge of asking her opinion about which heart defect Jolene must have had, what twisted unfurling of the chambers and vessels must have occurred when one flawed scrap of DNA misfired and finally, fatally, declared itself on my operating room bed. We could discuss it as equally educated physicians, as uncompetitive friends, talk through the physiology to find an answer. She would never tell. Surely she'll never be deposed against me—she wasn't even in the hospital that day. But what look will cross her face when she realizes I might have missed a diagnosis that could have saved a life? What will be her own verdict?

I carefully refold the damp dish towel and place it on the counter before I turn to face her. "I don't know, Karen. I may never know for sure."

Karen ducks out to collect dishes and I slip into a spare bedroom to call a taxi. Sitting on the bed by the phone, damp coats piled beside me, I wait on hold and study the room, paintings of hunting dogs above the bed, Ralph Lauren plaid comforter and drapes. Family photographs are arranged on the bedside table and dresser: Karen and Ricky and their twin sons in front of a fireplace draped with Christmas stockings; Matt at his first T-ball game, his baseball cap so big on him his ears are folded in half and stick out like tiny pink wings; Karen in the delivery room just at the moment of birth. I've always sworn I would never display pictures of my own babies' births throughout the house like some public anatomy lesson.

Once the taxi honks, no one can protest enough to drive me home. The usual misting rain has progressed to a steady fall of tear-shaped drops and the taxi's headlights glint off puddles in the intersections.

The driver lets me off at the corner of First Avenue, just beyond the arching Gothic-carved stone doorway of the converted red brick factory where my top-floor loft collects Seattle's northern and western horizons and cityscapes through windows as tall as trees. It went to a bidding war, this loft, when it first went on the market. I paid 30 percent more than the asking price—already at the peak of Seattle's housing boom. I fell in love with its wood-burning fireplace, its exposed brick library walls and honey-colored cherry cabinets. It felt like a complete home to me, even if I didn't share it with anyone yet. Eight years later I'm still the only one with a key.

I let myself in and put hot water on for tea, watch the blue flame wrap the bottom of the kettle in a fiery flower. Then I pull the Seattle white pages off the shelf beside the kitchen phone and look for Barbara Jansen's address.

· 10 ·

Bobbie Jansen lives in Rainier Valley. Her address is not far from mine when measured in blocks or neighborhoods or even miles. But it falls across an invisible line that separates lives with leeway for art collections and exercise clubs and dinners out from lives of juggled utility bills and generic food staples and unsympathetic landlords.

She lives so close, in fact, that from my balcony I can stretch around the scarred redbrick corners of my building and look down the canyon of high-rises to the point where the rooflines drop to one or two stories, just beyond the dim globe of downtown lights. It makes me feel like I live in one of those glass spheres, and the hand of God might shake up a sparkly snowstorm while Bobbie's house sits darkly fixed.

My head throbs. I walk into my bathroom and twist my hair up, run hot, hot water over a washcloth until it stings my hands, drape it across my face and exhale a steamy plume. Water. Touch. Temperature. Contact with something soft and warm and moist, like skin, like breath.

I strip off my dress and it puddles to the floor, a sylph's scarf. It was a foolish choice for the evening, too early in the year. I was shivering half the night. My bathrobe hangs on the door hook, next to my jeans. I reach quite specifically for the robe, not surprised at all when I put on the blue jeans and an old sweater. There are some things you know you are going to do despite the voice screaming at you to stop.

I drop my car keys into my pocket without even bothering to pick up my purse. Does some part of me think I'm more anonymous without my wallet? The only pen on the kitchen counter skitters dry in the middle of her street number, so I rip the "Jan" page out of the phone book and fold it twice, three times over. I'm in my car and leaving the garage before I start talking out loud to myself. Who will even notice me—one car circling the block, one woman out for a midnight drive on a Friday night? What are the odds that Bobbie will be awake and outside on her porch (if, indeed, she has a porch), or watching from her upstairs bedroom (if her house has stairs), or sitting by the living room windows (if they face the street)? What harm could I cause by trying to attach some concrete image to the ones I can't quit imagining? Halfway there I cut closer to the bone. What *is* my goal here? To see if her house has a For Rent sign? To see if she has wiped out any clue that a child ever lived there? To see if, maybe, there is some chance, some small chance, that she isn't in that house alone night after night?

I'm at a stoplight three blocks away when a siren screams through the intersection, and my heart races until it hurts. I feel illicit, thieving, deceitful, desperate. And still I don't stop. I make it all the way to the corner of her block. I am turning, I can almost see her house.

And then . . . What? God! What am I about to let myself do? Walk up to her door? Ring her bell? Wake her up? Ask her to forgive me? I press one foot on the brake and one on the accelerator, squeeze the steering wheel until my knuckles are white and the two halves of my mind slam together, fuse in shame, and I force myself to turn my car around.

· 11 ·

I'm on call. A Sunday. A quiet day. The techs have a Mariners game on in the lounge and the ER staff invites me down to a potluck. I pull a chair into the corner, behind the lunch tables, and call my father.

"Hey, Dad. It's me."

"Lori?"

"Marie."

A pause. "What's all the noise?"

"A baseball game on TV. I'm at the hospital today—in the lounge. How are you?"

"All right. Same as always."

My legs are tucked into a knot beneath me; my foot tingles and starts to cramp. I get up and walk around, trailing the phone cord. "You said you had a doctor's appointment this week—any news?"

"Good news is no news. I try not to listen to him. How's your job?"

In the background a line drive sends up a swell of rowdy yelps that sound more like I'm in a bar than a hospital. "Great, Dad," I lie with an audible smile. "Challenging." Closer to the truth, at least. "Your birthday's coming up soon. What's on your wish list?"

He pauses again, so long that I think I've lost the connection. "Get me a new pair of eyes. Maybe there're some spare ones rolling around in those operating rooms."

I order a HoneyBaked ham, a basket of flowers and season tickets to the Houston Symphony, and try not to wonder who he could share them with.

By midnight I have only two labor epidurals running. The corridors are silent except for the hum of cleaning crews and the occasional sleepless patient pushing a rattling IV pole on his way to the vending machines; I could actually sleep for a while.

Instead I find the isolated elevator to the subbasement. The elevator is scuffed and dented from the wheeled metal carts used to shuffle volumes of data from storage to clinics to hospital wards to operating rooms and back to storage, thicker each trip with coded diseases. The sheer weight of paper becomes a quantifier of suffering. The secretaries' desks are deserted, dried coffee grounds ring Styrofoam cups, incomplete charts are piled in metal trays and stacked in leaning towers on shelves and folding chairs and sagging laminated tables.

Jolene Jansen's medical chart is alphabetically filed among the thousands—tens of thousands of charts packing miles of metal racks in First Lutheran's basement records department. It is a part of the hospital I've never visited before—a part usually reserved for transcriptionists and the tapering levels of administrators who convert illness and disability into thick paper files of diagnostic codes and insurance billing numbers. Ten letters down the alphabet, dozens of rows into the racked aisles, I almost miss it because it's so thin, a half-inch pile of paper describing the medical facts of Jolene's short life. The majority of pages deal with the day of her death.

I've turned on only one light; it barely penetrates this deep into the room. I walk to the end of the rack, under a single overhead spot, and crouch with the folder across my knees.

The elevator shudders inside the wall and startles me. I clatter against an empty metal shelf to catch my balance and hold my breath until the elevator stops somewhere above. If discovered here in the desertion of midnight, I could say I'm looking for my own uncompleted charts, lacking the signatures that might stall insurance reimbursements or incite punitive fines from hospital inspectors. I could say that I have to review a chart for an upcoming surgical patient, or the past anesthetic records of all craniotomies. But I came here to see if any doctor before me wondered why Jolene couldn't run as well as other children, whether her impaired mind and small stature cloaked an impaired heart. And I came here to learn more about Jolene Jansen's mother.

Bobbie and Jolene had been connected with First Lutheran's medical social workers, as commonly happens with Medicaid patients or handicapped children. The overwhelming job of finagling governmental regulations and pharmacy coupons and mental health evaluations and home care plans would have swallowed the allotted time and patience of Jolene's doctors. So she was passed to the idealistic and bureaucratically talented assistants capable of unscrambling the loopholes of subsidized medical care. Their notes are filed at the end of the chart under a tab labeled Miscellaneous. The room is silent as a vault now. I relax my crouch enough to sit cross-legged on the thin carpet and read.

The one-page summary of Barbara Helen Jansen's life tells me she moved to Fairbanks, Alaska, from Florida at the age of nineteen. She supported herself as a cook for the North Slope oil field workers. After four years of cooking and cleaning, Bobbie earned enough to move to Yakima, buy a house and begin taking occasional classes at the community college. Jolene's father, a supervisor of migrant field workers for one of the large apple orchards in eastern Washington, walked into Bobbie's life relatively late. Shortly after Jolene's conception her father was reported missing. Bobbie was thirty-one years old at the time. His disappearance fell on the heels of a major labor dispute with the orchard's owners, and the social worker writes that Bobbie Jansen believes her husband was a victim of the violence and corruption scorching the farm labor community at the time. The police recorded his disappearance as abandonment.

Jolene's mental retardation was diagnosed when she was three, when she had still not begun to talk. Over the next several years Bobbie's money was consumed by doctors, psychologists, speech and occupational therapists, and specialized teaching programs until she had no more to spend, no more to sell and trickled out of mainstream health care to join the voiceless swell of public health patients. Jolene's infected cyst had reconnected her to the medical and social services available to her tier.

I rifle through scrawled Urgent Care Clinic notes and a few faxed pages from the public health clinic. There is no mention, in this abbreviated, summarized medical review, of any confirmed heart defect. But there is also no hint that any doctor ever listened carefully enough to consider the possibility.

· 12 ·

I know Bobbie Jansen's neighborhood. Ten years ago, after my internship, I worked in her public health clinic for six months.

My original plan had been to go to Africa and work with AIDS patients for a few years between internship and the three-year residency required for anesthesia. My father was stone-faced when I told him— not that I'd expected him to like my decision, but as a history professor he would at least appreciate, I'd hoped, my desire to see the world from another culture's point of view. If my mother had been alive, I know she would have been distraught and anxious and even skeptical, all the while helping me pack my bags with unconditional support.

But I had only my father and Lori. And below his impassive disapproval I sensed, or wanted to sense, a need to keep me at least somewhat closer to home. After four years of college, four years of medical school and the near poverty-level wages of internship, I was too far in debt to even buy the plane ticket. So I compromised. I answered a small ad in the back of a public health journal and moved to Seattle to work in an understaffed and poorly supplied clinic with some of the most irreverent, dedicated doctors and nurses I've ever met. I found the third world in the middle of urban America.

The clinic was part of a loose network offering medical care to the increasing numbers of uninsured people in the region. I had to postpone my anesthesia residency to work there, a decision my program director and certainly my father considered pointless. What use would primary-care medical experience be to an anesthesiologist? Pap smears and family planning were skills I would never need in my future. But the work quieted some loss I felt about specializing in anesthesia, a more anonymous field—most of my future patients would sleep away the time I spent with them. I would never get the Christmas cards and homemade brownies that *real* doctors might receive from the families they cared for.

Anesthesia was the antithesis of the complete, personally involved physician I had idealized to myself and my parents for all the years I studied chemistry and physics and biology alongside music and literature. It came as an unexpected, almost uncomfortable surprise to me when I discovered the immediate gratification of my specialty— injecting a local anesthetic at the precise nerve plexus to relieve the unrelenting pain of strained backs or injured limbs; calming a terrified obstetrical patient rushed into an emergency cesarean section, keeping her pain-free and hopeful, so her infant could make the miraculous transition from fetus to newborn uninjured; pulling the sleeping heart bypass patient back to consciousness and the inexpressible relief that they are still among the living. All of this, I discovered, was in contrast to general medicine, which could often do little more than shift the incessant, declining slope of mortality that begins the day we are born.

The patients I treated at the Rainier County Clinic, Bobbie's neighbors, were a mixed group—some unemployed and uninsured, some who'd tumbled down the social ladder to a bewildered state of neediness they'd never anticipated or saved for and many who were employed in low-wage jobs that gave them no health insurance and no sufficient means to pay for their own care. A lot of them came to us long after their early symptoms had ballooned into unchecked diabetes or hypertension or heart failure or metastatic cancers, because the balance of debt versus illness had to tip before they could risk visiting a doctor.

This same mix of crises meant social and psychological care became as fundamental to their cure as medication or surgery. I loved that part of it—opening a window into the back rooms of other lives, lives I walked past every day at bus stops and McDonald's and Wal-Marts;

the hidden rooms of the people who served me restaurant meals, kept the floors of my local grocery store swept clean, restocked the clothes littering my fitting rooms—even the people tucked into doorways at dawn wrapped in donated blankets, sleeping through the shuffle of early commuters. I was still young enough to see myself in their lives.

At night, when I come home from work and should collapse into bed, I sit in my living room and stare out across the swallowing blackness of Puget Sound. And I envision Bobbie's house. Maybe a white clapboard bungalow with chipped green trim around the windows and front porch columns. Maybe a chair on the porch, the old kind of outdoor metal chair with curving arms and a curved metal tube for the base, so she can rock while she watches a swing set rust in her front yard. Maybe she sits there at dusk listening to the new emptiness in her life and looks out to the lights of downtown Seattle, the lights of Pioneer Square, my home, dangling like pearls out of reach.

It has been five weeks now, and I still dissect the choices I made in the hours between singing Jolene to sleep and telling her mother that she was dead. I imagine myself on a witness stand, before a jury or before Bobbie Jansen, explaining the sequence of my thoughts on that day, trying to convince my listeners that each decision was issued from a calm and confident physician, detached and objective, clinically critical, never stalled by emotion for the pivotal moment that might have made all the difference. Had I waited too long to turn her over and start chest compressions? Had I given too little epinephrine, too much anesthetic gas, too much narcotic? And if Jolene had a congenital heart defect, one of the dozens of malformations described in any anesthesia textbook, what would I have done differently? If her autopsy proves I missed that diagnosis in the pre-op interview, does it prove I caused her death? Even if any physician might uncouple her heart from her death, I doubt any lawyer would.

I fill a mug with sweetened tea and carry it into the bedroom. There are only five more hours left in the night before I will turn off my alarm clock and go back into the hospital for another day of colon resections, cataracts, hysterectomies and hernias. All those patients are now tossing sleeplessly somewhere, suppressing the natural trepidation that accompanies surgery, the reluctance to give oneself up to the control of others and trust them to do their best, to be well rested, well trained and alert.

I lie on my back and watch the streetlight glint off the slowly rotating ceiling fan, and I try to lull myself into sleep by counting my breaths, letting the growing number crowd out background voices. I let my rib cage lift up and expand, my diaphragm suck down into my abdomen, my nostrils flare and pull in the largest volume of air I can hold. Then I close off my vocal cords and listen in the night to the rocking flush of blood in my carotid arteries. I watch the seconds pass in glowing blue on my bedside clock. I can't even make a minute. I can't force my body to fight its own reflexive terror of oxygen starvation for one full swing of a second hand.

It is an impossible thing to commit suicide by voluntarily holding one's breath. In psychiatric hospitals and jails we remove the occupants' belts and scarves and sheets—all possible bridges to death—but no one dies of self-suffocation. Because as soon as the mind goes black, reflex kicks in and volition is superseded by the natural dominance of survival.

· 13 ·

Lori calls more frequently than usual these days. We talk about whether her recent bouts of nausea could be her gallbladder, the cough Gordon brought back from the Far East, an Alaskan baleen basket I found in a nearby gallery, the latest news on my father. The noisy chaos of her household in the background is comfortably distracting, my borrowed family. She laces her conversation with oblique allusions to the lawsuit followed by pregnant pauses that I leave empty. One night I finally ask her what he would think if she found out it had been my fault.

"But we know it wasn't," she immediately answers.

"But what if the autopsy proved it was?"

"How could the autopsy prove that? You said this was an allergic reaction or something."

I take a deep breath and hold it for a second, then plunge ahead. "It could have been her heart. I think Jolene might have had a heart defect."

I can hear Lori thinking, almost picture her biting her lower lip. "Where did this come from? You've never even mentioned this."

"I had a dream about it. And I woke up just *knowing* it."

"Knowing it? You're deciding this because of a dream?"

"Yeah. Well, not really just the dream. I was thinking about how her heart slowed down right before her oxygen level started to drop. It would make sense if it had gone down *after* she ran out of oxygen. But not before. That's always bothered me. I just never really separated it out from the whole scene."

"I don't get it."

"Kids' hearts are strong. When things go wrong in pediatrics it's almost always a respiratory problem first, and then the heart gets starved of oxygen and fails. Before that a child's heart should be beating faster."

"Have you told your lawyer this?"

"No. Not yet."

"Good. Don't. I can't even understand all you're saying and it doesn't sound reasonable. Don't tell him. You want my honest opinion?"

I don't answer her. I know she'll tell me anyway.

"Your subconscious came up with this to justify how bad you feel. This was a dream, Marie. A nightmare."

I gradually cleave my day into two parts—work and the solitude of my home. Of these two, work evolves into a restful escape. It's odd, I think, because at the hospital I have to see all the people who were part of that day: Stevenson, Mindy, Alicia. I have to watch the faces of my patients as they sink beneath the spell of drugs and know they believe I will keep them safe, that I will wake them at the end of their surgery to rejoin the people they love. At work I have no choice but to wrap my guilt and anxiety in a tightly bound shroud and place them far away from mental reach. If they tumble from their high shelf for a moment, I might become too much the frightened defendant, too little the collected and confident physician. And then, it might happen again.

At home, the shroud tends to snag and unfurl, and my mind races into black corners of recrimination. I clean my house, dusting the tops of ceiling fans and closet shelves, scrubbing out refrigerator drawers and bathroom drains, organizing food pantries and file cabinets, arranging the books in my library by subject, then again by height or binding color. I polish the sterling my father finally gave me when I finished my residency—tired of saving it for a wedding gift. I alphabetize my CDs and walk from room to room wearing headphones, deafened by Prokofiev and Bizet and Bono. I watch old movies, bundled up in my bathrobe, until I fall asleep on the sofa buried beneath a down comforter. Even if I don't like the movie, the steady prattle of stilted dialogue blocks out the noise of my memory. And every evening I decide I will ask Donnelly if he has the autopsy report back yet. And every morning I decide to wait one more day.

It occurs to me late one night that Bobbie and I are more alike than it would seem. We are both without a partner or child.

Joe calls to try to coax me out of social exile. He leaves unanswered messages three nights in a row and then starts talking to me through my answering machine, cajoling me to pick up the phone.

"Marie, I know you're in there. Come on, talk to me. Be my friend tonight, I need one. What are you watching? You're gonna run out of movies soon."

I knew it. He's spying on me. I wrap the comforter around me and shuffle over to the rain-streaked windows. He is there, hunched into his glossy yellow parka with the hood pulled up to cover his cell phone, squinting against the streetlight as he waves at my TV-silhouetted shadow. I place one palm against the cold glass and he holds his up in return, spreading the fingers into a victory V.

"Gotcha," he says when I pick up the phone.

"Joe—respect for privacy, please. Can't I escape from the world for a night?"

"You've been escaping for weeks. I want to go out. I want to go out with you. Hell, I want to drink. Things aren't always so perfect in my life, either, you know. Come on, friend." He pauses, listening to my hesitation. "I miss you."

There is a familiar note of loneliness in his voice that always makes me want to take care of him. He surrounds himself with male friends for the sports betting and bashing, the single malt scotch ratings, the prideful litany of conquered women—but when any real pain starts he seeks me out. What is it that compels women to guard men's secret frailties?

"I haven't even showered," I say, hearing myself give in to him.

"What do I care how you smell? Isn't that the beauty of being friends with your ex-lover? At least when I tell you I love you for your mind, I really mean it."

"Joe, please? I'm not very good company these days, anyway."

"Marie, please? Would I turn you down in your hour of need? Besides, I'm getting blasted by the rain and my phone's about to die."

"Big surprise." Joe is notorious for being unreachable outside the hospital. He's lost three cell phones in the last year. "Meet me at Larry's in fifteen minutes. But I'm not staying out late tonight. I'm on call on Wednesday, since Sandy had to trade. Order a lemon drop for me."

Despite my reticence I smile. The fact that we were lovers once has made our friendship strong enough to bear fallibility, intimate enough to tolerate imperfection. When Joe started at First Lutheran he was thirty-seven, I was thirty-three, we were both single, both apparently straight, and it seemed the entire department assumed we would become a couple—the very fact of which we turned into a private joke, falling into a flirtatious friendship that was secure because we were both utterly committed to separating work and love. It made it easy to counsel one another in matters of romance, easy to fill empty Saturdays with a ready-made, obligation-free date. There was no tension about income or personal habits, no whining about schedules or domestic tidiness.

There was a man I'd liked—seriously liked—when I first moved to Seattle, an avid kayaker and runner who owned a bookstore deep in the bowels of the Pike Place Market. Then I got my job at First Lutheran and started canceling dates when emergency surgeries kept me late, or when my low seniority put me on call three weekends in a row. Soon he quit calling, upset that I didn't seem to have room for him in my life. I think it was the first time I wondered if my generation had tried to leap a little too far, plunging into the wilderness of equality without our trail of bread crumbs, turning around on the brink of infertility to discover that, enticing as the woods were, we were unaccountably lost. What I needed was some Microsoft executive who could accept my hours and retire early to raise our children. But not Joe. Never Joe. Joe was too close a friend to risk loving. In the meantime he could fill my weekends with bike rides and movies and the occasional symphony he would reluctantly allow me to drag him to—if I let him leave at intermission to smoke a cigarette.

Then we went camping. Friends of his were coming in from Boise, two men and a woman, and we were all going backpacking up at Harts Pass. We would meet in Winthrop, the closest town, and head up the precipitous twenty-two-mile forest road chiseled into the nearly vertical mountainside below Slate Peak. Joe and I packed on a hot, late-August day; camping gear littered his living room floor under huge south-facing windows. Butane stove, water filter, kerosene lanterns, cooking pans, a portable espresso maker, Therm-a-Rest sleeping mats, and enough warm clothing to summit Rainier. Joe had a list that ran two pages. I sat in the blazing afternoon glare squashing thick polyfill sleeping bags into bright-colored nylon stuff sacks with sweat trickling down my arms and face. Joe crammed bulky packages of pasta, tubes of pesto, imported Parmesan cheese and bottles of Chianti into the crannies of our backpacks, sculpting an ergonomically balanced gourmet restaurant to be hauled upon our backs. He would carry the heavier men's tent and I would carry the women's.

Joe got up to find more gear, a compass and waterproof matches and Capilene underwear (he should be an honorary Eagle Scout, I teased). I hefted my pack, and took out the fleece pants and jacket and tossed them behind his couch, pulled a wine bottle out from the bottom compartment and stuffed it under the sofa cushions. He found the wine bottle and put it into his own pack, but he missed the fleece. We both missed the fact that my tent stakes were wrapped up inside the jacket and pants.

We rocketed across the Cascades in Joe's dented white Jeep to Pearl Jam and the Talking Heads and Van Morrison and, my own contribution, *Puccini's Greatest Hits.* I'd never been this deep or this high into the mountains before. Highway 20 is surely among the most beautiful in America, only open in summer, swooping through the brash young mountains in manmade defiance of winter avalanches and rock slides. We passed Diablo Lake, a glacial sapphire blue, like a fragment of tropical sea exiled to a prison of cement dams and mountain walls. We got to Winthrop an hour late and went into the Duck Brand restaurant to meet his friends for lunch. The waitress took our name and said, "We've been waiting for you."

"All your life?" asked Joe.

"Your friends called. They left a phone number."

Joe's friends weren't coming. Their car had broken down eighty miles east of Spokane. He looked at me and shrugged, hanging up the pay phone on the nearly deserted street that ran through the middle of the three-block town. "Lotta food for two people. Hope you're hungry." And we headed up to the top of the pass.

We trudged four miles in to our campsite, hiking along the spine of the Pacific Crest trail with wildflower meadows and broken rock scree and blue-green pine forest falling away on either side like a grand embroidered skirt. Joe set up the tents under a single enormous evergreen. Then we discovered my tent stakes were still safely hidden behind Joe's sofa, inside the fleece that I would also dearly miss. I was too exhausted to cut new wooden pegs, so I lodged stones about the corners of the tent fly and fell asleep before the sun set, before the wind herded massive clouds down from the Canadian plains, before the temperature dropped thirty degrees. In the night I was startled awake by a profound, absorbing silence, and a moment later my tent humbly collapsed under the weight of the first autumn snow.

Joe's geodesic shelter was as unfazed by this anachronistic winter as any Russian onion dome. I hobbled to it in my sleeping bag. There had been wine for dinner, there had been schnapps and hot chocolate for dessert, and I suspect for Joe there had been a neat whiskey or two to replace the cigarette I had forbidden.

We began apart, crept closer for warmth, zipped bag to bag as the night grew colder, and finally pressed skin next to skin, not for warmth but because it was what we both wanted and could excuse as an emergency. We lay together in mutual, unspoken acceptance that we would not discuss whether this was wise or rational or intended for eternity. And for the next eight months we continued as the best of friends and the best of lovers.

In retrospect I recognize the nearly invisible barrier we both defended, careful never to discuss whether we were actually headed to the same place, acting as if time would stand still while we dallied with companionship and soulful conversation and purgative sex. We were so careful, during our eight-month entanglement, to be lovers without being in love—each of us poised in a waiting game for something more real to follow.

At twenty it would have been expanding. At twenty-eight it would have been explorative. But at thirty-four it begged to be nurtured or abandoned. Did I consider him a vibrant lover but unlikely father? Did he shudder at the glimmer of lost freedom? All I know is that we reached the precipice of those conversations and backed away, both of us, me when I noticed he still noticed other women, he when I told him I wanted more time to myself.

There was a sting, for a while, when he dated other women, when I wanted someone to wake up with. It is amazing, though, what pains your subconscious will undergo to achieve sustainable peace. It is amazing how quickly I was able to convince myself that the possessiveness of love would have inevitably suffocated our friendship.

I pull on a wool sweater and blue jeans, rake a brush through my hair and lick my fingers to wipe the mascara smudges from beneath my eyes. But under the white lights in my bathroom I see an aging face that doesn't bounce back from a seventy-hour workweek. I put my hands flat up against my ears and pull back to remember what I looked like ten years ago. If I squint a little, even the uneven skin tones blur. I push the right hand up and the left hand down, then put my thumbs in the corners of my mouth and pull them back. There. Now I can see what I'll look like in seventy years at age one hundred and seven, assuming I'm not cremated. I spritz perfume over my hair and neck—you do what you can in this world.

I jaywalk diagonally across First Avenue and up three blocks to Larry's. Posters of hip-hop and reggae bands flank the century-old brick and stone doorway. Odors of smoke and beer and the soft clink of heavy glass tumblers make the long, dark room feel oddly intimate—a dozen or so customers clustered over tables or half hidden behind high booths, the bartender easy with the pace of drinks, sloshing glasses through soapy water with up-rolled sleeves.

Joe is at the end of the bar and he's thrown his electric yellow parka across the next stool to save it for me. My lemon drop stands on the polished counter. I sit on the damp bar seat and point to the two emptied shot glasses in front of him. "That won't fix it, whatever it is. So why aren't you working tonight? Seems like every time I look at the schedule you're on call."

"You're one to talk. I think you beat my hours this month. I'm just trying to pay off all my creditors."

"Financial or romantic?"

He lets out a short, sardonic chuckle.

I sip the sweet martini over the sugar-crusted rim, looking for whatever opening he needs. "Joe, if you're going to drag me out of my bathrobe into the rain to console you, at least let me hear the truth."

"Oh, it's no one thing, really." He grins his crooked, almost sad "Joe grin" that has always made me want to protect him. "Maybe just that. Too much work."

"Is it Claire?" I ask.

He draws circles in the water droplets beading up on the dark mahogany bar. It's funny. I didn't understand him nearly as well while we were lovers, but now that the risk of heartbreak has been removed, Joe can tell me almost anything. Almost.

"She wants to cancel our trip to Mexico. Says she's too worried about leaving her kids with their dad. I don't believe her."

"I ran into her a couple of days ago. In the cafeteria."

He nods. "She came up to drop off my cell phone—I left it at her house."

"She said something kind of funny—I'm not sure I should tell you this. . . ." He glances up at me and I know I can't back out now. "OK. She said she didn't think she was as good at rescuing you as I was."

"Rescuing me, huh." Joe pulls his parka back onto his lap and fumbles in the inside pocket, then he pulls out a cigarette. "Pass me those?" He reaches across me toward a book of matches resting in a black plastic ashtray.

"No. I will not help you start smoking again. Smoking doctors! I should drag you through an emphysema ward. Will you remember this woman when you're plugged into a ventilator?"

"I used to work on an emphysema ward. And yes, I will remember this woman."

I can't help but smile, even though I know he's sincere. Joe is hopelessly appealing to women, and hopelessly attracted only to the few he'd never be able to handcuff in marriage. I've begun to doubt that he genuinely wants to marry, so his choices conveniently fulfill his secret dreams more than his conscious ones. I reach up and put my middle three fingers across his unlit cigarette and fracture it into a V. He pulls out another one and lights it anyway, squinting and drawing a deep draft of smoke and air into his lungs. He clasps his hands in front of his chin with the cigarette pointing up like a candle on an altar.

In the enormous gilt mirror hanging over the bar I see his face reflected back at me through the amber columns of whiskey bottles. "I never really saw Claire as being right for you for the long haul, if you want my opinion—and you may not."

He turns to look me full in the face, like he's either affronted at the offer of my negative opinion, or too curious to miss a word. "The long haul? Why not Claire for the long haul?"

"She's too domestically frivolous for you. She doesn't have an anchor."

"What the hell does that mean?"

"You need somebody who just makes you *worry* she's on the verge of deserting you—not someone who really will."

"You give me no credit for all the maturing I've done in the last two years." His eyes are smiling, but there's a bite of truth to this that makes me blush. He signals the bartender and crushes out the stub of his cigarette. I hear the soft thump and clicks of a cue ball splintering open a game of pool.

"I'll turn forty-two in sixty-three days," Joe says.

"So which is bothering you more right now, Claire or old age?"

He shrugs. "Maybe just an old age spent alone."

"I don't know, Joe, old age can stretch out for a long time if you're spending it with someone you only really liked for a few years of it." I lean over to take a sip of my drink. Now I catch Joe watching me in the mirror.

"Maybe you like your own company better than I like mine."

"What shocking insight coming from you! You must have gotten back into therapy." The line makes him laugh, which is probably why he called me out into the rain tonight. I ask the bartender for the check and push my half-emptied drink in front of Joe, the curl of lemon rind tossing like a tiny boat in a big sea.

"Just doing my best to support our psychiatric colleagues. Come on, I'll walk you home. You look exhausted."

"I *am* exhausted." I take my glass out of his hand and sweep out the lemon curl, lick off the last bit of sugar and wind it around his left ring finger. "There. You and I can have a lovely and long marriage of consoling talks and shared season tickets, and never have to watch one another floss our teeth."

He turns to me with a serious look. I see a haggard tug around his mouth, a strain that I haven't noticed in my own gloomy preoccupation.

"So how are you holding up with all of this investigation? Have you heard anything?"

I gently place the glass on the bar and compose my face, look up at him, look into his eyes, look all the way through him to find an answer he doesn't have, no one has. "I'm not supposed to talk about it. You know that. Especially to you—another doctor."

He shrugs. "Darryl Feinnes talked to me for ten minutes before I was totally dropped from the suit."

"Sure, but you're an anesthesiologist. My partner. Anything I say to you can be considered discovery. Maybe we really should get married, then you'd have immunity and I could pour my soul out."

He doesn't smile. I look down to break his gaze. He covers my wrist with his left hand, the lemon curl still encircling his finger. If I look up again, I will cry, and he knows that.

"I'll walk you home," he says, graciously leaning over to pick up my coat so I can avert my face.

· 14 ·

By the end of May the sun is coming up early enough that I no longer fix my breakfast in the dark. I wait for eggs to boil and bread to toast, sipping coffee while I watch the sunrise, mirrored pink and orange on the still snowy Olympic Mountains. It still excites me, coming from Texas, to stand at my downtown living room windows surrounded by concrete and steel, this urban compactness of humanity, and see such splendor so detached from civilization. Sometimes I look across at the peaks and try to imagine the cold, the deep crevassed glaciers, inhospitable and threatening and glorious.

I try to move back into the rhythm of a normal life. In the evenings it's light until after eight o'clock, and I begin running again after work. It has always been my preferred form of exercise, but one I drift out of in the dark rainy months of winter. I pack my gym bag in the morning and change before I leave the hospital, then drive to the Arboretum, or the shores of Lake Washington, or the serpentine bike paths winding through the University District and Lake Union. If I run long enough, far enough, fast enough, I become too fatigued to think about anything except the next breath, the next bend and what might lie beyond it.

Donnelly calls one evening when I have just walked in the door, sweaty and rejuvenated after five miles along the waterfront dodging T-shirt vendors and tourists and an occasional alcoholic curled in fetal self-protection on the broken sidewalk. My hands start to shake when I hear him say the word *autopsy*. I grip the receiver and prepare to explain why I didn't insist on getting Jolene's records from Yakima before I put her to sleep, why I didn't insist she see a pediatric cardiologist if I had the least suspicion, why I didn't tell him I was worried about her heart the minute it occurred to me so he could repair my defense. Then he blithely continues, saying the autopsy report is probably taking longer than usual only because it contains nothing significant. Nothing to worry about. He'll be sending over some more forms to sign but the suit won't be resolved for months—I should relax and get on with my life.

I thank God we are not talking face-to-face and sink onto the floor still holding the phone, connected to a dead line. But over the next few days I almost unconsciously appropriate his banal assumption, persuading myself that Jolene's heart was fine, and my paranoia is born of bad dreams.

The hospital schedule becomes more fragmented as summer approaches, surgeons taking off chunks of time for children's graduations and family vacations. Those left behind work later into the evening, picking up the slack. Joe and I seem to be vying for those rooms—hours my other partners are willing to pay us to cover so they, too, can see the sun.

Fritz Leyman, a urologist, has drawn the short straw for his group this week, and we are working together in room 9 for fourteen hours of scheduled operations. I like Fritz. He joined the staff about the same time I did, and I've gotten to hear the unfolding of his five children's lives ever since Daniel, his oldest, was ten. Now he's graduating from high school.

We're in the middle of removing the right kidney from a fifty-one-year-old financial planner whose executive corporate health plan paid for a whole body CT scan as part of his routine physical. They found a mass, and he chose Fritz as the surgeon to remove it. The patient is healthy and slender, which makes all of our jobs easier. There is a lull as we wait for Pathology to examine the mass and tell us if it's cancer.

"Why did you decide to take this out?" I ask him. Both of us know that it's almost certainly a benign growth.

"I talked to him about the likelihood that this was never going to cause him any problems, and the risks of the surgery, not to mention the time he'd be out of work. He listened and decided to leave it alone. Then, a month later, he comes back and tells me he hasn't slept a full night since his CT scan. Keeps waking up and wondering if it's growing, keeps looking at his pee to see if it's different. He finally got so convinced he had something fatal, he wanted it out just to put his mind at rest. So here we are."

The pathologist calls back into the room to tell us there is nothing suspicious in the mass, and Fritz starts to close him up.

"Don't feel bad about it, Fritz. The CT scan did diagnose a problem—fear of death. So now you've returned him to a happy state of denial for another decade or so."

Fritz laughs.

The day winds through prostate biopsies and resections, bladder tumors and kidney stones. My patients are personable, resilient men, some surprised to see a female anesthesiologist, all looking forward to fixing their medical problems and getting back to the day-to-dayness of their lives—a monotony often more appreciated after illness. It is the kind of day that can restore the pleasure and gratification I used to enjoy in my job.

When I interview my next-to-last patient, he confesses to having eaten lunch and we have to postpone his surgery, so I have an unexpected break—time to go to the cafeteria and still give a few of my partners a moment out of the OR.

The cafeteria aisles are narrow and crowded with clinic patients trapped in wheelchairs and walkers, rushed doctors and nurses reaching through the waiting lines of other customers to grab wobbly Jell-Os or domed scoops of drying carrot salad cooling on beds of ice. I pick up a yogurt and wait at the cashier behind a frail woman with thinning orange hair who plucks coins from her change purse with intense concentration. I wonder if I will look like her someday.

On the way back to the operating rooms I detour through the hospital lobby just to stand for a moment in the sunshine. For the first time in weeks I find myself looking forward to the weekend. Maybe I can convince Joe to go kayaking. He's in the heart room today. When I walk in I inadvertently startle him—he drops a syringe on the floor and I hear him curse. For the fleetest moment I see annoyance in his face when he looks up.

"Hey, I've got some time before my case starts. Do you want to get out for a few minutes?"

"How come? Fritz usually packs the day as tight as possible."

"Yeah. My last patient ate lunch so we had to delay. And I swear I didn't feed him." Joe and I have a running joke on hectic days that we're going to open a McDonald's in the pre-op area so somebody will eat and we can cancel their surgery.

"I'm gonna go without for now. This guy's heart is working on twenty percent, and I've had a hell of a time with his blood pressure." I look up at the monitor and scan the multicolored lines of light streaming across it in waves of arterial pressure, venous capacitance, ventilation, oxygen saturation—colored ribbons floating against a dark sky, as ephemeral as the life processes they tally. The surgeons are quiet, talking only when they need more retraction or another instrument. No wonder Joe seems tense.

I lower my voice. "OK. Come with me to the Arboretum Sunday? It's supposed to be sunny."

His eyes are the deepest blue, almost navy around the perimeter—a lovely sight to wake up to, once upon a time. He must be tired; his right eye is just slightly off center. Once he told me he actually put his amblyopia to good use in college. He could carry on a conversation with one girl in the cafeteria, and simultaneously observe another girl he liked more sitting at another table.

He shrugs one shoulder, and seems to warm up. "Let's go flying. We can take a picnic up to San Juan, huh? Give me a call after you wake up and we'll see what the weather looks like."

"Flying?"

"Flying?" he mimics in falsetto. "Hey now, don't go wrinkling up your nose that way."

"You can't even see my nose!" I clap my hand over my mask.

"I don't need to see it!"

. . .

Sunday dawns cloudless and mild, blooming into one of the brightest and warmest May days I can remember. At this time of year the *New York Times* usually bumps the latest war from the headlines to broadcast sunbathers in Central Park, while Seattleites are still wearing wool. Joe swears it's the best of days to fly. "A monkey could fly a plane on a day like this. I might even get you to fly."

Joe lives in a contemporary condominium rescued from the former classrooms and laboratories and study halls of one of Seattle's oldest schools. It caps the city's highest hill. A century ago horse-drawn trolleys were dragged up the steep slope using weighted pulleys. Now the neighborhood of Queen Anne perches like a floating island of domesticity above the scurrying masses of downtown. His building is surrounded by renovated turn-of-the-century homes, their tiny yards stuffed with plastic slides and climbing gyms in bright primary colors; tricycles and parked strollers clog the cracked and pitching slabs of sidewalk.

I ring his condominium from the front entry and wait, then ring again. Finally he buzzes me up and opens the door in a ragged bathrobe, his hair still wet from the shower.

"Hey. Sorry I'm running behind. You should have used the extra key. It's still in the same place. Have a seat."

"I forgot about the key. Take your time. Mind if I grab a Coke?"

I sit on the couch in his living room while he gets dressed. The room is sunny, almost too warm, collecting the eastern and southern light. A typical bachelor's flat, even at this stage in his life. The walls are bare except for a few framed pictures of his airplane and a large reproduction of Gustav Klimt's *The Kiss*, its mixed planes and textures reflected in the glass dining table. An earlier girlfriend gave him that, probably his cue to flee.

Beside the couch a stack of anesthesia journals is mixed in among yellowing *Mother Jones*es and bookmarked biographies of various dead men: Ben Franklin, Da Vinci, Freud, Jim Morrison. His bicycle leans against the dining room wall, the calligraphy of its scuff marks lacing the white paint. The furniture is limited to what's functional and necessary, as if he's expecting to move again. In truth it always left me feeling hollow when I stayed with him.

In the corner is his most prized collection, vinyl LPs of jazz classics and early rock. I know for a fact he's spent endless Saturday mornings combing garage sales to find these. When we were dating I was dragged out of sleep—and away from my personal goal of reading the arts section of the *New York Times* with fresh cinnamon rolls—to cruise foreign corners of Seattle looking for some hidden cache of Sonny Rollins or Hank Mobley. It was a good way to learn about a Seattle I otherwise never saw, but maybe an example of the better aspects of staying single.

His home is noticeably absent the slew of family photographs that fill my mantelpiece and library shelves. I met Joe's mother only once, when she came to Seattle for a medical procedure. She needed a stent placed into one of the arteries supplying blood to her heart and Joe, her only child, convinced her to see a cardiologist he knows here. She struck me as hesitant, pausing between her words and phrases as if she might withdraw them should I disagree, as if someone had convinced her that her opinions could never have an impact on her world. It surprised me, in a way. Joe's sarcastic wit and intellectual aplomb seem to have bloomed as a contrary reaction to his upbringing rather than as lovingly fostered traits. He never talks much about his childhood. His dad died years ago—the opposite of my own parental loss. I used to wonder if this truncated family left him more reluctant to have children of his own. It was a discussion we were never quite ready for.

Half an hour later Joe comes into the living room carrying a canvas backpack filled with crackers, dried apricots, leftover Ezell's fried chicken—my favorite—and a stainless steel thermos. He smells like pine soap and has nicked himself shaving; there is a fleck of blood on the cuff of his shirt. He has slipped in the small gold bead of an earring he wears in his right ear when he's not at the hospital. The first time I spotted it, that tiny piercing had seemed like a flashlight beam shining in a dark closet, exposing hidden rooms and unexplored spaces tempting me forward against my better judgment.

• • •

Joe squeezes my hand as he pulls out onto the runway and waits for clearance. He sounds different talking into his headset, a clipped song in the shorthand lingo of flight. My breath jumps high into my throat when we leave the ground. He banks out over the sound—the city looks like it's cupped inside the protective palms of encircling peaks: the eastern Cascades and western Olympics, the northern and southern volcanoes of Mount Baker and Mount Rainier. From this height the geometry of bridged lakes and islanded ocean sprawls like a rumpled quilt in greens and blues. It's worth the price of fear.

He goads me into holding the copilot wheel and I'm almost surprised by how responsive the plane is, so easy to skate across ripples of air. The plane shivers in a patch of light turbulence and I grip the wheel and look at Joe for help. He groans and clasps his hands to his head, then tumbles sideways into the space between us. Gravity turns over in my chest and I scream his name, let one hand leave the steering wheel to reach out to him, discover him shaking with laughter, thrilled with the effect his fake attack has produced, and soon I am also laughing and he has to take the wheel back from me.

We rent bikes and end up in an open field above the beach overlooking the straits. Joe spreads the blanket in the full flood of sunlight that's turning the entire meadow yellow-green. There is enough breeze to soften the sun's heat, enough heat to coax a drowsy relinquishment of time and responsibility. He opens the backpack and pulls out the thermos and two plastic cups. In the sunshine his face is reflected across the cylinder as a distorted caricature of himself, blurring the clean, proportioned angles of his jaw and nose, the reddish gold hues of his hair and skin that stand in such contrast to his dark humor. He was easy to fall for.

"Cheers." He holds his cup level with his eye, lining it up with the horizon of ocean and sky, the mountains now rising through the plastic as peaks captured on a golden lake. "Look. Now I have Mount Olympus right in the palm of my hand. Probably about how we look to God, or at least to an alien spaceman. Perspective, Marie. It's all about perspective."

I pull out some chicken and peel off the plastic wrap. "So why are you working so hard to remodel your kitchen when you haven't even furnished your living room?"

"A better investment. Women are always more attracted to a man's kitchen than to recliners and coffee tables. Besides, isn't gourmet cooking the requisite hobby of the financially secure professional these days?"

"The last time you cooked for me you had to ask what *deglaze* meant. Besides, there're no dishes if you eat out—that ought to appeal to you. Are you worried that's what drove Claire off?"

He's swirling his wine in the sunlight and doesn't answer. "So are you getting out of town anytime this summer? I mean can you, with the lawsuit and all?" he asks.

"I'll probably have to make a trip to Houston at some point."

"What for?"

I sit up and lean over crossed legs, plucking up slender blades of new grass and weaving them into a fragile braid.

"Is it your dad?" he asks, after waiting through my silence.

"Yeah. I guess it's coming to a crisis."

"How much of his sight has he lost?"

"I'm worried he'll be functionally blind before long. He was a medieval history professor for thirty-eight years." I look up at him. "Did I ever tell you that?"

"I knew he taught history. You've been pretty quiet about him."

"Hmm." I cast for some memory or description that won't tarnish this splendid day. "Well, my father is a man who's built his entire universe on books—deciphering them, teaching them, creating them. And now he can barely see the words on a page. He's losing the one thing that has ever really mattered to him—besides my mother."

"Is he still living on his own?"

"Not only that—he's still driving. I'm waiting to hear from the police that he's wrecked his car."

"Maybe you should have his license taken away."

"I'd have to have his car taken away. Not having a license won't stop him. But you're right. Pretty soon we'll have to force his hand."

"Can you get him to move up here?"

A short laugh escapes me at this, struck by how very little I must have relayed to Joe about my father and myself. "Funny to think that after I move to the farthest corner of the country he could end up next door. My dad would never accept being dependent on me."

I sense him pull back from the obvious question of why not. "It's a hard thing to learn, asking for help."

"Impossible to learn—for him, at least," I answer. "I don't think he'd ever let me take care of him, even if that's just his own kind of passive suicide."

"Yeah, but at least if you take his license away he can commit suicide without murdering a flock of pedestrians."

I slap his hand for that comment, and he reaches up and brushes my hair back from my face. "I'm sorry. I shouldn't have said that."

"No, you're right. I think it's the first time in his life he's faced a situation where he couldn't rationalize or debate or write himself out of trouble. In fact 'faced' is exactly the opposite of how he's dealing with this—he's ignoring it."

"Isn't there anybody he'd talk to? A priest" He's Catholic, isn't he?"

I shake my head. "He used to be."

"Why'd he quit?"

"Oh, it's complicated. Like most family stories."

"What about your sister?"

"I'm the doctor, I'm the logical one to figure out how to help him."

"As a doctor, or as a daughter?" Joe asks in a quiet voice.

"Oh, I think it's a bit late to fix the daughter role." My lap is littered with tiny green braids of grass. I sweep them off to wither among the weeds and twist the cap off a soda, but it's hard to swallow. I wait for the emotion to subside, then ask, "So what about you? Are you planning any trips?"

"I want to get some flying in, maybe down to California. Katz has been scoping out a bike trip, if he can talk his wife into it." He squints against the noon sun. Droplets of sweat glisten on his forehead and upper lip. "So has it gotten any easier, since your deposition is behind you? Isn't most of it handled between the lawyers from now on?"

I bite my lip and consider how much to lie. "I don't expect to hear much until the mediation date is set. It could be months. I don't know if that makes it easier or harder."

"I thought it was all just a financial negotiation at this stage."

I look him square in the eye and try to envision his expression if I tell him my concern about Jolene's heart. Would I see shocked empathy? Academic curiosity? Pity? Blame? Then I take a deep breath and answer in the most neutral tone I can manage, "Well, Donnelly's suggested that the more responsibility they can pin on the hospital and the staff—me—the higher the dollars will go. I know he wants to keep it out of court. I think he assumes a jury would slaughter me *and* First Lutheran, given the outcome."

He's quiet for a few minutes after this. He can hardly tell me it will all work out just fine.

I hear shouts and roll over on my stomach to look up. Four or five young boys are running across the field in front of us, dragging a newspaper kite along the ground, the string tangling in grass and twigs. It jolts and bounces into the air, then cartwheels down against the dirt as they clamor at one another to run faster, pull harder, let go of the string. Joe is propped up on his elbows and shades his eyes to watch. A second later he is up and running through the grass, circling the children and swooping the kite up from the earth. He hunches close to the ground and sweeps his hands across the sky. Now he's up and sprinting, the kite held high above his head, rattling and teasing against the wind. He is loose and ageless and accepted in their midst, a child among children. I am reminded of the time we went to the Oregon shore in October and he took advantage of a rare sun break to race straight into the icy waves, coming up suitless—naked and blue and hollering—sending a nearby family tearing for their car.

I watch him run, holding the kite's wooden cross and wheeling backward, shouting to a brown-skinned boy to let out the string more, more, and more again, until it breaks out of his grasp and arcs skyward. It is so obvious to me, here, at this moment, that we have had hopes for the same things in life: a family, a reason to come home from work. Why couldn't we make that step? One of us, both of us, pulled everything back inside, back into neutral territory, where it has taken root and grown into what it is now, what it will always be—this lovely, multifaceted friendship, immutable in its maturity.

He comes back hot and happy, innocent in his momentary oblivion to all but the present.

"You're drenched. Why didn't you wear a T-shirt?"

"Need less sunscreen." He looks at me and smiles, then falls on his back to stare at the infinite blue light.

"Hey, any idea what time it is? Should we be heading home?" I ask.

"Always back to earth, Marie. Always in control, aren't you?" He looks at me fondly, acceptingly, for which I am thankful. Otherwise the remark would have stung. "OK," he says, "we'll find out the time."

He rolls me onto my back and scoots around to lie head to head in a long line, then he tells me to lift my arms up and he grasps my hands so our four arms rise vertically, throwing a narrow shadow across the grass, a flesh-and-blood sundial. "There," he says, "how much more do you need to know about time?"

Our arms drop and we lie in silence and warmth until I can almost slip away from here into sleep. Just as I begin to drift I hear Joe say quietly, " 'Time held me green and dying/Though I sang in my chains like the sea.' "

· 15 ·

On the drive home I glance in the rearview mirror and see that I've sunburned my nose and cheeks. I check my mailbox—overflowing as usual. The phone rings as I open my front door and I run to the kitchen, dumping the armful of magazines, newspapers, bills and solicitations on the counter.

It's Lori. "Hi. Where were you? I've been calling all day. Sorry I left so many messages. Gordy's out of town and the kids are at the club with Olivia. It's my first moment of peace all week. How are you?"

"Better. I just got back from San Juan Island. We've had incredible weather the last few days—it's been up in the eighties." It relaxes me to be able to answer with something other than "Fine, and you?" "So where is Gordon this trip?"

"Dubai—trying to drum up investors. He's missing Neil's first Cub Scout hike."

"Dubai? They invest in Texas shopping malls? Couldn't you go with him?" She used to travel with him, but as their three children have come along, his schedule has become a burden she grudgingly accommodates.

"Even *his* plane ticket's probably wasted money. And we'd have to hire another mother. Speaking of which, why don't you plan a trip here soon? They're growing up fast, Marie. Elsa's got a better figure than I do now."

I laugh. "Oh come on." In our phone calls I still imagine her as the slender girl she was two years ago.

"I swear to God. You could fill me in on things. I'm tempted to eavesdrop outside her closet door one of these nights."

I feel a twinge of disloyalty. "She's a great kid—you know that. Should I be reporting more?"

I can almost hear her stand up straight. "No! Then she'd stop talking to you and start taking advice from her friends!" She sighs and adds, "I'll get this figured out by the time Lia's fifteen. You did pretty well by me after mom got sick." She brightens again. "So why not come down later this summer?"

"Who comes to Texas in the summer?"

"You could come here and then we could drive down to Houston together, if I can get Gordon to watch the kids. I talked to Dad yesterday. He saw his ophthalmologist again last week and the news wasn't good. I had to drag that out of him, though. I wish you would call him again. Maybe he'll tell you more of the medical stuff than he tells me."

As close as we are, Lori and I diverge around my father the way rushing water parts around a boulder. Instead of tempering our discrepant experiences with him, age has made them harder to talk about, at least for me. "Last time I asked whether he could still manage the house on his own he pretended the line was cut off and hung up on me. I don't know which he values more, his independence or his sight." I sort the mail as we talk, pitching Lands' End and Nordstrom catalogs, Valpak coupons and platinum credit card offers into an overflowing recycle bin.

"He's got to start making some plans. Are you going to wait until he shouldn't drive at all, which was probably months ago?" There is a weighted silence on the line as she slides the responsibility for my father's future into my lap. We've had this conversation numerous times, but always leave the painful conclusions unresolved. "Marie," she adds when I don't answer, her voice halfway between angry and sad, "I can't keep translating everything between the two of you. We're not that young anymore."

"No. You can't. At some point you may have to admit that some things just aren't translatable." I feel bad about the remark as soon as it leaves my mouth. "Look, I'll call him later this week and try to get him to let me talk to his ophthalmologist. And I'd love to see you all if I can get away this summer. I just can't plan anything until I know more about this legal settlement, OK?"

"I'll turn up the air conditioning for you. Will you call me after you talk to Dad?" She waits for my response through a prolonged silence. "Marie? You still there?"

"Lori, my pager's going off. I have to go." I hang up the telephone and sink cross-legged onto the tile floor of my kitchen. In my hand is the last piece of the day's mail, a thick white envelope with my formal name and title typed across the front and the return address of the King County Medical Examiner's Office. My hands are shaking so, I knot them together on top of the envelope, wanting them to stop quivering like the heart of some small and terrified animal trapped in my lap.

Right now an identical envelope must be sitting in Don Stevenson's hospital inbox, waiting in John Donnelly's office, slipping through Darryl Feinnes's mail slot, stacked with all corners rigidly aligned on Caroline Meyers-Yeager's spotless desk. If the contents conclude that Jolene died from irreversible complications of anaphylaxis—a presumption I have propagated since the day of her death—they will file the pages into a cabinet or an overflowing cardboard box, along with the thousands of other pages to be reviewed by the mediator. Nothing will materially change for any of them.

But everything will change for me. Either way, no matter what the autopsy discovered, everything will change. I will be freed by the knowledge that Jolene's death was a tragedy of nature, or awake in the nightmare that it was my fault.

I could wait until I get the phone call from Donnelly or Caroline and not go through this alone. I could drink enough wine to blunt the impact or celebrate the absolution. But even while I rationalize how to delay I slip my forefinger underneath the sharp crease and rip through the sealed envelope.

It is at least ten pages, thirteen when I actually flip to the back and see the final number. The first page is filled with known facts: the date and time of Jolene's death, the date and time of her autopsy, her diagnosis at admission and the type of operation. The name and title of each participant is listed like the opening credits to a movie. Halfway down the first page, in bold type, is the section heading **Final Anatomic Diagnosis**. I'm almost thankful it is right here on the front page, too late now to pretend I don't see the answer.

"Coarctation of the proximal aorta. Bicuspid aortic valve." Time breaks into a thousand finite particles. I am here reading the words, I am above myself, watching myself. I am conscious that I only have a few more stunned seconds before everything falls apart.

I scan through the lists that follow, the weight of her heart and the congestion noted in the ventricles, the edematous fluid in the alveoli of her lungs, the color and texture of her liver, her kidneys, her intestines, her spleen, each quantified in grams and centimeters. Her ovaries are small and atrophic. Her physical stature is noted to be smaller than her age-matched norms. There is a subtle laxity of flesh at the nape of her neck, a nominal lowering of her posterior hairline. And the last bit of data listed, which explains the delay in her autopsy report: a chromosomal analysis confirms that many, though not all, of Jolene's cells carried only one X chromosome. Jolene had Turner syndrome.

I have stood on crowded street corners and watched thyroid goiters ebb and flow above shirt collars when women swallow. I have waited behind men in espresso lines examining darkly pigmented flecks for the ragged edges and mottled coloring of melanoma. I've spotted the swan neck deformities of rheumatoid arthritis, the spidery broken blood vessels and yellowed sclera of liver disease, the fleshy nodules of neurofibromatosis, the broad, flattened fingernails and barrel-shaped chests of pulmonary disease, the butterfly rash of lupus.

I have lost the ability to look at a stranger's face without estimating the ease or difficulty of intubating their trachea. I have forgotten what it was like to be ignorant of the telltale clues that failing internal organs and multiplying infectious organisms surreptitiously display. Physical diagnosis is the study of optical illusions, the art of seeing through what is expected in order to detect which part of the picture is changed, what hidden shape hides in the shadows and creases of familiar scenes. Since I began medical school fifteen years ago this second sight has seeped into me the way tea stains dental enamel or cigarettes color smokers' fingers. To read Jolene's autopsy report is to slap my forehead—my own moment of "Aha!" The lamp becomes a lady, the young woman an aged hag. The clues were minimal to be sure—I should be comforted by the fact that every other doctor who's cared for her missed them as well. But if I'd recognized them, if I'd listened to her heart despite her crying, if I'd pressed Bobbie for more details, I might have caught it. I might have stopped it. I might have changed everything.

· 16 ·

Monday morning we operate on a fifty-two-year-old grade school principal who came to our emergency room last night with cramping abdominal pain caused by a blockage in his intestine. When he wakes up his surgeon will have to tell him he has metastatic colon cancer. His plight should help me keep my own in perspective, but I have lain awake most of the night waiting for my lawyer's office to open.

Mindy watches me like a mother cat with circling coyotes, smelling my distress. Bless her. I wonder if she would feel so protective if she knew what the autopsy report proved. Finally my pager goes off and flashes Donnelly's number. At a quiet moment in the surgery, my patient gliding safely at cruising altitude on an infusion of drugs and gas, I punch his number into the telephone behind my anesthesia machine.

"You've read the report?" he says.

"Of course."

There is a long pause, as if he's waiting for me to volunteer something more. He must hear the high rhythmic beeping of my patient's heart monitor in the background, the chatter of the operating room staff. Finally he clears his throat. "Well. This changes things. But don't get too discouraged. I'm contacting a pediatric cardiologist to address the heart thing. We can mitigate the impact."

"Mitigate?" The surgeon asks me to tilt the operating table and I put the phone down to make the adjustment. When I pick it up again Donnelly is already talking.

"... right expert can mitigate anything. Call Anne and set up an appointment for the end of the week. We'll go over the report, talk about how we'll be countering it."

"I don't have any time off this week. Could I meet with you on Saturday? It's hard to keep dropping out of the operating room to come to your office." My voice is tight. I feel like a child complaining about assigned chores or homework.

"Scoble knows how important this is. And not just to you. I'll leave Friday open until I hear from you. Call Anne with whatever time you can work out."

Am I imagining it, or is he sounding annoyed with me? I struggle to compose myself. "Fine then. I'll see you on Friday."

I'm about to hang up when he adds, "Marie, this isn't going to be resolved quickly, and it isn't going to be low stress. We're here to help you, but I'd advise you to get used to the fact that a mediation process can be as rough as a trial."

Mindy looks at me from her desk in the corner. I pull on new latex gloves and dive underneath the sterile drapes to adjust my patient's breathing tube and IV lines, avoiding her eyes. I wish I worked in an office and could abruptly excuse myself to go to the bathroom. I hear her walk up behind me.

"I brought you another liter of fluid. Your IV's running out. You OK?" She knows I don't usually talk on the phone in the middle of surgery. She reaches above me to hang the clear plastic bag of saline from the pole above my patient's outstretched arm, the loose skin above her elbow sagging in the way of a fit but elderly woman, a body losing pace with its own repair work.

"Thanks, Mindy. Maybe you could turn the music down some." The forced rhymes of early eighties hits are grating on me.

"No problem."

I hide my face over the anesthetic record on my table and start filling in the past few minutes' worth of blood pressures and pulse rates, then realize I've messed the time lines up and have to correct each tiny mark. Ten minutes later Joe comes into the room and leans over my shoulder.

"Hey there. Why don't you let me cover for you for a while."

I jump back, startled, and realize how distracted I am by my conversation with Donnelly. My face flushes. "Mindy called you in, didn't she? Thanks, Joe, I'm OK. I could use a favor, though. I have to go to Donnelly's office sometime on Friday, and I'm scheduled for a late day. If you can get me out for a couple of hours, I'll pay you back. I could take your late day next Tuesday."

"Don't worry about it." He bends low over my desk so the others can't overhear. "Look, there's not much I can do to help right now. Someday it might be me who's talking to lawyers and you can pay me back then."

His sincerity makes me want to tell him about the autopsy, about this sense I'm getting that ultimately I will have to be my own defense—Donnelly's goal will be to negotiate the lowest possible settlement, if he wants to stay on the hospital's payroll. But all I can do is squeeze Joe's hand.

I schedule another appointment with Phil Scoble, to talk about how to structure the time off I need for legal meetings. He sits on the corner of his desk dangling one leg over the side so his scrub suit pants scrunch up above his black socks and I can see the shiny, taut skin over his tibia. He rolls a crystal paperweight from palm to palm and every fourth or fifth pass it fractures the sunlight into a rainbow across the white walls.

"Why don't you give more thought to taking a leave of absence? We could take it out of your sick leave—even hire someone temporary to fill in. Nobody would think less of you for it."

"There's no one out there to hire. Look how long it took you to fill the last vacancy. I love my work—I need my work. It may even look better to the mediator if I keep working. I just feel bad that my partners have to work harder when I'm away."

Phil places the paperweight on his desk and folds his hands in his lap. He shifts and the sun silhouettes him so I can no longer read his expressions. "Donnelly tells me he doesn't expect to go before the mediator for another few months. Marie, don't underestimate the stress this might put on you. I want you to be considering all your options."

"My options? What, like running away under an assumed name?" He doesn't laugh—not that I'm sure I meant that as a joke.

"Do you want me to arrange for some counseling? Somebody from outside of the hospital?"

It's certainly not the first time someone has suggested I talk to a counselor. I've thought of it myself. I *want* to talk about the academic facts of Jolene's death. I want to discuss Turner syndrome and her cardiac abnormalities. I want to be adamantly, miraculously persuaded by another physician that in spite of those cloaked abnormalities my anesthetic management could never have killed her. Whatever collision of anatomy and medication occurred on the operating room table would have happened with any other anesthesiologist—Jolene was flawed, but I was not. I need to be told that the work I do sixty and seventy hours a week, the work I trained twelve years to master, is worthy. But I have no desire to probe the blurred boundaries that hinge my working life to my personal choices or my past.

"I want to keep taking care of patients, Phil. Just give me that chance, and let's arrange some kind of payback for any time off I have to take."

He stands up from the edge of his desk and walks to his chair on the other side. As he sits down and faces me again I can see all the features of his face, the deep-set creases of his professional, courteous smile, the parallel grooves above the bridge of his nose that reflect the gravity of his responsibilities. He answers me in a consoling tone. "Then you need to stay. You should stay. The hospital will stand behind you in whatever way we can."

· 17 ·

On Friday Joe comes in to take over my case so I can make my appointment with Donnelly. He seems studiously nonchalant as he picks up my chart to look it over, protecting my privacy in the face of the surgeons and techs who wonder why I'm leaving in the middle of the day. But I notice a fine tremor across the papers he holds in his hand.

"Much blood loss so far?" he asks.

"Five hundred. But his starting hematocrit was forty-three and his heart rate's stayed in the sixties. He's typed and screened for two units if you need any. Thanks for covering for me, Joe."

"No problem. Leave your pen, huh?" I'm almost out the door when he says, "Marie, let me know how it goes, OK?"

The women's locker room is deserted between the eight-hour shift changes. I drop my scrubs into an overflowing laundry bin and put on a linen suit and high heels.

Donnelly's office is only seven blocks down from First Lutheran. The plaza of his building is jammed with chattering coworkers headed out for lunch in the sun; I seem to be the only one going inside. I catch an elevator up to the twenty-second floor and step into the deep-carpeted, reverent hush of the reception area. Each of the firm's eighteen partners has his name displayed in stainless steel relief against a cherry-paneled wall. The receptionist offers me coffee or tea or sparkling water, and then

117

I wait, the two of us silent as churchgoers. She looks vaguely familiar to me and I wonder if I have ever anesthetized her. I open a *National Geographic* and begin an article about the space shuttle, but give up after reading the first paragraph three times. The cover photograph is of our cloud-enshrouded Earth drifting in a black universe. What speck am I, down there, on that spinning mass? What instant of my life passed as the camera shutter snapped closed? The instant of Jolene's death?

Finally, on some hidden cue, the receptionist stands and leads me down the hall to Donnelly's office. I hear the soft purr of an air purifier. The walls are lined with leather-bound legal books so densely packed and perfectly matched they could be hiding a secret panel, maybe a room from which other lawyers, other experts can observe our conversation. Donnelly folds his reading glasses on his desk and greets me pleasantly enough, closing the thick file folder in front of him and standing until I am seated in one of the silk-upholstered wing chairs facing his desk.

"Marie. Thank you for making the time. Can I get you anything to drink? You look well."

I haven't eaten or slept well in days, and I know my hair looks crushed and limp after being encased in a surgical cap all morning. But his voice has a reassuring resonance that recalls the invective prose of a Southern Baptist preacher.

"No. Thank you." I scan the room and notice for the first time that nothing in here gives a clue about the personal life of John H. Donnelly, other than framed Ivy League degrees and original artwork. No pictures of wife or children, no golf trophies or gym bags, no photos of him shaking hands with mayors or sports figures. It's as if he had been born and bred of law school and expensive, solicitous privacy. I wonder what the *H* stands for. He is looking at me, waiting for me to breach the polite chitchat and get to the point. I ask, "Have you talked to the pediatric cardiologist yet?"

"Extensively. He'll be testifying for us."

My mouth is suddenly dry. I find myself wanting to apologize for the missed diagnosis, as if he were a board examiner about to fail me. "John, I've spent every free minute since I read the report studying

Turner syndrome and coarctation—Jolene's heart defect. I feel terrible about missing it. It's terrible every doctor who's ever treated her has missed it. But I'm not convinced I would have changed my anesthetic. It made anesthesia riskier for her, and I would have gotten a cardiology consult and an echocardiogram. I concede that. But I might still have done everything the same way."

I keep waiting for him to nod, or scowl, or smirk—give me some hint of his reaction to this. "Do you get what I'm saying? I don't think Feinnes can prove it ultimately made a difference in her outcome."

Donnelly leans over his desk and flips open a file folder. "The pediatric cardiologist agrees with that. But the real issue is that now the plaintiff, Darryl Feinnes, has something definitive to pin on you."

"Wait. If an expert can testify that I still made all the right choices, even without knowing about her heart, how can I be any more liable than I was before we had the autopsy?"

"It goes to 'breach of duty' and 'proximate cause.' The autopsy gives Feinnes a much stronger case to argue that you failed to conform to the relevant standard of care by not recognizing the child had a heart defect, and that such breach of duty resulted in her death." He cocks his head and watches me trying to process this. "Unfortunately, medical malpractice isn't just about what is absolutely right or wrong. It's about how successfully you can persuade a jury."

"But there is no jury."

"Not at this point. Hopefully never. But a mediator can be equally influenced. We're in a betting game. It all comes down to who holds the strongest cards, and these autopsy results dealt Feinnes a royal flush."

The absurdity and gut truth of it make me want to cry. They argue, all of them, as if any amount of money could repair Bobbie's life or mine. What would all the lawyers do if I went directly to Bobbie, begged her to sit down with me, if she could bear being in my presence, and together we settled on the sum of money that would allow her at least a chance in life?

Donnelly says, "The plaintiff's side, of course, has deposed their own expert. Do you want to see it?"

"See it?"

"The recording. Of his deposition. Then you can get an idea of what we'll be rebutting." He tucks his loosened tie back beneath a gold tie clip. The painting behind his desk rises to expose a flat-panel screen—he must have pressed something. A video begins playing with an initial jerk of the camera from a man's folded and manicured hands up to his face, the focus moving in and out until it gels.

"Pediatric anesthesiologist from the East Coast," says Donnelly. "Double-boarded in both specialties. Makes his living now traveling the country testifying in cases like this. Costs them a bundle, but he's got an amazing track record."

The witness starts talking, answering Feinnes's questions in a rapid, certain voice that leaves no question of ambiguity or opinion. He has re-created the scenario from the operating room record, my anesthetic chart, pharmacy notes, and time estimates made by the multitude of extra hands who poured into the room when the code was announced—all composed after the tumult.

"I see no documentation that Dr. Heaton recognized this child's preexisting cardiac abnormalities—a lapse in her responsibilities to her patient."

"Dr. Heaton clearly misdiagnosed the earliest moments of pulmonary edema and impending cardiovascular collapse. Had she responded promptly enough, with more precision and familiarity with pediatric emergencies, Jolene Jansen would almost certainly be alive today."

"Dr. Heaton has failed to recertify in pediatric advanced life support. While not required, it is a readily available course of instruction that could have saved this child's life."

He is as at ease with courtroom persuasion as I once believed myself to be with a difficult anesthetic. By the end of an hour of such unfaltering damnation I have lost any rational measure of my own competence or negligence. I cannot imagine facing these accusations before a jury or judge.

When the video ends I sit quietly, pulling at a loose thread on my blouse until the hem begins to unravel. The declining afternoon sun is making the room uncomfortably warm. Donnelly rubs an open palm over his face, then picks up a pen and begins turning it end over end against the polished desk; it clicks as rhythmically as a second hand.

"Well, you can see why he makes a profession of this."

"Sure. He makes his career by ruining others." I recrease the blouse hem, unwilling to look up until I can compose myself.

After a pause Donnelly answers me with the first tinge of empathy I've heard today. "Look, Marie. I realize how vicious this feels. And I won't minimize it—Feinnes will make this as painful as he can for you and the hospital. Your record has been clean until this. The nurses and Stevenson have said you handled yourself well in there. And of course we'll be deposing our own expert. But a dead child. That carries so much emotional weight. We're really scrambling for containment here."

After a deep breath I meet his eyes. "Has Jolene's mother seen the autopsy report, and this video?"

"She was at the deposition. Yes."

I involuntarily cover my eyes with my hand, as if I could shut out the image of Bobbie hearing that her daughter died because of my mistake.

I can't face the possibility of running into someone in the garage, of having to respond to anyone's cheerful "How was your day?" I walk the ten blocks home. I'll take a cab back to work tomorrow. The streets wind down past galleries and bookstores where hip young musicians and artists share sidewalks with unshaven men whose mongrel dogs wear signs asking for spare change or spare jobs, down to the piers where Seattle meets the sea. The deepening sky has lifted Mount Rainier right up off the horizon, a melting scoop of ice cream suspended in the city smog.

From the western-facing windows of my loft Elliott Bay casts the last blue reflection of sky, and the outer world is more visible than the interior. I don't turn on any lights. I want to watch the glassy line between sky and reflected sky blacken and disappear. Tomorrow is Saturday, and I don't have to work, I have no family responsibilities demanding my time or my money. I can stay home and sleep as late as I want, sit in my living room in pajamas until the sun is full up on the mountains, then walk down First Avenue to my favorite bookstore for espresso and the morning *Times,* or wander through Occidental Square to the antique stores—buy the Curtis photogravure I've been eyeing. I can drive my reasonably new and fully-paid-for car out to Whidbey Island or Port Townsend and go for a long run along the shore, then find a small inn where I can get a massage and have fresh oysters and a tiramisu brought to my room to be consumed with one of the unfinished novels stacked beside my bed.

I have worked and studied long enough and hard enough to have the luxury of options, sweet choices from a banquet of homes and vacations and cuisines. I have chosen my career, spiced with intellectual challenge and prestige and succor, conveniently garnished with a substantial salary. I have chosen the select friends I allow to become close, and packed the empty niches in between with framed professional degrees and purchasable clutter. If the mediation fails and we go to a juried trial, I could lose it all. And if all the money and possessions were stripped away, what, exactly, would be left?

· 18 ·

The Fourth of July. Friends are setting off firecrackers and drinking mojitos at a colleague's waterfront home on Mercer Island, where docks thrust into Lake Washington, hundred-thousand-dollar footnotes on the multimillion-dollar mansions. I am on call at the hospital.

The day has dissolved into a stream of emergency laparoscopies, labor epidurals and C-sections, until a late evening lull sends me back to my call room to try to catch a nap before the usual onslaught of holiday emergencies begins. As soon as I curl catlike on top of the rough cotton bedspread my pager beeps; the LED screen flashes the seven digits of an office line somewhere inside the hospital. A surgeon, most likely, calling about an upcoming case. My energy sinks as the night's work piles up, and I have to remind myself I asked for this additional shift.

"Hey, I saved you the best seat in the house to watch the fireworks. Meet me on the fourteenth floor."

"Joe. You nutcase. What are you doing here—don't you ever get sick of this place? And there is no fourteenth floor. Where are you calling from?" I get a giddy lift hearing his voice on this endless day.

"Sure there's a fourteenth floor. You just have to know where to look for it—like a lot of life's more exalting vistas."

He could only mean the roof. The highest patient floor is eleven, and above that is a maze of storage areas—sort of a grandmother's attic stuffed with wheelchairs, ventilators, traction devices and braces for all manner of fractured and failing skeletons. A medical junkyard. There is no thirteenth floor—not in a hospital.

"Which stairs should I take?"

"Depends on whether you want to watch the sunrise or the sunset."

"I'll come up through the south wing. Then we'll have both options."

The stairwell rises in a cloistered shaft parallel to the bustling patient wards, its thick concrete walls cool and sweaty. I push against the silver bar of the metal fire door that seals the dark stairs from the building's rooftop. The flood of slanted evening sunlight is jolting after the white lights and hard surfaces of the operating rooms. It catches Joe in a wash of gold—gold glinting off his reddish hair and the thick soft hair of his arms, that half-shaven beard casting an inverse halo of gold under his jaw.

He is leaning back on elbows cocked over the cement rooftop wall, staring directly at the door as I exit, grinning like a colluding, teenaged prankster. How old is Joe? Forty-two or fourteen? How can he not make me want to pretend life holds no consequences beyond the joy of the moment?

Sitting on the hot asphalt roof among the detritus of cigarette butts and foil gum wrappers is a tiny chocolate cake. I recognize it immediately as a Fran's chocolate torte, one of the few delicacies of Seattle guaranteed to plump me into my larger pair of blue jeans. A single sputtering sparkler is fizzing into sulfuric smoke on top of the torte.

"Sorry. The ice cream was melting, so I had to eat it myself."

"Hey, if you feel like you have to be at the hospital on the Fourth of July, why not just take my call day? I could have gone to the beach for you and let you know how terrible the weather was or how bad a sunburn I got or something."

"I already did that this weekend. Then I wanted to watch the fireworks and I figured the best view would be from the Aurora Bridge, but I might get unexpectedly depressed about something and decide to jump off. So I came here instead."

When I pick up the shiny dark torte it releases a seductive aroma through the summer air. The sparkler has melted a tiny black pond in the circular center of solid chocolate. Joe runs his pinkie along the outer rim, gouging out a moat of chocolate, then licks it clean. Everything is magnificently shadowed in the horizontal sunlight. The roof is deserted, despite the sweeping scape of Seattle's surrounding mountains and sea.

"Scoble should move the anesthesia call room up here and glass it in. He'd have people begging to work weekends," I say.

"You can see Lake Union from here, if you lean around the ducts at the end of the roof." He grabs my hand and pulls me to the eastern end of the building. The twilight is deepening and the landscape is taking on the indefinable blue of near darkness, the blue of transition. He's right. By stretching around an air-conditioning tower I can just make out the shimmery surface of Lake Union, the clustered lights of party boats rocking in the breeze, waiting for the first crack and whine of fireworks to spread in the blackness like fiery peacocks.

"I met you right out there, four years ago tonight. Do you remember that? I'd just moved here—I had a huge U-Haul parked in front of my condo and I was supposed to start work the next day. And I'm obligated to go to this welcoming party."

I remember. I'll always remember that night. The anesthesia department had rented a boat out on Lake Union, anchored right in front of the fireworks barge and Gas Works Park. It was an evening when we all saw perhaps too much of each other's unprofessional sides, drinks flowing unfettered and weather hot enough to justify—or rationalize—minimal clothing. All the tension of the operating rooms seemed to be uncoiling in the heat. Joe was a reasonable excuse to throw a party. By sunset I was tucked into an isolated booth beneath a clouded porthole. Then Joe was sitting next to me, handing me a beer. He put a plate of iced jumbo shrimp on the table in front of us. The fireworks were just starting and he said almost nothing to me, besides his name. It felt like the only honest conversation on the boat.

It's almost dark now. Around us the hilltops are episodically lit with tiny colored explosions and to the west the ferries, ringed with tiers of brightly lit windows, stream across the bay like floating birthday cakes.

The air is a perfect balance of light humidity and heat, my skin a fluid component of the atmosphere. My eyes begin to sting and the city lights blur into melting stars.

Joe watches me, sensing the shift in my mood. He doesn't say anything, no flippant remark that I could nonchalantly punt back. Instead he reaches out and squeezes my shoulder.

I turn away from him and see the fading silhouette of the Olympics simplified to a two-dimensional cutout. "I suspected you weren't just randomly roaming by the hospital with a Fran's chocolate cake in your front seat."

"It's a torte, not a cake. They charge five dollars extra for the torte."

"Whatever."

He leans back on the ledge, watching the sparse bursts of bottle rockets before Seattle begins its show. "Quite a view, isn't it?" he says, allowing me the moment to compose myself.

"So why does it make me so sad? To be this intensely alive for an instant?" I release a weakhearted laugh at the absurdity of the question.

Joe stares at the dimming horizon. He answers so quietly I almost miss it. "Because you never really look 'til it's almost gone."

Below us the city grows tense with the anticipation of fireworks.

He looks over at me. "Marie, you need to let go of this. You have to stop blaming yourself for this girl's accident. You've been carrying this around alone for so many weeks now."

I hold my face in my hands and sorrow surfs against my eyes. "Let go? How do I do that? I think about it every time I sit still for more than five minutes. I go over every single step of it, every blip of the monitors, every drug I gave. Every time I introduce myself to a patient I see that woman's face, her mother's face. It's not just about the little girl. Death might be a blessing if it means you never have to face this kind of grief. To lose your baby? I don't see how she . . ."

Joe breaks in. "Listen to yourself. This little girl, be realistic. What kind of a future did she have? I'm not trying to be cruel—I'm sure it's been a huge blow for her mom—but stand back a little. What could you have done differently?"

"You don't know . . ." I stop, wiping tears away with the back of my hand, avoiding his eyes. I have to bite my lip to keep from shouting the autopsy results at him. I understand now why criminals feel compelled to confess their crimes.

"What? What don't I know?"

I shake my head, then answer in a hoarse whisper, "I see her mother in these depositions. She looks even more lost than I am. She had to watch that expert of Feinnes's—he made it sound like her daughter was all but murdered by my incompetence. Can you imagine trying to find the truth in all this when you don't understand half the medical words? God, this whole gruesome legal process has taken on its own perverse momentum."

"Not without the help of her lawyers, I'm sure."

I stare out at the glittering party boats on the lake. A light breeze is dropping the temperature and I start to shiver. "My own lawyer would hang me out to dry if he knew I was talking to you about this."

"Screw the lawyers."

I answer him in a flat, defiant tone. "Right. Screw the lawyers. You know the pitiful thing? I'm almost rooting for Bobbie Jansen's side just so she at least comes away with enough money to start another life."

Now he steps around in front of me and grabs both of my shoulders squarely in front of him, the balls of his thumbs pressing into my clavicles. "Marie. Anesthesia is not perfectly safe. Neither is flying or driving a car or taking over-the-counter cough syrup. Whatever happened to Jolene—and you will probably never figure out what happened to her—was going to happen no matter who was taking care of her. Regardless of how this settlement comes out, she is dead and you are not the reason. The biggest battle you have in front of you right now is to forgive yourself. My God," he says in an exasperated tone, "for all anybody knows she was going to die at that moment whether she had surgery or not. If you have to blame somebody, pin it on Brad. He had a chance to change things if he thought you were doing anything wrong."

"Brad's paid enough for this already."

"My point exactly. So have you. Don't make yourself the next victim in this tragedy."

I shove his hands off my shoulders and shout, "Have you ever been responsible for a child's death? Sure, you've lost eighty-year-old heart patients, but a kid? I was the one in charge when she died." I back away and restrain my voice to a quiet storm. "Think about it. This was the only child of a woman who's already lost her husband. What fills her mind every evening when she comes home to a house with that empty bedroom? More than one life was lost in that operating room."

At that moment the northern sky begins fracturing into a rainbow of colored fire as rockets are shot from a barge in the middle of Lake Union. We watch the lights in silence until I tug his sleeve. "Come on. I'll walk you down to the lobby. I've got to check on some people in Labor and Delivery."

· 19 ·

I think about Bobbie Jansen every day. I imagine her house with its empty rooms and silent dinner table. I imagine her dressing table mirror rimmed with photographs tucked beneath a peeling wooden frame—pictures of a baby holding a furry teddy bear, a toothless infant smiling drunkenly at the looming camera, a toddler splashing in a plastic wading pool, an eight-year-old girl blowing out the candles on her last birthday cake.

This is what I should have screamed at Joe before he left. The rest of the night I rescript our conversation, berate myself for what I didn't say, regret what I did.

Will shows up at seven thirty to relieve me. "Hey, rough night, huh?" he asks. There is a deeper layer to his concerned look; he must recognize more strain than one bad call night should forge.

"Death by perpetual paging—you know. The sheets are clean on the bed. I never even pulled back the bedspread." He grins at me but studies my face.

I turn away and stuff my hairbrush and socks into a shoulder bag. "So, there are still three epidurals running, one VBAC, but she's almost fully dilated and her tracings look good. I got a couple of calls about add-on cases for general surgery, but we should be able to work them in at the end of the day. Two rooms are running light."

"Want to grab a cup of coffee before you take off?"

"Thanks. I think I'll try to get some sleep so I can go for a run later. Looks like it should be beautiful today." The sunshine through the narrow window near the ceiling flickers off a river of dust motes flowing between the two of us. We are in the brief hour of direct natural light this makeshift room gets before the sun passes behind the looming wings of clinics and laboratories that have been patched onto the original building. It must be like this in prisons: a slot of sun each day that inmates follow across the floor like heliotropes rooted in concrete.

"Great, great." He is standing in the doorway and I have to gently push past him to leave. "Well, have a good one. See you tomorrow."

The curbside gutters are cluttered with spent firecrackers and plastic American flags stapled to little wooden sticks; an empty beer bottle rattles across the street like the last drunken partygoer. I lock my front door behind me as if I suspect I am followed.

Two messages are on the machine from Lori about my dad. He has burned a pile of books in his fireplace and set off the smoke alarm—a neighbor called her to say the fire department nearly broke down his door before he answered it. Gary's called asking when he can reschedule his visit, wondering if it's a new romance that's made me so hard to reach lately.

And the third voice is Donnelly's. It's short and cheery. "Call me as soon as you get a chance. Tell Anne to put you right through to me." My heart starts racing. Anne never puts me right through to his office. I always have to wait for him to call me back. In fact, it had been of some nominal relief to know that my case fell low enough in his rank of threat to keep me on hold. Something has changed.

It's only 7:45 in the morning. No one will be at his office until 8:30 at the earliest. I have forty-five minutes to play out scenarios of professional crucifixion. I pour coffee beans into the grinder but spill most of the bag onto the floor. My hands are numb. I wish time were a physical body I could grasp and yank forward. I fill the bathtub with hot water and slide down under it like a blanket, my nose just above the water. The clean line of it divides my face—a line of hot and cool, water and steam, breath and suffocation. The clock barely moves.

At 8:20 I start dialing the phone and ring back every few minutes until the receptionist finally answers, her voice as manicured as a re-cording.

"May I speak to Mr. Donnelly, please?"

"Could I tell him who's calling?"

"Dr. Marie Heaton. I'm returning his call."

Next I should hear Anne telling me Donnelly's in a meeting and he'll get back to me. But instead she sounds almost fawning. "Dr. Heaton, thank you for calling. I'll put you through."

"Marie. How are you?" His voice is too considerate. "Glad you could get back to me so quickly—I thought you might be out of town for the holiday. Listen, a couple of issues have come up that we need to talk over. Can you come by my office sometime today?"

So whatever it is he won't tell me over the phone. I clear my throat. "Sure, John. I'm free. What time would you like me to come?"

"I'm open all morning. How about ten o'clock?"

Anne appears in the doorway minutes after I arrive.

"Good morning, Dr. Heaton. Mr. Donnelly is expecting you. I've just brewed some coffee if you'd like a cup."

"No thank you, Anne."

"Perrier?"

"I'm fine, thank you." Has she ever been so solicitous of me before? I can't remember.

Morning clouds outside the office windows feather the arc of mountains and islands; the earth is a discernible sphere from this height. Donnelly shakes my hand and gestures at one of the two high-backed wing chairs. Caroline Meyers-Yeager is sitting in the other. She stands up and waits for me to be seated.

"Good morning, Dr. Heaton," she says. "Mr. Donnelly thought it would be best for us to meet together this morning." She holds my eyes a second too long, and I catch a flash of sympathy.

My face burns as I sit down; a sense of dread rises that makes my knees weaken.

John and Caroline exchange an indecipherable glance and then John starts talking. "We appreciate your coming in on such short notice. I know you have a busy schedule." He pauses, waiting for me to return some pleasantry, but I can't even smile.

"Well." He coughs lightly. I see his eyes narrow for a second. "Let me get right to the point. Some issues have come up that make it necessary to change our tactics. We're going to broaden the team. The thinking is that we'll have a stronger position if we separate your defense from the hospital's at this juncture."

I look at Caroline and try to read her face. "Is this about the autopsy results?" I ask.

Caroline steps into the conversation, sounding unperturbed, even a little distant. She is nearly swallowed by the enormous chair, sleek in a peach-colored silk suit. From this angle I can detect the tucked cheek muscles of a face-lift when she talks. "When this malpractice suit was initially filed against both the hospital and you, an employee of the hospital, it was reasonable to defend you as a unit. That decision was made when it appeared this would be a fairly straightforward financial negotiation with Ms. Jansen and her lawyers. In answer to your question, yes. The autopsy results make your defense more complicated."

I nod, trying to look like I have faith in their logic.

Now John starts talking. "First Lutheran, or more specifically Frank Hopper, your CEO, is concerned that any divergent issues would be better handled separately, to make sure we keep everyone's best possible outcomes at the top of the agenda. Caroline and I agree with that."

"Divergent issues," I repeat, focusing just past him through the window where a seagull is diving among the updrafts, its beak yawed in a muted cry. "What you're telling me, if I'm understanding this right, is that the hospital is intending to blame Jolene's death on my mistake. To lower their damages."

He leans closer toward me over his desk, all pretense dropped. "You can't get a fair defense if the same lawyer is defending both you and the hospital. Not with the autopsy results. It might have been wiser to separate your teams from the start. I think Caroline would probably agree with me on that." He raises his eyebrows and looks at Caroline, who nods, and gives me a quick, uninterpretable smile.

Donnelly opens a manila folder in front of him and slips a pair of reading glasses out of his pocket. "The insurance company is recommending another lawyer for you. Charlie Marsallis. Firm over near the federal building. Good group of people—I've worked with him before. Caroline has a list of other lawyers if you want to interview them."

I start to write his name down, but my hands fall into my lap. After working all night I don't have any more energy to filter this. "So you're telling me that I'll be starting with a new lawyer? In the middle of the case? And you'll still be representing the hospital?"

"No. I'm dropping out altogether. Too many confidentiality issues. The hospital will also be starting with a new legal team."

I feel Caroline watching me and turn to her. "What do you think I should do? I don't have any idea how to choose a lawyer."

She relaxes her perfect posture for the first time today, leaning toward me. "It's a tough spot for you, and I'm sorry. I wouldn't recommend Mr. Marsallis unless I completely trusted him. He's excellent. I've already discussed your case with him and he's more than willing to represent you." Then she stands and shakes hands with John. "I have to get to a meeting." Turning back to me, she says, "Call Marsallis. If you don't feel comfortable I'll get you a list of other names. Let me know what you decide." She collects her briefcase and bag and is gone.

John rocks back in his chair. The room is quiet.

I finally break the silence. "I don't know what to say."

"Well. I'll be sure Marsallis gets every scrap of paperwork we've generated so far; we'll take care of all the data transfer."

"John, could you clarify some of these 'divergences' for me? I feel like . . . like more is going on here than anyone's telling me."

"Listen." He looks right at me again, but his eyes expose a separation of allegiances that has already happened. "The figures for this settlement are running into the millions—way beyond the limits of your policy. First Lutheran has to do everything it can to protect its future, its capacity to care for the people of this community." He takes his glasses off and folds them closed. "Marie, have you prepared yourself for the possibility that, if this settlement exceeds your coverage, you will become financially liable for the residual?" He raises his eyebrows as he waits for my response, appears surprised that I don't have an immediate answer for him. "Your only other option here is to go to trial and hope the jury finds in your favor, but I can guarantee you the hospital will fight that."

"You can reassure the hospital that I won't pursue that option." My voice is an emotional void.

He taps his folded glasses against the desktop and hesitates a minute. "Well. Marsallis is an excellent attorney and I'm sure you'll come out of this just fine. Stop at Anne's desk on the way out and she'll get you set up with him this afternoon, if you like. He's expecting your call." He stands up to walk me out.

Charlie Marsallis is in court all week and his secretary, who is clearly unfamiliar with my name, judging by Anne's having to spell it out for her twice, schedules an appointment for next Monday at 10:30 AM. I'll have to find somebody to cover for me again at the hospital.

Donnelly reaches out to shake my hand. I'm suddenly conscious of the weight of my arm, reluctant to touch him. "Phil wanted this, too, didn't he? Frank wouldn't have asked for this without telling Phil." My spine tingles with the ugly truth of it.

Donnelly lets his hand drop. "You'll need to talk to Phil about that. Good luck, Marie. I hope things turn out all right for you." Anne breaks in with a stack of messages. Our meeting is apparently over.

· 20 ·

The dream begins *as a nightmare I've had countless times since medical school, a dependable thief of my sleep. I am in an operating room crowded with nurses and technicians and surgical assistants. The surgeon paces beside the table with a scalpel in his hand, ready to cut. My patient looks up at me for reassurance and I promise I will keep her safe.*

Nothing is prepared—no drugs are drawn up, oxygen tubing dangles from the ceiling, disconnected and useless. I search through drawers filled with broken glass vials, dirty needles, empty syringes. Everyone in the room is waiting, staring at me. I inject a milky white liquid into the IV line and watch my patient's eyes close in a slow, hypnotic saccade. Then, at the moment the knife draws a blood-red welt down her belly— the only point of color I can see in the dream—she opens her eyes and screams.

In every dream it's the same. I frantically break open more glass vials and flush more drugs into her bloodstream, but nothing puts her to sleep. Her screams go on and on until I wake up in a tangle of sweat-soaked sheets with my heart pounding, groping for the light switch.

But this time I don't awaken, and the dream changes. The operating room doors swing open and I am in a small room, locked in—no, out— locked out, standing in front of a rectangular slab of rough wood, some kind of shed. Someone is crying inside, an infant maybe. Or a cat—it's a cat crying to be let free. I rattle the iron latch and wrench the handle until my hands ache; the work of it drains my strength. I hammer my fists

135

against the boards; my arms flail—heavy, impotent, as if pushing through a wall of water.

I know this place now. It's the rotting garden shed on my grandmother's farm. My sister and I have come here with our father; it is the last time we will see my grandmother until her funeral. We are young still, nine or ten—an age when we were equal—and we've come to adopt a kitten, the lone survivor of a premature litter of four. But by the time we arrive this kitten, too, is dead, caught and mauled by the scarred tom who dominates the feral cats of the barn and fallow fields. My grandmother has locked the tom in the garden shed as punishment. She will leave him inside this slat shed for three days with only water, to teach him compassion for the weaker strains of his own species. Lock him up for three days beyond any fleeting link a cat could make between the crime and the punishment, her cruelty blind to the hard truth that empathy for the offspring of strangers is a uniquely human quirk.

My father tries to explain when my sister and I cry over the imprisonment as much as for the lost life. "It's the way on a farm. The natural world doesn't lean toward coddling."

But this last dream is not a dream, it's a memory. I remember the cat and the mauled kitten. And I remember the shed.

It is 4:15 AM and my pager is blaring from the bedside table. I had to trade call days in order to meet with Charlie Marsallis on the following Monday, so after one night of unfulfilling sleep I am back at work for twenty-four hours. I jump up and turn on the light, disoriented and squinting at the row of numbers glowing in the glass window of the hard black plastic case. It's the emergency room. I dial the number, shielding my eyes from the overhead bulb and clearing my throat, hoping to sound more awake.

"This is Dr. Heaton, anesthesia. Someone paged me." Two minutes later Jim Dahl picks up the phone. Jim is head of the Emergency Department, a young athletic guy who juggles his work shifts around various world marathons. He has a sort of flat-out stamina that serves him well in both arenas.

"Hey, Marie, sorry to drop this on you at this hour. We've got a ten-month-old who aspirated a peanut—don't ask me how the kid found a peanut at three AM. His airway's patent right now, but he's stridorous. Noonan's the ENT guy on tonight. He says he'll be here in ten minutes. Wants to have the baby waiting for him in the OR, so we've got staff setting up now."

His words come at me in a blizzard in this half-awake state. I have to pause for a minute to align the facts into the proper keyholes of automatic anesthesia protocols.

"When did he last eat anything?"

"You'll love this. He drank eight ounces of formula just before he found the nut." So now his airway will be further jeopardized by the risk of vomiting when he's put to sleep.

"I don't suppose he's got an IV yet." I reach for my stethoscope and twist my foot under the bed to rake out my shoes.

"We tried, but one cry and his breathing got worse. I was worried he might close off completely."

It is a balance of risks. If we struggle to put an IV in the baby while he's awake, his crying could suck the peanut farther down his tiny trachea, effectively strangling him. If he stops breathing I'll have to push oxygen into his lungs, forcing the peanut deeper—its damage as random and unpredictable as a brick tossed by a tornado. But without the IV in place I can't give him emergency drugs if he gets into trouble.

"Do you want me to get him over to the pre-op holding area?" Jim asks.

"No. If he's at all unstable just keep him there and I'll come talk to his parents and transport him."

I am awake enough now to move into my professional zone, generating a list of emergency equipment and personnel I'll need. As I pass the mirror in the call room I see my hair splaying in every direction. Mascara smudges look like matching bruises. Not exactly a reassuring face for distraught parents to relinquish their child to. I twist my hair up into an operating room hat and scrub away the black smudges with a paper towel. I'm shivering in the dark, chilly room, as if I've run out of the basic energy it takes to keep my body warm.

The emergency room smells of ethanol and body odor, bleach and ammonia. The hallways bristle with damaged bodies. My pager goes off again. The six-digit code swimming in the luminous green LED like some tropical aquarium specimen is for an outside call. It's Noonan.

"Who?" he asks when I say my name. "Oh right. Anesthesia. I'll be there in five minutes, so go ahead and take the foreign-body kid into the operating room. I also just got word of a tonsillar bleed on the way in, so we'll have to do him right after this one. Hey, and make sure they have my peds tracheostomy tray there—they totally fucked that up last time and gave me the standard tray." A change in the static on the line tells me he's hung up.

The baby, Toby Earle, is in the cubicle nearest the admissions desk, where he can be observed more closely than the migraines or vague belly pains that stack up for hours behind more threatening emergencies. He is sitting up in a padded metal crib clutching one of the stuffed animals handed out by the staff to disconsolate children. Sam, a respiratory therapist, holds a misting oxygen mask near his face.

Toby is still pink, but his right chest wall contracts slightly with each breath, so the peanut has probably slipped past the trachea into the right lung. That could be good—it means his left lung should be clear. But any coughing might jolt the nut back up into the main airway and then both lungs could be blocked. His mother is leaning across the lowered crib rail, rubbing his back and singing softly to him. She doesn't look more than twenty to me, but she's keeping the panic in her eyes from infecting her voice. The child's father appears less in control. He stands behind the pair of them, rigidly rocking from side to side in paint-splattered work boots, his hands leashed under tightly crossed arms.

Toby is a round, wide-eyed child with a scant sheen of blond hair and prominent ears. He has an incongruously mature face, like a Renaissance image of the Christ child. From several feet away I can hear the work of his breathing. He is assessing me, slotting me into the jumbled mix of alarming sights and noises that surround him, deciding whether I represent a safe zone or another threat.

"I'm Dr. Heaton. I'll be Toby's anesthesiologist this morning." I make my voice sound reassuringly rested and secure. In this next min-

ute I must become, for these terrified parents, the healer whose authoritative hand will lead them off the ledge of despair. His mother stares
at me as if what she reads in my face will define the rest of her life. Her
son's survival is not up to God, or fate, or the unconfessable parental
lapse that left a peanut lying like a bullet in their baby's reach. I am
the determiner of her child's fate. It feels like the clutch of a drowning
swimmer.

Toby sways with the currents of his breath, which push and pull
against the blockage. I want to race with him through the labyrinth of
empty hallways to the operating room, to cross magically into the moment when Noonan will lift the peanut, clasped like a diamond between
the tines of his fiber-optically guided grasper, and drop it ringing into
a metal bowl. We'll laugh with the relief of tension, wonder at the way
children harm themselves—that any survive the risks of childhood. I'll
wake him up and carry him, pink and vital into the recovery room.

I ask his mother about his medical history as quickly as I can. Does
he have any drug allergies? Any heart or lung problems? Was he born
prematurely? Has he ever been hospitalized or under anesthesia before?

Then I hold her eyes, looking into a well of maternal fear I've never
experienced. "I need to take Toby to the operating room now. I'll be
there with him every moment. I will do everything possible to keep
him safe."

She stares at me, struggling, hoping this foreign medical world
holds all the power it promises. "Take care of him. Take care of my
son."

Elaine, the circulating nurse, helps me roll the metal crib down the
hall. Toby has begun whimpering at the separation from his mother.
Sam walks with us, holding the oxygen-enriched mist just below Toby's
face, and the two of us are supporting him so he can sit forward,
hopefully keeping the peanut from shifting position. I grab a warm
blanket from the heating unit and enfold him. Holding him so close,
I hear his faint, quick wheezing as the peanut wafts and rubs deep
inside his airway, hovering like a menacing bird on his shallow breaths.

The finest vibration passes through to me with each exhalation, the smallest contraction of his upper body with each inhalation. His hair is so smooth and warm I have to press my lips to it; he smells of baby shampoo and the moist, inviting scent of new unblemished skin—a sensation as much as an odor.

He is calmer now, soothed in the soft folds of this blanket and my arms. He is safe for this dangling moment, balanced between breath and suffocation. His risks loom when I begin to put him to sleep, when I enclose his nose and mouth in the cold blue plastic of the anesthetic mask and turn the dial on the gas canister, flooding his lungs with the sweet-scented cloud of chemicals that will suffuse from lung to blood to brain. During that infinite instant of time any mistake I make could be fatal.

Sam slips the oxygen monitor onto Toby's toe. It's beeping high and fast with the pulse of oxygenated blood pumped from a frightened heart. We are taut and still, waiting for Noonan to arrive—a stage set waiting for the curtain cue. I look over my shoulder to see if he is here and spot the room number above the doorway.

Three months ago I was in this room with Jolene Jansen. I was standing at the head of this operating room table and Jolene was slipping from life into death while I tried to pull her back across to this side of consciousness. Her heart was pulsing on this same monitor. I can still hear the high tone of the monitor's beep, then the steady drop in pitch as her airways closed and her oxygen level fell.

It's hot and sweat collects under my arms. My head throbs with the rush of my own blood. The carefully planned sequence of actions I have mapped out to put Toby to sleep doesn't make sense anymore. In the next five minutes whatever I do, or forget to do, or do incompetently may kill this child. In half an hour I could be standing in front of Toby's mother telling her that Toby died. That I let him die. That I made the wrong choice at the wrong moment and he died because I was his anesthesiologist instead of the doctor who may have worked last night or who might work tomorrow.

I look up and see Elaine watching me, waiting for my signal to begin Toby's anesthetic.

"Elaine." My mouth is so dry I have trouble forming the words. "Page Dr. Hanover. Page him stat and tell him to get here as soon as he can."

Noonan comes banging in through the operating room doors and sweeps his eyes over the collection of nurses, technicians and me, ready to spring into action at his dictatorial order. "OK, let's get this on the road." He pulls on latex gloves and checks the fiber-optic scope, looks over the instruments fanned across the surgical table. He glances up and scans the faces of the crew, stopping at mine. He is waiting for me, staring at me standing motionless behind Toby, my hands wrapped around the baby's panting torso. Heat rises into my cheeks. Noonan drops his gloved hands to his sides, the flexible scope swinging like a snake between them.

"I've called for backup," I say, looking away from him. There is a tight knot just below my vocal cords that makes me gasp for enough air to speak. "We have to wait. The baby's stable right now and my backup is on the way."

Noonan looks as baffled as if I had spoken in tongues. "You're kidding. It's five in the morning, this kid's got a frickin' peanut stuck in his lung, and you're gonna wait for backup to drive in?"

I look directly at Noonan with my last fragment of control. "We're waiting for backup. I'm not putting him to sleep until Dr. Hanover gets here."

Five interminable minutes later Will Hanover arrives, sweating and red, banging the OR doors open so they slam against the tile walls. He must have run all the way from the parking garage. "Marie," Will says, breathing hard from his sprint. "What's the story?" He is looking at Noonan, Toby, me, trying to piece together the medical emergency I have called him in for.

"Toby is a ten-month-old who aspirated a peanut about an hour ago. He's got a full stomach, no IV yet. He's otherwise healthy, no allergies or medical problems."

"Right," Will says, catching up on his breath and stepping in to take the oxygen mask from Sam. "How can I help?" I hear the deeper question in his voice—why have I delayed this procedure to call him into the hospital? Why can't I, an experienced anesthesiologist, handle this case by myself? But I can't answer him. I can't explain to him why I have to leave this room right now, before Toby goes to sleep, before I might hear his oxygen monitor go down, before I hear any strained and frantic commands of an anesthetic emergency.

"I can't do this case, Will. I can't do this." I slide my arms away from Toby as Will brings the anesthesia mask gently up over his nose and mouth, calmly telling Sam to begin turning the dial on the anesthetic gas, telling Elaine to get ready to start the IV. Everyone is focused on Toby as he begins the slow slide into sleep. I turn and leave the room before I have to know any more.

· 21 ·

I sit on the edge of rumpled bed coverings and grip the sides of the mattress. What will I say to Phil Scoble when he hears, to Noonan and Will and Jim Dahl—each of whom have just watched my professional competence splinter?

Below the call room window an ambulance is wailing up the street to our emergency room. Already, hearing the siren, nurses and doctors will be organizing to rush this patient into the treatment room, pull the curtains clattering across their metal rod in a facade of decorum as shirts are ripped open and pant legs split so that wounds can be exposed and sutured, abdomens can be percussed and siphoned of fluids, and bare chests can be slathered with conductive jelly before electrical paddles are discharged over quivering hearts. We are righteous in our mission to challenge the limits of life, scratching every last breath from flesh. It is our job to rage against the dying of the light. To hesitate for an instant—to question if perhaps the grasping hand is not reaching for more time on earth but rather for glimpsed paradise—is truly to move from being a doctor to being God.

Will Hanover will be able to finish my shift for me, tired as he must be. He is unquestioningly responsible—probably even relishes this chance to flaunt his devotion to work. In a few hours Sandy will be here to start Friday's coverage, followed by the nearly interchangeable slew of anesthesiologists rolling through the coming days and months and decades. In a few years, this will become amusing gossip, the anesthesiologist who froze with fear in the middle of an induction, and I will have blurred into an anonymous memory of someone who can no longer imperil patients with unpredictable panic.

I change into blue jeans and a T-shirt. Now, as I go down the elevator to the basement garage, I can blend with the faceless throng of hospital employees and visitors.

It almost seems odd to see my car still parked in my usual space, yesterday's morning coffee remnants still wet in the bottom of the cup. At the first intersection I hesitate about which way to turn the steering wheel. Where does one go to run away from a life? I weave and drop through the deserted streets toward the waterfront. At the end of the pier, I pull into the empty lot next to a green tendril of public park that stretches up the coastline beneath the massive silos of a grain terminal.

Toby is probably recovering in his mother's lap right now—I am sure Will took excellent care of him. Better than I was capable of giving. Deserting Toby in the operating room was not any random act of fate, as might have occurred with Jolene. No lawyers or mediators will be needed to judge this.

Twelve years I trained for the work I do. Seven years more I have coaxed fact and experience into talent and skill. I've learned how to make the few waking moments I spend with my patients feel personal and reassuring. I have discovered how to sense my patients' rise and fall in consciousness and pain beneath their chemical sleep and mechanized breaths. I have earned my rank among First Lutheran's staff. I matter here. That can't dissolve in one mistake.

Someone raps on my window, startling me. A security guard points to the reserved parking signs. I begin backing out of the space and someone shouts, "Hey," and bangs on the trunk—two women push jogging strollers just behind my car. I jerk to a stop as they pass, and wait for my pulse to slow down before starting out again. The guard glares at me until I leave the lot.

Cresting the hills above the lake, the glare off sun-glittered water stings my eyes and I raise my arm to shield them. I pass beneath the mansions of Denny-Blaine and Madison Park and wind west again, toward the city. Now the streets stretch along vacant sidewalks and the dust-colored blocks of subsidized apartments—buildings born of thrifty bureaucracies, fortresses of poverty. At the intersection of Beacon and Sixteenth I turn left and park opposite a dark green bungalow.

Bobbie Jansen's windows are still shuttered against the night. Black metal railings brace the sloping, shadowed porch. Someone, maybe Bobbie, has started a vegetable garden along the side yard—early tomatoes and beans crawl up skeletal frames. There is a single narrow window under the peaked eaves with a colored-glass unicorn dangling inside the lower panes. The shade is pulled down. Like a waking dream this house replaces the inventions of my guilt. Now, when I stare at the dark, unable to sleep, I will know this place.

A screen door slams and I jump to start my ignition; two men stand outside the neighboring house. Their voices pitch and rise in some quarrel before one slams his fist against the siding and stamps down the plank steps. The other slips back inside. He peers out of a front room window at me before shutting it and dropping the blinds.

I still sense someone watching me, a face behind a curtained window or cracked door—or perhaps my own conscience. Then I turn back to look at Bobbie Jansen's house, and she is standing on her front porch, a straw bag and summer jacket over her arm. She is looking right at me. As I drive away I see her in my rearview mirror following me with her eyes, looking as if she has been waiting for me to find her.

· 22 ·

Exhaustion finally overcomes my resistance and I drive home. All I can think about is sleep. There's already a message from the hospital—Frank Hopper wants me to call him as soon as possible. I'd expected the call to come from Phil. I should have guessed that a professional lapse as dramatic as I'd displayed last night would rocket right up to the hospital's CEO.

Frank is on another line when I call him back, and I wait on hold trying to invent a reasonable explanation for why I'd walked out on a patient in the midst of an emergency.

"Marie," he answers at last. "Thank you for calling back so promptly. I spoke with Dr. Noonan this morning." He pauses, as if to let me preempt him with my own justification. After a silence he continues, "Well, we've been discussing the case you had together last night. The baby. He's concerned about you."

I sit on the floor next to the phone and listen, wishing I'd had the courage to call him first, waiting for him to say what I can't.

"Marie? Are you on the line?"

"Yes, I'm here."

"Listen, this is a difficult subject, I know. But we're all aware here of what you're going through. The strain must be terrific . . . it would undermine anyone's composure. We want to help you get through this. I'm not calling to take your job away—you've been a valued member of our staff for a long time and we're backing you. But I

146

think it would be in everyone's best interest—in *your* best interest—to take a leave of absence for a bit. Don't you think that's a sensible thing to consider?"

I fold into a knot, lift my chin to keep my voice collected. "Yes, Frank. It's a sensible thing to consider."

"All of us reach points in our lives, in our careers, when some time off could help us maintain perspective. I think it takes a lot of professional integrity to address that, out in the open. Don't worry about this affecting your standing with us—your job will be here for you. *We're* here for you. And, Marie, if you're interested in seeking some professional input—you know, some counseling—the hospital can arrange for that."

"How much time away are you thinking of?"

"Well, let's see how things stand once this suit is behind us. It shouldn't be more than a couple of months at the most. We've already got a locum anesthesiologist lined up, so the workload will be manageable for the rest of your team."

I want to ask him how he can pretend to so much empathy when he has just cut our legal defense in half. I choke on the words, stumbling over the dawning awareness that, of course, he couldn't have hired another anesthesiologist overnight. That must have taken weeks.

"Erin's buzzing me about a JCAHO meeting I'm late for. We'll be in touch about your return date—don't hesitate to call me anytime. My door is always open here."

My bedroom is quiet and dim. The blinds are still drawn against the sun; the comforter still billows over the empty space in my bed where I last lay, a day ago. I drop my clothes to the floor, slip into the soft nest of sheets and struggle at the boundaries of consciousness, begging sleep to drag me into a temporary peace.

The phone is ringing again. I've unplugged my bedroom extension but the noise radiates across my kitchen wall and through the pillow I've wrapped around my head. Four rings and then a pause, in which I know my most cheerful and self-confident voice, eternally imperturbable, is telling the caller to leave a message.

It's dusk outside now; I must have slept all day. The street noises are picking up with the flirtatious laughter of college students opening the bars on a Friday evening. The ringing starts again and I fumble down the hallway into my kitchen to pull the cord out of the wall. Outside my living room the towers of downtown are glittering shadow boxes—squares and rectangles are illuminated as cleaning crews replace secretaries.

And there is Joe. Staring up at my living room from the street corner, waiting for my lights to go on. Waiting for me to finally pick up the phone. I coil my fingers around the braided cords of the slatted blinds and lower them to the floor. But fifteen minutes later when I hear him at my front door I unlock it.

"Hi." He stands with his hands tucked into the fraying pockets of his old blue jean jacket. He is exactly what I need right now, though I would have denied that a minute ago.

"How'd you get into my building?"

"I still have your key. Karen called me after you left this morning—she was worried. The baby's fine. He went home early this afternoon." He lifts his shoulders slightly and says, "So, should I come in?"

I reach out and take his hand and lead him inside. We walk to the sofa, he sits and draws me down against him, my back curved against his chest, his arms wrapped across my abdomen. I sink into him and remember his solid weight, the comfortable arc of his neck along the back of my head.

"Marie." He hugs me closer as he pulls words together, his breath so soft through my hair. "This . . . this little girl's death has been terrible for you. Harder than the malpractice suit. But it's eclipsing everything else in your life. It's overshadowing all the care you've given a thousand patients before her death. It's jeopardizing all the patients you'll take care of in the years ahead." He rocks me, quietly and rhythmically; his beard lightly brushes my ear. He waits for a response, but I have none.

"This time will pass. This lawsuit will come to an end at some point. None of the OR staff hold you responsible—the nurses and techs think the world of you, you know that. The hospital is behind you. You've got a great legal team. And you have a life ahead of you filled with work I know you love—work you do superbly."

I stare into the darkening room, lit only by wedges of city light gleaming between the blinds. Familiar paintings and sculptures take on odd shapes in the gloom.

"There's something I haven't told you yet," I say at last. "No one knows about it yet. The hospital is cutting me out of their defense. Donnelly isn't representing me anymore."

Joe stops rocking me and we both sit still, locked together as if we shared equally the weight of this news. After a moment he says, "What did Donnelly tell you?"

"As little as he could get away with. He never should have represented both of us, probably. But if the hospital can prove I caused her death, they come out blameless."

Joe seems to grow heavier against me. His hands beneath my hands are dry and rough from sport and sun. I trace the hard, sleek curves of his nails and the winged bones of his clasped fingers—so fragile and so strong. I imagine myself small, a bird, crawling into the refuge of these cupped palms.

In the streets the hoarse calls and hearty cursing of an older crowd has displaced the rollicking college crew—men who drink to forget life rather than enhance it. I get up from the sofa and raise the blinds; a checkerboard of lit windows brightens the room like candle glow. I walk to the kitchen and pull a bottle of wine from the rack and bring it to the living room with two glasses and a corkscrew. Joe twists the spiral down into the cork and pulls it free, then pours the glasses full.

I haven't eaten all day and the first half glass feels potent and soothing. It makes me understand why people drink too much. Joe sits opposite me now, backlit by the skyline. He narrows his eyes for a moment as if considering his words. "Have you ever figured out, more or less, why we stopped seeing each other?"

My pulse gives a small jump. "We still see each other."

"All right. Are you telling me I shouldn't go there?"

"No," I say, fighting an urge to fend this off. "I don't know. Is that always something you can analyze? Sometimes love just finds its own way, doesn't it?"

"Does it? Maybe." He swirls the wine in his glass and stares into it as if it held some hidden message. "Maybe. Or maybe neither of us could trust that much friendship to a lover. Maybe we both suffer from the same fault there. We do keep our secrets, don't we, Marie."

Tears collect in my eyes as he says this. All the pain of these last weeks, and now this is what threatens to make me cry. And even though I can't answer him, I don't want him to leave. I am worn out by it all— by the mediation, by the betrayal, by the lonely bearing of my remorse.

The wine begins to loosen me. I want it to take me further. I want it to sweep time and strain away. Joe hardly seems affected by it at all, and pours us each another glass. I reach out for his hands, even if I can't meet his eyes.

"Stay with me tonight, Joe. I want you to stay with me. Just to sleep. I can't . . . I don't want to sleep alone tonight."

He hesitates for the barest instant, then brings his hand to my face and traces the outline of my cheek with his finger, the soft and the rough paired. He rises and leads me into my bedroom. The bed is rumpled from my day's sleep, and he lifts the covers, lofts them up to float down, smoothed and waiting. He takes off his jeans and unbuttons his shirt. I turn out the light and let my bathrobe slip from my shoulders to the floor, then slide beneath the sheet.

When I close my eyes the room spins and I have to open them again. I've had too much to drink. As Joe lies down next to me, I turn toward the wall and he wraps his arms around my waist. The long muscle of his thigh cradles my hip; his shoulder rises above me like a guardian. Each breath he takes presses his chest close against my back.

I'm not aware I'm crying until my tongue tastes the salt, and then I curl against the waves of tears, shudder as they overtake me like some physical being of flesh and bone. Joe strokes my hair from my temple and murmurs, "Shhh, shhh," his mouth so close to me his voice is inside my mind. He holds me until I'm quiet, and we breathe in a slow and deep union.

Tears of grief are unique. They contain chemicals that aren't found in the more mundane droplets of moisture that bathe the eyes, as if our tears wash us free of some noxious cause of sorrow. And tonight, after crying until I am empty, I have a rare glimpse of my own interior landscape—wounds piled like tiny skeletons into the reef of conscious adult life. I am aground amid my conquered traumas, stranded as a consequence of my achievements.

Joe tightens his grasp around me, or perhaps he is asleep and dreaming of his own struggles. Late in the night—the clock reads 3:30—he is tossing restlessly, hot and sweating. He throws the covers off and gets up to go to the bathroom. When I wake again at dawn, my head throbs and I have an acrid taste in my mouth from too much wine. He's no longer beside me.

Out my window the summer sun is buried behind dense clouds; they fold upon one another all the way out to the rim of the mountains. I climb out of bed and walk into the living room expecting to find Joe brewing espresso and reading the morning paper—or at least to find a note. But his jacket is gone.

· 23 ·

Charlie Marsallis is tall; his olive-colored eyes are draped by full lids that curve downward at his temples. He stands back against the open door to let me walk by, one long arm cocked across his waistband and the other extended to show me into his office. My head barely reaches his shoulder. He indicates the cushioned Windsor chair opposite his cluttered desk. A gold basketball trophy stands on the bookcase below his framed degrees; every other surface on the tables and shelves is stacked with legal briefs and medical charts and thick white sheaves of stapled papers. The files I can read from my chair are labeled Jansen vs. Heaton. A framed picture of a young woman and a boy paddling a kayak balances on top of a pile of memos stamped with Donnelly's letterhead.

"Did Jean get you anything to drink?" he asks, turning to slip off his suit jacket and hang it on the rack behind him.

I shake my head. "I'm fine, thank you."

"Well. Where to start?" He settles into the rolling desk chair and pivots toward me, raking long fingers through his loose blond hair so that it splays in odd angles across his brow. His youthfulness is disconcerting; it almost makes me miss Donnelly's stern, paternal self-confidence. "I met with Ms. Meyers-Yeager and she's given me a summary of your case up to last week." He lets his words hang between us for a moment, as if inviting me to jump in with my own version. He clears his throat and continues, "I haven't been through everything yet, but she assures me—and I can see from Mr. Donnelly's notes—that your initial deposition is pretty solid. You don't have any earlier claims against you or problems with your credentials or complaints on your record at First Lutheran. The autopsy results are a hurdle, but I've read your comments about the child's heart problem. We'll be calling an expert witness to back that up." He pauses again. I nod at him, wondering how many meetings it will take to cover the ground I thought was safely behind me.

He continues, "I have two academic anesthesiologists in mind. But obviously the direction we take will depend on what we learn in the next few weeks."

More time. It has already been six weeks since we got the autopsy results. In a profession enriched by hourly billing I suppose Darryl Feinnes has every incentive to uncoil his next attack as slowly as possible. I should feel the heat of adrenaline surging into righteous anger, a demand for prompt justice that might bond me to this young lawyer. But I'm drained by the idea of more weeks of waiting.

Across from me his office windows face the neighboring building, cement walls blur into a stone-colored sky; illuminated cells of backs and shoulders hunch over flickering computer screens. Marsallis stops talking for a minute, and when I glance back at him he is studying my face. This man is a stranger to me—a stranger who has access to more facts about my life than I would share with a lover. Or perhaps I have become the stranger, on the brink of conceding a life I thought I'd earned.

His voice drops a notch, almost as if he'd read my thoughts. "I know it must be hard, starting with a new lawyer at this juncture."

My eyes suddenly sting. Donnelly's formality had made it easier to mask my feelings. I wait until my throat relaxes and force myself not to think about the autopsy. "Truthfully, my only goal now is for this to end. If it were up to me, I'd settle it for any sum they want. But I don't suppose the insurance company will let you do that, will they?"

He hesitates a beat, then nods. "I hear you. Neither law nor medicine are that uncomplicated these days, are they?" He rocks forward in his chair to lean on his elbows, the knobbed bones of his wrists jutting beyond his sleeves. His hands are large, even for his big frame—with long, almost gangly fingers that must feel more natural branching over the sphere of a basketball than curling about the shaft of a fountain pen. "Why did you choose anesthesia?" he asks.

The question lands so far outside the realm of litigation and legal defense that I am caught off guard. "What?"

"Why anesthesia? Why did you decide to become an anesthesiologist instead of a surgeon, or a psychiatrist, or—for that matter—a chemical engineer?"

"Oh, I don't know." I hesitate. "I'm good with my hands, I guess. I like doing the procedures. I aced pharmacology and physiology and so my dean suggested anesthesia." I'm giving him the rote reasons I always give to friends and patients when they begin such introductory small talk. But then I notice how he's looking at me, waiting for more, and I reach further inside to reasons I haven't thought about in months now. "I like helping people through a critical time. Everybody always thinks anesthesiologists are just there to watch you sleep, but it's the preoperative part, when patients are anxious, that makes the difference. That's what I went into it for. I always shake their hand—just as an excuse to hold it for a minute, right before their surgery, and see them let go of at least a little bit of fear. I like seeing, just as they go off to sleep, how their faces get almost young again, as if they're escaping the stress of work or their illness. Even if it's because of a drug. Even though they'll wake up to the same problems, at least I can give them some temporary relief. I love figuring out how to take away somebody's pain. I get to meet people I'd never even talk to otherwise—hear a little about how they live, what matters to them." Suddenly I feel self-conscious and trail off, shrugging my shoulders.

Marsallis nods to himself, oblivious to my embarrassment, as if assimilating this blurted testimonial as thoroughly as he might evaluate my board exam scores. "I like that. I'd like people to hear that." He raises his eyebrows and looks me directly in the face again. "Of course, this latest twist will complicate things for a while. But, even before I hear any new evidence, I can promise there's a good chance this will get thrown out."

"Thrown out?" I look him straight in the eyes for the first time since entering the office, ready to hear what Marsallis has learned in one week that has eluded Donnelly for months.

He looks surprised at the animated relief in my voice. "Definitely. It's hard to make this type of charge stick unless they have really irrefutable information—something concrete. As much frustration as the public professes toward health care, juries are still very unlikely to convict a doctor. I wouldn't be surprised if the district attorney refuses to even consider it."

Something turns over inside my chest. "The district attorney? What are you talking about?" I know I've misunderstood him, but blood rushes into my face. "We're still going to mediation, right? Why would this change to a juried trial just because of the autopsy results?" I want to ask him if he has my case mixed up with someone else's.

He sits motionless—I wonder, for a moment, if he's heard me. Then a creeping flush mottles his neck and cheeks, and I know instinctively that some secret hand has been played.

"I'm sorry. I thought you'd been told." He drops his head and stares down at his clasped hands resting on my case files, pages flagged with bits of colorful tape signaling that here a mistake occurred, here a judgment was passed, here a decision was made that exploded into three ruined lives.

"You thought I'd been told what?"

"Dr. Heaton, what did John Donnelly tell you about your case at your last meeting?" He says this so softly I have to lean forward in my chair to understand him.

"John Donnelly told me that I needed to get another lawyer. Because Jolene's heart defect made me more liable," I answer, my voice brittle as glass. "He told me that the hospital and I were no longer on the same side of this suit. Without saying it outright, he told me the hospital was going to get out of this by blaming me."

"Nothing else?"

"Nothing else? That's not enough?"

"Did Mr. Donnelly tell you—did *anyone* tell you—that a criminal investigation is under way?"

Behind Marsallis the rain heaves in gusts against the windows, which bow and shiver with each pulsation of air. My stomach rolls and I have to swallow twice, and then again, to keep it settled.

"I need a glass of water. Could you get me some water?"

"Of course, just a minute." He leaves the room and I lower my head to my knees, terrified for a minute that I might throw up. The clink of ice on crystal startles me. He is crouching beside my chair, and when I lift my head our eyes are at equal levels—there are lines across his brow I had not noticed before. "Here. It's okay, just take a deep breath."

I take a sip of the ice water, so cold my teeth ache. "Explain this to me. What are you talking about?"

He puts the pitcher of water on an end table and sits down in the chair next to me. Now we are both on the same side of this desk laden with reams of legal dictums—the counterbalance offered against a lost life. He takes a breath and says, "Someone has filed a complaint with the district attorney accusing you of criminal negligence resulting in the child's death. You should have already been told about this."

"How is that possible? How can anyone claim that—even if they want the money, even if they believe I made mistakes? Where does a tragic mistake become a criminal charge?"

"You aren't *charged* with anything criminal at this point." He leans over his knees toward me, his tone more like that of a sympathetic consoler than a legal adviser. "But someone has approached the district attorney with allegations—true or false—that the state is obligated to pursue. If they don't find any substantial evidence to back up the claim, then no charges will be filed. And that's very likely."

I wrap my arms across my abdomen and rock forward. "Who's behind this? Who's saying this about me?"

"I don't know that right now. And I don't know what evidence the DA has—they aren't required to tell us unless they actually file charges. It could be anyone who thinks they have new information the state would be interested in. In truth, it could be anyone who wants to see you take the entire blame for this."

"But how can a doctor be charged with anything criminal?"

"It's rare. Usually something extreme—like alcoholism or drug abuse, or some blatant misuse of equipment."

The muscles of my abdomen are so taut it's hard to take a breath. I look over at him, this solemn-eyed man I must now depend on, his tie skewed beneath his collar, his bangs frayed along his forehead as if he'd forgotten to comb his hair. "Listen, this has blindsided you," he says. "I had no idea you didn't know. But there is a very good chance, like I said, that we can get this thrown out, even if the state does file a charge."

"What, then this whole thing finally ends?"

"No, the mediation still has to be settled. But it ends any question of criminal wrongdoing on your part."

We are both quiet. "What should I do now?" I finally ask.

"Try not to worry too much. We have to wait until we hear from the district attorney to plan any specific defense. Be sure you don't talk about this at work, of course."

I look up. "I'm not at work anymore. Frank Hopper, the hospital's CEO, asked me to take a leave of absence. Didn't you know that?"

His face colors again. "No."

In the building across the street, workers gather briefcases and umbrellas, chatting in small groups as the day winds down. Someone in his partner's office behind us laughs, and the noise reverberates until a door slams and all goes silent.

"So there's nothing more we can learn today?" I ask, wiping my cheek with the back of my hand.

"I'll let you know as soon as I hear anything." He stands and puts his jacket on.

I walk to the door before he can open it for me, then turn and look back at him. "Can I leave town?"

"Leave town?"

"Am I allowed, I mean? To leave the state?"

He hesitates and looks as if he wants to ask me another question, then slips his hands in his pockets and nods. "Sure. But you should leave a phone number."

As I'm about to close his door behind me he begins talking again and I turn to face him. "My son . . ." He stops and takes his hands out of his pockets, folds them across his chest. "My son, he's six now. He was born with a birth defect. His trachea had a narrowing in it, and he stopped breathing right after his delivery. He's . . . well, he has a mild palsy, most likely as a result of that episode. But my son is alive because an anesthesiologist was working at the hospital that night."

He stands there watching me, so lean and athletic, so resilient with his freshly framed degrees and untarnished willingness to lope into this medical-legal labyrinth. "I'll let you know where I can be reached, Mr. Marsallis," I say, while I can still speak without my voice breaking.

Lori is ecstatic when I tell her I'm coming for a few weeks, if a little surprised that I'll arrive tomorrow. In the middle of our short conversation she is already telling Elsa to get her stuff out of the guest room, and Neil to clear his toys out of the bath. I don't try to explain to her that this is not purely a long-postponed pleasure trip. I pull a kitchen chair to my closet and drag dusty suitcases from the high shelves to the floor. The effort exhausts me, as if age had slipped in at dawn and thrust me decades forward by dusk.

Except for some short naps and a long shower I am up all night paying bills and stopping the newspaper and sorting through my mail. At least I've no cat to kennel, and I'm willing to let my lone philodendron wither away. At 6:00 AM the taxi driver rings me from the entry gate and I bump down the hallway with my bags to the front door, backing through it to wedge my suitcase past the hinge. I nearly stumble when my heel catches on the ribbons of a small white box sitting on the mat just beyond my threshold.

My arms are so full I have to nudge the box into the elevator with my foot and drop my purse before I can pick it up; the weight of its contents gaps open the cardboard lid, and chocolate suffuses the air. I slip its silver ribbons free, and inside is the ebony torte; a floret of chocolate frosting glues a slender gold chain to its lacquered coating. The chain loops beneath the flap of a sealed envelope. I tease it open without dislodging its chocolate tether and free a pink sapphire pendant and a note.

I think I like these tortes so much because
they are the color of your eyes.

· 24 ·

From the airport I call Charlie Marsallis's office and leave my cell phone and my sister's home numbers on his answering machine, in case any charges arrive from the district attorney while I'm away. The second call I make is to my malpractice insurance company. After punching in an endless string of automatically answered and forwarded numbers I land in Caroline Meyers-Yeager's voice mailbox. Her recording informs me she is away from the office for more than a week but her assistant would be happy to help me, or I may leave a message at the tone. I begin with a polite summary of my meeting with Charlie Marsallis and end with a barely restrained rant about unethical legal charades, which is amputated midstream by the beep concluding my allotted digital space.

The jet engines fight the tenacious grip of gravity—a battle I always marvel at surviving—and the supernatural feat of soaring five miles above the earth takes hold. I am, for the moment, unavailable to prosecutors and accusers. Thousands of feet below, the Rocky Mountains slough into farms and deserts; the Colorado River is siphoned into perfect green circles stitched across brown land. Just before we descend I take the white box from beneath my seat, open it and release the slender gold chain from its chocolate rose, then clasp it around my neck.

Lori lives in the plains just west of Fort Worth, where cattle drives used to camp on their way to the transcontinental railroad and settlers laid claim to Indian lands with barbed wire. Now, a grid of pavement allots quarter-acre swatches of azaleas and scrappy live oaks to home-owners who coax green growth out of the dust. The lushly watered lawns invite barefoot play, until the Texas sun slaps you back inside. The moment I step out of Lori's car the heat swallows me like a blood-thirsty beast. It takes my breath away.

Behind me the *tick, tick, tick* of a sprinkler reminds me of summers spent racing through their spray. In the two years since I last visited, the sprawling brick and stucco homes have seeped toward the flat horizon to claim more open space for the seemingly endless array of families able to afford them. The sidewalks are deserted.

"Is it OK that I put you in Lia's room tonight? I didn't have time to get the guest room ready yet—I'm using it for an office and papers are spread out all over the bed." She is scooping up baseball mitts and LEGOs and balled-up socks as we walk in. "Sorry about all this junk. You look hot."

"Seems like I can't handle Texas summers anymore. Too long up north in the rain, I guess. When did you cut your hair? It's cute." It cups her chin at the front, and the highlights pick up the pale taupe hue of her skin, her dark eyes.

She ruffles the feathery fringe at the nape of her neck. "I cut it all off around Christmas. I'm coloring some of the gray—can you tell? Now we don't look so much alike, huh? Sit down, I'll get some iced tea."

"Where is everybody?" I call out to the kitchen.

"Neil's at a sleepover and I made Elsa take Lia to the pool so I could pick up the house—you should have seen it in here two hours ago." The room is sprinkled with evidence of five lives, scattered like excavated artifacts of the modern American household, a maze of plastic toys and polyester clothing, a cornucopia of synthetic abundance. Lori brings in the iced tea and settles opposite me across a vast, beveled-glass coffee table stacked with home decor magazines and real estate journals. An abandoned game of Monopoly spills to the floor when she sets down the tray of tea and frosted glasses. "They're excited to see you. Elsa is beside herself."

"I was hoping she'd be at the airport. I wonder if Lia will even remember my face—I haven't seen her since right after her third birthday."

"We look at your picture. She knows you." Lori crosses her legs beneath her in the armchair and studies the swirling ice cubes in her glass, then looks back at me and smiles—her smile so like our mother's. "So, should I ask you how you are?"

"Probably not." I pick up my tea and focus on squeezing the lemon wedge, stirring the tea with the yellow rind. "I think, right now, I want to feel every one of the two thousand miles between me and Seattle. Thanks, though, for letting me come at the last minute like this." I smile, looking back up at her. "And for asking if you should ask."

"You're welcome. You're *always* welcome." After a pause, she adds in a brighter tone, "Well, you look good."

I have to laugh. "No I don't. I look haggard."

"All right, you've looked better. You must have been up all night, getting things pulled together. Do you want to take a nap before everybody gets home?"

Even the suggestion makes me aware of how exhausted I am. Lori leads me down the hallway, lined with her own black-and-white photographs of the children, into Lia's bedroom—an altar to Walt Disney. Snow White, Sleeping Beauty and Belle crowd the pillow and I place them next to the bed before turning back the quilted spread. Last Christmas I gave her a pink tulle princess costume with sparkled plastic high heels. Lori told me she wore it to bed every night for weeks, despite the scratchy lace.

Above me a canopy floats on four wooden pillars, and ruffled curtains swoop back into braided ties like Rapunzel's locks. What a dreamy five-year-old bed—enclosing its sleeping treasure in a safe and private kingdom. I pick up an oversized picture book from the floor and browse through it, waiting for drowsiness to settle. The illustrations are luminous, the pages framed by interlaced ivy and climbing roses, bodices and dancing slippers embroidered with filigreed golden weaves. Every story describes evil vanquished by good, loneliness banished by love, wrapped up with a final triumph of royal nuptials. At what age did I notice the fairy tale always ended with the wedding? At what age did I begin to question the unwritten conclusions of women's lives?

I'm awakened with a start when Lia jumps into the middle of her bed. I shriek and then roll her over to tickle her belly, doughy and soft beneath her T-shirt. How sweet that she can love me in the flesh after knowing me mainly as a voice over the telephone.

"Look how big you've gotten," I say, brushing her brown hair back from her face. Her eyes are dark and shiny as coffee beans. "Your mother must be feeding you too many vegetables to get you so tall in just two years."

"Come outside, Aunt Marie. You have to see my secret garden."

She stands and pulls me to my feet with five-year-old urgency. Lori is basting chicken pieces in barbecue sauce as Lia leads me, arms over her head grasping my hand, through the kitchen and out the screen door, letting it slam behind us. Their terrier circles in a whirl-wind to get her attention. The concrete is still warm, radiating back the day's heat. Lia steps catlike across the prickly coolness of spiky grass; the naked soles of my feet tingle with this unaccustomed con-tact with earth.

She guides me around behind the garage to a fenced enclave of gar-bage cans and redolent grass clippings. There rises a pyramid of sand, abandoned after some recent landscaping venture, an adult's forgot-ten project converted to a child's wonderland. We crouch side by side, conspiratorially, and the seemingly solid mound of sand discloses cas-tles and moats, Tupperware lakes and twig forests, winding mountain roads and intersecting tunnels carved by her small hands. Caverns of sand shelter plastic knights battling rubber dragons, and fat pink po-nies with blue manes parade inside a pencil-fenced corral.

Lia crouches in the way of little girls, heels flat against the ground, knees accordioned against her chest, a flexibility granted before the pel-vis wings open for childbearing. A breeze of evening air, moist and still warm, lifts off the Texas prairies; her fine hair feathers across her eyes and she sweeps it aside with a clutched fistful of princesses. Her skin is pure in the shadowy evening sun, a downy gold, unmarred by whatever strains will engrave themselves on brow and chin in her future. I reach over and stroke her face. Her body, at this age, is an efficient machine of DNA repair and well-regulated cell division, birth upon birth of re-freshed generations of perfect tissues. By the age of twenty it will begin to lose the race with time, sliding slowly into the decline of age, ceding itself unto the next generation.

"Aurora's going up to her bedroom now. She's changing clothes for her birthday party."

"I see that," I say, squatting beside her in the dirt until my legs begin to ache and I sit down cross-legged. "How old will she be?"

"She's sixteen. This is her pony and she's just a baby. She's one years old."

"Well, we should help her get dressed up, then. Will she be wearing her crown?"

Lia smoothes the nylon hair and wedges a glittery tinfoil crown over the doll's forehead. "She's getting married on her birthday."

"She's mighty young to get married, isn't she?"

Lia is absorbed in stretching a tiny blue gown over Aurora's inflexible arm, her breath staccato with each tug at the material.

"Aunt Marie, when will you get married? Mommy says I could be in your wedding someday."

"Did she?" I reach over and loosen the Velcro waistband impeding Aurora's vestment. "Well, I guess I haven't found the man I want to marry yet."

She jams sandy high heels onto Aurora's feet, and sticks her upright in the sculpted castle. Then she rocks back over her heels in the dirt and looks up at me, squinting slightly against the setting sun. "Are you looking?"

"Looking?"

"Looking for your husband?"

She scans my face with serious purpose, curious about how this distantly admired aunt has missed such a critical benchmark. I prepare an explanation of the twenty-first-century woman's choices in life, and then surprise myself with an abrupt and uncalculated answer. "Yes, I guess I am."

This seems to settle some mild disturbance in her view of life's natural order. Then she frowns slightly and says, "But not at night."

I smile at the ease with which I can resolve this final puzzle about my world. "No. It's too dark to look for him at night."

The screen door bangs shut, and Aurora and her pony are abandoned to the fate of the night as Lia runs to the back porch. Lori is arranging chicken and hot dogs on the propane grill. She hands me a Coke and sits down in a canvas sling chair, dragging another beside her for me. The evening has cooled to a tolerable heat as long as I sit still. I roll the Coke can against my cheek to steal the cold.

Thousands of cicadas hum as twilight arrives; the sound inhales and exhales as one unified creature, hovering like an aura without visible source. It invokes barefoot summers playing in the open field behind our house—a field in which my sister and I once buried a mangled rabbit we'd found in the blackberry brambles, victim, it appeared, of some neighbor's dog. A shopping center covers that field now; car radios have replaced the cicadas' mating calls.

"I told Elsa to be back for dinner," Lori says, turning her wrist to glance at her watch. She shakes her head and adds, "Her best friend has a big brother she's got a crush on."

"Yeah, I heard about that one. Do you know him?"

"No. But I've seen him and I don't blame her. I swear, it happens overnight. Thank God she at least talks to you. I'm not sure she hears anything I say."

I take Lori's hand across the dark space between our chairs. "I'd tell you if I heard anything you needed to know. Promise. I don't think you have to be worried."

Lori gives me a wry smile that I remember signaling, decades ago, some secret held over me, the older sister. "I know. I count on that. But you start worrying about your children the day they're born. Sometimes, when I'm waiting up at night for Elsa to come home, when she's pushed her curfew to the last second, I ache for her to be a baby again. I ache for the days when I was the center of her universe, even though I know it's selfish to want that. It's almost cruel that we're hardwired to love our children this intensely."

"Does it bother you? Our phone calls?"

She looks bemused, wise about a realm of life I can't fully comprehend. "It's the best, Marie. We hardly even had one mom at her age. She has two. It's been a hard year for her. Gordon's last development flopped—over half the units are still empty. Then the investor for his upcoming project backed out on him. It's turned our finances upside down—I'm managing his books now. I think it's affected Elsa more than the others. She's old enough now that she picks up on the stress—not to mention the cutbacks in all the clothes and makeup she wants at this age."

"I can't believe it, Lori. You never said anything about this to me."

She flashes another strained smile. "Survival through denial. Works every time. Besides, you've had your own worries. We'll get through it. Commercial real estate is that way—remind me to drive you past some of our deserted strip malls while you're out here. But I confess, this one's been a steep tumble."

Lori lifts her soda to her mouth and sips with a soft gurgle of air and liquid. Lia flashes low and high on the swing set, pumping hard with her bare, dusty legs. I am ashamed at discovering how stoic Lori has been with her own trials, at how I've insulated myself within my crisis.

She swats at a mosquito on her neck hunting blood in the dusk and then flicks the crumpled insect into the long grass, sweat glistening over the rhythmic undulations of her carotid pulse. After a quiet minute she looks back at me. "Don't say anything to Gordon about it, would you? Unless you decide you'd like to open a strip mall outside of Irving, that is. I'm sure he'd make you a deal. Not as much job security as anesthesia, but you could get a great buy on computer parts and acrylic nails."

"Well, how serious is it? Is he worried about his business? I mean, you're OK, right?"

She looks back at me. "Let's just say there's more demand for face-lifts and appendectomies than nail salons and Domino's Pizzas. I have to admit I miss the maid." She swashes her hands at more mosquitoes and stands up. "I give up—they win. Let's eat inside. Lia, come in for dinner. Wipe off your feet before you open that door."

At this cusp of night it would be after nine o'clock in Seattle; late summertime dinners are eaten in full daylight. But here, nearer the world's girth, it is almost dark at seven thirty. Lori sets a platter of chicken and hot dogs between two sterling candelabras on the glossy wooden dining room table.

"You don't mind paper plates, do you?" she asks, fanning out white, crimp-edged Dixie plates and lighting the tapers. "I love it. Candlelight and hot dogs—only in Texas. Elsa should be here any minute. She almost canceled her plans today to stay home—a miraculous concept. You're her idol, you know, a female doctor living in a swank apartment in the city. Not some stodgy suburban housewife like her mother." She squinches her nose up in humor, such a characteristic Lori expression, connected with a thousand shared experiences. Like the way she hitches up her right shoulder whenever she exaggerates the truth, bites her lip in contemplation, or laterally flares her hands before she offers her frequently obstinate opinion on what's right or wrong for the people she loves. I am flooded with a sense of belonging, to be so intimately aware of another person's unique watermark on the world, connecting us like the secret insignia of clans.

The front door slams with a clank of the brass knocker and Elsa bounds into the room. I know it's Elsa—she has my little sister's face. Otherwise I would barely recognize her from the girl I saw two years ago. I don't see any of my sister in the billowing figure of my niece—the miraculous mixing of genes has strayed far from the lean, functional physique of the Heaton line. I wrap her in my arms so tight she lifts into the air. Her hug invokes the luxurious sensation of falling into a plush comforter, round and warm and inviting. No wonder Lori's worried.

"Aunt Marie. Oh my God, I'm so glad you're here. I couldn't believe it when Mom said you were coming today. My Spirit Club had a car wash so I had to go out before you woke up. We made tons of money, though—over two hundred dollars. But I swear tomorrow I won't leave the house so we can talk. Well, I mean, I have to go out tomorrow night, but that's, like, just for a few hours."

She has no idea how beautiful she is, I can tell. Her hair, wet from what must have been a water fight after the car wash, has been haphazardly swept into a tangled knot skewered with a gnawed pencil. Her T-shirt clings to her cleavage. Only her voice, the part of her I know best, is still childlike. Truly, the fecundity of young womanhood has been launched, and she seems delightfully unaware.

Lori raises an eyebrow at me from across the table. "Hi, sweetie. Grab a plate and sit down. Have you eaten anything yet?"

"I gotta run, Mom. Sierra's picking me up in twenty minutes to go to the mall with her and Dakota." She plucks a chicken leg off the serving platter and gives me a kiss, fragrant with suntan lotion and Juicy Fruit gum.

"Sierra and Dakota," I comment, as Elsa bounces out of the room, Lia following in her wake like an adoring fan. "Is it a family or a geography class?"

"You should hear the lineup of Neil's baseball team. It stops just short of a world atlas. So, maybe you could rent a car and follow her—tell me what goes on at the mall."

"She hasn't gotten into any really dicey stuff, has she?" I have to remind myself I usually hear only one side of Elsa's world.

"Maybe I should be asking you! I mean, what would I have done with a body like that at her age? Our parents were blessed with two scrawny, flat-chested wallflowers. Whatever happened to the 'Heaton Late Puberty' gene? Maybe it's hormones in the milk—it makes me want to give them Coke. Do they talk about that at any of your fancy medical meetings?" She sweeps the dining table clear of paper plates and knots the red plastic ribbons on the trash bag with a fierce tug. "Maybe I'll get lucky and Lia will stay little forever."

"How can that much time have passed? All this year on the phone, I've been picturing her as a child," I say, stacking up the emptied plastic cups.

"It's been two years since you've seen her, Marie. Two years of estrogen and internet chat rooms. And Abercrombie and Fitch—or whoever decided it was indecent to cover your navel. Biggest problem is that she *is* a child. She just doesn't look like it anymore. Maybe it used to be easier when girls got married in adolescence—less open ocean to navigate between childhood and moving out."

"You're kidding, I know." She shrugs her shoulders and keeps clearing the table.

"Of course I'm kidding. Most of the time. Or at least the few hours of the day when she doesn't seem to hate me. Did you and I argue with Mom very often, though? I can't imagine she ever contemplated spyware."

"They didn't have spyware when we were growing up. What makes you think she hates you?"

"Oh, just the fact that fifty percent of our dinners and breakfasts end up with all the napkins being used to wipe tears instead of spilled milk. I feel like I'm walking on glass around her. I hand her a hairbrush because I assume she hasn't gotten around to it yet and she bursts into sobs."

"Here. Let me take it." I pull the trash bag out of her hands.

She sighs and releases her hold on the garbage. "I'm sorry. You don't need to hear me vent. Just remind her there's more than one side to her issues."

"I do. And it does me good to hear somebody else's problems for a change. Do you want me to take this out back?"

"It's a toss-up. In here it starts to smell, outside the dog rips it up all over the yard. And you thought only doctors faced tough choices. My life is filled with fascinating dilemmas like this. Just stuff it under the sink for now and come sit down with me. Want some ice cream?"

"Just water," I say, jamming the trash into the overstuffed can and coming back to sit next to her.

She divides the last of the pitcher into two plastic cups and sets one down in front of me. "Now, you complain for a while. I'm tired of hearing myself moan."

"Trust me on this. You'd rather hear yourself," I say, my pulse notching up at the threat of revealing that my medical-legal nightmare has escalated to a realm I'd thought reserved for perpetrators of corporate frauds and investment schemes, if not just common thieves.

Lori is quiet, tracing tiny crosses and circles in a pile of spilled table salt, then she leans toward me over the table and takes my hand in hers. "I know you didn't leave Seattle just to appreciate our summer weather. And I know they don't give away extra vacation time at that hospital. Is there any settlement in sight yet?"

I shake my head and focus on the lacy crystal patterns of salt. "That's a long way off. It's gotten more complicated in the last few weeks."

She gives me time to tell her more, then asks, "Complicated in what way?"

"You know the dream I told you about? The one about her heart?"

Lori waits, open, ready.

"I was right. Jolene had a heart problem. They found it in the autopsy. She had a coarctation of her aorta—a kink in the biggest blood vessel leaving her heart."

She groans and covers her eyes with her hands. "Oh God. Is that why she died?"

"I don't know. I don't think so. But it gives the other side a reason to blame me. I missed it. I didn't know about it before I put her to sleep."

"Did anybody else know? She'd been seen by other doctors, right? You said she'd been sick off and on since she was three or four."

"She was mentally retarded—that doesn't automatically make anybody look for a heart defect. Her mom didn't say anything about her heart when I talked to her before the operation. There's no record in her chart that anybody knew about it."

"So why do you get the blame? Besides, you just said you're not sure this is why she died."

"I'm not. I mean, I might have put in an arterial line at the beginning, but—when I'm objective about it, really think it through—I still don't think it explains her death." I tuck my hands together between my knees, torn between leaving the room and telling her about the criminal investigation. "There's more." I stop, and bite my lip. After a minute I twist my mouth into a false smile and add, "I think I'm not ready to talk about it right now."

She looks so sad, as if my inability to share this represents her failure. "How are you getting through your workdays?" she asks gently.

"Honestly?" She nods for me to continue. "Every time I introduce myself to a new patient I wonder if they've heard about what happened. I feel like a charlatan. I can't take care of children anymore—I can't stomach the idea of telling some mother that her baby would be safe with me." I look up at her again, see the concern in her eyes. "I keep seeing her mother. Seeing her face when I walked into the waiting room to tell her what had happened. I keep imagining that if I could talk to her again, find out how she's surviving this, I could somehow fix it. Not fix it—I know it will never be fixed—but, I don't know, somehow take part of her pain into myself."

Now I have brought Lori near tears, spilling my tragedy into her own turbulent life. I see her struggling to respond when the garage door suddenly squeals up on its metal rails and we both jump. She sighs. "Gordon's home." Then she leans over and kisses me on the cheek. "So here's what I want to know, Marie. Who's taking care of you during all of this? Who's listening to this when you come home at the end of the day?" Then she walks into the kitchen, smoothing her hair, to greet her husband.

The refrigerator opens and closes, and I hear the hiss-pop of a bottle cap, the brush of cloth against cloth. Murmured fragments of words crescendo and fade through the walls. After a few minutes of silence Lori comes back into the dining room, followed by Gordon, my brother-in-law of sixteen years.

"Hey, Marie. A house call from the doctor at last. How are you?"

"Great," I say, forcing a smile. "Great. Wish I'd brought some of our Northwest weather, though."

"You guys just need to discover real climate control. Be as proud as us to build houses with windows that don't even open. No kidding, though. It's good to see you. The Heaton progeny need to get to know their smart aunt better. Got to get you down here more often, now that Southwest Airlines flies to the hinterlands of Seattle." He gives me a one-armed hug, and swings out the chair at the head of the dining table, then leans back in it, loosening his tie. Since I saw him two years ago, Gordon has increased his belt size by nearly the same percentage his hairline has receded. Lori sits down in the chair next to him and rests her hand on his sleeve.

"So how is it in the land of nod? Still putting people under, are you?" Gordon asks.

Lori winces and interrupts him. "Gordon's always so fascinated by your job. I think it's because he's terrified of anesthesia." She rubs his arm. "I saved dinner for you, honey. Hungry?"

She sets a plate full of microwaved barbecue on the table. As he leans forward to take a bite I watch the throb of his temporal artery snaking across his brow and wonder what his blood pressure is.

"I'm not terrified of anesthesia. But I'm sure Marie deals with plenty of people who'd rather be anyplace but unconscious under a knife. Don't you?" Gordon asks.

I draw in a breath to answer him but Lori deflects the conversation again. "Tell Marie about the idea for your new project, Gordy. That one you want to start on the Holtman property. I thought I might drive her by there tomorrow."

Gordon beams at her, then looks down at the whorled patterns of wood on the dining room table and raises his palms above the reflecting surface, as if preparing to conduct an orchestra. He clears his throat and draws his eyebrows together, apparently mesmerized by his internal vista. "Imagine you're an artist," he finally begins. "Imagine that you're a sculptor, or a woodcarver, or a weaver." His eyebrows are rising higher with each image. "A fiddle maker, a potter, a . . . a whatever. You've got talent." He clenches his fist in front of me. "And vision. Skill. You can create beautiful, one-of-a-kind works of art." He fans out the fingers of his thick hands and looks me right in the eye. "But how do you create your art and still have the time—and the business savvy—to find the market for it?"

"Well." I try to sound optimistic about what might be coming. "I don't know. I never really thought about that problem before."

"No. Of course you haven't." His forefinger jabs the top of the table. "You doctors are always too busy shopping at Neiman Marcus or Saks Fifth Avenue or some such. So maybe you hit a street fair now and then for some pottery toothbrush holder or soap dish, or you go to a fancy-pants gallery where the painter has to whack off half his price to the gallery owner in commissions before he even slips a dollar into his own pocket. Am I right? Am I right?"

I nod at him after an inquiring glance toward Lori, who stares into her empty plastic cup. "Now, what if you could get your buyers to come to you—in masses—instead of a random trickle lured in through some homegrown scrap of advertising you stuck on a telephone pole?"

I open my mouth to answer but he slaps both beefy palms down on the table so the silver candlesticks shiver. "Now. Look up." I widen my eyes in anticipation, but this proves to be short of the physical reaction to his vision he's hoping to provoke. "No. Up. Up. Look up." He points at the ceiling. I shift my eyes toward my hairline and notch my neck back a degree. He seems happier.

"Staircases are winding up amid platforms and alcoves. Wooden staircases, branching and twisting and spitting you out into the very studios, the laboratories of creative invention, for hundreds of craftsmen. And women, of course. Turn left, and an ironsmith is forging one-of-a-kind andirons or towel racks. Turn right, and watch angora goat hair being carded and dyed and woven into a handspun scarf. Behind you a kid is silk-screening dragons and unicorns onto the panels of box kites. No sir, you won't find that at Neiman's." His hands fall back into his lap as if the weight of his ideas has drained them of strength.

I look at Lori again, and with a quick pursing of lips she lets me know it's my moment to respond. "Wow. Gordon. What an idea. I mean, it's a great idea. Christmas would be huge—handmade gifts and all. I'd love to see it while I'm here."

"And I'd love to take you to see it. But I can't. It doesn't exist." He taps at the serpentine pulsation along his temple. "Only here. Only exists right here. Until I get the investors together, that's where it stays."

"Oh. Well, it does sound like a great idea, though."

"That it is. That it is. And a great investment for anybody who acts early. Get your money working for you in the ground stages of this and you'll see it skyrocket. I know that for a fact. This is my business. Spent my whole life in it—well, you know that—and this one's a winner right out of the gate. Right from the blocks. You've got to think of your money as one of the artists—working to craft a unique thing of beauty. Can't go wrong, if you look at it like that."

"I'm sure it is. I mean, it sounds, well, I mean, if I were ready to invest in real estate—commercial real estate—it would probably be an opportunity."

"I've already got the projections mapped out. The return you will see on this makes your Dow Jones index funds look like lunch money."

Lori pushes her chair back from the table. "Marie, let me make sure you have some fresh towels and soap in your bathroom. She's been up all night, Gordon. I don't think she can wrap her head around all your numbers right now." She puts her hands on my shoulders and gently forces me from my chair.

"I'll be more lucid tomorrow, Gordon. Sounds like you're working on something really interesting, though." I move toward the stairs with Lori herding me in front of her.

"Give it some thought. Ground floor is where the money is to be made." And with that he pulls a pair of folded reading glasses from his pocket and snaps open the business section of the *Star-Telegram*.

As soon as we slip behind the door of Lia's bubble-gum-pink room Lori sits down on the edge of the canopy bed and picks up a ruffled pillow, hugging it against her middle. "So what do you think?"

"Oh God, Lori, I'm not in any frame of mind to think about real estate investments."

"I'm not asking about real estate. What do you think about Gordon?"

"What do you mean, what do I think?"

"I mean, I think he's losing it. I mean, I can't believe my husband was sitting at our dining table hitting up his sister-in-law for a loan."

"I'm not sure he meant it that way, Lori. He's done awfully well in real estate around here. Maybe he's onto something."

Lori nods at me but her eyes narrow and she leans forward over the pillow like she's sharing a scandalous secret. "He's asking you for a loan."

In truth, I had not heard my brother-in-law string so many illustrative adjectives together since I was his bridesmaid and he overdosed on champagne. Lori's gaze drifts softly out of focus over my shoulder. One and a half years younger than myself, and so similar in appearance we have been mistaken for twins—she has the same deep-shadowed eyes, too large for her narrow face, the same hint of cleft in her chin. She is still pretty, to me. But I see in her face the wear that must be equally etched on my own.

"Are you two OK?" I ask her. "You haven't said anything about how *you're* handling his financial problems."

She turns her eyes back to me, scanning my own new creases of worry and time. "We're OK. For better or worse, and all of that. He's been the strong one for me when I needed it. Now it's my turn." She relaxes against the wall, pushing the pillow behind her back. "So how's your friend Joe? Do you still see him very often?"

"Sure, Joe's still a good friend." I say it evenly enough, but my face warms. "What made you think of him all of a sudden?"

"I think about your love life a lot. I just figured out a long time ago that the less I ask, the more you tell me. But since it hasn't come up lately, I decided to intrude."

"Am I really that secretive? Even with you?"

"Yes."

I laugh. "Maybe that's more out of consideration than privacy. My love life is boring."

She narrows her eyes, not giving up. "Joe is the only guy you've ever dated whom you didn't describe as 'nice.'"

I fold my legs up and rest my chin on top of my knees. "How *did* I describe him?"

"I can't remember. But I'm sure you used adjectives with more than one syllable. How can you work around all those male doctors and have a boring love life? Jesus, serial soap operas run for years on hospital romances."

"Most of the men my age are married."

"Does that matter?"

"Very funny. If a man *is* still single at this age, there's usually a reason for it."

"So why is Joe still single?"

I shrug. "He's not an easy one to figure out. I probably know him better than anybody else at First Lutheran, and he still surprises me. He says he wants a relationship, but he only goes for women who stay one step out of his grasp."

"He sounds like you."

I raise my head up. "Do I have to pay for this analysis? Come on, I'm not that bad. I'm just busy. I have a great home, good income. No dirty socks or underwear to pick up."

"Picking up dirty socks and underwear gives you humility, a fine attribute and a valuable tool for personal growth, I find. Besides, men can learn to pick up socks if you're patient with them."

"You could always place a personal ad for me, if you're that intent on getting me coupled," I say, smiling at her. "What makes you think Joe's the right guy?"

Her voice drops to a more serious note. "Because you were happy when you were dating Joe. You were content in a way that I haven't seen you since. Because Joe's the one that makes you blush."

"He's too good a friend, Lori. He doesn't feel like a lover anymore. I don't know how better to explain it." I've said the same to myself over and over. There should be no catch in my throat, no jump in my pulse. I run my finger over the delicate chain suspending the sapphire, then lock my hands back around my knees.

"Your lover should be your best friend, Marie. Love can be a choice as much as an accident."

"That doesn't exactly ring of passionate romance, you know."

"The choice is everything that comes after the passionate romance. It's the durable part—the part they never follow up on in movies. And for somebody who's as into control as you are, it might turn out to be the best part."

"Thanks."

"Well, you are, Marie. I mean, God knows I want my doctor to be in control. But love isn't a career. It isn't a degree you earn or a formula you pull out of a textbook. It's bumpy and blotched and painful and completely irreplaceable. Aren't there times when it might be better to let go? Sometimes the best part of life grows out of what you have no say over."

I reach over to hold her hand and whisper, "If I let go now, Lori, I will become completely unable to function."

She clasps my hand in hers. "Well, what better point in life to be with people who care about you?" She hugs me then, holds me close and tight before she stands up. "I love you, Marie. I've missed you. Let me know if there's anything you need, and sleep as late as you want." She closes the bedroom door behind her and a faint puff of air flutters the pink taffeta canopy like the wave of a fairy's wand. I run my tongue over my lips and taste quiet tears.

Beyond the walls of Lia's bedroom the shudder of sneakers on stair treads, the rush of bathwater and muted singsong of bedtime stories at last diminish and settle into sleep. Half a continent away, Joe is probably home from the hospital. I imagine him sprawled on his sofa with Chet Baker and a cold beer, hair tumbled and sweaty after biking up the steep hillside of Queen Anne. Or sleeping already, his arms wrapped tight around an oversized pillow the way he does, the sheet tangled at his feet. I wonder if he has called me yet. I wonder if he has missed me. I wonder if he even knows I have gone.

· 25 ·

My eyes open at dawn. I'm too programmed to the early hours of my profession to sleep in. Or perhaps it is my ex-profession. For the fourth time since my plane landed I check my cell phone for messages, turning it off and on to be sure it's working. In the hushed corner of Lori's sleeping household, enshrouded in Lia's princess bed, I dial my own number and whisper, "What has happened to you?" then play it back to myself as if I might hear the answer instead of the question. Trying to forget that it is only 4:00 AM in Seattle, I pull on running shorts and shoes and hope to pound the catcalls of my conscience into silence. Besides, this early, perhaps I can tolerate the heat.

By the time I return Gordon has trundled off to the office and both of my nieces and my nephew are gathered together, hypnotized at the breakfast table watching TV. "Well, hey, guys. How's the clan this morning?" Neil breaks into a huge grin that encourages me, until I realize it is directed at the cartoon action hero flying across the television screen.

"Neil. *Neil!* Your aunt Marie is here. Say hello to her, please," says Lori, clad in a stained bathrobe that testifies to years of maternal duty rife with bodily fluids. Tugging against the mesmerizing force of the flickering light, Neil's head pulls toward me until I occupy enough of his visual field to steal his focus. Then he leaps off the stool and throws himself around my neck.

"Aunt Marie. Did you bring me anything?"

"Neil!" says his mother. "Maybe you want to tell Aunt Marie about

the sleepover. Or she might be able to help you put your bike back together." I catch her hopeful suggestion that I might rescue her garage
floor.

"I fix people, not bikes. Hey, you've grown two skinned knees since
I saw you last. So you were at a sleepover last night?"

"Yep. Tyler's. Oh, Mom, Tyler's got this swimming pool in his
backyard and he got this mechanical shark for his birthday that swims
around the pool trying to eat you. It was so cool. Can we get a swimming pool?"

"Not today, honey," Lori says distractedly, sorting piles of mail and
magazines with a cup of coffee balanced in one hand and the telephone
crooked against her shoulder. She drops the phone below her chin and
whispers to me, "Sorry, I'll be off in a minute. School auction stuff. . . .
Two hundred and fifty, set up in tables of ten. . . . There's juice, Marie.
. . . No, I never told you one hundred. . . . Neil, feed your dog and get
some clothes on. . . . If you'll send me your menu, as I requested two
weeks ago . . . Neil, *now!* . . . I've already given you my address." Her
chin dodges up and down over the mouthpiece as she targets us each
in turn.

Hanging up, she says, "Oh God, it's not even eight o'clock and I'm
already worn out. Sit down, I'm making a fresh pot of coffee."

I pull out a chair at the breakfast table, still slick with sweat from
my run. Lia scrambles down from a high stool at the counter headed
for my lap and knocks her plastic cereal bowl to the floor in a waterfall
of milk and puffed rice. Lori slumps against the sink. "Lia, I've asked
you not to leave your bowl so close to the edge of the table. Let Bella
inside—I guess you don't have to feed her now, Neil."

Elsa appears in shorts and a T-shirt. She kisses my cheek and wag-
gles a hand at Lori. "Bye, Mom."

"Bye? Where are you going? You know you're babysitting this afternoon."

"I'm going over to a friend's."

"What friend's?"

"Sierra's."

"Not wearing that, you're not."

"What's wrong with what I'm wearing?" Her voice climbs ever higher.

"Your shorts are shorter than your underwear. Have you looked at yourself in the mirror from the back?" Lori turns Elsa around by her shoulders and pushes her ahead of herself out of the kitchen. Elsa's pleas spill into tears before they are across the living room. Lia and Neil slip off their stools at Elsa's first wail and escape to the swing set in the backyard. I finish making the coffee and pour a cup for Lori when I hear her return.

"Welcome to my life. I'd hoped we could spare you for a few more days before you had to see the truth," she says, taking the cup. She wipes a splatter of milk off the chair before sitting next to me.

"Would it help if I went to talk to her?" I ask.

"Oh, don't bother right now. She's furious but she's changing clothes." She holds her coffee cup wrapped between her hands, elbows propped on the kitchen table, and stares out the window at her younger children. Neil spins Lia's swing until her hair whirls straight out from her small face; the dog yaps at his feet. *Families,* she says to herself, shaking her head, as if the word both asks and answers all the riddles in her life.

She looks back at me, appearing to measure my mood. "Dad called the other morning, before you got here."

I sit up straighter in my chair. "Did you tell him I was coming to Texas?"

"No." She raises her eyebrows emphatically. "No, I didn't tell him. I figured you might not want him to know yet."

I'm almost embarrassed by my relief. "Thanks. I'm not sure I'll be able to get down to Houston this trip, so I didn't call him."

"Lia did."

"Lia did what?" I ask.

She squints her eyes like she's bracing herself. "Lia told him you were coming. She picked up the phone before I got there."

I slump back into my chair and look up at the ceiling. Lori gives me a minute to adjust before she adds, "He'd like to see you, Marie."

"Did he actually say that to you?"

"No. But I know he would." She puts her cup down and leans closer. "You could fly down for a couple of days while you're here." We're both quiet for a minute; Lia's laughter outdoors is the only sound in the kitchen, bouncing like an echo as she twirls around. "When was the last time you saw him?" Lori asks at last.

"It's been a long time."

"How long?"

"Three years." I see her bite her lip to keep from reacting to this fact. "I know. I know I need to go."

"He's aged a lot in this last year, Marie. We flew down a couple of months ago—Gordon had a meeting there in May and I went down for the day. I couldn't believe how much he'd changed since my last visit. He just seems to have run out of energy, like he's giving up. I think part of it is that he's convinced he'll be totally blind soon."

"Most people with macular degeneration don't ever go totally blind."

"I know that. You told me that. So I told *him* that. He wouldn't even let me finish the sentence. How do you get out of bed in the morning when you can't even hope that today might be better than yesterday? He's going to fall soon if he stays in that house alone. Fall and break his hip, or hit his head—if he doesn't burn the place down first."

I shift uncomfortably in my chair, staring out the window at the children clambering across the top beam of the swing set, the morning sun cutting sharp shadows across the grass. "Maybe that's his own choice. Maybe he'd rather have that happen than give up his independence and let other people take care of him. Do we have the right to ask him to move?"

Lori doesn't answer immediately. I turn to face her, waiting. "I don't know," she finally offers after the silence has become almost awkward. "Maybe he's not the one who's struggling with that question." As soon as she sees my face fall, she says, "I'm sorry, maybe I shouldn't have said that. It's just that . . ." She hesitates. "It's just that before long you're not going to have the option to make things better between you."

I swallow back the mix of anger and fear welling up. A string of defiant words comes into my mind but I know they're not really meant for her. "I can't." I shake my head. "It's been so long since I've had a genuine conversation with him I get knots in my stomach thinking of going there. And besides, I don't know how long I can be away from Seattle."

Lori absorbs this without comment, though I see her mouth tighten for an instant. "I'm not trying to push you," she says. "I'd rather have you here with us. But, especially given that he won't tell me anything about what his doctors say, your input could make a difference. To me, anyway. And to him. He might actually listen to you about his health." She lets all this sink in for a minute, and then optimistically tacks on, "It's a short flight from here. Planes leave every hour."

I drop my neck back on the hard rail of the chair and stare up at the light fixture, where a mosquito is strangling in a filmy spider's web. "Oh God, Lori. I'll think about it."

"Thanks, Marie. I wouldn't pressure you if I weren't concerned about how much time he's got."

I lift my head and look at her. "Are you that worried?"

She nods her head, but any words are aborted as the screen door crashes open. Neil bangs into the kitchen dragging a plastic garbage can. "Mom, where can I find another can like this?"

"Neil, that thing is foul. Why are you bringing it into the house?"

"If I get another one, I can put them together, like this, see?" He joins his cupped fingers in a cage before his face. "It'd make a cool submarine."

"I guess that does kind of look like a submarine. Look in the garage. But wash it out—with soap—before you climb into it."

"And if I had a big pipe I could make that into a periscope. Can I get some duct tape?"

Lori opens a drawer crammed with coupons and screwdrivers and fishing line and jimmies out a wide roll of gray tape. "Here. Put it back when you're done." She brings the coffeepot to the table and pours more into each of our cups, ignoring the black streaks that trail the garbage can as Neil bumps back across the floor and out into the yard.

A minute later she jumps back out of her chair, black coffee sloshing over the table. "Neil. Neil, get back in here."

He stomps up the porch steps to the door and presses his face into the wire mesh. "What?"

"What are you planning to do with this submarine?"

"Play in it," he says, incredulous at the unimaginative density of grown-ups.

"Are you intending to play submarine in Tyler's swimming pool?"

"Well, yeah."

Lori whips open the door and pulls Neil in, plunks him into the chair facing her. "Neil." She leans across her knees so her face is inches from her son's. "Promise me. You will *not* make a submarine out of garbage cans and climb into it in Tyler's pool."

"But, Mom . . ."

"Promise me! Look me in the eye and promise me. Honey, if you go under the water inside those cans, you might not be able to get back up. Every year kids die from games like that."

"No, it's OK. It's going to have a trapdoor on it, Mom."

"Neil." She holds her wristwatch up in front of his eyes. "Take a deep breath. Now hold it as long as you can. Keep holding it. Keep holding it. Look at the second hand on my watch and keep holding it . . ." Neil's face, puffed out like a blowfish, grows pink, then red, and finally explodes in a spray of spit and air.

"That's how long you have to get two stuck-together garbage cans apart before you die in Tyler's pool. Get it? Now put the garbage can back behind the garage."

· 26 ·

When my cell phone finally rings I'm in the shower and almost miss the call. I've left it perched on the edge of the counter and the vibrations shimmy it off to the slate floor, where it hums in a shallow splash of bathwater. I lunge for it, leaving the shower still running in the background, water streaming off my hair over the mouthpiece.

"Dr. Heaton?"

It's Charlie Marsallis. I sit down on the closed toilet lid in a slippery puddle and try to sound collected and professional, or at least clothed. My heart rate must have doubled. "Yes. Hello, Mr. Marsallis."

"Good morning. How are you? Are you in Texas now?"

"I'm in Fort Worth. At my sister's house."

"Hopefully with better weather than we have in Seattle today. Or at least warmer. Is it raining there, too?" I shut off the shower, grab a towel from the shelf above the toilet and drape it over my lap. "Did you call to ask about the weather, or to tell me the district attorney filed charges?"

"Actually I *really did* call to see how you were." He sounds almost amused at my snippiness.

I picture him swiveling around in his desk chair with the telephone cord looping across my stacks of files, his hair probably raked in all directions. So different from Donnelly. Donnelly would never call just to see how I was. I bite my lip and hunch down over my knees, fighting an urge to cry. "Sorry. I guess I'm in limbo—that's how I am. Have you heard anything yet?"

"I'm calling the district attorney's office as soon as they open to set up a meeting. Things can move slowly in the public arena, though. Especially in the summer. It still might be weeks—or more—before we know any details."

"Yeah. I guess murderers and rapists trump me for court time. I should be happy about that." My voice catches at the end.

"Let me worry about this, Marie. That's part of my job."

I think of all the times I've told a terrified patient that same thing, "Let me do the worrying," before I roll them into the operating room. I'd never appreciated how empty such a claim could sound. At least in my own profession I can wield the power of benzodiazapines and narcotics. Marsallis has to depend on words.

"OK," I whisper, and then swallow and say it more clearly. "OK. Thank you—I appreciate your calling me."

"I'll let you know as soon as I learn anything."

Lori wants to take me to lunch at her country club. We wind through streets lined with sprawling brick homes; they loom monstrous behind juvenile shrubs and sticklike trees that swim in optimistically oversized rectangles cut through the sidewalks. The entryways rise two stories above cut-glass front doors, as if anticipating their owners will grow into giants over the coming decades. Bicycles and baseball mitts and Frisbees are strewn across grass lawns, abandoned to the midday heat. We drop the car with the club valet and walk through the chilled lobby to the blinding blue glare rippling off the pool. Lori shields her eyes to scan the deck and someone taps on the window from inside the dining room.

"Oh, it's Charlotte." She waves and takes my elbow to lead me back inside. I sink at the thought of making small talk with Lori's friends but follow her to the table where three women sit, cool as summer sherbets in pastel dresses and lipstick that matches the color of their nails. She introduces me. "My sister—the anesthesiologist, from Seattle."

Charlotte says, "Oh, you're my favorite kind of doctor. Ever since I got an epidural with my last baby, I'd never been so glad to see anybody walk into my hospital room as that anesthesia doctor. I wish it had been a woman, though."

"Thank you. I enjoy obstetrics."

The woman to Charlotte's left adds, "It must be wonderful to go home every night knowing you'd made somebody's life better. I mean, everyone's always so particular about choosing their surgeon, but it's really the anesthesiologist who keeps you alive. My daughter wants to be an accountant—I wish I could get her to think about medicine."

Charlotte says, "Lori is one of my favorite people in this town. She does half the work for the school PTA—if they paid her she'd be a rich lady! How long will you be visiting Fort Worth?"

"Just a few days. It's great to be with her children again. Could you excuse me a minute?" I let Lori settle into conversation and wander down marble-tiled hallways to find the bathroom, where I run a brush through my hair and pray that she won't ask me to sit through lunch with her friends. I don't think I could make it through an hour avoiding any reference to the history of my recent working life. I lean toward the mirror to reapply lipstick and freeze with the tube halfway to my lips. I look so normal. It's almost startling. I half expect to see my secret spreading like a stain across my face.

I can't help wondering, if Bobbie Jansen had been born among these women, had attended their private schools and colleges, been included in their churches and their country clubs and their dinner circles, if her teeth had been straightened at the proper age and her hands had been regularly manicured, she might have discovered herself here, flowering in the heart of suburban America. Even now, these women would be kind to Bobbie, if they met her and learned of her loss. They would politely shift their glances away from her broken fingernails and dated hemlines, be kind enough to offer her work, perhaps, cleaning their homes or tending their gardens or caring for their robust children. And then I stop myself, hearing the callous judgment in my own mind.

When I return Lori has been seated at the other side of the room.

"I'm sorry, I probably embarrassed you. I feel like I've lost all my social grace," I tell her.

She opens her napkin into her lap and studies me for a minute. "Have you always been this hard on yourself, or did it start in medical school? I wish you saw yourself the way other people see you."

"Other people? Maybe we should ask Jolene's mother how she sees me."

Lori covers my hands with hers in the center of the white tablecloth. "Marie, you've been a doctor for, what? Eleven or twelve years? This is *one* event. One patient out of thousands. Don't let this accident wipe out your faith in yourself. You're a good anesthesiologist."

"How do you know that? I know you're saying that to make me feel better, because you love me. But how could you possibly know if I'm a good doctor or not?" I shake my head, almost challenging her to defend her trust in me. "I make mistakes. And even if I can't figure out what it was, maybe because of her heart or maybe not, some mistake I made might have killed this little girl." I untangle my hands from hers and clench them in my lap. I remember a professor I had in medical school, an oncologist. He was from India, and he had that musical British-Indian accent. His whole working life consisted of poisoning people with the hope that he could kill the cancer and then pull back in time to rescue the patient. I told him I could never specialize in oncology, I wasn't brave enough to make those choices every day. He answered, "To be an excellent physician you must accept the possibility of failure. A doctor who considers himself infallible is a most dangerous creature." So here I am, facing my own fallibility. I say to Lori, "God, if you only knew the latest turns this suit has taken."

"I *would* know if you'd tell me," Lori says, leaning back against her chair as if she had all day to listen.

"My latest lawyer asked me not to talk to anyone about it. I'm not sure that applies to sisters, but I'd hate to expose you to perjury charges."

"Your *latest* lawyer?" Her eyebrows rise beneath her wispy bangs. "What happened to the guy with the great view of the Olympics?"

"I love the details you remember. But actually, now that he's out of it, I wonder if that view wasn't the best thing he had to offer."

"So what's the best thing about this new lawyer?"

"Maybe just the fact that his offices are closer to earth. Maybe that he seems to see me as a human being more than a yacht payment. He may need my case as much as I need his defense. Look, I'm not trying to be evasive. I'm just trying to get some distance from it. Try to keep me busy enough that I can't think too much, OK?"

"Hardly possible, knowing you."

The waiter comes and takes our order. Lori asks him to bring us each a glass of sauvignon blanc. When it arrives she lifts her glass and clinks it against mine. "Happy Anniversary."

"Is this your anniversary? No, you got married in spring."

"It's Mom and Dad's anniversary."

I glance at my watch. "Oh my God. You're right. I'd completely forgotten. Forty-seven years, is that right? It is. Forty-seven years. They had a good marriage, though, didn't they?"

"They did. I'm envious sometimes."

"Do you ever wonder if they would have been happier if they hadn't had kids? Dad, at least? I know Mom needed us, but . . . they had a connection that went way beyond parenting."

Lori looks thoughtful, perhaps maternally enlightened. "She'd be proud of you. I hope you know that."

A desperate laugh escapes me, imagining the district attorney signing criminal charges against me.

Lori continues. "She would. You're so much like her. Calm in a crisis. Private. Intent on making the world better. I've wondered, sometimes, if she might have become a doctor if she'd been born later."

"Can you imagine Dad married to a doctor? Cooking his own dinners or doing his own laundry?"

"No. I guess not. But I know he's glad to be the father of one. "

I take a sip of my wine and set the crystal glass carefully in front of my plate. "I needed him to be glad to be my father a long time before I was a doctor."

"He loves you, Marie. He's always loved you. He's just not so good at showing it."

"Well, maybe I got tired of having to work so hard to see that."

"You know, you told me once—you'd just started practicing on real patients, was that your third year in med school?—you said you'd have to learn to be less sensitive once you were a doctor. That you would need to start compartmentalizing your feelings so you could take care of sick or dying people. And then, when Mom was so sick and you were with her, I remember wishing I could step back from how much it hurt. You were so strong for Dad during that time. For both of us. You got us through it."

I remember talking to her about that, almost fifteen years ago. I remember the naive sense of power it had given me to imagine such emotional maturity. When I first started medical school we had a few lectures about the personal toll of mixing into the inevitably fatal consequences of biological processes—the perpetual unraveling and reorganization of chemicals as they evolve from life to mineral and back into new life. It would be a purely awe-inspiring miracle if love and loss didn't have to be part of it.

I nod. "I was stupid enough to think it would be a voluntary thing, somehow. An emotional switch we could turn off and on. But you just wake up one day and discover new walls inside yourself."

Lori watches me quietly for a minute. Then she says, "Maybe this is one of those times you need to figure out how to knock down the compartments, Marie. People can change at any age. Even Dad. But you'll never figure that out if you can't talk to him."

Our food is delivered, the perfect excuse to shift our conversation onto easier topics. I take a sip of my wine and thank God I am left with this sister in my disrupted family, someone who can be honest with me. Someone who can believe in me more than I believe in myself right now.

After lunch, Lori hands the valet a folded bill when he pulls up with the car. "I'm going to miss this," she sighs. "Maybe more than the maid."

The metal buckle on my seat belt burns hot against my pelvis and the tires crackle across bubbling asphalt. The neon green of the golf course yields to end-to-end strip malls as we drive. "You have nice friends, Lori. I'm sorry I didn't talk to them longer. I can tell they care about you."

"I'm lucky, I know."

"Luck doesn't earn friends."

"How's your obstetrician friend? Is it Karen?"

"Karen Leece. She's fine. I don't see how she does it—she works at least sixty hours a week, and it's not like her husband is home flipping pancakes."

"I remember meeting her." When Lori was pregnant with Lia she came up to visit me, and started having Braxton Hicks contractions. I took her to Karen's office. "She had warm hands."

"She's a warmhearted soul."

"No. I mean literally—her hands were unusually warm. I even remarked on it and she told me she holds her hands under hot water for a minute or two before each exam. Imagine in this day and age—she's probably losing one whole appointment slot every day just so that her hands feel comfortable against your skin."

Lori checkerboards through traffic with the unflappable agility required to survive the leagues of freeways that connect Dallas–Fort Worth's burgeoning suburbs. She whips between two massive trucks to an exit ramp that I don't recognize. Five turns later we park beside a field pocked with tumbled blocks of reinforced concrete and wooden stakes flying orange plastic flags that wilt in the late afternoon heat.

"Where are we?"

"In the middle of Fine Furs, Lord & Taylor—I think. This is Gordon's last project. Looks like only the lawyers will get any payment for it, though. It's bankrupt before groundbreaking." She reaches down and scoops up a handful of loose rubble, then hauls back her arm and chucks bits of concrete at a metal sign announcing the coming glitz and glamour. "Bingo," she says as a rock bounces square off the middle of the sign. "This one's for college savings. And this one"—she throws a rock so hard I duck instinctively as it ricochets back toward us—"is for half of our retirement savings and a second mortgage."

I bend down and pick up my own dusty pile, then toss the entire handful at the sign. Lori takes my hand and says, "I can tell you haven't been a softball coach anytime recently. Wind it up, girl, this isn't a bride's bouquet. The harder you throw it, the better it feels."

For the next onslaught I pick up a golf-ball-sized stone and cock my whole body back, then fling it with enough force that I skitter forward and am saved from falling only by Lori's quick grasp. I am repaid by a sizable dent in the middle of "Elegant Dining." The metallic whack makes me smile.

"Now," says Lori, "every time you hit it focus on one particular gripe." Her voice catches as she heaves another rock. "That one was for the adviser who convinced Gordon the NASDAQ was at an all-time low." She laughs and reaches down to collect more rocks. "Here, Marie. Pitch a few at the lawyers." I hurl a clotted mass of studded concrete in Donnelly's name. It feels revengeful and cleansing.

"Now I understand why you see all those signs pocked with bullet holes," I say. "Here's one for the expert witness, may he rot in his Brooks Brothers suit. And this"—I cock my arm back behind my ear, gripping a particularly vicious chunk—"this one is for the smirk on Darryl Feinnes's face." The stone clangs against the metal sign and reverberations radiate across the pockmarked field like the prize bell in a carnival game. Lori clutches her stomach in laughter and throws her arms around me. Sweat is running down my cheeks, sweat and tears both, and I can't tell if I'm crying with laughter or desperation but it doesn't matter, because either extreme is better than staying helplessly numb. We sit on the hood of her car and she hands me a Kleenex.

"Here. You're striped," she says, taking the tissue from me and wiping my face. The Kleenex turns gray with construction dust. "You know, it means a lot to me that you've come here. Now, I mean—when things are hard for you. It means a lot to me that you consider this a safe haven. At least, I hope that's why you're here." She is the one being on the earth who most intimately shares my history and my genetics. As divergent as our lives have grown, I know I may never be closer to another human.

We're both quiet for a while; the sunlight is tingeing the deeper gold of late afternoon. Lori slides off the car and walks across the littered ground, pulling up one of the orange-flagged stakes. "Do you remember that day we were riding one of your friend's horses through that cornfield? And we found all those surveyor's stakes?"

"Oh yeah. Mary Ann Coker's horses." Her dad had a place east of Dallas. The corn truly had been "as high as an elephant's eye." All three of us loped bareback down a farm road into the forest of ripening stalks, horse sweat and girl sweat making dark, slick ovals across the horses' backs, yellow froth working up and down along the arcs of rein. The land was at the fringe of a much younger Dallas, downtown spiking the horizon, and ageless, sun-crackled farm shacks waiting for the creeping sprawl to bring bulldozers and cement. We wound through the rustling corn, a symphony of dry leaves, and emerged into a flat dirt yard before three bungalows, gray slats shedding white curls of paint.

An elderly black man rocked on the nearest porch, lifted a hand in greeting as if we were expected. "Evenin'." A woman stepped into the doorway, cast in the half-gloom of the interior. And there in that cornfield clearing, like some glitch in the linear track of time, we all passed our simple greetings and moved on.

Winding back toward the stables, we crossed, I remember now, a small cemetery plot, stone grave markers bare but for bits of moss clinging to depressions that were once the names of grandparents and too-fragile infants. All along the ride home we pulled up the wooden surveyor's stakes and flung them randomly throughout the fields, like children raising hands against a tidal wave.

"I haven't thought of that in years," I say. "Decades now, I guess. Where were we?"

"Out past Greenville Avenue. Gordon and I went to a dinner meeting near there a couple of years ago. There's a Hooters restaurant in the middle of that cemetery now."

"So what will happen with this land?" I ask. "Has Gordon completely lost his option on it?"

She shrugs. "I haven't asked him lately. I don't know, maybe you should write him a prescription for one of those fancy new antidepressants. Don't they fix just about everything?"

"Is he any help with the kids at all these days?"

She shakes her head and tucks her skirt between her knees, staring out at the dented and broken signs promising her financial security. "Sometimes I lie awake at night and decide that, starting tomorrow, I'm going to stop telling anybody to get dressed, get in the car, pack your lunch, do your homework. I'm going to quit using the words *get up* and *pick up* and *hurry up*. I'm just going to shut my mouth, stand aside and see if the whole family really collapses."

"What would happen, do you think?"

"Well, either the Health Department or Child Protective Services would lock me up within a couple of weeks, or I would find out that everybody figures out how to take care of themselves just fine without me. And I'm not sure which one of those is scarier."

"It's hard, what you do. Being a mother. Harder than I give you credit for, I know," I say.

"It's hard. And wonderful. But I'm not saving lives every day, like you."

I smile at her generosity. "You're saving lives."

She squeezes my hand and whispers, "It'll happen for you, too, Marie. It could still happen."

I squeeze her hand back, hard, and feel tears coming again. "It's funny. Anesthesia is filled with all these algorithms, planned pathways you're supposed to follow in an emergency so you never find yourself trapped in a dead end where you can't rescue a patient." I stop for a minute and wipe my eyes. "I should have planned one out for my life. How did I forget that, somewhere along the way?" At this tears begin to fill her own eyes and she hugs me, rocking me gently back and forth.

"Lori?" She looks up at me, ready to accept whatever I want to tell her. "I think I should go to Houston."

"Good." She nods, as much to herself as to me, then hugs me again. "I think that's great. When do you want to go?"

"Well, never. But since I could get called back to Seattle anytime, I think I should go tomorrow."

"Tomorrow? Wow. OK. How long do you think you'll stay with him?"

"I don't know. Long enough to figure out what he needs. Or at least as long as I can stand it."

She studies me for a minute, thoughtfully. "You were so close to him when you were little. You were his dream girl, Marie. Smart, organized, always on top of everything—destined to do something impor-

tant with your life." She says this hopefully, without any note of jeal-
ousy, as if urging me to reclaim some personal history I have let slip
away. "He was so protective of you, almost doting. Do you remember
the day you cut your back on the rake? He was tossing us into the leaf
pile after he'd raked the backyard, and he'd left the rake buried under
the leaves, and you landed on it. I remember him carrying you into the
kitchen; his face was white. He looked so shaken, I thought you must be
dying. You must remember that day, don't you?"

A recollection stirs, and then sinks under other memories. That day
is hers now more than mine. When do we stop crying over our injuries?
When we get old enough to swallow our tears, or when the people we
love stop responding to our cries of pain? "Not clearly," I answer her at
last. "I guess I remember other days."

We are both silent then, until Lori asks, almost whispering, "You've
never felt forgiven, have you?"

"Well. Forgiveness has never exactly been his strong suit."

"No. It hasn't. We needed Mom for that." She slips off the car into
the dust and takes my hand.

Elsa awakens me by softly blowing on my eyelashes. I startle and grab
her arm, dreaming I've been paged for an emergency, and we both
laugh.

"I forgot where I was." I push myself up to a sitting position and
pull her toward me. She drops her face onto my chest, as if she were a
little girl again.

"You're leaving tomorrow."

"You got my note."

"You just got here." A whispered plea.

I stroke her hair and press a kiss on the crown of her head. So sweet
to replenish the physical memory of her smell, her shape, the resonance
of her voice through my flesh instead of a telephone. "I know. It makes
me sad, too. But I need to visit Grandpa, and I can't be away from Seattle for too long. I have an idea I talked to your mom about, though.
Want to hear it?" She sits up and I catch a tear trailing down her cheek.
"What's this? All because I have to go?"

She shrugs and more tears fall; her lips and nose are plush with emotion. "Hey. Tell me."

"Have you ever . . . ?" She stops until I nod. "I hurt Sierra's feelings. I said something really mean, and I don't even know why."

I pull her near again, so her head is tucked under my chin. "Want to talk about it?" She shakes her head. "Was it about Dakota?" She doesn't move. I cradle her next to me, give her all the silence she wants. Her length is startlingly equal to mine. After a time she talks, though not about her regret, telling me about the dance routine she has to learn for the Spirit Club, and how they finally took a vote on their costume design because nobody could agree, and the iPod she's saving up for, and, finally, as if she'd almost forgotten, she asks me what I talked to her mom about.

"Well, we thought maybe you could fly up to Seattle at the end of the summer for a week. Before school starts."

"By myself? *My* mom agreed to that?" I smile and she jumps up, electrically happy. "Oh my God, I have to call Sierra. She will never believe this—she loves Pearl Jam. Can we go shopping together?'

Before she leaves the room, practically ready to pack, I take her hand. "Hey, Elsa. Remember: sometimes just saying you're sorry can make things a whole lot better—for both of you."

· 27 ·

My father's house is old, built of brick, as all the old houses in the neighborhood are. Up and down the street big, boxy new homes with circular driveways are crowding onto the expensive lots once occupied by small bungalows and grand oak trees, the sidewalks and street curbs buckled by their heaving roots.

I reach up to press the doorbell and feel the weight of a million disappointments and silent quarrels settle over me like accumulated drops of water, none of them burdensome alone, but their collective mass suffocating. It is finally the professional part of my mind, the part that has practiced how to keep emotion out of decision making, that lets me push the small brass button. I hear his hard-soled leather slippers scrape across the worn oak entry. Then the heavy door swings back.

"Hi, Dad."

"Well. You made it at last."

"The traffic coming in from Hobby was awful. I should have called you." It feels sadly fitting, somehow, that I should begin this visit with an apology. "It's good to see you." I lean toward him to brush his cheek against mine but, stretching over my suitcase, it becomes easier merely to press his arm with my hand.

It is almost frightening to see him—his eyes rheumy and distorted behind the thick lenses of his glasses, his head tilted to capture my face in the ring of remaining vision that surrounds his central core of blindness, like a ring of cherished light being sucked down a well—alarming to discover his stooped frame and stiffened gait. Three years at this end of life, as at the beginning, rush parabolically along the axis of physical change.

"Well. No harm. Let me help you get your things inside." He reaches for my suitcase and together we lift it across the threshold and into the dimly lit hallway. The smells of the house tell their own story—earthy coffee and cigars, his pleasures, barely mitigating the tinge of urine and stale eucalyptus, the hint of mildew and Mentholatum; the scents of his residual comforts nip at the odors of decay.

"Dad, let me take this. Do you want me in the twin bedroom? Go on and sit down. I'll unpack and be out in a minute."

"I'll carry it. I'm not dead yet. Thought you might prefer the double bed, so I made that up. Better light in there, anyway."

I allow him to take the suitcase from my hand and bump it down the back hallway ahead of me, cringing as he hauls it onto a low brocaded chaise at the foot of the bed; the heft of it upsets his balance and lands him on the cushion beside the bag. Behind him a window-unit air conditioner groans and sweats against the humid air; I am reminded of midnight pushing matches with Lori to drape ourselves over an even older model, pleading for some relief from the heat before the whole machine froze up like an ice-encrusted ship waiting for spring thaw. Most of my memories inside this home, though, are limited to college holidays. My parents moved from Dallas to Houston at the end of my junior year of high school, when my father took a professorship at Rice. I have always felt like a guest in this house.

"Have you eaten yet? Let me take you out to dinner," I tell him, brushing a damp strand of hair off my face. "I thought you might enjoy getting out for some Mexican food. Do you still like Mexican?" His eyes roam over my face like the sweep of a lost traveler's lantern searching for the road home. He squints up at me and I can't tell if he's angry at the suggestion or just trying to focus.

"Mexican food?" The words seem to make him weary, as if the experience required packing and flying to the country itself. "You want Mexican food?"

"Well, no. I mean, only if you do. I thought *you* might like some.

Is that little place in University Village still open? The one Mom liked so much?" I sit next to him and try to catch his roving pupils, to meet his eyes directly. I watch him struggle with even the notion of the effort it might take to back his old Buick out of the narrow garage and weave through traffic to the restaurant. How is he getting his groceries? How does he make it to his doctor's appointments? In the still, musty room with the ticking heartbeat of the painted porcelain clock on the bedside table, the shifting weight of responsibility presses me into the thin cushion.

"Only if you want to, Dad. Or I can run to the store and pick up something to cook here."

"Suit yourself." He shrugs and braces his hands against the chaise, his fingers arched with knotted joints. "Get yourself unpacked and I'll start some tea water. Lie down if you want. Rest after your trip."

"Thanks. Maybe I will lie down for a few minutes."

He pushes up from the chaise and steadies himself with a hand on my shoulder. Or is it a gesture of affection? As he shuffles toward the hallway I catch myself diagnosing him, ticking off a list of clinical signs—the awkward angles of arthritis that skew the pendulous swing of his limbs; the slight swoon when he stands, until his aging vestibula settle his center of gravity; the gradual compression of his vertebral discs that has lowered his looming stature, dropped his face nearer my own. Even his dampened smiles and scowls, and the barely visible tremor that could be Parkinson's. As soon as he leaves the room I close the door and lie down on the bed, stare up at the ceiling. What will we talk about hour after hour?

I pull the telephone onto my chest and dial Lori's number. "Hi. It's me," I say as soon as she answers. "I'm at the house."

"He's bad, isn't he? I can hear it in your voice."

"He's just gotten so old. So suddenly."

"It's not so sudden, Marie. You just haven't seen him in three years."

"I know. I mean, I didn't know. That he'd have changed so much. I didn't expect it would be so dramatic."

"How dramatic is it?" Her voice has a ping of alarm in it, a familial radar scope raised to detect impending cataclysms. "Is he OK? Should I fly down there?"

"No. No, it's not anything like that. I don't know, he may have been this way when you saw him last. I just wasn't expecting this much decline. This much frailty."

Lori sighs and seems to reach for words. She answers with a tone of sympathy—for me more than our father, I think. "I know. I never would have believed I'd be describing him as frail someday." We both sit silent as the gulch of our father's neediness tests our undeclared boundaries of accountability. "So are you going to talk to him about moving?"

"God, Lori, first I have to figure out how to talk to him about what to eat for dinner."

"Sorry."

I reach over to turn on the bedside lamp and my fingers are entwined in the dusty threads of a spider's web and its long-desiccated occupants. "I think I'm going to spend every day cleaning. Maybe before I leave I can at least arrange for a regular housekeeper to come in."

"How are you going to get him to agree to that? He's never even paid to have the oil changed in his car."

"I'll pay for it, then."

She doesn't answer immediately, and I try not to imagine judgment in her pause. "Well, I suppose money can fix part of this." The background sounds of her house—children calling and the dog barking, a television set turned up too loud—are muffled as she covers the receiver. "I have to race. Call me later tonight or tomorrow and we'll talk. Try not to stress about it—we'll figure something out."

"OK. You too. Tell everybody 'hi' for me."

As I'm about to hang up I hear her call out. "Hey, Marie? I've never said anything to Dad about, you know, about the lawsuit. I've never told anyone at all."

"Thanks, Lori. Thank you."

I cradle the receiver and rest my head against the wall. This bedroom had been Lori's once. I remember this wallpaper, embossed with pink rosebuds and English ivy, remember running my fingertips over its textured pattern in the dark when Lori and I lay awake talking, while the house cooled and eased back down onto its footings with the weight of the night, as if it, too, had to settle down from the bounding of teenaged girls in and out of the wire screen doors, bounding across the thresholds of womanhood. We hated that wallpaper, both of us. Its femininity mocked our liberation from hair curlers and petticoats and folk music—an era before the word *ladylike* was sarcasm. Mother chose the decor for her room when Lori was away at a music camp, and I remember her vigilant supervision over the handyman, insisting the seams be perfectly matched so the vines could twine unbroken across the wall. Maybe, in a funny way, these roses bonded the two of us in our conspiratorial pretense of satisfaction with our mother's idealized view of our tastes and our world—poised as we were in the aftermath of Vietnam and Watergate, emerging from the trough of student protests and Black Power and Woodstock, ready to strike out after a decade of national rebellion had mellowed, offering us some choice about where on the measuring stick of sexual freedom and political activism and domestic duties we might pin ourselves. So in the middle of the night we would wait until my parents slept and turn the volume down low on the Grateful Dead or Pink Floyd and imagine what our lives would become, my fingertips tracing the ivy and roses across the wall behind us as we talked of college campuses, and the meaning of life, and boys. The darkened circles of paper behind the bed mark where our heads had rested, the graying knots of the fringed white bedspread where our heels had crossed. Everything in the room is stained and worn out, well past its prime.

In the corner of the living room the grandfather clock chimes, muffled through the walls of the house. It is five thirty in Seattle. Charlie Marsallis might be home already with his wife and son, waiting for dinner or watching the news, or preparing briefs for some other impugned doctor. I claw my cell phone from the bottom of my purse. The unblinking light assures no message is waiting, but I still punch in the code for voice mail just to hear the recorded voice declare that I have "No. New. Messages." Something about the flat, mechanized tone sounds like a jeer: "There is no news for you, Dr. Heaton. No end in sight."

I dial Marsallis's office, not even knowing what I'll dictate into his answering machine. I'm completely caught off guard when he answers the phone.

"Oh. Mr. Marsallis."

"Yes?"

"I didn't expect . . . It's . . . This is Marie Heaton. I wanted . . . Were you able to schedule a meeting with the district attorney?"

"I have."

"You have? You've got something scheduled? You said you'd call me."

"I got off the phone with him twenty minutes ago. I was about to dial your cell phone. Is that where you're calling from?"

"I'm in Houston today. At my father's. Yes, on my cell phone. What did he say?"

"I'm meeting with him next week, Tuesday. He said he doesn't have anything definite yet—hasn't finished reviewing whatever evidence he's been given. I didn't pick up any cues from him. I don't think he's bullshitting about that. You don't need to be there for this meeting, but if the state does file a charge I'll want to get things moving quickly. Is that going to be a problem?"

"I can fly back whenever you want." I have to hold my breath for a moment to try to slow my heart rate down. Suddenly the threat of eternal purgatory seems more palatable than the possibility of a conviction. "Did you get any information from him?"

"No. Nothing. Which is exactly what I'd expected at this point. Remember? You're letting me worry right now."

"Mr. Marsallis?"

"Charlie."

"Charlie. Could I go to jail? I mean, is that absolutely crazy? Or could I go to jail if I were convicted of negligent homicide?"

He doesn't answer me, and I can almost picture him standing with his thumb hooked on his belt, throwing his head back at my ridiculous question. I hear him suck his lips against his front teeth before he answers me. "Yes. That's conceivable. But unlikely. Extraordinarily unlikely."

. . .

In the kitchen my father has set two mugs of steaming water on the counter and rummages through a drawer. "Can't find the damn tea bags." He pulls forth bottle openers and broken clothespins and boxes of toothpicks and an ancient book of Green Stamps. The wings of a dead moth flutter to the floor.

"Dad, let me help." I open the upper cabinet and rifle through rusted tins of paprika, curry powder, more toothpicks, and a swollen carton of salt before spotting a package of reasonably new Lipton tea bags on a lazy Susan.

We sit at the yellowed Formica table with its gold boomerangs and silver trim, and concentrate on dipping the bags in and out of the hot water. "Are you still lecturing up at the museum now and then?" I ask, pouring some milk from the quart he has set out. Congealing curdles rise up from the bottom of the cup to float like tiny white birds across a muddy lake. "Or for any of the local schools? Weren't you doing something for the school district?"

"Oh, golly. I haven't done that for years now." He stirs and sips, stirs and sips. The kitchen sink faucet taps out a slow drumbeat of drips.

"Lori and Gordon are doing well," I say. "Her kids are beautiful. Really. Elsa isn't even a child anymore." He nods and stirs and sips his tea. "She looks, just a little bit, like pictures of Mother at her age."

"Is that right?"

I clear my throat and trace the handle of my ceramic cup with my finger, run it along the rough seam of a crack threatening to split clear through and drench me in hot tea and curdling milk. "It looks like a lot of new houses are going up in your neighborhood." I can't tell if he doesn't hear me, or doesn't care to comment. "Do you still keep up with that couple in the corner house? The gray house?"

He shakes his head. "They moved three or four years ago. She had some memory problems. I think he found one of those apartments with nursing care." With each sip he takes, a thin brown trickle meanders from the rim of his cup to the prominence of his chin, until it bleeds onto his shirtfront. I clench the napkin in my hand to keep from reaching across the table to blot the damp fabric. I wonder if he would engage in the conversation more avidly if I told him I was facing criminal charges and might not be able to visit him once I was in prison.

"So, Dad, I'd like to meet your ophthalmologist while I'm here. I thought maybe we could try to get an appointment and I could go with you."

He stops stirring and searches the vicinity of my face. "What for?"

"Well, I thought maybe I could help translate some of the medical stuff. Just make sure all your questions were answered."

"Why do I need a translator to tell me I'm going blind?"

"Dad, macular degeneration doesn't leave you completely blind. Most patients can still function . . ."

"Function? Can't read, can't drive, can't find the damn tea bags, even. How is that functioning? That's as blind as anybody carrying a white cane, far as I'm concerned." He stares out toward the late afternoon sunlight streaming through the kitchen window, his hands curled limply around his tea. I wish I could slip off the prisms that warp his eyes and make them unreadable to me. Instead I reach across the space between us and cover his hand with mine, struck by how thick and gnarled his joints are, how thinly protected by his papery skin.

He turns his palm over and briefly squeezes my hand, grips it the way you might tighten the knot of an anchor line with one fierce tug before casting off to the open ocean. "Well. Nothing to be done." He draws both hands back into his lap.

In the morning he is already sitting at the kitchen table when I come in. I pour a cup of coffee from the Mr. Coffee pot and walk to the windows, pull a little U in the aluminum blinds to look into the backyard, where the sun is still morning soft, rose and peach across the peeling wooden fence posts. The grass looks like a little boy's unruly hair—tangled with thick budding blades. As a girl I loved it when Dad let the grass grow long so I could pop out the tiny elliptical seeds along the stems and sprinkle them as seasoning over my mud-and-leaf stews.

I let the shade flip back into place and take a sip of the coffee, go back to the sink to brew a new pot, twice as strong. Dad sits in slivers of sunlight shimming through the closed blinds, holding the handle of his empty coffee cup. Where the light falls I can see all the details of his skin, rough brown patches of seborrheic keratoses, mulberry-colored stains of ruptured capillaries, sparse white hair. Alternating slashes of shadow camouflage the flaws.

"Do you want more coffee? I made a fresh pot."

He shakes his head. "No. I've been up since four. Can't sleep anymore, it seems. Old age."

"Your body makes less melatonin as you get older. Have you tried anything for it? Ambien sometimes . . ."

He waves the advice away like an annoying fly.

A mockingbird calls from the oak outside the back door, a sharp, impatient sound that defines his turf. I twirl the plastic wand that dangles from the end of the blinds and the gaps of sun flood together. "Do you remember the mockingbird that lived in the pecan tree in Dallas? Remember how he used to dive-bomb that orange tabby cat we had?" He looks at me but doesn't contribute to my childhood memory. Was he aware we had a cat? "I can still see him crouched at the bottom of the tree and that bird would go straight for his head. Mom kept a bottle of hydrogen peroxide on the washer to swab his scalp—his ears were covered with nicks. What was that cat's name?" His name was Chester, I know quite well.

Dad shrugs and keeps staring toward me, gazing somewhere over my left shoulder. I fight an urge to turn around. "It was Chester, I think. Do you remember Chester?" There is an unintended edge of accusation in my voice I find unsettling. "Listen, while I'm here, let me help out with things."

"What sort of things?"

"Whatever you need. Shopping. Organizing. I could clean out some of your closets or shelves, get the place in better order. Maybe we should get you some pill dispensers to help keep your medications straight. You're on a blood pressure pill, aren't you? Do you still take that?"

He cocks his head at me as if I puzzled him. I go on. "And your ophthalmologist must have given you some vitamins, for the macular degeneration. Are you taking them? I read a study a few months ago that showed a benefit . . ."

"Marie? Can you stop being a doctor for a day or so here? If you don't mind?"

I turn away from him and start scrubbing dishes. "Fine, Dad. I'm not trying to meddle. I just . . . I don't know how many days I can be away from work and I want to be useful to you. I like being useful."

"Don't they know you're on vacation?"

"Of course they do." I keep my face toward the sink. "But we've been short-staffed this summer. I could get called back. Let's at least go shopping for you. Get out of the house. When was the last time you were outside? Let's make a list." I dry my hands on the stained tea towel and go into his office at the front of the house, still so dark I have to turn on the light. The desk is heaped with articles about medieval city-states, academic journals, junk mail flyers and newspapers. The one on top is dated two months ago. I pull open the middle drawer to hunt down a blank notepad and crumpled papers and letters jam the uneven wooden slides. I jimmy out a ripped envelope from the electric company. The paper with Dad's address showing through the cellophane window is bright pink.

"Dad, what's this?" I say, all but storming back into the kitchen.

"What's what?" he asks, scraping his chair back to stare at me.

"These bills? From the electric company? Have you paid them yet?"

He takes them out of my hands, flips through them page after page. After a minute or two I take them away from him and sort through to retrieve the summary page. "They're going to turn off your lights in another week if you don't pay this. What about your water bill? And sewer bill? Have you just given up trying to keep on top of this stuff?" I feel like I'm dealing with a child. Was he thinking he would just hole up here until the house gradually went dead around him? I sit down at the table with the papers spilling off my lap and stare at the boomerangs dancing over the dingy Formica surface. How did such a ridiculous design ever get so popular?

After an empty minute of silence I look up at him, see him frowning out toward the green weedy lawn, the rotting fence, the caving garden shed, the leggy wands of my mother's roses, grown amok. I press the heels of my hands into my eyes and let out a broken sigh. *I* am the blind child here. "Oh, Dad. I'm sorry. I'm so sorry. You can't make out the numbers anymore, can you? I'll call the electric company later today. Maybe we can get you set up on an autopayment or something."

I scramble some eggs and cheese and we eat, patching together a safe conversation that doesn't reach too far back or too far forward in either of our lives. His mind is still sharp. I can see that. I wonder if it is more painful to be so acutely alert to the progressive failures of your body, whether it would be easier to lose cognition before corporeal function. After we eat I strip down his bed and carry stale sheets and mildewed towels into the laundry closet. The linen cabinet is empty, so I begin a search for fresh bedding and wind up at the back of my parents' walk-in closet. Twelve years after her death, all of my mother's clothes and shoes and sweaters and nightgowns are still here. They look like she changed out of them last night, has slipped out only to run to the grocery store or a garden club meeting.

I remember asking her once, somewhere on the cusp of childhood and adolescence, when I was beginning my own search for reason, what happens to us when we die. She avoided the standard Catholic text my father would have given, and said she didn't know for sure if there was a heaven or a hell, or whether we had to earn eternal life. But she did know that if heaven exists, we get there by being as kind to one another as we can be. And if there *isn't* a God, then what matters most is that we are as kind to one another as we can be.

I pull my fingers down the length of her blue flannel robe, plunge my face into the lining of her woolen coat, place my hand deep into the sole of one shoe, where her sweat left a perfect imprint of her toes. And like some short circuit of memory triggered by her aromas I crumple to the floor in the dark cove beneath her hanging dresses and sob.

After a dinner of frozen lasagna (the stamped expiration date is at least within the last year), I shower in the same pink tub I bathed in twenty years ago, waiting impatiently for hot water to drizzle through the calcified pipes. We will need to have some safety rails put up in here if he doesn't move.

The dimly lit hall leading to Lori's bedroom is lined with photos. One of my father showing off his first car—he looked so limber and wavy-haired—these days only skin and gray stubble cover the interlocked plates of his skull; Lori in her bassinet as a newborn, me standing next to her on tiptoe to peer beneath the baby blanket; three pictures of Dad accepting handshakes and certificates from now long-dead senior faculty; a framed oval portrait of my grandmother holding my infant father on her lap. His new teeth bite on a heavy gold crucifix suspended from a chain around her neck. It's the same crucifix he fastened around my mother's neck as she lay in her casket, and finally buried with her. I want to ask him if he abandoned God because he believed his religion could never forgive me. Did he, at the end of one grueling year, choose me?

I hear him snoring through his partially closed door, grateful he's fallen asleep before I came to say goodnight. His loneliness permeates everything in here—the faded slipcovers and dusty vase of crumbling dried flowers, the burned-out bulb in the side-table lamp. On every wall, from floor to ceiling, beneath the window ledges and above the fireplace mantel, are bookshelves. Bookshelves he used to stand in front of after dinner, running a finger along the leather and cloth and paper spines to pluck out the exact chapter or paragraph or single quotation that supported whatever discourse he had engaged my mother in, or lecture he was outlining on the Smith-Corona typewriter in his cluttered office. I would watch him sometimes, standing in the middle of the room, hands cocked on the back of his belt, looking over the rows and rows of titles, the chronologically cataloged stacks of journals and professional papers, his authored writings among them, searching the crowded and sagging shelves for no particular textbook or thesis or biography, but in unadulterated admiration of the accumulated wealth of human intellect bound up in the printed page.

These books, these words—*these* were his connection to the world. Every evening he was locked to his desk in reclusive silence, dissecting and digesting and rearticulating some translated parchment or fragment of doctrine he'd scavenged from a dead society, while his living daughters saw only the frown of his intellectual tangle, saw his eyebrows knot together as he unraveled some bit of historical minutiae, saw only a vague recognition of our own dilemmas if we interrupted him with our personal quandaries. His life was inside his mind and inside these books. Maybe he loved the words in these books more than us, or maybe these books were the tactile offering of his hidden mind, the only offering he knew how to give. My mother understood that, I'm beginning to realize. My mother understood that this was not a man of spoken and physical displays of love. These books, letters printed black against white, were the link between his internal world and the world our small family shared. And now he can't read them.

· 28 ·

A small mountain of soggy paper towels is growing in the middle of the floor and still the white weave turns brown after each swipe of the kitchen cabinets. I climb onto a chair to dislodge the bottles of Worcestershire and A-1 steak sauce and cooking sherry that are glued to the wood in a gum of spilled syrup. Scraps of the newspapers my mother had used to line the shelves chip off in a time warp of advertisements for Bee Gees music and campaign speeches for Jimmy Carter. The telephone rings again, the third time in half an hour, and I look over my shoulder at Dad. He turns up the volume on the television set and continues eating his tuna fish.

"Dad, do you want me to answer your phone?"

"I have an answering machine to answer the phone. I'm eating my lunch."

I jump down from the chair and reach over to pick up the receiver just before it clicks into the recording. "Hello?"

"Hello." There is a pause. "I found you."

"Hang on for a minute." I put the receiver down and say to Dad, "Could you hang this up after I pick up in the bedroom?" He seems to be dissecting his tuna salad, searching for some palatable bit of celery or egg, and then I realize that his eyes are directed at a blank space beyond his plate, and he's sorting through the mixed textures of food with his fingertips.

I run into the bedroom and take the receiver off the hook, then back to the kitchen to hang up that receiver, then back to the bedroom. "OK. You could have called me on my cell."

"You didn't answer it."

"You could have left a message."

"I guess I didn't think you'd return it."

"So how did you find me here?"

"You weren't at any of the first thirteen Heatons in Houston that I called." Joe gives me a minute to respond before asking, "Why? Were you hoping I *wouldn't* find you?"

I sit down on the edge of the bed. "Oh, not you in particular."

He laughs at this. "Glad I wasn't singled out. I thought maybe you'd gone to your sister's, but I didn't know her last name. Easier to start with your father."

"Would have been even easier to just knock on my door when you left the cake."

"Torte. So you got it."

"I got it."

Neither of us says anything then; each waits for the other to start some thread of conversation. I hear him breathing, a rhythm of small waves washing down thousands of miles of telephone line. Finally Joe says, "Should I hang up yet? Or should I just shoot myself?" He adds this last bit in the hick Ozark drawl he always teases me with.

"Well, if you shoot yourself, leave me your record collection. I can sell it to pay my legal fees."

"This will be long over before my record collection is worth that much. Did you meet the new lawyer yet?"

"Just before I left town. He's nicer than Donnelly, I think. Not sure that's a good thing in a defense attorney, though."

"I was wondering why you'd left so quickly. Everything OK?"

I twist the phone cord through my fingers. "Why? Have you heard something?"

"No," he says, almost too quickly. Then more gently: "Just offering to listen if you need to talk."

"Thanks. I'm OK. Tolerable, as Dad would say. How are *you*, now that you tracked me down?"

"Lonely. I was supposed to go on a bike trip this week with Katz, but he bagged out on it."

"What happened?"

"Some piddly-ass plans his wife made without even talking to him. She went into early labor."

"Oh wow! I didn't know Katz was having another baby. Is she all right?"

"She's fine. I think she's thirty-four weeks, so they're not too worried. But now I have a week's worth of gear packed in my panniers and no place to go. Which, coincidentally, ties in with your covetous designs on my records."

"How so?"

"I found a guy on eBay who's selling three hundred albums he found in his dead father's attic. Mainly Blue Note."

I turn over onto my stomach bunching a pillow under my chest, holding the phone up to my ear on one propped elbow. "And you got them?"

"Thanks to a good bottle of single-malt Scotch to lubricate my bidding frenzy, I did indeed. I'm flying to New Orleans to pick them up."

"Why can't he just ship them?"

"I haven't flown any long trips since I went to Toronto last fall. Besides, if you knew what I paid you'd know why I want to pick them up in person. At any rate, I thought I could stop over in Houston for a night on the way back."

I sit up again and push the bedroom door closed with my foot. When I don't answer immediately he asks, "Marie? Are you there?"

"Yeah, I'm here."

"I won't come if you don't want me to."

I take in a deep breath. "Come. You should come. It would be good to see you."

· 29 ·

"**How was the flight?** No close brushes with death?"

"Of course not. You have no faith in aerodynamics, Marie." Joe swings his battered leather satchel over his shoulder and pushes open the double glass doors exiting one of Hobby airport's fixed-base operator lobbies.

"No, I have no faith in humans. At least within the margin of error for flight."

"It was fine once I crossed the mountains. Clear skies all the way."

I haven't seen him since the night he slept with me, a few weeks and a lifetime ago; haven't seen him since I fell asleep in his arms and woke up to an empty bed. The memory of it twists and leaves me tongue-tied. He holds the lobby doors open for me and we walk out into the wavy heat toward the parking lot. At the car he leans forward to toss his bag onto the backseat and then turns toward me. Cupping his hand around the curve of my neck, he bends to kiss me, lightly, ambiguously. Still, the physical contact of his lips relaxes, somewhat, the unsettled status of our companionship.

"I looped down over Galveston Bay on the way in. It's nice out there, with the jetties going out into the water. We should fly over tomorrow. I could teach you to do some dives."

I laugh. "Be happy with getting me to fly at all, Joe. Sometimes I wonder how well you really know me!"

"To know someone is to try to change someone, isn't it?"

211

"That, Joe, may be why you've never married."

I shut the door after he slides in and walk around to the driver's side. "I made you a reservation at the Sheraton, near Dad's house. Is that OK?"

"Sure. Whatever. I can stay with you at your Dad's place, if you want me to."

"It's a mess over there—smells kind of funky. I don't even know where you'd sleep. Well, you'll see. I was going to pick up some barbecue and take it back there for lunch if you want to come. He's expecting to meet you. Besides, you can't fly all the way to Texas and not have barbecue."

"Arkansas has barbecue." Joe angles the air-conditioning vent upward so that it blows his sandy red hair away from his face, a tangled, freeform breeziness that suits him. A small gold stud glints in his earlobe. Thankfully, Dad's vision is too far gone for him to notice it.

"Maybe after he gets settled tonight we can go out for a while. How much time have you spent in Houston? I can't remember."

"I interviewed at the Texas Medical Center—Methodist. I was thinking about a cardiac fellowship. They run quite a show down here, don't they? I changed my mind when I saw the giant bronze statue of Michael DeBakey's hands—a little too godlike for my tastes."

"I'd forgotten you considered cardiac. You're not stuffy enough for cardiac."

"I had a great case yesterday—guy who'd had laryngeal cancer and I had to do a retrograde intubation over a cardiac catheter wire."

"Wow, I haven't done one of those since my residency." I rev the engine up the access ramp and onto the freeway, capturing a rare space between speeding vehicles. "So, any special requests while you're here? Any famous Houston landmarks you can't fly back without seeing?"

"What can you offer me?"

"Let's see. NASA? Neiman Marcus? The Astrodome? Lone Star Cafe?"

"Can't do Lone Star—didn't bring my cowboy boots. Take me to Astroworld."

"Are you serious?"

"I'm always serious, Marie. You know that." Around us cars and pickups and eighteen-wheelers ricochet around hundreds of miles of looping intersections and concrete ramps and construction barriers, driven with the brazen blind trust of contemporary frontiersmen. Joe sucks in his breath when a van cuts in front of me. He adjusts the sun visor and rolls the sleeves of his shirt halfway up his forearms, reaches across the cracking vinyl of the Buick's bench seat as if he might take my hand, then pulls away to scratch the nape of his neck.

I feel him look over at me but don't look back. He asks, "How've you been, since you got here?"

I keep my eyes fixed on the traffic. "I don't know. Distracted, at least. I'm too busy cleaning my dad's house to think about my own problems. He didn't even keep it up when he was younger—sort of the absentminded professor type. He ought to just sell the place so somebody can tear it down—the land is worth a lot these days. He could afford an extended-care apartment for as long as he needs."

"Have you talked to him about that?"

"I'm not a masochist, Joe. Or a hypnotist—which is what it would take to convince him to move. Oh, let's get off here." I grip the steering wheel with both hands and whip into the right lane between two cars with a bumper's width of room between us.

"Jesus, Marie." Joe braces himself against the dashboard. "You're starting to drive like these people. Slow down."

"You should have your seat belt buckled," I say. He looks agitated and pulls out a cigarette. "I'm worried you have a secret death wish, Joe. Seat belts, cigarettes, private planes . . . There's a great barbecue place down this block, if they haven't torn it down."

He cracks the window so the silvery trail of smoke snakes up and out over the top of the car. "I'll take a plane over these freeways any day."

"What for? Traveling or dying?"

"Either." He draws on the cigarette and exhales the smoke like a visible sigh. "Either one."

The freeway dumps us into a nest of prewar bungalows huddling below the glass and metal giants of downtown. The houses are painted

in the vivid Easter egg yellows and blues and lavenders my mother always associated with the Mexican barrios that percolate up through the
soul of all Texas cities like boiling springs, their mariachis and jalape-
ños and Spanish seared into our cultural palate.

It's still here, unchanged from my nights as a medical resident when
we would draw numbers to see who got to break away from the emergency room or intensive care unit to haul in greasy sacks of ribs and
cornbread. I pull the car up over the sidewalk onto the packed dirt of
a makeshift parking lot. Washboards of pork and beef ribs and whole,
brown-basted chickens are smoking in pipe-vented, half-barrel cook-
ers lined up behind a clapboard shack. A massive elm cuts the sun, its
sooty umbrella of boughs as cured and aromatic as the smoking meat.

"Dad and I both love this stuff. Clogs your arteries even to smell it.
Best barbecue in Houston. What do you want?"

"Baby backs." He crouches down to scratch the chin of a ragged-
looking cat with swollen teats. "How is your dad's eyesight?"

"He can get around the house. He hasn't tried to drive since I got
here—that's another conversation we're putting off. He doesn't want
me to talk to his ophthalmologist."

"Can't you call him anyway?"

"Not while he's competent—you know the laws on that."

Joe sits down at the nearest picnic table; the cat twines between his
legs and then jumps into his lap. He rakes it back to the ground and it
slinks across the dirt to a bank of garbage cans.

"Joe, don't hurt her! She must have kittens somewhere."

"Damn cat clawed me."

A young boy in barbecue-stained overalls comes out of the house
with two large grocery bags stapled across the top. Joe stretches out one
leg and digs into his jeans pocket. "I'll get this. Hey, *niño, aquí. No, no.
Todo es para usted*," he tells the boy, folding a fifty-dollar bill into his
hand.

He's appeasing me now, about the cat. He opens a corner of one of
the bags and peels off a shred of chicken that he tosses into the shrubs
where she is crouched and she pounces on it, starved. The car is even
quieter on the drive home. I point out landmarks; he comments on the

weather. I turn on the radio to fill the silence. We are both wondering why he is here.

"Dad?" Joe follows me into the living room and drops his duffle on the end of the sofa; dust motes spiral up from the cushion. "He must be in the bedroom. Wait here a minute."

When I come back he is leaning over the TV cabinet studying a photograph of my mother. "She looks like you."

"No, I look like her. Dad's just getting up from a nap. He'll be out in a minute. Want some tea? Coffee?"

"Beer?"

"Don't have any." He waves away the offer and roams through the living and dining rooms.

"This is just how I'd imagined it," he says.

"And how is that?"

"Oh, a history professor's home. Shades drawn, solid, practical furniture. Books and books and more books. How old were you when you lived here?"

"They moved here from Dallas when I was in eleventh grade. I hardly lived here at all."

"Doesn't look like it was a home that ever held kids."

"I guess our house in Dallas didn't ever really look like any kids lived in it, either. I think my parents sort of expected us to be adults a few months after we got out of diapers. My father, at least."

"Oh, oh, oh. Now look at this." Joe slides back the door of a battered wooden cabinet beside the fireplace. Inside it is the stereo my father bought at Millard's Hi-Fi on Lovers Lane when I was in seventh grade, infuriating my mother, who was coping with a flooded washing machine at the time and scraping nickels together for repairs.

He squats down to look at the records standing on the bottom shelf. "He's got an original Burl Ives in here. I wonder if that's collectable."

"Don't tease him, Joe."

"Who's teasing? You can sell anything on eBay. My God, and *The Best of Lawrence Welk*!"

"Diamond needle on that. Weighs less than one gram," my father says from the doorway. He stands in his undershirt and loose trousers watching Joe leaf back the albums beneath the turntable. "No computerized, digitized music can match that for resonance."

"Dad, this is Joe Hillary."

"Nice to meet you, Dr. Heaton." He rises and walks over to shake Dad's hand. How funny to hear the address of "Dr. Heaton" directed at someone other than myself—I wonder if anyone has called him that since he stopped teaching.

"Tall son of a gun, aren't you?" my father says.

"Joe's flying back to Seattle from New Orleans, Dad. He's a pilot."

My father studies Joe frankly, scanning his features, unconcerned with the social graces of smiles or small talk. "Which carrier do you work for?"

"No, Dad, Joe's a doctor—an anesthesiologist, at my hospital. Remember? He's an amateur pilot, I guess I should have said. He flew his own plane down."

"That's quite a haul, Houston to Seattle. You can run into to some weather over the Rockies. What do you fly?"

"Piper Navajo, twin engine. I can make it in a little over eight hours if conditions are good. I stopped overnight in Salt Lake on my way to New Orleans, just to break it up. Do you know planes?"

"Had a brother that flew the F-86 in Korea. Took me up one time in a T-33 trainer."

Joe lights up at this. "Now the F-86 was a plane I would have fought to fly."

"Well, that's what he thought, too. Didn't make it through to the end, though." He stares up at Joe, his mouth partially open and his brows low over the top of his glasses.

Joe slips his hands back in his pockets. "I'm sorry to hear that."

"Long time ago now." Dad waves the memory away as if it were a gnat buzzing around his face. "Well, make yourself at home. I'm headed out to the store, so Marie can get you settled in."

"Joe's staying downtown, Dad. I'm gonna run him over to his hotel later. Why don't I do your shopping for you after that? Then you don't have to go out."

"I want to go out." Dad looks from me back up at Joe. "She wants me to stop driving. Probably told you that already. How about a beer—always good on a hot day." He heads off into the kitchen, leaving us to follow or fend for ourselves.

"I brought back some barbecue for lunch," I call after him. "I don't think we have any beer."

"Doesn't want me to drink, either. All right. How about some barbecue and water?"

Joe shrugs his shoulders at me and follows Dad out through the dining room into the kitchen.

"So you have to fly IFR to get here? Got your instrument rating?" Dad is filling glasses at the sink and Joe is peeling cardboard lids back from the tinfoil pans of ribs and chicken and sauce. The smell of barbecue beats back vague odors of bacon grease and bruised bananas and a dank wisp of mold rising from the graying sink sponge.

"Yeah, they require IFR over the mountains. We have enough cloudy weather in Seattle I decided to go for instrument training after I moved up there. Marie tells me you were a history professor at Rice."

"I taught there until 1987."

"What was your concentration?"

"Medieval European history, leaving me little enough in common with my doctor daughter here. Marie, sit down and eat, would you? It's ruining my appetite to watch you sterilizing the counters. We're not going to be operating on anybody in here today."

"Fine, Dad. I'm just trying to be helpful."

He scrapes the wooden legs of his chair around on the linoleum floor to face Joe. "Haven't seen her in three years—all she wants to do is clean. Do you get much opportunity to fly? Frederick—my brother—used to say doctors made lousy pilots. Said they were always too busy to put in enough hours, and too cocky to know when to get the hell out of the sky."

I'm cringing at this but Joe laughs. "He was right, your brother. We tend to have more money than common sense, I guess. I get to fly three or four times a month. That's another good reason to take long trips like this one—to keep my skills up."

Dad purses his lips, unabashedly judging Joe, sizing him up. Joe is unfazed, smiling back at him as if he welcomed the appraisal. "Well, Lordy. Must cost you as much as a ticket to fuel that plane this far."

"Yes sir," he says, slipping easily into the courtesies of his Southern upbringing. "More actually. Maybe my funds outpace my own common sense. So did your brother get to fly the P-51 in Korea?"

"No, they only flew those in the earliest part of that war. There was one on his base up there at Bergstrom, though. Back when it was still military. I would have been over there with him but for my eyesight— even back then I needed Coke bottle glasses. Too much reading. You from Texas?"

"Arkansas. We just sound like we're from Texas. I grew up on a farm outside of Little Rock."

"Flying planes and being a doctor is a long way from farming, is it not? How did you come to study the sciences?"

"My granddad considered himself a healer. He was Cajun—moved up from outside of New Orleans to Arkansas just after the Depression. He started planning for me to study medicine before I was born, I think."

I lean back against the kitchen sink and watch Joe draw more words out of my father than I've managed to since I got here. I watch the two of them coasting above simple questions of social introduction into something that seems basic and genuine—an easy exchange of personal facts and interests unpolluted by decades of unmentioned injury, their conversation absent the awkward stalls of my obligatory questions and his recalcitrant replies. My father, this widowed scholar, who has always, always kept his mind so locked up from me; who has never, as far as I can recall, bothered to ask me why I, the daughter of a history professor, would prefer the calculations of chemistry and pharmacology, would choose a profession where mathematical models were applied to comprehend the human condition. He has never asked why I would choose to find my answers in the objective manipulation of facts and formulas instead of his own endless parsing of the fragmented scraps left by doomed populations groping to find godly design in random famines and plagues.

Joe leans back on the rear legs of his chair, balancing his glass on his knee, the damp circle of it bleeding in a dark ring. After looking forward so to Joe's arrival—the first thing I've been actually happy about in weeks—I feel lonelier with the three of us than I did before he got here.

"Dad, I'm going to run to the grocery store now, while Joe's here with you. Do you guys want anything? Besides beer?"

"Get me some more of those frozen pies, would you? A couple of the chicken pies. I'll have one for my dinner." He looks back over at Joe. "Not bad, those pies. Have everything you need for a complete meal right in the one tin."

"I'll make you dinner. Take a break from the frozen food while I'm here," I say.

"I like frozen food."

Joe drops his chair back on all fours. "Hey, I've had those pies. They're really pretty good, Marie. The turkey's even better—get him some of those. So did you ever fly yourself?" Joe turns his attention back to my father. I slip my purse over my shoulder and walk out the back screen door to the car.

An hour later I stand with my arms full of grocery bags and kick the bottom of the kitchen door hoping they'll open it for me. After minutes of silence I slide one paper bag down and wedge it between my hip and the door jamb so I can wiggle my key into the lock. Inside, the kitchen is empty. Joe's half-drunk glass of water sits on the floor beside his opened duffel bag, and the dismantled skeleton of a barbecued chicken lies on their empty plates. Through the living room archway I can see Joe's leg stretched among stacks of record albums, my father's brown wing tips planted below his upright recliner.

"Artie Shaw, now he was a great bandleader. You probably never even heard of him."

"Oh, he's heard of him. Joe, you look like you're in garage sale heaven."

"This is still in the original dust jacket. Even has the band's flyer. Did you see this, Marie? He's got a whole closet full of vinyl. No rock and roll, though, huh?"

He looks like Peter Pan awash in plunder. A tall and golden boy sprawled across my father's filthy, sculpted pink carpet—a provocative mix of insouciance and potent masculinity. Even my father is charmed.

"It's four forty-five you guys. What's the plan for this evening? Should I start some dinner?"

"Good Lord, Marie. We just finished lunch. Why don't you show this young man Houston after he flew all the way down here for a two-day junket." Pushing himself up from his chair, he gyrates in a tiny circle before reclaiming his balance and stepping over a pile of Gene Autry and Jeanette MacDonald. He tugs at the waistband of his pants; a thinning clump of white hair sprouts from the V of his undershirt. He was Joe's age the year I was born.

"All right. That sounds good. We can drive him around and then go out for dinner somewhere. Anywhere you want, Dad. My treat."

He cants his head back to angle a look at me through the periphery of his glasses. "Hell, I don't want to go. You go." He raises his arm in some gesture between good-bye and disgust. "You go."

"What will you eat?"

"Same damn food I've been eating for the last twenty years."

Joe is holding a record between his palms as if it were a black diamond, tilting it back and forth to catch the few rays of sunlight coming between the perpetually closed living room drapes. "Johnny Hartman. Not a scratch or speck of dust on it. Amazing."

"Where to?" We are stacked up at a red light behind matched convertible Jeeps filled with teenagers calling back and forth to each other over the roar of Friday rush hour traffic. A girl in groin-high cutoffs and a tank top is flicking popcorn into the backseat of the other car and bits of it catch in the evening breeze to settle on our windshield. She stretches over the gap to dump her red-striped paper bag into the driver's lap just before the light changes, perfect curves and gilded hair arresting the cars behind her.

"Hey, I think I like Texas. What did you ask me? I don't care where we go. Wherever you want to take me," says Joe.

"I'm not sure I've ever been the one to take *you* anywhere," I answer, jerking forward through the green light with a screech of tire.

"What's bothering you?"

"What makes you think I'm *bothered*?" I ask, immediately wishing I could take back my sarcastic repetition of the word.

"Well, aren't you?"

All I can do is shrug a shoulder. We weave through the racetrack of the freeway, a thousand cars flooding bumper to bumper at seventy miles an hour, each an instant away from an accident. I let the traffic push us up the ramp onto the massive cement loop that ensnares Houston like a belt straining against the paunch of the city's middle age.

"It's your dad, isn't it? You're annoyed at me for hitting it off with him."

"I think it's great you hit it off with him. You cheered him up more in two hours than I have in three days. You're the son he never had! Why should that bother me?"

He just looks at me for a minute, then whispers barely above the volume of the surrounding traffic, "I didn't grow up with him, Marie. He didn't raise me. It's easy for me to like him."

"So now I need a psychiatrist in addition to a team of lawyers." My eyes start to burn and I reach over to my purse and feel around inside it for my sunglasses, but after I put them on Joe closes his hand over mine and holds it quietly in his own. Our hands lie interlaced between us on the car seat. Joe watches the city, the sunset igniting the glass skyscrapers into beacons of commercial American triumph.

"Look!" he shouts, breaking his hand free to point at a green highway sign. "There's the exit for Astroworld."

I don't answer.

"My one request. Seriously."

· 30 ·

"I can't believe I let you talk me into this. God, I haven't been here since I was in high school. It's gotten bigger. Disneyland may be cleaner, but Astroworld has a raunch factor that's kind of hard to beat."

"Raunch factor?" Joe asks, pushing through the metal turnstile behind me.

"Oh, you know, spilled beer and tight tank tops. Plenty of bare skin and Texas twang. Everybody wanted to come here on a date—all those scary tunnel rides where you could neck without being caught."

"Who did you come here with?"

"Well, I mainly came with girlfriends hoping we'd leave with boys. I didn't date much in high school."

Joe stops walking and pulls me around to face him. "Really? I'm surprised. You must have been pretty, even as a gawky kid."

"Not really. I didn't think so, at any rate. I was more the type that won the blue ribbon at the science fair."

He keeps looking at me, like he's rummaging through the decades of my life before he knew me. Then his eyes move down to my neckline and he reaches out to press his thumb gently over the pink sapphire. "You're wearing it. Thank you."

"No, thank *you*." I bring my hand up and cover his own at my throat, holding it there for a moment before swinging it back down to the more neutral territory between us. "I never thanked you for it, and

222

it's beautiful." We turn to walk down the packed aisles of postcard vendors and game arcades. I jump at the sharp flack of gunfire where pim-
pled boys vie for plastic bears and girls' affection. Joe wraps my hand in
his large palm, calm and floating above it all, more relaxed than he was
when we were driving in from the airport—like some broken fragment
of himself has floated back into place, settling some internal argument
with the world. If I hold his hand long enough, knit my fingers tightly
enough into his, could I also come to peace?

"Hot dog?" We stand in the smoke of a massive iron grill, the heat
of charcoal folding into the heat of the summer night and the allur-
ing aroma of roasting meat. I pull my hand out of Joe's and wipe my
face on the end of my shirt. The cook, a black mountain of a man unflinching in the splattering grease, forks hissing sausages, peppers and
onions onto two white buns. Joe slips ten dollars into his apron and
takes the hot dogs, then leads the way to a patch of green grass sloping between asphalt pathways. I have to lean far over my crossed legs
to keep the grilled onions from oozing onto my lap. Next to us a tat-
tooed boy buries his face in his girlfriend's neck. The lights of the mid-
way flash against the darkening sky and the volume of all of it—the
carousel music and laughter, the blazing neon and the smoky smell of
sweat—pulsates. Arcing across the skyline, a mammoth roller coaster
shoots cars filled with screaming riders like a jet of blood through the
great vessels of the heart.

"Come on." Joe grabs my arm. "We gotta ride that thing."

"Uh-uh. I don't do roller coasters, Joe. I hate roller coasters." I plant
my feet against the asphalt, blocking the crowd.

"Oh come on, you're kidding. You can't leave here without riding
that! That's like dying without trying sex."

"No, no, no, no, no siree." I lock both my hands around his wrist
and throw my weight against him.

"Come on." He slips his fingers through mine again. His voice drops
to a supplication. "Come with me. Please."

I tug against him once more, but then let myself be led to the line
at the bottom of the concrete ramp winding up to the ride. My pulse is
starting to race. It's ridiculous. I know riding this roller coaster is safer

than driving in my car, safer than swimming in the ocean or running alone in Lake Washington parks on early winter evenings—all things I would never give up. And I'm panicked.

Joe stands behind me and folds his arms across my clavicles, brings his head down to the crook of my neck to whisper, "I met my first girl-friend at a fair in Little Rock. Spent a week's worth of lawn mowing money just to get her on the roller coaster, imagining she'd have to hold tight to me the whole ride." The striped cotton sleeves of his shirt are rolled up over his forearms, exposing the ropy twist of blue veins braided over the muscles—so much power in a man whose work de-rives from the strength of his mind. His arms feel good around my neck, solid and decisive, like something that lasts, something that could bear a burden.

"And did she? Is that where you got your first kiss?"

He laughs. "She was my first kiss, as a matter of fact, but not on that ride. She got sick. Threw up on me right at the top of the third loop." We laugh until we are folded over and the teenagers around us look as if we have infringed on something sacred to youth, we who are old enough to be their parents. And *this*, I remember, *this* is why, for at least a brief time in my life, I had wondered if I could let Joe change my life. The giddiness of it tumbles into the tremor of anticipation at catapulting along the spiraling tracks of the coaster, and I am abruptly drugged with life, drugged with the aliveness of the present, electrified and forgiven, temporarily, for the death of a little girl.

The silver railing hisses back and Joe steps into the car, clasps my hand and pulls me in beside him. A padded steel bar clamps down across my knees. Joe's hand presses into the back of my neck as if he can read my panic. "You'll be fine. Let your muscles relax." His fingers massage the taut bands running parallel along my spine. "Look, do you trust me?"

"Sometimes." I try to swallow, but my mouth is too dry. "Until now, maybe!"

"Let me cover your eyes."

"Are you crazy?" I yell, my heart starting to pound so hard I'm lightheaded, and the roller coaster at a standstill.

"No, really. Lean against me." He brings his palms up over my eyes. My eyelashes brush against his skin like butterfly wings skittering against a closed window. The world condenses into the cupped flesh of his hands. The train jerks forward and I try to pull his hands down. "No," he says, his mouth just beside my ear so his voice comes from inside of me. "You're all right. Focus on this one instant in time. This single split second."

The car rolls smoothly into the first turn, a gliding arc that draws me deeper into the seat, swooshes the air against my arms and cheeks, feathers the hair back from my face. My weight melds into the sliding curve of the track, my stomach and intestines and liver and spleen drop deeper into my pelvis. Now the curve opens out into a straight line and now the wheels catch and grip onto a chain hauling us forward and up-ward, up to what must be the first plunge back toward the earth. I tense and reach up to Joe's hands again.

"Ah, you're thinking. You're anticipating. Try to be right here, in this moment. You're safe—it's the perfect chance to let go."

The car hovers at the top of the peak, teasing, then with a silent re-lease of the brake it tips across the edge of balance. Screams rise up in a noisy plume, and I hear my own voice mixed among those of strangers. With my eyes covered the fall is endless. It is as terrifying as my worst repetitive dreams, scrambling to claw a purchase in the air, shrieking to the ground knowing this is the end of my life. I hate Joe right now. The car twists and dips in a spiral to the right and then whips back to the left, and I'm trapped here, choking with panic.

Joe is laughing, clearly having the time of his life. "Marie," he says in a jovial scream that makes me want to push him over the side. "Try it. Just give yourself up to it."

And so, trapped and blind beside Joe, I force myself toward the conscious act of letting go, and wind inwardly closer and closer, tighter and tighter into this moment, this fraction of an instant, this incan-descent flicker of time even before the electrical synapse of thinking blisters into a concept of individual being. I exist only now. A now of atoms more vacuous than solid, transiently amalgamated into human form before splintering into mineral and water and air, like a personal diaspora, a random dispersion of all that was Marie. The completely profound senselessness of my own existence explodes into its own blissful freedom. There is no impending moment, no past moment, only this one, and without past there is no sorrow, and without future there can be no loss.

· 31 ·

I pull under the awning at the Sheraton and Joe squeezes my hand. "Come up."

"All right." I return the pressure of his hand and smile at him. The valet approaches my window and I nod, then pop open the trunk for Joe's bag. The glass doors of the lobby, wide as a wall, swoosh open, and refrigerated air pours out into the night with oil-rich Texan abandon. As soon as we step through the entryway the sticky glaze of humidity evaporates from my skin.

"Wait in the bar for me and I'll check in."

I sit at a small table in the corner and try to look upscale enough to pay the bill, despite my cotton candy and grease-stained blue jeans and shirt. I should have at least brushed my hair. The waitress doesn't even bring the drink menu until Joe joins me.

"I'll just have sparkling water, thanks," I say, pushing the menu across to Joe.

"Really? I want a good, crisp martini. I love these dark hotel bars. Make me feel like Humphrey Bogart."

The minute the words are out of him a lithe woman in skintight black sequins taps the microphone on a small corner stage and sways into a torch song. She has a fluid, chesty resonance that could express the anguish of sexual longing even without words.

" 'Pretty Strange.' "

"What's strange about her?" I ask.

227

Joe smiles at me. " 'Pretty Strange.' It's the name of the song."

"Back when you were in your prime/Love was just a waste of time," she sings, holding the microphone close to her mouth. The piano player behind her is crinkled with age and cigarettes.

Joe reaches out and taps the waitress as she's turning away. "Vodka martini. Stoli. And a lemon drop."

"I'm driving, Joe."

"One is legal. Man, she's got this song nailed. Listen to her timing." He leans back, lost in her throaty spell, his fingers unconsciously drumming the beat against the bar table. Our drinks arrive at the end of the song, and he lifts his glass to toast me. "Hey, cheers. To your first fearless roller-coaster ride." He clinks the rim of his glass against mine and looks over the icy vodka into my eyes. "May it be the first of many."

Two lemon drops later I follow him into the elevator and up to a plush room that looks out over the city lights, wrapped like a sparkling package in ruby and platinum ribbons of roads. In the distance, lit up like a city unto itself and crowned with a jet of blue flame, a refinery churns the carbon of ancient swamps into jet fuel and gasoline.

Joe stretches his long frame across the window. "OK, I am completely disoriented up here. Is that where your dad's house is? Isn't that over near Rice?" He nods toward the farthest cluster of lights within the beltway.

"No, it's just beyond those towers, in the darker area." I tuck my hands into the front pockets of my jeans. "So what *did* you and my dad talk about while I was at the store?"

"Music, mainly. And airplanes. You, a little."

I look up at him. "Anything I wouldn't want to hear about?"

He scowls briefly, almost as if the question were irritating, but then winks at me. "Nah. All safe stuff." He walks over to the mini bar and comes back with two plastic cups and a miniature bottle of Beefeater.

"No thanks, I'm spinning as it is," I tell him when he holds a half-filled cup out for me.

He takes a sip of his own and asks, "What do *you* talk to him about?"

"Oh, things get pretty quiet once we venture beyond food or weather. Can't you tell?"

He smiles and raises his glass as if to toast my honesty. "It's palpable, the tension between you two. Is he just getting defensive about needing more help?"

"Oh no. This has nothing to do with his eyesight or his health. We've been like this since I was in my teens. Even now, with me here to take care of him, we have the same stiff conversations we had when I was young. It's so ingrained it takes over when I talk to him, like some automatic motor memory, the way your hands can play a piano piece you haven't thought about in a decade."

Joe empties his cup and sets it on the round table beside the draped floral curtains, then turns back to study the view. I seize the chance to switch the subject. "That's the Texas Medical Center over there. Those towers back behind Rice."

"Wow. It looks as big as Seattle. I bet it's doubled in size since I was there."

"Yeah, it makes First Hill look pretty paltry." We're both quiet for a minute, and then the question burning at the back of my mind breaks loose. "How are things at First Lutheran, anyway?" He tenses his shoulders in a quick shrug. "Has anybody heard about . . ." I sit down on the edge of the bed and hold my breath for a second. "About the criminal charge?"

"Marie, there *isn't* a criminal charge yet—if ever."

So. It's out. "How did you hear about it?" The words come in a hoarse whisper. I stare at his turned back and see his shirt stretch taut across his shoulders as he inhales and seems to brace himself. "OK," he says. "There was something in the newspaper. Just a short clip—your name wasn't even mentioned. They called Phil Scoble for a quote and he pretty much punted it. Just said the hospital was investigating."

I fall backward onto the bed and draw my knees up. "It's in the *newspapers*? The Seattle newspapers?"

"It was just a blurb on the inside pages. Nobody outside First Lutheran would ever know what it was about, that it involved you at all."

"What did it say? Did you cut it out?"

"It just said the death of a child undergoing routine surgery was being investigated. That's all. They didn't name anybody except Phil, and he gave them some pablum shtick that wouldn't raise any eyebrows."

I lie on the bed with my arms locked across my abdomen, closing my eyes to keep back tears. The light beyond my lids flickers as Joe walks over, the bed yields to his weight when he lies down next to me.

"Has your lawyer told you anything?"

"He's meeting with the district attorney on Tuesday. Even then he might not know if I'm charged. I'd thought at least, if this got dropped, no one would hear about it."

Joe seems to flinch. He says, hesitantly at first, "Maybe it's worse for you to be here, with so much time to think about it. I mean, don't you think the criminal charge is just a Darryl Feinnes gimmick? No jury's going to be convinced you've done anything criminal. For Christ's sake, you're a doctor." He turns my head toward his face. "Marie, go easier on yourself. You're not the only doctor at First Lutheran who's gotten hit with a malpractice suit. It's like you've become a martyr for this girl."

"Maybe she needs a martyr. Maybe I'm just the only one thinking about something other than the money," I say, almost sharply.

"Or maybe your grief goes way beyond this one accident in your life." He drops his voice down a notch. "Come on. Don't get mad at me. I know the money seems like all Hopper and Scoble care about anymore, but try to look at it another way. That girl's mother is about to walk away with more dollars than she could spend in a lifetime." I start to get up off the bed and Joe puts his arm across my waist. "Wait. I'm not saying that fixes it. Don't look at me like that. But she does have a future, at least. She can move. She can buy her own house, wherever she wants. She never has to work at a job she hates. She'll have choices she never would have had."

"It makes me sick to talk about it. It sounds so callous."

"I don't mean it to be callous. But even if you only half believe it, couldn't you stand some relief from guilt? It's OK to stop hurting for her." He takes my hand in his and I feel the ridged texture of his fingertips, the rebounding, giving fullness of the veins crossing his tendons, their persuasive strength—and I relax against him.

"Sometimes I think hurting for her is the only part of me that's still alive. People keep asking me how I am. I feel like they should be asking *what* I am. What am I if I can't be a doctor? What will I be if they take that away from me? I used to know, before medical school and internship and residency. Before First Lutheran and its sixty-hour workweeks. My career, becoming a doctor, was supposed to be one stop along the way to a whole life—this great, altruistic job where I could help people live longer, or live better. Or at least live with less pain. All so they could go back to whatever truly mattered in their lives—their husbands and their mothers and their kids—the things that were supposed to be waiting at home for me, too, at the end of my workday. And now I don't even have a workday. Oh God, listen to me. Don't ever let me drink two lemon drops on an empty stomach. I drink too much when I'm with you, Joe."

He rolls up on one winged elbow so his inky blue eyes are right above mine. "You're beautiful when you're drunk. You're beautiful anyway," he responds to my scowl. "Just . . . shinier, somehow, when you drink."

"Shinier?"

He shakes his head and hesitates, then says, "You let more holes open up in your cloak." He focuses past me, into some distant inner place. His cheek resting against his closed fist deepens the furrows at the corner of his eye and around his mouth, so that his face seems divided in two, one half etched with the inelasticity of age, the other half youthfully forgiven in the soft bedside lamplight.

"What are you talking about?" I ask.

"Hmmm," he murmurs. "It's this theory I have about death. About what happens when we die." He refocuses on my face and brushes my hair from my throat, winding his fingers into the tangled strands, fanning it out onto the pillow around my head. "Haven't I told you about the 'Big Oh' theory I have?"

I give a short laugh, glad to be distracted again. "The 'Big Oh'? Great name!"

"It *is* a great name. When I was eight . . . I can't believe I haven't told you this before. . . . When I was eight I went to a Halloween party as a cigarette—give me a break, more people smoked back then. Anyway"—his eyes drift into space again—"I'd wrapped myself in a cylinder of cardboard and cut out eyeholes. I could hardly see. I forgot to cut a slot for my hands—couldn't even put candy in my mouth, so you can guess the costume didn't last very long. All the sounds were muffled through the cardboard. Couldn't smell anything. And I remember, really vividly, how different my house looked and felt to me. Everything cropped down to a fragment of itself. My folks . . . I remember my dad's belt buckle jiggling up and down while he was yelling at my mom, and the buttonhole just above it straining against his big old belly. And my mother at the sink washing the dishes. How every time she made some point to Dad in whatever they were arguing about—I couldn't hear all the words—dribbles of soap streamed off her arms onto the floor. All I could see were these foamy globs dangling from the bony point of her elbow while she jabbed away at his chest.

"Then my father yanked the costume off over my head and all of a sudden the room, our kitchen, just exploded around me. Huge, and brand-new, and kind of . . . luminous. The light was so bright, everything looked almost crystallized. And the smells. Everything that had looked so splintered suddenly snapped back together into my whole, comprehensible world." He leans over me, his fingers laced through my hair to press against my scalp, looking intently into my eyes, as if he had to transmit this concept of universal order directly from mind to mind without words. "And for that split second, in a house where nothing ever, ever made sense to me, I suddenly understood it all, at least for a moment. That was my moment of the big 'Oh.'"

I try to picture his face as it must have looked at eight years old, without the rough stubble of beard, without the sun- and cigarette-creased lines of skepticism and self-reliant defiance, without the almost perfectly camouflaged shard of pain flickering in the deepest recess of those deep, deep blue irises. I want to shelter it, this exquisitely wrapped gift from his life, delivered from a time he never talks about. "And how does this become death, your moment of 'Oh'?" I whisper.

"Well, that's how we stumble around all the time, isn't it? So cloaked and fettered we can't really make sense of any of it. Believing it's so complicated. Here, alive, we have five senses. I think maybe there, after we die, we have . . . millions. Billions."

It is such an uncharacteristically hopeful suggestion coming from Joe, to be honest. How gratifying it would be to have faith that all this muddling through we do—the missed opportunities and mistaken blame—might eventually worm its way out to an answer. Maybe with a billion senses unleashed I could understand why Jolene died—not just what caused her death, but for what reason, for what purpose. Maybe with a billion senses connecting us, Bobbie Jansen and I could explain to each other why our lives ever had to intersect, why she gave birth to the child I won't have only to lose her in my hands. But how would a billion senses compensate an eight-year-old girl when she had yet to discover her own life? Even eternal bliss can be robbed by such brevity of experience among the living.

Joe cups his palms around my face and turns it back toward his. "You're thinking about her, aren't you? About Jolene." I stare past him to the ceiling, finding pictures in the nubs of plaster like tea leaves— both of us are looking for answers outside ourselves.

"She's everywhere I go." I say it too softly for my voice to break. "She and her mother. She's in every school yard I pass, in grocery lines and the car next to me at traffic lights. I didn't just kill Jolene. I killed her mother. I killed her reason for being. All the money in the world can't change that." I reach up and put my hand on his cheek, making him listen to me as if he had to live inside my conscience. "Joe, I want you to find her. Bobbie Jansen. I want you to find out what's happened to her. Where she goes, if she has any friends. I know where she lives— it's in south Beacon Hill." He is shaking his head. I push myself up from the bed onto my elbow and grip his shoulder. "It's not stalking, Joe. It's not illegal, or even immoral. I can't go there myself anymore—she saw me once. I just . . ." He is looking at me as if I have tipped over some balance of sanity. "Oh God. Don't you get it? It doesn't matter what the judges say. It doesn't matter if I'm totally cleared if I know she . . . How can I go on with my own life when I've destroyed hers?"

Joe lifts my hand from his shoulder and brushes it against his lips; he sweeps tears off my cheeks and chin. "Sweet Marie. A death behind you and a death before you." I close my eyes and try to will the tears to stop. Joe leans back on one arm and braids his fingers through my hair again, softly combing it away from my face. "You and your father don't know each other very well anymore, do you?"

"I'm not sure we ever knew each other very well. Certainly not past adolescence. It always felt fragile, his loving me. As if it was an obligation instead of an emotion."

Joe strokes the planes and curves of my face, tracing the lines of my forehead and the folds of my eyes, the arc of my jaw. Now the silence between us feels as patient as time. He starts to tell me something, then stops himself, plainly considering his words, and begins again. "Your dad said something to me about you this afternoon, while you were out. He said—" Joe hesitates and looks away from me, as if that might make it easier for him to keep talking. "He said he never understood why you hadn't gotten married, that he thought you were too lovely and too smart to have so much trouble with love." His hands are still now; only his breath brushes against my skin. "He said he blamed himself. It was his own fault."

I curl away from Joe into a tight knot and he wraps himself around me, laying his head next to mine. "What?" he asks. "What happened?"

His mouth is so close his whispered question fills the room, floods my mind, unravels my life back to a place I'm still learning how to leave, a time I've spent twenty-two years apologizing for. He is so close I barely hear my own voice when I tell him, and the raw flesh of that year bleeds out of me again. "I got pregnant when I was fifteen." Joe doesn't move, but I feel his arms grow stronger around me. My throat constricts and I have to consciously let go before I can keep talking. "I was a counselor at a summer camp and I met a boy there, another counselor; we both worked in the stables. He was from Arkansas—near your hometown. I didn't have any experience with boys. I'd never even been asked on a date. I would have been too shy to go. And, I wanted to be *liked* by him. I needed him so much he couldn't stand me by the end of the summer." I'm quiet again for a moment, listening to Joe's even breaths.

"I found out I was pregnant after I got home. There wasn't any question about keeping it. Not in my mind. I told Mom—she drove me across two counties to a clinic just to be sure nobody would recognize us. There were protestors outside carrying signs with pictures of fetuses. Shouting at us when we went in. Something hit the back of my coat and my mother started crying behind her sunglasses—I'm sure she thought I didn't see her.

"She wanted me to talk to my father about it—begged me to. She couldn't stand it, having this ugly, hidden thing unspoken among all of us, but I made her swear not to tell him. And then about a week later I started bleeding. I must have had endometritis—I had a high fever and horrible cramping. They had to take me into the emergency room in the middle of the night. I remember my dad carrying me into the waiting room wrapped in this pink ruffled bedspread, his arms trembling under my weight when he lifted me out of the car. And as sick as I was, I still remember being terrified he'd find out.

"Before the doctor even came in, my dad asked me straight out. He asked me what I'd done. So I told him. I told my Catholic father about the boy from camp, and the clinic. And how sorry I was. I remember that examining room as clearly as if we were in it right now, a small white box of a room with this fluorescent light glaring down over us, and the smell of disinfectant everywhere, and my nightgown sticking to me with blood." I hold my outstretched hand before my eyes, as if I could blot out that blinding light, then clutch it back across my chest. "My father didn't speak to me for an entire year. Not one word."

Joe lies still, curved along the length of my back. He brings his hand up to my face, haltingly at first, brushing his fingers across my brow, light as the shimmer of music down the strings of a violin, even the slight roughness of his skin like the singing of a musician's calluses along the corded length of the frets. My face tingles where he traces my eyelashes, my eyelids, my temple and cheek, the ridged curve of my ear, the vermilion boundary of my lips.

I turn toward him, and now he traces each again with his mouth, dry and soft and breath warmed, my breath inhaling his, the eddies of our lungs intermingling. His fingers move over the buttons and bands of my clothing and slip them from my body, so I need him against me, crave his heat. His palm presses into the small of my back, lingers along the column of my spine to the nape of my neck, strokes the hollow between the twinned tendons there. The uncertainty of what we are together hums like an electric presence between us; the anticipation of becoming lovers again almost surpasses the act of physical connection.

His body is exactly the same temperature as mine, not varied by a tenth of a degree, blurring the planes of us, now moist and interlocking, rocking together, not penetrating one into the other, not conquering or yielding, but woven so that the coupling itself is complete fulfillment, with no climactic ending to separate the experience of uniting. This must be as close as two lives can come outside the realm of death. And for me it is both passion and forgetting. I am not exposed or vulnerable, but freed. How brilliant that this is the natural act to create a new life.

It is not even gray outside when I wake up. Joe lies next to me beneath the sheet, the crest of his shoulder dropping to the deep cleft of his waist, the rising slope of his hip and thigh like a landscape—a continent of a man, solid enough to sow and reap a crop of progeny and personal hope. And isn't that what it takes to make love last? Taking the risk to say this may be all but this can be enough? Yielding to the finiteness of what is *really* possible? Declaring that *this* will be my allotted plot of earth to till and harvest over the startlingly short course of my life?

He stirs, stumbling toward the surface of sleep, the flickering of his lids and brow warn me he is close to waking. Then, like a sea creature, he sinks again into slow and even breaths, beneath even the level of dreams. And this time, before he can awaken and leave me, I slip out from under the sheet and quietly gather my clothes from the floor, leaving him before the next dream comes.

For one entire year my father and I walked through the same rooms, ate at the same table, drove in the same car and spoke to each other only through my mother or Lori. For one year my mother sat between us at every meal, linking our hands over grace and filling up the silence with monologues about my father's research articles, and my track meet times or college application essays.

In that year of silence our house trembled with shrieks beyond the range of human hearing. Supersonic shockwaves ricocheted across the breakfast table, screeched through the living room over homework papers and Walter Cronkite's "way it was," screamed above the hiss, hiss, hiss at the end of a record album while my father hunched over his manuscripts engrossed in footnotes and bibliographies. The apocalyptic boom of that silence should have shattered the brick walls of our house, leaving us exposed to gawking neighbors as we sat in orderly oblivion around our dining table, replete with pot roast and mashed potatoes and perfect table manners.

It is amazing how something so abnormal can gradually blur into the background of day-to-day life so thoroughly that its cruelty is no longer apparent. The best of us are capable of selecting what we will see and what we will ignore. It would be inexcusable if it had been a conscious choice.

In the fall, quite near my seventeenth birthday, I won a scholarship to college based on SAT scores. My father congratulated me, and we proceeded with our lives as if the previous year had been imagined. In that same year I began making nearly perfect grades, my mother became noticeably weaker, and my father stopped going to mass.

That year has been thoroughly dammed up behind decades of glossed chitchat about college courses and medical school applications, behind score cards filled with scientific trivia I could recite that finally gave me a notch up—a topic I understood and he didn't. But just before my mother's heart attack, as I sat diagramming the flow of blood through her heart to persuade her to have her valve replaced, she told me why my father broke that silence. She made it clear to him that, despite her love, she would leave him if he didn't. I wasn't yet mature enough to remind her that he was not the only one who had refused to speak.

· 32 ·

The sun has edged far enough above the horizon to spark hot and yellow-orange across the grass, already steaming away morning dew and softening tar on streets and sidewalks. I close my father's front door behind me and I'm almost blind in the gloomy living room with its perpetually drawn blinds and dark furniture. How can he live here and not become depressed? The smells inside this house hang like limp flags of age and decay—smells of household neglect, and my father's physical decline, his unlaundered clothing, his unwashed body.

I dance-step down the hall around the creaking floorboards to Dad's bedroom door. It hangs open, too swollen and warped with coats of paint to close anymore. He is lying on his back under the wheezing air conditioner, snoring away in stuttering gasps. The arch of his rib cage caves into the wide bowl of his pelvis. He can't be eating enough. I can almost trace his skeleton under the bedsheet, practically see his heart beating through the thin cotton of his undershirt, rocking along in its seventy-ninth year inside a chest grown from the flexible balloon of a baby into broad-shouldered manhood, and now, finally, shriveled back into the spare bones and flesh of his old age.

His snore clogs into silence and I count the seconds, waiting to see if he'll roll his tongue clear and gasp for air, or if, maybe, I should run to him and press my ear against his mouth, my fingers against his pulse. Then he curls onto his side and the irregular, staccatoed whoosh steadies into an unobstructed, rhythmic flow—fourteen breaths a minute, twenty thousand breaths a day. Could I count the breaths he has left in him? How low has the number dwindled from whatever seemingly infinite quantity he was allotted at birth? And how many breaths would he need to tell me, face-to-face, that he regrets the course of my life? How many breaths to elaborate on the prejudicial word *fault* when I point out that a woman *can* remain lovely and smart without the validating stamp of marriage? Or would any words beyond the secondhand apology he offered to Joe take every last breath he has?

The air conditioner has been off all night in my room; I'm clammy with perspiration even before I crawl across the bed and punch a button under the metal grill. The machine thuds once and shivers to life, and the fan cranks out a tepid stream of air. I open up my shirt and try to trap any coolness.

"Marie?" I hear Dad calling through the walls. "Marie? Is that you?"

I scramble back across the bed and up the hallway to his room, re-buttoning my shirt. "Yes, Dad. It's me. I'm sorry I woke you up."

"What time is it?"

"Early. It's not even six thirty yet—go back to sleep."

"You didn't come home last night."

"Joe and I had a lot to talk about. I thought it was too late to drive back, so I stayed there."

He brings his hand up over his face and rubs his palm, dry and rough against the stubble on his cheeks. He exhales in a deep sigh and lies still, as if he is orienting himself to the task of living through another day. "Well, long as you're all right."

"I didn't mean to worry you." I shift in the doorway and twist my hair up off the back of my neck. "I guess I should have phoned. I'm not used to somebody waiting up for me." I try to remember if he ever waited up for me in my early years of dating, listening and awake in his bed when my mother called out to be sure I locked the front door, to be sure I was safe.

He grasps the bedpost and pulls himself up to sit on the edge of the mattress, pauses to catch his breath. "Come sit with me a minute. Would you?"

I walk over and sit beside him on the sagging bed, self-conscious to be this close. The details of his room are lost in morning twilight. A fly is trapped behind the closed window blind, battering its wings against the glass pane in a desperate hum.

I'm on the verge of offering to make his breakfast or run a bath for him when he clears his throat and says, "I'm not going to drive anymore. If you or your sister could put the Buick up for sale, I would appreciate it. Lori can have it if she wants to drive it up to Fort Worth." He is staring into the dark hallway beyond his bedroom door, not even trying to make out my features in the unforgiving shadows.

"Dad . . ."

He cuts me off with a wave of his hand. "I don't want the liability anymore."

"OK. All right. I'll call Lori later this morning. How will you get your groceries?"

"There's a bus at the corner. I can get that far."

"Have you thought about a housekeeper? I could take care of that."

He shakes his head and seems to sink heavier into the mattress. "Damn. I can hardly believe it"—this said to himself more than to me, and I can't tell if he is surprised about succumbing to his infirmity, or the fact that the vast majority of his life is concluded, like the last toast at an elaborately planned party when it becomes clear that the anticipation has surpassed the event but sped by unappreciated. "Well. I suppose that would be best."

He leans over to his bedside table and pulls out the drawer, groping through pill bottles and dried-up ballpoint pens and broken bits of cigar. I am about to get up to turn on the lamp when I remember that it would make little difference.

"You should have this," he says, holding a silk embroidered lipstick case in his outstretched palm. In an Instamatic flash I see my mother snapping it open to angle the doll-sized mirror at her mouth and slip the gold cap off a tube of Passion Flower, sculpted into a creamy red Eiffel tower by her lips. Something smaller than a lipstick rattles in the box. Inside I find the diamond engagement ring my father gave to her

on their tenth wedding anniversary, an apology for the academic poverty of their early years together. "Your mother would have liked you to
have it."

"Dad, are you sure? What about Lori?"

"I'll give her your grandmother's earrings. Besides, she's got a
ring."

"Thank you. It's beautiful. It reminds me of Mom." I try to twist it
onto my right ring finger. "I'll have to have it sized." I smile at him. "Are
you just afraid I'll never get my own?"

"I don't know what your young man, Joe, is planning. I'd be giving
this regardless."

I shrug my shoulders and slip the ring onto my little finger.
Even there it is tight. "Joe and I aren't planning. We're friends. Good
friends."

"Your mother was my friend."

"Yes. You were the best of friends, weren't you?" It's true. And being
able to share such an honest fact relaxes some of the strain between us.
My mother's love for both of us still has power. "It was a good thing to
watch, growing up. A good model."

He shifts his weight on the bed, bracing his hands on either side
of him for support. Then he surprises me by saying what I couldn't. "A
good thing to watch, maybe. But better to have been included. I spent
so much time deciphering the minds of dead men I wasn't much good
at listening to young girls. Left that to your mother." He grips the cord-
ing on the mattress. I reach over and close my hand around his. The
cool metal of his wedding ring is loose around his flesh, locked forever
behind his burled knuckle.

"So. Here we are," he says, a stutter of cracks running through his
voice. He clears his throat. "I taught my students that there was usually
a hell of a lot more to be discovered in what was omitted from a textual
translation than in what was inscribed—typical of human nature, I've
come to believe. Now I have to content myself with what I can hear,
what people say or don't say in the few conversations I have these days."
He pauses, and grips my hand, the hard knots of his joints pressing my
fingers together. "Why did you come?" he asks me, not sounding angry

or taunting, but genuinely interested, willing to admit that we are awkward together.

I stumble for a minute. "It's been a long time since I've visited."

"Yes. It has been a long time," he affirms.

I start to offer one of many justifications, but end up letting the sounds of the house fill the space between us. I'm suddenly afraid of what he wants to talk about. Everything I told Joe just a few hours ago rushes back at me. "I came here because I thought you needed help." Strain makes me sound almost accusatory, as if I blamed him for aging. He doesn't react, waiting for me to choose whether this will be an argument or a resolution. I say it again, genuinely now. "I want to help you, Dad."

He turns to look at me. "You're very like your mother, you know. She was a caretaker. I never fully figured out why she married such a solitary type. You also came here, I believe, to leave something behind. Whatever that is, it's your own business to tell or not to tell."

"Did Joe say something to you?"

"Not a word. You left your portable phone here—I found it at the bottom of one of the grocery sacks." It must have fallen out of my purse when I dropped the bag. I had managed to go half a day without checking messages—a reprieve granted by knowing Marsallis won't meet with the district attorney for another three days.

"Did it ring?"

He nods his head. "I did not intend to pry into your affairs, but the fourth time it went off I opened it."

"You answered it?"

"I didn't know I was answering it. I opened it to try and shut the thing off and someone started talking. A man named Charles Marshalls asked me to have you call him back."

"Marsallis. Did he say why?" My heart rate has skipped ahead so fast I feel short of breath.

"I told him you were out for the evening and he said you should be at his office as early as possible on Monday morning."

"And he didn't say anything else?"

"I got the impression he expected you to know."

Without even processing the possibility that this might mean good news, tears begin to run down my cheeks. I let them fall onto my neck so my father won't be aware of me wiping them away. I swallow to steady my voice and ask him, "Is that how you knew something was wrong?"

He shakes his head. "I've heard it in everything you haven't talked about since you got here. Like I said, I'm learning to listen the same way I used to read." He stretches across to the bedside table and pulls a Kleenex out of a box, steadying himself against the bedpost. He pushes himself upright again and folds the tissue into my hand. "If it helps you at all, I'd like to listen. I am past due on that account."

I blot my face with the Kleenex and clench my teeth to bite back more tears. My father waits for me; his breath almost imperceptibly rocks the mattress. Minutes of silence pass before I begin to talk. "I'm involved in a malpractice suit. Somebody died in the operating room, a little girl." He doesn't say anything until I've told him the entire story. For once it's almost cathartic to dictate the whole thing from start to finish without the constant interruptions and provocative questions of a deposition. Not that there is a finish—I have almost begun to define my life by everything being taken away, like a handprint in the dust. Even when I tell him about the criminal charge that I'm convinced must be waiting for me on Marsallis's desk right now he only takes in a deeper breath.

At the end we both sit quietly on the edge of the bed. I am wrung out by the retelling of it all, and the crashing of memories through this house, and the lack of sleep.

"Are you all right?" he asks me.

"Oh, I don't think the whole thing will be settled for months. Regardless of the criminal charge."

"I meant now. Are you holding up right now?"

I don't have an answer for him. Daylight slices through the window blinds. The ticks and sighs of the house have submerged beneath street traffic and dogs and neighborhood kids. My father starts to say something else, and stops himself. Then he blurts, "Joe is an interesting character," as if changing the subject is the only safe reaction.

"He is interesting. And certainly a character."

"He was there that day. The day the girl died?"

"He was working that morning. He'd already gone home by the time her operation started."

"He had nothing to do with her care, then?"

"No. I mean, he helped me get ready for her case, but he'll be fine—the lawyers barely even questioned him. I'm glad you like him."

"To be specific, I said he was interesting. Don't know whether I like him."

I wait for him to go on, but he doesn't offer any more. "Did he say anything to you about the lawsuit?" I ask.

"No. But I think he could have." He pauses for a breath and adds, "He strikes me as a man who says a lot less than he says."

"What do you mean?" I look at him, but he is staring off into the still dark hallway.

He shakes his head and lowers his voice. "Nothing. I don't know what I mean. At my age that's often the case." He sighs and lifts his shoulders, brings a hand up to rub over his face and scratch the back of his neck. The intersecting ellipses of his biceps and deltoid stand out beneath the slack skin of his arm. I have a momentary flash of him as a young father hoisting Lori or me in an arc over his head—the threat of falling had been a game in those strong arms. Did he feel betrayed when we outgrew his ability to heft and carry us, when protecting us became a task of conversation, and we turned to our mother?

I take his hand again. "I'm sorry I've got to leave like this. I'll talk to Lori. We'll get the housekeeper figured out, and the car. I'll try and get back as soon as all this gets settled."

"Well. Some things don't ever get settled. You just make a place for them. Learn to let them sit there with you, side by side with the good."

· 33 ·

On a fading Sunday afternoon in August, First Lutheran echoes of escaping employees. I sometimes wonder if Seattle's spectacularly brief summertime doesn't suppress disease until the rains return. Despite threatening skies the offices and lounges are deserted but for the emergency staff. As I'd hoped, I run into no familiar faces on my way into the mailroom.

Envelopes and flyers are so crammed into my box I have to seesaw a thick cardboard mailer out to decompress the lot, uncorking a drift of paper. I sit in the midst of the pile and pull the recycling bin beside me. It's a treasure hunt to find the fragments of information that matter. Ads for anesthesia equipment and conferences and journals and textbooks, newsletters from city and county and national and international societies, solicitations from investment brokers and real estate agents and political lobbyists. Call schedules and vacation schedules and committee schedules—meetings that have come and gone in my absence like seasonal birds winging over the landscape, mattering only for the moment. The more I get, the less I read.

Resting on top of a mound of new Medicare guidelines is the slip of white paper I'm looking for, folded and stapled and addressed to me in the cursive script of a human hand. I pull it open and read a jotted note from Matt Corchoran, First Lutheran's pharmacist, asking me to stop by his office to discuss the matter I'd called him about before leaving Houston.

The pharmacy office is tucked into a windowless closet of space behind the cavernous storage rooms of surgical equipment. Matt's office
door is split, Dutch style, and from down the hall I see the bottom half
closed; the glow from his computer monitor illuminates the close walls
and ceiling like a huge aquarium. The top of his balding head bobs
above the lower door. He sees me and jumps, as if discovered among
secrets, then laughs at his own startle.

"Dr. Heaton. I get so used to being alone back here on the weekends—only chance I have to work in peace. I didn't even hear you walk
up."

"Hi, Matt." We fall into the hierarchy of address so common in the
medical world, a taboo against using doctors' first names even after
years of working together. "I got your note. That was quick—thank you.
I hope you didn't spend your whole Saturday reviewing files for me."

"No problem. Have a seat." He wedges open the door and I squeeze
around it to reach a blue plastic chair tucked beside him under the narrow Formica desk. "Sorry—they keep promising me a new office when
we remodel the ORs, but equipment gets more space than people around
here." His Midwestern vowels protrude unabashedly into his language.
They suit him in a way, straightforward and methodical—a man used
to the meticulous measuring and counting of chemicals. He opens a
dented metal file drawer and flicks through cardboard folders until he
plucks one forth, stuffed with the pharmacy's copies of all the anesthesia
records I've turned in over the last several months. These yellow pages,
filled with blurred blue carbon check marks and numerals, are the third
sheet of a triplicate form divided among the patient's chart, the billing
clerks and this office. My name is typed across the folder's plastic tab. It
is chilly in here and I tuck my hands in between my knees.

"I looked through them," he says.

Of course; he must have reviewed the records himself, at least cur-
sorily. I should have guessed he'd do that. I nod at him, finding it hard
to look him in the eye. "I know it's an odd request. With my leave of
absence, I just . . . maybe I've had too much time to worry about details
lately. I thought I should go over everything."

He gives me an understanding smile that almost immediately tightens to a professionally polite mask. "I came up with some discrepancies." He glances up at me over the open folder in his lap. "We almost always find a couple, you know—usually just a recording error in dosing or dilution." Seven years ago when I started at First Lutheran I'd had a similar conversation with Matt after I mistakenly wrote the number of milligrams of Dilaudid I'd given to a patient on the wrong line of my anesthesia record, and his rigid cross-checking had flagged the gap between drugs used and drugs returned.

Then Matt slips twelve different anesthesia records out of my folder and hands them to me. Twelve records. I'm flustered for a moment—maybe he's handing me the whole department's errors. All twelve couldn't be mine. But my signature is at the bottom of each page. I look back at Matt and see him patiently waiting for my reaction. I've made no errors in seven years and now twelve in six months?

My face gets hot and I keep my eyes down on the papers in my lap, encoded with a jumble of dashes and scribbles. "What kind of errors did you find?"

"In a few, the drugs missing from your narcotics box didn't match up with what you recorded using. That's an easy enough mistake." He scratches at the side of his temple and then loosely clasps his hands across his knees as he leans toward me. "But what caught my attention is the amounts you used. Calculated out by the body weights of these patients, some of them shouldn't have woken up for days. Not unless they had quite a drug habit already." He slips the sheets out of my hands and deals them out across the desk like a poker hand.

I shuffle the pages on the desk and in my lap, picking out numbers and words. My eyes fly over them until they tangle in a jabberwocky of drugs and procedural notes, blood pressures and pulse rates. Matt's unasked questions burn through the top of my head as he waits for me to give him some rational answer—something he can believe, anything that will let him shrug away the doubt materializing like a third entity in the room. He's right. It's plain. The doses are way out of line, two and three times what would be normal. The silence between us is becoming tense. Then one fragment of print in the bottom corner of a record makes me suck in my breath.

"Matt." My voice sounds muffled by my own pulse. "Can you give me a couple of days to look through these? I want to look back at the charts. Maybe there's an explanation I just can't recall without seeing the whole record."

He's still watching me. He has hazel eyes—kind eyes; he wants me, I sense, to find a way out of his oblique accusation, knows I wouldn't have set myself up for this by asking him to pull these records. It seems to take him forever to respond. I can almost see him weigh how much to believe, how much faith he can afford to invest. He looks at me for such a penetrating moment I have to concentrate to keep from turning away. Then he gives the smallest nod. "Two days, then."

"Can I make a copy of these? Please?" I ask, sweeping the papers up.

He takes the pile to a desktop copier in the corner of the office and its rhythmic whir and zing churn out duplicates of the shorthand scrawls that sketch twelve people's surgical histories. I watch the pages peel out in a neat black and white stack and suddenly, without thinking at all, I know his discovery is no coincidence.

"Matt, you'd already started an audit, hadn't you?" I ask, before considering whether I can endure the answer. I must have given over six hundred anesthetics in these last six months—it would have been impossible for Matt to review all those surgeries since I'd called him yesterday morning.

His mouth goes taut, just for an instant, as if tempering self-censorship. "You were flagged. I was asked to start an audit two weeks ago."

I feel like I've been slapped by a friend, even though I'd already guessed the truth. I want to ask him who it was, but I know he won't—or can't—tell me. I've already compromised his job by asking him for two days of silence.

He holds the copies out toward me, gripped between his thumb and curled fingers. I start to take them, but he doesn't let go. "Dr. Heaton, you have a right to this information, as far as I'm concerned. But I can only keep this conversation confidential until Tuesday."

"I know. Thank you, Matt. I promise—no more than two days." Then he lets the papers slip into my grasp and I leave before he can question his decision.

· 34 ·

There is only one secretary working in medical records today. She is balanced on a stepladder, squeezing a chart back into its alphabetically regimented slot on a metal shelf. I ask her to pull the chart matching the name stamped on one of the twelve Xeroxed pages, and she frowns at me before thudding her girdled bulk to the floor.

"I need to see some ID." I dig through the bottom of my bag until I find my hospital badge. She glances from the picture to my face twice, readjusting a strap beneath her blouse. Then she takes the page from me and wanders into the endless, fluorescent-lit labyrinth of patient records. Five minutes later she slaps a chart into my hands and heaves herself back up on the stepstool with another armload.

Sitting against the broad end of one rack, I flip the chart open across my lap. The surgical notes are all together at the back; the graphed lines of the anesthesia record are easy to spot. With the records side by side, the discrepancy is so obvious. But, of course, the original top page and the bottom pharmacy copy would never be held side by side. They would be torn apart and sent on their separate pathways as soon as the patient left the operating room. So when extra doses of fentanyl were logged onto the pharmacy page later, no doctor or nurse handling the original would question the dose, and no pharmacist reconciling the narcotics count from the copy would find a gap.

Jolene Jansen's pharmacy page is not among the records Matt gave to me. I ask the clerk to pull her chart and she harrumphs in annoy-

249

ance, but drags her stepstool to the J aisle, then drops the manila folder into my hands. It is thirteen pages thicker than it was three months ago because the autopsy report, identical to the copy sent to me, has been added to the laboratory section near the back. I flip past the anatomical descriptions of Jolene's heart and aorta, past the chromosomal analysis that confirmed her Turner syndrome. On the last page is a list of chemicals found by the toxicology lab when her blood was analyzed after death. I hadn't even read it before today. Even if I had, I would only have paid attention to what was listed there, the drugs I knew I had given her—everything I expected to find. Today I see what is missing.

The secretary starts turning out lights. I stack up the sheets of paper and follow her out. At the doorway she takes the charts out of my hand and puts them on a table. "We'll be open at six tomorrow. If you need these, you can fill out a requisition slip."

Rain has turned the gutters in front of the hospital into milky streams and I splash through puddles with the pharmacy records tucked against my chest as I run to my car. I push the front seat back as far as it will go and hold the first record up in the gray light. The patient's name is only vaguely familiar; his surgery was months ago—a colon resection with Don Stevenson. My handwriting details an unremarkable anesthetic, the wavy horizon of checks and dots that reflect a sleeping brain's normal reaction to a surgeon's scalpel.

I search all twelve pages, looking at every mark on each page. The handwriting is all my own, and I've written these words so many times they've become interchangeable across a thousand anesthetic records. No extraordinary dissections were made, no raging blood pressures or skyrocketing heart rates are here. No reason to need so much narcotic. All of the pages are like this, cases so routine they have become as banal for the surgical team as they are unique for the patient. Only the illusion of a pattern coils at the base of my consciousness, daring me in my father's voice to read what isn't written there. Only the faintest difference in pen pressure, a slight shift in the curve of a numeral. No one but me would even suspect it. No one would believe it.

Beyond the windshield the flat gray sky gives little clue about what time it is. I start the car and pull into the sparse evening traffic. The steep streets dropping down to the waterfront feel unfamiliar, the way one's childhood home seems altered by the days strewn between then and now. Something inside of me is sinking with the landscape. My condo is close—four blocks south of here. But I turn north almost unconsciously. Five minutes later I am winding up again, toward the crest of Queen Anne Hill.

Joe's building dominates the hilltop neighborhood, massive as an overbearing monarch. Just as I reach for his bell at the entry gate a loose-limbed teenager hauled by four leashed dogs pulls the doors open and the tangled animals surge through.

The doors slam shut behind me and the halls are silent, as if the last living occupants had deserted. Joe loves the privacy of these thick plaster walls and solid doors. His own is locked. I ring his buzzer. After waiting five minutes I step into the nearest fire escape and reach under the metal railing above the top step, working my fingers into a crevice between the handrail and the wall support. His key is still tucked into the notch there, as it was years ago when I came and went from this home as frequently as my own.

The western wall of glass in Joe's living room lets in more sound than comes from either neighboring flat. Children holler from a jungle gym in a nearby playground; a woman begs them to stay out of the mud. Such a contrast, these high young voices singing through this half-furnished, unattached man's home. Breakfast dishes—several days' worth, I suspect—clog the sink, and half a pot of cold coffee stands on the stove. The leather duffle he brought to Houston is open and unpacked, slung over the back of a kitchen chair.

I walk through the rooms, touching nothing, noticing everything: a battered box holding the harmonica he bought on an earlier trip to New Orleans—I remember him cupping it at his mouth, warbling an off-key accompaniment to Charles Brown; a reading lamp I gave him one Christmas so his midnight insomnia would no longer waken me. His favorite terry bathrobe, frayed to transparency at the neck and cuff, is draped over the claw-foot bathtub rim. Traces of his aftershave hang in the air and ruffle my memories like the breath of passing spirits. It is the expected bachelor's home, decorated with the clutter of daily living.

I begin opening drawers—aspirin and Motrin and Tylenol and crumpled, uncapped toothpaste tubes, prescription bottles of antibiotics and antihistamines and antacids; empty toilet paper rolls and plastic boxes of dental floss; a razor with dried blue shaving cream clotted between the blades. The linen cupboard is stuffed with mismatched towels and sheets—plaids and stripes all wound into the crumpled piles of a man who doesn't have to share his cabinets and closets.

In the kitchen I paw through spatulas and paring knives and plastic forks and bamboo chopsticks. Wedged behind the silverware caddy is his old baby spoon, rubber coated at its tip and engraved with a teddy bear and his initials. He used it at a New Year's party once, I remember, for caviar. A tea bag has spilled open and the drawer smells of jasmine.

The bedroom closet is filled with his standard apparel—T-shirts from bike races and music festivals and 10-K runs, jazz clubs and local microbreweries. A few pairs of pressed trousers are still in their plastic dry cleaning bags. Four ties are knotted around the neck of a wire hanger. The top shelf sags beneath a jumble of canvas backpacks and battered luggage, one jelly jar of small change and another of pastel-colored beach glass, dust-covered medical textbooks on biochemistry and cell biology and pathology. I drag his desk chair over to the closet and balance on it while I grab the bags and suitcases and heave them onto the floor. When the shelf is cleared I push the books aside and look behind them, grope into the corners I can't see. Then I step down and begin to unzip the packs, unlatch the clasps and buckles, unsnap the flaps of toiletry compartments and shoe pouches and collapsible handles.

Tucked into the bottom of a nylon shoulder bag is a black leather fanny pack embossed with a pharmacy logo—one of the thousands handed out by drug companies at national meetings and annual conferences. There is a rattling of plastic when I turn it over to find the zipper. The sound startles me out of my crouch and I sit back on the floor, leaning against Joe's unmade bed. Light as it is, the weight of the pack presses against my thighs. I want, more than anything I've wanted in years, to be wrong about what's inside.

I unzip it and the two halves fall easily open across my lap. Laid out upon cotton gauze are five syringes—neatly tucked inside this small black womb, unlike the casual neglect given his other possessions. I lift up one plastic cylinder and hold it up to the light. The crystal clear fluid inside casts a tiny rainbow over my leg—pure and sterile, invisible as water, odorless and tasteless and lethal. I place the syringe back into its nest.

In a movie, hours would pass until Joe comes home. The room would grow dark and I could spring out of some shadowy corner surprising him with my find, or slip unseen out his door to keep his secret. But it's only minutes later when I hear his key slide into the lock and pivot, hear the door open and then shut behind him. He walks into the kitchen and opens the refrigerator, then the freezer; a cabinet closes, rattling the glass panels. Ice clinks into a tumbler and liquid splashes in a rising pitch, the frozen cubes crackle in the clash of temperatures. I hear him turn the pages of a newspaper. The carpet is so dense I can't tell he's come into the bedroom until he says my name.

"Marie!" Pure, honest puzzlement is in his voice. But then he doesn't say any more and I know he's seen the open bag in my lap. I can't look up at him, even when I feel the bed sag beside me under his weight.

I turn the leather pouch over in my hands and run my finger along the stitching, smooth out the buckled strap across my legs. "I called Matt Corchoran yesterday, before I flew back. I asked him to pull my narcotics records for the last six months. Turned out I didn't even need to call. He'd already been asked to audit me. He can't account for all the fentanyl I've been using in my cases. In a couple of charts the numbers didn't add up right. But in almost a dozen, the doses were out of line—way more than anybody who wasn't addicted could take. I checked the pharmacy copy against the original, and I could tell someone had tried to match my handwriting. Did you figure nobody would ever compare them? Or did you just count on them blaming me for it?"

My voice sounds like it's coming from a stranger. I scrape my finger along the zipper of the black bag until it hurts, trying to feel something. "My dad saw it. Not the fentanyl—just . . . that something was off with you. It's kind of amazing I've been so blind. I don't think I believed it even after I talked to Matt. I could see how you'd tried to keep it hidden—using my pen, never signing the chart where you'd given me a break. I never called you on that, despite all the rules. I only knew for sure because of the way you mark your blood pressures—with a heavier stroke right at the end, almost like you're impatient with it all. It's such a little thing, nobody else will see it." I wipe tears off my cheeks with the back of my hand. They've come before I'm conscious of an emotion, like the empty expanse of shore before a tidal wave. "You're so good, such a good anesthesiologist, I never worried about my patients when I left the room."

Joe is silent. He seems to sink more heavily into the bed. Then he speaks so softly I almost can't hear him. "I didn't mean to do this to you, Marie. I didn't . . . I didn't single you out."

I put my hand up to stop him. "How long? How long have you been using?"

He leans over his knees holding his head. "I don't know. A year, maybe more."

"While we were dating? Were you using fentanyl while I was dating you?"

"No. It started after that."

"What do you mean 'it started'? 'It' didn't start anything, Joe. You started. You put— You injected this drug into your veins. God, what were you thinking?" Tears roll over my face, dampen the front of my blouse. I don't try to wipe them off anymore.

"I got off work one morning. I'd been up all night. You know what it's like. I could hardly drive home I was so exhausted. I didn't even change clothes at the hospital—came home in my scrubs. And I found it in my pocket. I must have drawn some up for an epidural and then she delivered before I gave it. I don't know . . . I don't remember. It was just there, in my pocket. And I wanted to see what it felt like. I watch the faces of patients after I give it to them, how everything melts away. I wanted to feel that."

"And then you did it again. You kept on. You plotted and you lied and you stole this drug. You drew it up into a syringe and put a tourniquet around your arm, stuck a needle into your vein and injected it into your bloodstream. That takes a lot of conscious intent. That doesn't happen by accident."

"I never lost control of it. It's never hurt anyone else. It doesn't interfere with my work—you see that. You admit I'm good at what I do. It's *my* problem. My choice to use it and my choice to stop." He sounds like he's practiced these words, saying it all so persuasively.

My stomach turns over and something explodes inside. I hurl the bag against the closet door and stand up. The room spins; I almost lose my balance. "Don't talk to me about choices. Your choice is your delusion. You're an addict! That's why your hands shake. That's why you woke up sweating in my bed—why you left without a word to me. You had to run out and get your fix. You lied to me. God damn you, Joe. You set me up!"

He thrusts himself up from the bed and storms over to the doorway, braces himself in the frame as if to keep from coming at me. "I. Am. Not. Addicted," he shouts. "I've never let it go there. I used it sometimes. It made me feel good, it made things tolerable when they were intolerable. You want the truth? It made me better at my work. I focused better. I stopped worrying about how tired I was, or whether First Lutheran's endless political bickering would finally drive me out of my job. It's a drug. A medication. How many people do you work with every day who use Prozac or Xanax or Ritalin or caffeine or nicotine or their own nightly cocktail hour to get by? How many of them call themselves addicts? Wake up and look around you. We haven't been able to live with our unadulterated minds since we first brewed mead, too terrified to admit how fucking inconsequential it all is. I can quit whenever I want to."

"How? How will you quit?"

"I throw that stuff away and end it. Today. Now."

"So you'll turn yourself in. Go to Phil, or the medical board. Right now—with me."

"I can quit on my own. I quit the minute I saw you sitting here on my bedroom floor."

"This is classic, Joe. The classic addict's response—that you don't need help. You don't even see it, do you?"

He stares at the floor, the muscle along his jaw line trembling. And then the last bits of the puzzle fall into place, almost subconsciously, and I freeze.

"What happened to Jolene Jansen?" I say it evenly, so quietly I only know he's heard me by the way his shoulders tense against the doorjamb. "I asked you to draw up the fentanyl for her surgery before you left that morning. You put something else in the syringe." He shakes his head, his hands clenched at his sides. "Tell me. I know you took it. They didn't find any fentanyl in her blood at the autopsy. She died right after I gave her whatever you put in that syringe. What happened to Jolene Jansen?"

"Goddammit, I had nothing to do with Jolene's death." His jaw is so tight he nearly hisses. "Nothing to do with it. That kid died because of some problem, some medical problem nobody knew about and *nobody* could have predicted."

"You want to hear the rest of her autopsy report, Joe? You want to hear what medical problem she had? Oh God. It finally makes sense. Her heart rate slowed down after I injected it. Just like it would with fentanyl. But then it didn't go back up when her airway started closing. I could never explain that." I walk across the floor toward Joe. "You switched it for a beta-blocker! That's why it acted like fentanyl. It lowered her heart rate and her blood pressure, the same as if I'd treated her pain. The dose would have been way too high for a kid her age . . . She had Turner syndrome, Joe. She had a coarctation of her aorta. Aortic stenosis. The beta-blocker killed her."

My thoughts are streaming out loud. But Joe knows as much as I do. The narrow stricture across Jolene's aorta acted like a kink in a hose, and when an adult dose of beta-blocker weakened the force of her heart's contractions, blood backed up into her lungs, flooded the delicate air sacs that absorb oxygen and suffocated her.

"I did not kill Jolene Jansen." He speaks slowly, precisely, taking a breath between each word. "You are describing the hypothetical. Even if she got a few milligrams of a beta-blocker—it's almost unthinkable that would kill her."

"A few milligrams? I thought the fentanyl was diluted. I gave her half the syringe!"

"You're saying crazy things. I never heard anything about this autopsy before today—you're looking for an answer that doesn't exist." He takes a step toward me and clenches his fists. Then he slaps the front of his chest so loudly I wince. "I did nothing to hurt that child. I've hurt myself with this. And you. I know that. I swear to God I will never touch the stuff again. But this is not what killed her."

"I have to go. I have to go home." He is still standing in the doorway and I try to walk by him.

He grabs me by the wrist and holds me against the wall. "What are you going to do?"

"I don't know. I don't know what I'm going to do."

"Do you know what would happen if anyone thought this was connected with Jolene's accident?"

I nod. "You would be accused of manslaughter." His fingers are sinew strong around my arm, anchoring me to this pinpoint of time, the only thing holding me upright in a world that is sliding out from under me. His face fills that world—the mouth, wide and pale, the half smile he makes when he perceives hypocrisy; his straight, almost regal nose; his hair, glinting as gold as the tiny earring in the soft, full lobe of his ear. And his eyes—deep-water blue, almost imperceptibly askew, just enough to leave a question about what he sees when he looks at me.

I wrench myself out of his grip and try to get through the door, but he grabs my arm and pulls me back against the wall. Then he swings his balled fist above his head and slams it toward me, just past my face, hitting the wall so hard the Sheetrock caves. "Get out of here then. Get the hell out of here." He slumps to the floor and his shout breaks into a sob. "Oh God, Marie. Please go."

· 35 ·

The streets are empty now, people driven from the summer night by the fine pelting spray. I cross to my car and peel a sodden parking ticket from beneath the wiper blade. I keep expecting Joe to splash through to the passenger door, expect or wish or fear—I'm not sure. I look up at his bedroom windows, now dark, and drive away.

My balcony doors must have blown open; rainwater has bled into a damp crescent of carpet. In the distance, the black sea and black sky are slit by a necklace of man-made stars.

There is no ache, no welling of tears, no exhaustion. I can't imagine ever feeling hunger again, or thirst, or physical desire. I am hollow, scooped raw.

How many accident victims have I treated in the emergency room, slashed by power saws or crushed by cars or burned by gasoline spills? In those first minutes of shock they sail on a zephyr of endorphins that extinguishes pain and time like a snuffed candle. When they ricochet back into the horror of it all, it is only the narcotic—the morphine or Dilaudid or fentanyl I inject into their veins—that makes the pain bearable. And how many heart attacks have I prevented by giving a hypertensive or tachycardic patient a beta-blocker, a cardiac drug designed to regulate the rate and force of the heartbeat?

It was ingenious of Joe. His unique medical genius. In an unconscious patient the effects of the beta-blocker would mimic those of a narcotic—the heart rate would slow down, the blood pressure would fall, and there would be no suspicion that the clear solution in the syringe had been swapped.

In the morning I will make the calls I have to make, and tell the people who need to know. I imagine myself standing before hospital committees and department heads. Within days everyone will have heard—Matt Corchoran will have his explanation and uncover, almost certainly, other records whose sums don't tally, other anesthesiologists unwittingly used to channel fentanyl to Joe. Frank Hopper will begin garnering experts to defend First Lutheran's reputation, and prepare sincere and convincing press releases. Don Stevenson and Mindy and Alicia can all take deep breaths of confirmed innocence. Even though they have long been dropped from the suit, an unexplained death haunts anyone whose signature is on the chart.

I'll tell Phil Scoble everything. He can salvage my career and see that Joe gets treatment along with punishment. Our profession is so adept at planning, so proficient in controlling even the seemingly uncontrollable, that we have developed protocols for handling the "impaired physician." In only a few hours I will call Charlie Marsallis and hold out the key to my vindication. I will flay Joe's betrayal and expose him to the hospital and the lawyers and the state medical board. Joe's demise will be my rescue.

I'm finally free. All the nightmarish hours I've spent retracing my choices in operating room 5 while Jolene Jansen died are over. I don't have to struggle any longer with what natural phenomenon might have taken her life, or what unnatural catastrophe I might have caused. I won't have to sit before a grim-faced jury listening to my own pronouncement of guilt. Maybe, someday, I will even stop seeing Jolene's mother swallowed in an empty life. And the only thing I have to pay for my freedom is Joe, and the life we might have made together.

Joe, this many-layered man whose determined will and fortressed privacy define him. If I've loved his strong reserve, his dimly lit corners, then I have also loved his secret demons. And perhaps in loving them I have allowed them, even nurtured them, making me complicit in his dependence.

I reach up to my neckline and slip the sapphire pendant from beneath my blouse. It is warm from my skin. The finely woven gold chain reaches just to my mouth and I trace the outline of my lips with the sharp surface of the stone, run it along the sensitive boundary. I squeeze it in my closed palm. What did Lori say about love? "Love is a choice"? What choice do I have? Even to save him by staying silent is to sacrifice him. I know the pitiful statistics of doctors who abuse their own drugs. Like every other anesthesia resident, I sat through the required hours of education telling me the mortality figures, when those who believe they're in control edge too close to the margin between peace and death, and inject too much narcotic. Euphoria must settle like a thick cloud, calm their conscious frontal lobes, quiet aggression in the amygdala, then sink like a stone into the brain stem until it becomes too numbed to trigger the automaticity of breath. They suffocate in their pleasure.

Only the lights of the shipping port are bright now. An orange and white skyline of cranes floating on the black horizon. Finally I am washed through with fatigue and begin to drift in and out of sleep. Just before I close my eyes for the last time I think of the other person who will be told that Jolene did not die inexplicably, that her asphyxiation in the operating room was the consequence of a deliberate drug swap by a doctor entrusted to take care of her. I try to block an image of Bobbie Jansen's face when she hears this news.

I wake from sleep as if being dragged from underwater. It's only 7:40—too early for Charlie Marsallis's office to answer, but not too early for an anesthesiologist. I sit up and pull the phone into my lap, begin punching the numbers to my own department. At the sixth digit I press my finger on the button and cut the connection. My hand trembles. I dial again and wait for Phil Scoble's secretary, Pamela, to answer, practice the words I'll use. When I hear her voice I almost hang up again, then tighten my fingers into a fist around the telephone.

"I'd like to speak to Dr. Scoble, please."

"May I say who's calling?" Pamela asks.

"It's Dr. Heaton, Pamela."

"Oh. Dr. Heaton." A catch of surprised embarrassment in her voice. "Good morning. Can you hold for just a minute?" I cringe hearing her stall. I wish I hadn't called now. I should have waited until I could see him in person.

Pamela clicks onto the line again. "Dr. Heaton, Dr. Scoble won't be in the office until late tonight. He's out of town. Can I take a message?" An almost imperceptible tension edges her voice, like a veil dropped between us.

"No. Wait. Yes," I stutter, caught off guard. "Tell him I need to speak to him as soon as he gets in. Tell him it's urgent, please."

Three miles across town Joe is waking, if he slept at all, knowing I have the power to expose him, knowing that I'll have to tell someone, time cinching around him like a noose. The only person I can trust besides Phil is Charlie Marsallis. I throw on slacks and a jacket and brush my hair in front of the mirror. Deep lines are etched between my brows. What is the French saying? "After a certain age, each of us wears the face we have earned." I press my thumb against the two furrows above my nose, to see if they have become a permanent scar.

Charlie's building lobby is just opening. A man in faded blue work clothes sprays the sidewalk clear of cigarette butts and city soot and vagrants' urine. He turns the hose into the gutter to let me pass, rivulets of water jigsawing across the cement. Counselors and clients, prosecutors and plaintiffs are already lined up at the espresso stand outside the front doors. They chat in hushed morning voices and scan newspaper headlines. I wonder if I will ever again feel connected to the world they are reading about. I scan the crowd for Charlie, but see instantly that none here are tall enough to be him.

Charlie's office is still dark. Saturday's mail is spilled across the carpeting beyond the letter slot, and a blinking red light on his secretary's desk reflects off the back wall. I pace in the hallway, conjuring a purgatory of anticipated scenes. Who will talk first? Will Charlie rush to tell me whatever news called me back from Texas—the name of my accuser and my alleged crime, perhaps? Or an offered settlement? Or will I be the first to declare news and tell Charlie that indeed Jolene Jansen's death was needless and completely avoidable, the result of a selfish and senseless compulsion by a doctor I trusted, a man I believed I knew—a man I'd begun to believe I loved.

At 8:35 the elevator opens and I hear Charlie's secretary detailing appointment conflicts and court dockets before I see her. Charlie answers. Both stop talking as soon as they see me leaning against the glass panel of his door.

I stand up and pull my purse higher on my shoulder, feeling unexpectedly awkward about surprising them. "Hello, Mr. Marsallis."

He lifts his briefcase up under his arm and holds his hand out to me. It is warm and dry and I am uncomfortably aware of my own perspiring palm against his.

"I hope it's all right that I've come without calling first."

"Of course. I guess this means you got our message. I'm glad you've come." He reaches into his pocket and pulls out a set of keys to unlock the door, a jarring clatter in the stillness of the hallway. "Jean, could you get us some coffee? Come on in." He steps across the scattered envelopes on the floor, then squats and scoops them into a stack, which he deposits on Jean's desk.

"Let's sit in here," he says, and clears some files off the long wooden conference table in the room adjoining his office. He pulls out a rolling chair for me, takes off his coat and hangs it on the rack, folds his long frame into his own chair.

"I'm sorry we had to call you like that. So urgently. I had to be sure you got the message. I appreciate your getting back here so quickly." I recognize in his tone the same intentional serenity I use to interview a frightened patient: a tone of comfort offered to calm someone who can't even hear the words. He clears his throat and snaps his briefcase open, pulling forth a sheaf of papers.

Jean comes in with a tray of coffee and doughnuts. She sets ceramic cups on saucers and fills them. Charlie draws in a breath to speak, and suddenly I know that I have to speak first—that whatever he has to tell me, before he condemns or consoles I want him to have already heard the truth. I put a hand out to interrupt him. "Wait." I inhale and look directly into his eyes. "I know you must have news for me. I know that's why you called. But I have something to tell you first." Charlie sits back in his chair and pushes away from the table to turn toward me, patient and expectant. "I've learned something new. About what happened that day in the operating room. Something that changes the whole suit."

Charlie watches me as I tell him about Joe, his face a receptive but unreadable mask. Words rush out of me almost uncensored, laying out what I know about the fentanyl, and what I suspect about the beta-blocker causing Jolene's death. I talk faster and faster, trying to explain how only this makes sense physiologically, how only a drug swap could answer the questions I could never figure out, questions no one else has even seemed concerned about. The room pulsates with silence after I stop. I feel myself flushing. I try to look at his face but can only watch his hands, steepled fingertip to fingertip across the arms of his chair. He sits impassive and still for a long while. Then he exhales, as if he'd been holding his breath while I spoke.

"This changes everything, doesn't it?" I ask.

He nods before speaking. "Yes. Yes, it changes things." He sits quietly again, and I look up into his eyes, search his expression for some glimpse of what I expect—a complete relinquishment of any fault. He places a hand on top of the primly stacked papers sitting between us on the table; his fingers hover above as if beckoning the words forth, telling him what to tell me. "We've been notified by the district attorney. The state is filing a criminal charge against you. That's why I asked you to come back to Seattle."

My throat tightens, even knowing that I hold my own proof of innocence. "What are they accusing me of?"

Charlie slides the white papers toward himself, realigning their edges. "They are saying they have evidence you've been using narcotics, and that you were using fentanyl when you treated Jolene." He looks up at me as he finishes the sentence, color rising into his cheeks.

"Charlie." My fingers tighten over the seat of my chair and I lean closer, blinking back tears. "This can't just be coincidence. Matt Corchoran told me someone at the hospital had already asked to have me audited. He must have talked to someone about the drug discrepancy even before I saw him."

"Do you think he did?"

"He said he hadn't. But how else could someone come up with that accusation?"

"Maybe." Charlie flares his hands open briefly, then locks them together on top of my charges. "But now we'll have to prove this was Joe, not you. Unless you think Joe is willing to testify to that."

"I don't know." I shake my head. "I don't know."

"Well, if you arrange an intervention today, it's possible his urine would still test positive for narcotics. Do you think you can make a credible enough case to get support for that? Have you talked to anyone at First Lutheran about it yet?"

"I called the chief of my department, but I didn't reach him. He would believe me."

"The chief of anesthesia. That's Phil Scoble, right?"

"That's right."

Charlie's expression doesn't flicker, but his eyes darken, like some fraction of light has been extinguished. "Marie, Phil Scoble is the one who's filing the charges against you."

· 36 ·

It is after 12:30 by the time Charlie finishes detailing for me the impact of the charges and his plans for my defense. He is assuming that Joe will deny my claims and that the hospital staff—my own chief, who knows my record at First Lutheran better than anyone—will be denouncing me as an untrustworthy addict. This, at least, is how I have understood his words. I try to focus on the hearings and jurisdictions and deadlines he's telling me about, but I keep searching his eyes and listening to his tone of voice, wondering if he still has faith in me.

He offers to take me to lunch but I've no appetite. He escorts me to the door just as Jean opens it to tell him his next client is waiting, a pallid-faced man seated across the foyer. Charlie swings the door closed again and says, "Look, Marie, you've gotten hard news today. I wish I could tell you that all we had to do was expose Joe and everything would be settled. But unless he's intending to turn himself over to the state and admit his actions harmed Jolene, we still have a lot of work ahead of us."

I want to answer him with affirming self-assurance. I want to square my shoulders and tell him how much confidence I have in the judicial system and the overbearing weight of truth. He waits for my response, looking directly into my eyes.

"Do you believe me?" I ask.

He holds my gaze, equal and unflinching, and nods. "I believe you."

. . .

I can see my hands clenched around the steering wheel. The skin is blanched across my knuckles but I don't feel them gripping anything at all. My car seems to be following a line of traffic on its own; pedestrians walk in front of me through crosswalks and somehow the car stops and then goes again. At the top of a hill an ambulance screams through the intersection and I realize I am at First Lutheran. And then I am in the elevator. I squeeze around two orderlies maneuvering a patient's bed; the brass valve on the oxygen tank must have scraped against my arm—there is a pencil-thin scratch of bright red blood. Every button between one and nine is lit, so at the second floor I get out and take the stairs. By the time I reach Phil Scoble's office I'm sweating and out of breath.

Pamela is startled when the door opens. She jumps up from her chair, knocking a wooden box of pens onto the floor. "Dr. Heaton! Dr. Scoble's in a meeting right now."

"I thought he was out of town."

"Well, his schedule is so full. I can ask him to call you later today."

"I'll wait."

"There's no point, really. The executive board is meeting until two, and after that . . ."

"I'll find him." I walk past her to the door that leads to the executive offices and meeting rooms. Pamela picks up the phone and pushes a buzzer as the door slams after me. I hear their voices rolling down the corridor through the closed doors, unchallengeable opinions vaulted back and forth interrupted by spurts of cozy insider chuckles. Phil's voice cuts through a round of muted laughter, bringing business back to order. When I push the door open the conversation stops so abruptly it sounds like a crack. Every face in the room turns to look at me. Every mouth closes and every voice stops. This is not the silence of surprise; this is the stony silence of exclusive secrets.

Frank Hopper is here, and Don Stevenson as head of surgery—all the department chiefs. Phil stands at one end of the conference table in front of the whiteboard. He must have been making some point with his hand. He lets it drop to the table like he's forgotten it's part of himself. Hopper's secretary, Erin, is taking minutes and her pen is poised, immobilized, above the notepad. Hopper is so red he looks like he's choking on his sandwich.

Phil initiates a polite smile. Then he cocks his head to one side and a frown cleaves his eyebrows. "Marie?" he asks, as if he wonders if he's seeing me for real, as if my audacity at showing up here affronts his leadership. Four or five other men and two women surround the table and they all look up at me, then at Phil, then over at Hopper, then back to me. A tennis match of confused and embarrassed glances is traded between those who clearly belong here, trying to figure out how the one who clearly doesn't got in the door.

Phil says again, "Marie," with no question mark now. "We're in a meeting here. Could you wait for me in my office?" Any tone of former friendship is smothered beneath assured superiority. "Are you all right?"

"I thought you were out of town. Pamela told me you were out of town. What's going on, Phil? I just got back from a meeting with Charlie Marsallis. My lawyer." My voice keeps getting louder, quavering. Now Phil has that slightly panicked look men get when they think a woman is about to cry.

Hopper stands up. "Dr. Heaton, why don't you have a seat. Would you like some water? Can we get her a glass of water, Erin?" he asks, turning to his secretary.

"I don't want to sit down. I don't want any water. I want to know what's going on. Marsallis just told me, Phil."

"Told you what?" Hopper asks, looking at Phil.

Phil breaks in. "Does Mr. Marsallis know you're here?"

"No."

"Because I don't think he'd be very happy to know you'd come here without counsel. You've thought about that?"

"I haven't thought about much of anything since I left his office except how you could be so concerned about my mental health, so supportive of my well-being, so encouraging, while you were going to the district attorney to accuse me of . . ." I break off and feel the heat of everyone's eyes on me.

Hopper's face looks like it's swelling above his starched white collar and tie. He looks at Phil and says, "We can adjourn for now, Phil, if you need to meet alone with Dr. Heaton." He raises his eyebrows at Erin and starts stuffing papers into his briefcase. With an inaudible sigh of relief the others look away from me and begin folding up sandwich bags and reaching for white coats.

Phil puts a hand up. "Don't adjourn. We need to finish the discussion. Give us a minute, would you, please?" He smiles at Hopper and then extends the smile around the room. Don looks like he wants to bolt. One of the women presses her lips together and stares at her plate. Some of the others relax back into their chairs, probably thanking God I'll be leaving the room.

"Frank, maybe you could discuss the preferred provider accounts from Blue Cross, those numbers we pulled together. I'll be right back."

He opens the door with one hand and takes my elbow with his other to usher me out, supporting my arm as if he were afraid I might faint. As we walk into the corridor he squeezes my arm tighter, pinching his fingers into the flesh just above my elbow, cutting off the blood flow to my forearm until my hand begins to tingle. He pulls me down the hall and around the corner into a small coffee room and slams the door behind us. He pushes me backward until I am pressed up against the sharp edge of the counter. His lips are a thin white rim and his face is a patchwork of red blotches.

"Have you lost your senses?" His grip almost lifts me up off my feet. "Don't you think you're in enough trouble as it is? What is a jury going to make out of your barging into a board meeting like some crazy . . . ? What do you think the district attorney is going to say when he hears about it?"

"You're hurting my arm." He clenches his mouth even tighter and shoves his hands into his pockets. "I know about the missing fentanyl. I talked to Matt Corchoran. I know what it looks like. But it wasn't me."

"Sure it wasn't you."

"It was Joe Hillary, Phil." His face blanches and I can see him ball his fists up in his pockets as if he had to lock them there. "He gave me a break in every one of those cases. I recognized his handwriting, or at least his marks on the page. Quit staring at me like that. Listen to me."

His eyes are narrowed and distant, as if he's already backing away from me. I stand up straighter. "Listen to me! I've got the records. I checked the pharmacy copies against the originals, the OR copies. They're different. Somebody wrote in more fentanyl on the pharmacy copy than showed up on the original. They changed it after I took the papers apart, to make the amount match what was missing from my narcotics box. You're looking at me like I'm crazy, but think about it. I wouldn't set myself up by forging my own cases."

I look him straight in the eye, watching for a break in his conviction. "Phil, if you go with me, right now, over to his place, we could do an intervention. I know it's not really set up, but if we go now, he'd almost surely test positive. Test us both! Whatever you want. Just go over there with me. I can't go alone. Please."

Phil brings his fist up, stabs his index finger at my chest. "There is nothing in those records to suggest that anybody other than you was ever near that drug or those patients."

"Phil, just look at what I've got, look at the records. If nothing else, even if you aren't doing it to prove me innocent, we should go there for Joe's sake. You know what could happen to him."

He puts his hands up and takes a step backward, shaking his head. "Maybe I shouldn't be surprised to hear you try to pass this off. But there's no way I'm going to drag another doctor into this mess."

I scream at him now, not caring if the whole boardroom hears me. "You've known me for seven years. How can you accuse me of this? For God's sake, Phil. If you really believed I was addicted to fentanyl, shouldn't you have tried to get help for me?"

"If you want my help, I'll give you my advice. Get out of here before I call Security. Go talk to your attorney."

I bring my hands up over my eyes, starting to cry. Phil sighs and clears his throat. I hear him walk toward me and he puts his hand on my shoulder, gently this time. I flinch and he withdraws.

"Oh God," he says, the anger in his voice collapsing. "This isn't my choice. Can't you get that? I'm sorry, Marie. I'm sorry for what's happened in your life. I wish that were the only thing I had to worry about. But there are bigger things on the line now. This hospital is on the line.

Everybody who works here and everybody we take care of. Look at what the facts point to. This isn't just about a drug habit. If drugs are involved, this is about manslaughter. And I'm not going to watch this whole institution collapse in a media fallout. You shouldn't be here. And I shouldn't be here talking to you."

When I get home the light on my answering machine is blinking, but I'm almost afraid to play the message. If it's Joe, would he be calling to accuse or to confess? To pass blame or plead for salvation?

I finally press the playback button, and it's Lori saying she hopes I've had a safe trip and returned to good news. The only other message is a hang-up, leaving me to speculate who might be struggling over some intended conversation with me.

Dusk is already coming sooner, the first perceptible shift toward summer's conclusion. I feel as afraid as a child of the night coming, afraid of spending hours alone here in the dark, tossing sleeplessly or searching for distraction in a book or a movie. I'm tempted to open a bottle of wine and drink enough to blunt my pacing mind, maybe enough to sleep.

Instead I stand by the windows overlooking the sound and watch the ships. The mountains are sleeping giants rimmed in purple and deep blue. In the street the neon lights of bars begin flashing on and couples are claiming tables out in the cooling evening air. On the corner opposite a young woman talks with animated gestures in the telephone booth, as if her hands could add to the intimacy of her words. How many times has Joe called me from that corner, watching my windows until I appeared?

Something rigid inside me fractures and begins to crumble, as if my bones are turning to ash even as my flesh bears on. I sink onto my knees before the glittering city, a knot in my stomach as if I had been physically struck, my cheek against the windowpane, my palms pushing hard against the vast expanse of glass that divides me from the immense, raw beauty of Puget Sound. I want to crash though the glass; I want to break it open and let wind and rain shriek through in a consuming fury. I want to hurtle down onto the million glass shards shattered over the concrete below until a crowd gathers around and someone cries for help. And in that instant the terror becomes real, the terror has a recognizable face and form. I am terrified for Joe.

I pull the telephone off the table and dial Joe's phone number, count the rings while I wait for his voice. He doesn't answer. I redial the number and wait again. The streetlights are flickering on, casting an unnatural light upward through my windows; my shadow stretches gigantic across the ceiling. The rings continue on and on.

I can't find my car keys until I empty my purse upside down onto the floor. The elevator ride down to the garage drags endlessly and I begin playing out scenes of what Joe might have done after I left him. Joe, the stable rock, the athlete and pilot, the quick-thinking doctor who's always walked above the petty politics of the hospital and the accepted dictums of day-to-day life. Joe, whose irascible, unflappable and impenetrable nature has rooted itself in the quick of my subconscious to become a part of me, a secret hope chest. What has he done in this crisis?

Crossing under the viaduct, I have to slam on my brakes when a trolley clangs and shrieks to a stop a few feet from my car. I drive up to Queen Anne hardly aware of the traffic and late-summer tourist crowds, barely noticing stop signs and traffic signals.

His windows are black and vacant. I dance impatiently at the front door until an emerging couple accepts my rushed excuse of having forgotten my key and lets me in. I pound at the elevator button with my thumb, then my whole fist, then run down the hall to the fire door and race up the stairwell two steps at a time.

I don't consider what right I have to be here, whether my coming alone here again is dangerous for both of us, whether it will only push him farther from help. I know there are prescribed steps for an intervention—that it should never be done alone, without a plan and without a place to go and professionals waiting to induct the cornered addict securely into confession and redemption.

I press Joe's doorbell. The hallway feels as still as death, frozen and waiting. I push the bell again, holding my finger there; the insistent, high-pitched tone sounds like an alarm. I pound on his door with my fists and call his name; I shout to him that it's me, that I've come alone, that I have to see him. When I stop the noise vanishes in a vacant space. There are no footsteps coming to the door, no vibration of movement. I run to the fire stairwell and reach up into the crevices beneath the railing, praying that, somehow, his key has been replaced. The ledge is empty.

Somewhere below a door slams shut in the corridor, voices hum and dissolve. I grasp the railing to pull myself up and run down to the first-floor hallway. The door to the right of the stairs leads into the furnace room; next to it is the building superintendent's apartment. The euphoric bantering and laughter from a television set disappears when I ring the bell. A voice calls out in Spanish and then the door swings open.

"Mr. Iglesia." I brush the hair back from my eyes and start to reach out for his hand but instead clench my arms across my body to stop their trembling. "Mr. Iglesia, I'm Marie Heaton. We met a few years ago—I'm a friend—a colleague of Joe Hillary. Dr. Hillary, on the fifth floor." He looks cautious, maybe alerted by my nervousness, until he seems to recall me and his narrowed eyes relax.

"I'm sorry to bother you at this hour," I say. "But I need to find Dr. Hillary. Tonight. He's . . ." I take a deep breath and hope I sound reasonable. "It's urgent. We have a staffing problem at the hospital. A family emergency came up for one of the other doctors, and we have to reach Dr. Hillary to fill in. He's not answering his telephone or his door, and we need to locate him. I thought I might see something in his apartment—an address or phone number." I wait for his help, trying to transform the furrows in my face into a look of trustworthy concern.

Mr. Iglesia brings his hand up to his mouth and shakes his head. "I can't let you in without Dr. Hillary's permission, Dr. Heaton. I'm sorry." He looks down at the floor and then back up at me. "You don't have a key?"

"I do have a key, at home, but I came here straight from the hospital. We have some emergency surgeries coming in later tonight," I say, holding my breath after each inhalation to slow my heart down, my face flushing hot with the lie.

He rubs the side of his cheek and the hard skin of his palm scruffs across the stubble of his beard. "Well, I'll have to go in with you. Wait just a minute." He leaves the door standing half open and walks out of sight. The light from within is yellow and warm; the smell of frying onions and red meat seeps into the hallway. Somebody, a woman, laughs inside, and Mr. Iglesia reappears with an enormous ring of keys jingling like Christmas. He walks ahead of me to the elevator and presses the button. We stand awkward and silent as the creaking weight descends.

"You work at the hospital up on the hill with Dr. Hillary? Yeah, I remember. You still drive that nice silver Audi, huh?"

I nod.

"I like cars. I always notice what kind of car people drive. So, looks like the fall rains are coming early this year." I am spared having to answer because the elevator doors heave open and we step inside. He circles through the crowded key ring searching for Joe's; the shrill clang of metal on metal is painful in this small space.

At Joe's door he knocks and waits for a moment, shrugging his shoulders at me as if shedding a guilty sense that this is an infraction of rules. Then he fits a key into the lock. It won't turn. He curses softly and clatters through more keys. When he inserts another I hear the smooth unhitching of the mechanism.

Inside it is dark and chilly, and the blinds are still drawn. As my eyes adjust to the faint blue wash of streetlights through the slits, I pick my way around the chairs, his bicycle, record albums and stereo speakers toward the bedroom.

The door is nearly closed and I reach up to push it open, but draw my hand away, hesitating, almost wanting not to know. His apartment feels eerily lifeless, but I fold my fingers into a fist and knock on the bedroom door. No one answers. I open my palm against the wood and push it back. Behind me Mr. Iglesia pauses in the living room, as if shy about venturing farther into his tenant's privacy. I stand just inside the bedroom, statue still, holding my breath so that I can hear if any other living being also breathes.

I should turn on the light, but in this gloomy room I still feel able to hide from something—what, I am not sure. Do I hope that I will find him here, sleeping so softly I can't even sense his presence? Or that a letter, perhaps addressed to me, will explain all this in some believable way that leaves hope for both of us? Or is it possible that all the tragic warnings I've read about the risks of suicide or overdose in the unmasked addict will include Joe? Had I thought of that when I left him here a day ago, stripped raw to speculate what I would do with my new knowledge?

There is the sound of a footstep behind me, and with a click the overhead light flashes on. Mr. Iglesia has stepped into the room and flicked up the switch. Joe isn't here. The bedcovers have been pulled up over the pillows and the bureau drawers closed; the floor is bare of its usual piles of laundry and running shoes. I walk across to his dresser looking for an envelope, a piece of paper, anything he might have scribbled, any notes he might have made. There's nothing. Neither is there any scrap on his bedside table or beside the telephone. But the room has changed since I walked out on him last night. The top of the dresser looks bare. Though I can't say what's missing, the usual clutter of watches and keys and coins has been picked through. I turn toward the closet and slide back the paneled hanging doors. A few shirts dangle on hangers, but it is obvious that Joe has packed and gone.

· 37 ·

Tuesday dawns a virtuous blue after all the rain. On the drive to Renton Airfield I see a few trees whose branches are already slashed with orange and red, spilling eagerly into fall as if forgetting winter will follow. The parking lot is almost full, even though it is early, and the sun is blinding as I walk up to the building—what a perfect day to fly, the sky washed clear, boundless and beckoning.

There are only men in this room. Men wearing T-shirts with biplanes embossed in shiny black ink over the breasts; men wearing navy-blue blazers and pricey aviator-style sunglasses; men wearing leather bomber jackets that would be fashionable clichés if not for their authentic purpose. I'm hardly noticed, standing just inside the double glass doors of the lobby, listening to their locker room stories of skirted thunderheads and midair stalls, their brazen landings on uncharted lakes and steelhead streams—so excluded from their jocular camaraderie I am invisible rather than strikingly out of place.

A balding man sits on a high stool behind the counter, his features clustered in the middle of his wide, ruddy face as if pulled taut by a string. He is talking to an older man who wears ear mufflers slung in a horseshoe around his neck, relating some story so hilarious he explodes in spitting laughter between words. If I'd paid much attention to procedures the few times Joe brought me here, I could look for his plane without interrupting them, without the risk of telling them my name and seeing them stamp it into a record book or permanent log.

The man finally notices me, called back to whatever official duty he is paid to do here. He sits cocked up on one hip, braked by a heel lodged over the bottom rung of his stool, still chuckling when he asks me, "What can I do for you, missy, on this gorgeous day?"

The older man pulls the padded ear protectors back on his head and slaps the balding man's back. "OK, Ray. Spot you a beer tonight." Then he heads out into the roar of landing and departing planes.

"I'm looking for a friend. He keeps his plane here."

He raises his eyebrows up the barren slope of his forehead, waiting for me to finish. "Who's your friend?" he asks at last.

"Hillary. Joe Hillary."

He punches the keyboard of a vintage computer on the counter and types the seven letters of Joe's last name with his index fingers.

"Hillary, Joe, let's see. Not here yet. When are you supposed to meet him?"

"Yet." What a generous, forgiving word, so opulent with possibility—the carrot perpetually dangled from the advancing stick of denial. I am tempted to leave now and cheat disappointment.

"He didn't . . ." I lick my lips, chapped after so much crying and so little sleep. "We didn't have a set time. I can't remember when he told me he wanted to leave."

The man clicks his tongue against his teeth once and shakes his head. "Leave? You need to be waiting for him to come back. He left sometime last night, and his plane . . ." He cranes his head back, stepping halfway off the stool to look out a back window. "Nope, plane's still gone." He flips a pencil back and forth between the fingers of his left hand while his right punches at more keys; each time the new screen lights up I get a clench in my stomach, praying he'll look and tell me some distinct spot where I'll find him, some obligatory time of return.

"Doesn't look like he filed a flight plan, but he might have left that with the tower. I can call over there if you want."

I cross my arms over my stomach, as if maybe I could force the muscles to loosen up. Why should I bother him to call, when I know Joe has no intention of being found. Not today. Not ever. "Yeah, sure, if you don't mind."

He dials the number and after a perfunctory introduction launches into the insider's dialect of flight. "No go," he says, dropping the receiver back down. "Couldn't be going too far if he didn't file, though." He falls silent then, tapping the pencil in a quick seesaw against the counter. He's looking at me closely for the first time since I came into the lobby, seeming to recognize the tight lines around my mouth, my locked arms. "Look, why don't you have a seat. We've got some coffee in the back if you want a cup. I'll check the bulletin board in the office— sometimes the guys pin a note up there for me."

"Thanks. No coffee." I cross my arms tighter. "But if you could check the board. Maybe I got the time wrong."

He's back before I can sit down in one of the folding metal chairs scattered along the wall. "You Marie Heaton?"

My face swims in heat. "Yes. I am."

"Joe left this on my desk with a sticky note asking me to drop it in the mail. Addressed to you. Good thing you got here before it was buried under a pile of papers—wouldn't have found it till Christmas." He laughs at this and I force a smile.

"Thanks." I take from his hands a rectangular manila envelope, and shrug one shoulder. "Must have decided to stay away longer." I am halfway out the doors when I turn back to him. "You can track a plane, can't you? I mean, if we needed to find him?"

He studies me for a minute before he answers and his smile dims a bit. He shakes his head. "That's the beauty of flying. It's a big sky. You can get lost in it if you choose to."

I make it halfway home, where I could hide in my own sanctuary with a lock on the inside of the door. But without really planning to, I pull off the highway and wind through the circles and lanes of tidy and obedient suburban Seattle homes to a bluff overlooking Lake Washington— the afternoon sunshine like a million faceted diamonds across the wilderness of water lapping between richly populated shores.

My name slants upward across the the manila in his looping, adolescent script. I hold the envelope beneath my nose wondering if I might smell his spicy aftershave. But there is nothing so personal from him to be here with me when I fold back the brass tabs and run the edge of my forefinger under the flap, opening it.

I turn it upside down and a white, business-size envelope slides onto my lap. It's not addressed to me. The return address is that of Columbia Hospital, in Florida, where Joe worked just before he came to Seattle; it's postmarked four years ago. Inside are only a few papers. The first is a copy of Joe's letter of recommendation from Columbia's chief of anesthesia to Phil Scoble. The second is Joe's request for privileges at Columbia. It's a standardized form I've seen a hundred times, filled out for every medical license renewal and every hospital membership and every insurance enrollment—a checklist of health limitations, rule infractions, revoked status or malpractice claims—the de rigueur form every doctor checks off so often we no longer read the questions, and run a long, straight line down the innumerable boxes marked "No." As always, in the lowest box, is the list of personal fallibilities and handicaps that might impair capacity or cloud judgment, the questions about physical disability and mental illness and substance abuse. Any question answered "Yes" requires an additional page of detailed explanations and therapeutic interventions.

The letter from his former chief lauds Joe's education and mental agility, his quick-wittedness and clinical acumen. It expounds on the procedural protocols he refined for Columbia's ICU and trauma response team. The last paragraph of the letter, just above his signature, equivocally exonerates Joe from the documented questions raised during his tenure there of addiction to fentanyl. "No such abuse was ever confirmed, although we were unable to reconcile some discrepancies," his chief writes. "Certainly we believe any suspected drug use was of limited duration. Dr. Hillary is an outstanding clinician, however I can only recommend him with the caveat that he be scrupulously monitored. It is unfortunate that we cannot keep him on our staff at this time." On the third page, Joe's own self-composed exculpations are equally convincing. Maybe I'm alone in spotting the anagrams of pain camouflaged in his apology.

One final page lies below the others. It has only a few sentences, beginning with my name, scrawled almost illegibly in Joe's handwriting. "Scoble and Hopper cleaned the originals out of my files before the lawyers talked to me. I was never monitored—never even reported to the medical board. They're selling you out to save First Lutheran." And below this, in a darker stroke that carves into the surface of the paper: "You are absolved."

· 38 ·

Charlie Marsallis takes me to lunch at Etta's in the Pike Place Market two days after I give him Joe's letter. The district attorney has already dropped the criminal charges against me, but there are still hurdles. The toxicology report in Jolene's autopsy didn't list a beta-blocker, so the mechanism of her death remains open for debate—a euphemism for persistent blame, I decide, without saying this out loud. Feinnes could still try to pin some responsibility on me for taking Jolene to the operating room without examining her closely enough to detect signs of her Turner syndrome, without listening to her heart and ordering a cardiology evaluation. Charlie uses the term "degree of negligence," as if death could be fractionalized.

Still, our lunch has an air of celebration about it. Our discussion of upcoming legal maneuvers and strategies digresses into a conversation about Charlie's son William, who has a precocious gift for music and a heart-stopping voice for a seven-year-old. I tell him about my father and his eyesight, and he talks about his own parents and the assisted living complex in downtown Seattle he's moved them to. But I still can't talk to him about Joe—*my* Joe, not the addict or the deceiver, but the Joe who always knew when I needed his sense of humor; the skeptic who was blindingly determined to live richly, intensely, eternally one step ahead of his own pain.

It isn't until a week later that Charlie gets a personal visit from the district attorney. He's received a letter from Joe, postmarked on the Tuesday I discovered his plane missing. In his distinctive, looping script, clearly signed, Joe confesses that he exchanged the fentanyl in Jolene's syringe for labetalol, a drug that is not on the list of chemicals automatically screened for by the King County toxicology lab.

I should have guessed. Labetalol is kept in the top drawer of every anesthesia cart—the most commonly used beta-blocker in the operating room. In the letter Joe plots out the simple math to show the dose Jolene would have received. In a normal child the dose would probably have done no harm. In a lower dose, it might not have harmed Jolene. But, Joe explains, in a scholarly description of cardiac physiology, the excessive dose Jolene received would have left her heart incapable of forcing blood past the stricture in her aorta. At the end of the letter, he applauds my medical sleuthing for having figured out the drug switch.

The police check with airfields up and down the coast, but no one reports refueling any plane with his N-Number. His credit cards haven't been used. His bank account was only partially emptied, enough money left behind for the authorities to question whether he was intending to run. His leather duffle bag washes up just north of Marin—some kids building a sand castle find it, half buried at the cusp of a low tide line. Inside are his passport, his wallet, stuffed with credit cards and ID, and some cash. The coast guard does a cursory search for wreckage or any reports of an Emergency Locator Transmitter. Nothing turns up. Eventually the police quit looking for him—his crime doesn't warrant that many resources in an age of international terrorism. They presume he is dead. But baggage can fall from a plane in any number of ways, I think.

Still, the depositions continue. I sit across from Phil Scoble with conflicting feelings: betrayal, anger, incomprehension, and, sometimes, sympathy, all spilling into an ocean of sadness I've hardly begun to navigate. In Phil's imperturbable, overconfident testimony I hear the same denial Joe must have used, the same unwillingness to stare down his destructive selfishness. If I hadn't known Phil for so long, if I'd never seen the unattainable expectations pressed on him by Frank Hopper and the board, if I didn't understand that he has pinned all of his self-worth to his job, it would be easy to hate him for the lies.

At first, Phil and Frank deny the role they played in Joe's hiring and his lapse back into drug abuse, and it's almost certain the lawsuit will go to trial. Charlie reassures me I'll be testifying against others instead of defending myself, but I feel queasy when I envision telling this story to a jury, watching Bobbie listen to the horror of her daughter's death again. After three weeks of accumulating evidence against them, the hospital's lawyers convince both that their likelihood of losing, and of facing even bigger penalties, is greater if twelve civilians—most of whom undergo surgery at some point in life—get to decide their fate. So a mediation date is set; a mediation in which I am no longer a defendant. I am allowed, at last, to plan my future.

One final day in front of a video camera, one last time I will sit at this conference table surrounded by lawyers. Then I will leave town, with Charlie's blessing and a release from any liability for Jolene's death. We take a break late in the afternoon and I walk down the hall to the bathroom, but it's closed for cleaning. I skip down one flight of stairs to an identical women's room on another floor lined with lawyers' offices and conference rooms. The single stall is occupied, and I stand at the sink running warm water over my hands, dampen a paper towel and daub it over my temples and throat, press it over my closed eyes. Then the stall door opens. Someone is behind me, waiting. I open my eyes, and Bobbie Jansen is looking at my reflection in the mirror.

She's thinner, older than she looked four months ago, when I saw her sitting at a conference room table like the ones we must have both been at today. She holds a comb half raised toward her hair. We could be two painted masks, we are both so still. One a mask of terrified anticipation, one a mask of tragedy. In her face I see unabated sorrow.

In the last few weeks Bobbie has learned that her daughter's death was the result of more than one doctor's incompetence. Jolene died because her Turner syndrome was missed in an underfunded and overcrowded public health clinic. She died when Phil Scoble and Frank Hopper chose to ignore Joe's suspect references so they could keep First Lutheran's operating rooms running at full capacity, and their spreadsheets in black ink. She died as she was passed down a chain of committed, conscientious professionals—her pediatrician, Don Stevenson, Mindy, Alicia, me—all of us wanting the best for her, all of us engulfed in a health-care machine that has outstripped our individual competence with its monstrous ambition and complexity. And, yes, Jolene died of an addict's false confidence, and his willingness to push blame onto whoever was most vulnerable. Even someone he loved.

A thousand words flood my mind. Words of condolence and empathy. Words of explanation and self-acquittal. Words that might approximate some altruistic blessing in the face of sacrifice. Even an openhearted plea to hear her bitterness and rage, if she needs to unleash that on me. The words feel like solid objects I could put in her hands—wood and velvet and sharp glass—tangible, vivid, durable gifts waiting to fall out of me.

Bobbie lets the comb drop into her purse. Her eyes recede, as if an interior light were shutting down. Then she turns away and walks out of the bathroom. Now there is only my face in the mirror, pale and shaken.

I grab my bag off the counter and run into the hallway. The elevator doors are closing and the down arrow flashes off. I punch the button and wait impatiently for the next car in the bank to open, cross the hallway and push the call buttons on the opposite wall.

It's impossible to stand and wait. I run to the stairwell even though I know I'll never be able to spiral down ten flights in time to catch her. The elevator bell sounds and I race back to thrust my arm between the doors just before they shut, then pound the parking garage button over and over during the descent.

By the time the doors open Bobbie is already at her car on the far side of the lot. She hears the sound of my heels crossing the concrete floor and turns around, her car key poised to unlock the door of the same badly repaired Ford sedan I saw at Jolene's funeral.

She doesn't even look startled, as if she had expected this brash attempt at contact. She squares her shoulders and waits, her keys swinging from her clasped hands, ready to hear whatever has compelled me to chase her. We are two feet apart, face-to-face, and she doesn't even blink. All the pain I thought I saw has been swallowed into a defeated worldliness, and, for the first time, I comprehend that pain is keenest when a person has a reason to live. Bobbie is not waiting for any resolution—from this lawsuit or from me. She has stopped, here in this deserted garage, for the sole purpose of allowing me to unburden myself. Everything I thought I could tell her is a prayer for my own redemption exacted at her expense. I want her to forgive me for taking her child into the operating room. I want her to forgive me for trusting Joe. I want her to forgive me for wearing the First Lutheran name badge that implied all the brilliance and infallibility of the American medical machine. I have no answers for her. I don't know her. My fantastic obsession has generated an illusion of intimacy. Her forgiveness is an endpoint I will never reach.

"Ms. Jansen," I start, and then my voice trails off. She looks down at her keys, as if she is embarrassed for my awkwardness, giving me a moment of privacy to collect myself. After an echoing silence she sorts the car key out from the jangling bunch in her hand, and looks up at me again. "What is it, Dr. Heaton? What do you want to say to me?"

I say the only words I can hear inside my mind: "I'm sorry." How simple. Two words. At last given the chance to tell Bobbie whatever I might have the courage to express, this is the one thing I understand about Jolene's death. "I never got to tell you before how very sorry I am."

Bobbie nods and slips her key into the door lock. "I know. I know you are." She says it as a simple statement of fact, without any hostility or trivialization. Then she gets into her car and backs out of the parking space, pulls around me and drives away.

· 39 ·

The girl now lying on my operating room table looks like some kind of dark angel. Her skin is young enough to be unblemished and smooth as browned butter. Her eyelashes sweep above her zygomatic bones in feathery black arcs. Her nose still has the full rounded tip of childhood, just beginning to lengthen and straighten, and her ears are as identically matched as two halves of a heart. Her hands curl in the relaxed posture of deep anesthetic sleep, the nails are tissue paper moons.

Looking down the length of her sinewy, proportioned body, her legs splayed just to the comfortable angle allowed by her pelvic girdle, it is impossible not to appreciate how inconsequentially minute is her single imperfection. How can I see anything except the miracle of the millions of bits of genetic code that cobbled together food, water and air into this almost perfect human being? An oxygen saturation monitor beeps with the rhythm of her pulse, its high tone reassuring me that she is safe in her suspended state—a sleeping princess awaiting her prince.

I have come to a place as steamy as any August day in Houston: Porbandar, Gujarat—Gandhi's birthplace, on the Sabarmati River. I accepted a job at a teaching hospital back in Seattle on the condition that I could spend three months abroad as a volunteer working with a small team of pediatric surgeons repairing cleft palates and fistulas and clubfeet.

Some days we operate on more than twenty children, in addition to running a pre-op and post-op clinic, and I go back to my single bed so exhausted I sleep through till morning without realizing time has passed at all. We brought crates of medical supplies from the U.S., and still the working conditions approximate an era decades before I did my residency: a finger on the radial pulse, a stethoscope taped over the chest wall, a glance at the nail beds or conjunctiva to estimate oxygen levels and hematocrits when the electricity blips off. We are a mixed group of doctors and nurses, six from the States, four from other re-gions in India, three from Europe. Over the few weeks I've been here we've become best friends, all of us, in the unique way that unusual circumstances and stress can foster extraordinary bonds.

Lori sends me letters every few days. They always start with a para-graph or two about Dad and how he's coping with her kids. He gives them history lectures at the dinner table every night. She writes that Neil actually seems interested, Lia usually falls asleep (but he can't see her clearly enough to tell, so his pride isn't hurt), and Elsa would rather hear critiques of fifteenth-century Medician social constructs than his criticisms about her clothes or musical tastes. From there on her letters ramble for pages about everyday domestic life—our correspondence seems to have evolved into a therapeutic journal for her. For me, the let-ters are movies and television and computers and radio. They have all those things here, in sputtering and intermittently transmitted Hindi, but I prefer the peace of pen and ink for a while.

Dad began calling me more often after I flew home from Houston to meet with Charlie—telling me how the repairs on his house were progressing, what great new frozen dinner he'd discovered, or com-plaining that the housekeeper I hired for him insisted on scrubbing out every stain in his carpet and every corner in the kitchen cabinets so the whole house smelled like white vinegar. One evening, at the end of a detailed discussion of the weather forecast, he asked me to help him sell his house. He said Lori had put him on the waiting list for an assisted living apartment in Fort Worth, and in the meantime he would stay in her guest room. But when Charlie told me there was an opening in the building his parents live in, I put a deposit on it. After I return from India I will help my father move to Seattle.

My father and I seem to be discovering, or perhaps inventing, a different relationship, rather than attempting to work through our history. We haven't said that to each other—he is not from a generation that talks things out to clear the air. But we are both learning to hear each other, finally, beyond our words.

There is a formula that calculates the delivery of oxygen to the tissues in the human body, a tidy package of numbers that attempts to quantify how much oxygen we can extract out of invisible air and squeeze through our nearly infinite capillaries with every beat of our hearts. Give me some measurable facts—the concentration of red blood cells, the inhaled mixture of oxygen and nitrogen, the volume of blood jetting out of the heart at each contraction—and with a few punches on a calculator I can determine whether or not the sum total is sufficient to sustain life. As long as no numeral slips too far toward zero, the calculation predicts we will awaken from our biopsies and arthroscopies and bypasses to return to work, create, love and reproduce, with only a scar to remind us of the violation.

Condensing it to a formula, of course, belies the art of my profession—tailoring the drugs and drips and pain relief, even my words, to conjure the ideal anesthetic, unique to each patient. An ideal anesthetic should be almost imperceptible, dissolving into the background like the painted blue sky of a stage set. It should appear as effortless as a ballerina's pirouette, or the volley of a tennis champion. When it works, when all the components blend in perfectly balanced proportion, my job becomes oddly intimate—a shared personal secret with a stranger, watching them wake up with an expression in their eyes I recognize as stark disbelief that time has passed and this frightening event is over. They have crossed this barrier and emerged intact, if changed in some indefinable way, opened up and explored, on the other side.

My dark angel, this almost perfect child, has a deep groove incising her palate and upper lip just to the right of the midline and extending up into the right nares. The surgeon has spent two hours opening the flesh and resuturing it along the fresh, raw edges to create a new mouth. It is not a perfect mouth, but a functional mouth that will allow her to eat and drink normally, to talk, someday to kiss. He puts antibiotic ointment over the interrupted line of black silk holding her stitched skin together, and I let her begin to breath; I turn down my anesthetic gas in the same way a pilot might glide onto a landing strip. As her sleep lightens, the effort of her breath rises up the length of her torso, from her abdomen, to her chest, to her clavicles and the sternocleidomastoid muscles that join her head and thorax. She is light enough now that I can carefully withdraw her endotracheal tube and place my fingers beneath the angle of her mandible to open her airway. She begins to swallow, her eyebrows flicker, and the lashes overlying her cheeks twitch as her brain emerges from anesthetic sleep into consciousness. She is almost here, barely below the threshold of response, just close enough to hear me, and I whisper in her ear: "*Ootho buchche, ootho. Aap kaa operation khatam ho gayaa hai. Sub kuch theek gayaa, aur aap bilkul theek honge.*" Wake up, little one. Wake up. Your operation is over. Everything went well, and you are doing just fine.

Acknowledgments

A novel is created in the solitary world of the writer's mind, but brought to life through the support of an entire community. I would never have started this work without the coaching and encouragement of author Michael Collins. He and other teachers at Field's End writing community on Bainbridge Island helped me turn a dream into words. Carole Glickfeld, Michael Byers, David Guterson and Priscilla Long all have shared their unique talents for the benefit of new writers. My thanks also to Loretta Barrett, Mark White, and my ever-patient writing partners Dennis O'Reilly, Suzanne Selfors, Jonathan Evison, Susan Wiggs, Elsa Watson, Anjali Banerjee and Sheila Rabe for wise feedback on language and storyline. Thanks to everyone at Inkwell Management and my agents, David Forrer and Kim Witherspoon, who believed in me enough to invest their time, energy and endless cheerleading. My editor, Marysue Rucci, devoted many patient hours sculpting my words closer to my personal best. I am so grateful for her vision and faith; she offered sage advice even when I was reluctant to listen. Ginny Smith, Victoria Meyer, Jonathan Evans, and the entire staff at Simon & Schuster have made this a superb and seamless experience.

Thanks also to my friends, who have read countless early drafts of this book: Anne Gendreau, Julie Kriegh, Bryce Holmes, Sherry Holmes, Beth Hendrickson, Doug Nathan, Helen Hendrickson, Mary Katherine Bywaters, Deborah Hickey-Tiernan, Cynthia Seely, and Zan Merriman.

I have attempted to write this fictional story as realistically as possible. For that I have depended on numerous advisers, all of whom generously offered their help. Thanks to Nancy Nucci, Kevin Trumbolt, David Steefel, Bob Ransom, Karen Roetman, Jon Ferguson, Manir Batra, Ann Marie Gordon, Dan Gandara, Katherine Galagan, Corrynne Fligner, Karen Weiss Hanten, Todd Schneiderman, and Prem Pahlajrai.

Without the lifelong support of my family I would have achieved nothing. All my love to Ray and Kathie Wiley, Marilyn Wiley and Ellen Bywaters. Steve, without you I would have no words and no reason to write. You make it all worthwhile.

Addendum

Fiction explores the boundaries of our lives, the *what ifs,* magnifying imperfection in order to wake us up to the majesty of the commonplace. This book is about no actual person and, if I have done my job, it is equally about each one of us. In the twenty-five years I have studied and practiced medicine I've worked with hundreds of doctors, nurses and technicians, and cared for thousands of patients. They have affirmed my belief in the compassionate core of human nature. As with any humanly engineered and delivered concept, the juggernaut of health care is both awe-inspiring and flawed. People are not perfect. But I am routinely humbled by the dedication, goodwill and endurance of the people who have chosen this career. They do it because they care.

About the Author

Carol Wiley Cassella lives in Bainbridge Island, Washington, with her husband and their two sets of twins. She is a practicing anesthesiologist and medical writer, and is currently working on her next novel.